The Good Muslim of Jackson Heights

Jaysinh Birjépatil

Fomite
Burlington, Vermont

ISBN-13   978-1-937677-16-9
Library of Congress Control Number: 2012935627

Cover Photographs by Kalie Kamara , Digital Illustration by Hilary Baker

Fomite
58 Peru Street
Burlington, VT 05401
www.fomitepress.com

For my parents
Meera and Dataji
Ajit and Shilu

Key Characters in Jackson Heights

Siraj (Siri) Amolini — Cambridge(UK) educated aristocratic Indian Muslim intellectual of Persian descent

Shabnam Amolini — his wife

Imran (Immy) Amolini — their son

Gulshan (Gullu) — their American born daughter

Sally — Immy's American wife

Maury Lee Carmody — An anthropologist friend of the Amolinis

Nasreen (Reeny) Babukhan — A Bangladeshi-American feminist college teacher

Amanda Carmichael — President of Kingman College

Miriam Shapiro — Amolini's Kingman Colleague

Gabriella — Amolini's opera loving girl friend

Bookstore-Nambiar — Originally from Kerala (India), runs a bookstore.

Mr Edulji — An Indian Parsi antique dealer

Qureshi — A Bangladeshi grocer often called Qureshi-chacha (uncle)

Rehana Qureshi — His wife

Thakorji — Dignified owner of a sari store called 'Draupadi.'

Chitral — An unscrupulous trader who runs 'Sari Palace'

Kanti Chitral — His alienated feckless son

Mr. Sampat — A smuggler of blood diamonds

Mrs. Sampat — His wife

Maya — Their hapless daughter-in-law

Durbar Singh — A successful attorney of Sikh Mexican ethnic mix

Dr. Maltilda Singh — His wife

Jaspal (Jessi) — Their son

Jit Singh — Head Waiter at Peacock Diner

Raj Kumari — His daughter

Abdul Latif —(Badé Miyan) Of 'Karachi Halwa' & sweets.

Ghaseetkhan — A halal butcher

Natthuram — A Jeweler

Yamini — His daughter

Who's turned us round like this, so that we always,
do what we may, retain the attitude
of someone who's departing? Just as he,
on the last hill, that shows him all his valley
for the last time, will turn and stop and linger,
we live our lives, for ever taking leave.

------Rilke-------

Prologue

It seems everybody's grandmother once lived in Jackson Heights. Utter the magical name at a Thanksgiving dinner and someone at the far end of the table is bound to say, 'Oh yeah, I know the place. My grandmother once lived there when she was a little girl.'

A lot has changed since grandma's time, when she came over with her family through Ellis Island. The difference between then and now is one of form; in substance it's still the same old rambunctious, hard-knuckled, toilsome place full of piss and vinegar with enough heft to carry every planeload of new immigrants through their first rite of passage.

Nine-tenths of life in Jackson Heights is a celebration, a jingle-jangle of tongues, a fishgig of disparate cultures, and an elegy for lost homes. In a couple of decades, this hardscrabble piece of real estate under the elevated E Train has acquired the mystery and aura of fabled streets mapped on historic memory, like Lahore's Anarkali or Chandni Chowk in Delhi. Today the name Jackson Heights is whispered with awe in the back lanes of every town of the Indian subcontinent.

On festive occasions, of which there are many, it shrinks to a crystal ball, a Gypsy stall, a mélange of gods, a jumble of kitsch and elegance, American dream coiled around neck forms in jewelry shops, in folds of filigreed saris, locked in jars of cinnamon, cloves, and cardamom, smothered in mounds of yellow turmeric, sneezing in the wake of blood-red chili powder. In shop fronts, classy and tacky stand hand in hand in morganatic marriage.

There is Durbar Singh the lawyer, giving a final swipe with a rag to his glossy black shoes. He takes in the scene below from his upstairs office, slips some documents into his brief case, before setting off for a hearing. His downstairs neighbor, Natthuram of Kohinoor Jewelers, is peering at a diamond brooch through an eyeglass like a one-eyed salamander. Across the road from the jeweler, Chimanlal, of drum-like paunch and snaggle-toothed smile, is giving a pep talk to his staff, judging by their yawning faces. Then with one swift motion he reverses the 'Closed' sign to 'Open' and a small woman pushing a walker comes in and disappears among fruits and vegetables. Chiman thinks she brings the store's profile down. He fawns on the upwardly-mobile IT crowd, investment bankers and other well-heeled folk who have been induced by fast-talking realtors to trade their two-room apartments on the Upper East Side for a house in Jackson Heights.

The scrawny, law-dodging lads on home delivery errands from the grocery, rags-to-riches suckers waiting tables at the Peacock Diner with its tinted windows and red and black awning, slink in with their INS-haunted look and are transformed into busboy princelings in embroidered livery with slip-on turbans in the cramped pantry behind the kitchen.

By lunchtime, coffers have half filled in almost all the shops except at Vidya, the bookstore at the corner of 74th and Roosevelt Avenue. Maybe someone will step in to buy an almanac. Word on the street is that the bosomy sister-in-law of Chitral Seth of Sari Palace is to marry that nice young man who works as his shop assistant. Also, Purushottam, the chemist from round the corner, is expecting his third grandchild and will be looking for a nice name for the infant. He said the other day he wanted a copy of the new translation of the Mahabharata to pick a suitable moniker for the baby.

In the afternoon, traffic is sluggish on 74th Street — renamed Kalpana Chawla Way, or KC Way, after the young Indian astronaut whose portrait hangs on the wall behind the cash register in the Peacock Diner. She'd tried to escape history, to remake it in space, until one sunny day her shy smile and large trusting eyes scattered unblinkingly over New Mexico (or was it Texas?) when the shuttle Columbia blew up minutes before touchdown.

Delivery trucks arrive, and the grocery and diner are blocked to the view from the jewelers. Lawyer Durbar Singh steps out and clicks the remote to open his locked car. Singh drives the only Mercedes on the street. Others make do with Ford Tauruses or Toyotas, and those who live on the back streets of Jackson Heights prefer to walk down, except when it's freezing cold. Then they get a ride from their wives; you can tell by the nervous horn as the car rounds the corner.

By the Korean store in the subway vestibule, a mendicant in mufti droops on a crate. Overhead, the E Train's rumble rises and subsides every fifteen minutes as it off-loads, at 74th Street, sightseers, bargain-hunting tourists, and nursing and hotel staff returning from night duty in Manhattan. For the latter, Jackson Heights means a bunk bed vacated by the day-shift guys, the chance to lie down while the E Train makes ruts through their hard-earned sleep. Fresh gnome-like faces at the checkout counters, and new student waiters appear at the Peacock Diner every summer and move to campus housing in the fall.

Patrol cars nose through the traffic at a leisurely pace; Irish, Italian, and black cops with bored Maytag-Man expressions fondly believe that Indians don't play hardball, rarely mess around, and there aren't any shoot-out splatter fests of any kind, as in the drug trafficking seventies. It always amuses the cops when one of these immigrant dudes does stray from the path. The entire community goes into a huddle, cowering as though a giant vat of shit is about to hit the fan. The cops have learnt during cultural diversity training at the 151st Precinct that the Indo–Pak–Bangladeshi types belong to what is called 'shame' culture. If one of them is caught with his pants down, the entire tribe stands guilty of collective flashing.

Qureshi, the Bangladeshi grocer, wipes his hands on his overalls and steps out to puff on his *beedi*. Most shops at the far end of 74th Street, bisected by 73rd Avenue, sell Indian and Afghani sweets, Bangladeshi groceries and halal meat. Mr Qureshi, who is well past sixty, attends night school to improve his prospects and be a contender. He waves to Mr Edulji across the street. The old man is sound asleep in his rocker under a framed photograph of Zubin Mehta conducting in his first season of the New York Philharmonic. The Eduljis have never met Maestro Mehta but are proud of him on account of his being a fellow Parsi.

Now almost eighty-nine, Edulji owns the only antique shop in Jackson Heights. It's called Mandalay, and until recently—that is, till Mrs Edulji's passing away—it used to be filled with colonial knick knacks, shipped by impoverished relatives from Poona Cantonment, Tardeo in Bombay, and hill stations like Matheran, Panchgani and Mahabaleswar. There were also a few bronze figurines from the Chola period, Ming Dynasty vases, Japanese fans, Staffordshire pottery and toy Redcoats picked up from decaying Parsi estates in Rangoon, Singapore and Hong Kong (Mrs Edulji's home town before her marriage), and other outposts of the Empire where the Parsis had followed the British and supplied them with genuine merchandise from home. Napping in his overstuffed leather chair, Mr Edulji looks like a fallen statue waiting to be carted away. In his pale brown eyes, some fading élan and world-weariness have long combated themselves to a stalemate.

On that block, Mandalay sits a bit awkwardly like a turbaned elderly relative in jodhpurs, with younger members dressed casually in shirts and jeans. Among the regular visitors are the Amolinis, Siraj and Shabnam. Ah, the Amolinis! What can one say about them? As a couple they are 'one for the book', so to speak, and cannot be co-opted in a prologue. It'd be like trying to capture in a grocery jar the aftertaste of consummately cooked Basmati rice.

At nightfall, Jackson Heights pulls up the ladder and the E Train levitates above the tracks, thunder and clatter deferred. Time is on 'pause'. Along Broadway Crescent, past Tivoli Cinema, pullulating like a mythical chariot, Aladdin's halal cart, griddle sizzling with boneless chicken, and the *Arepa de Queso* stand feed the graveyard shift. No one

speaks, mindful that in hushed groceries on streets criss-crossing behind them, even a slight exhalation might send blushing Alphonso
mangoes rolling down their pyramids and odalisques in colorful saris
scampering out of their *harims* of glass.

Book I

❧ 1 ❧

What is the color of memory?

Some say it is green. A moss-thick cottage sagging by a disused branch line.

I am still unable to vacate the ramparts of Inderpur, my memory town, still eager to unfold a tale. But who has time to listen? The night is full of ghostly voices whose time is up.

In Jackson Heights we live under another dispensation, a new plot line, a set of characters with different axes to grind. What the butler saw back then has no bearing here. Or so I imagine; only time will tell. The overhead train girdling this place of perpetual arrivals and departures yields no clues. There is no suspicious vagrancy or fly-by-night stealth at its core. A decent chance of ending one's days with children and grandchildren is all one can hope for.

We were the envy of Jackson Heights when we arrived here. Something of an oddity we were—one heart, one breath. When all around us marriages were tumbling like a house of cards, we were the odd couple, the Indian and his wife, always together, providing ocular proof that once upon a time marriages were made in heaven.

Our son Immy was too excited for words over going to America, but our steps were leaden, eyes lingering over every last broken brick of our *kothi*, every worn cobblestone in our courtyard. Going into exile we were heavy-footed, moved slowly, uncertain of our future in this strange world. You didn't have to be told there was sorrow in my heart; your eyes kept scanning my face for signs of muzzled agony when I pretended to be asleep in my seat during the long flight. I could feel your gaze passing over me like a consoling hand.

While Immy blathered on about going to the top of the Empire State Building, your grey eyes pleaded with me not to be annoyed. I obliged by playing the much put upon head of the family, gritting my teeth and rolling my eyes like a court jester. Nobody knew better than you what the stakes were.

We presented smiling happy faces even though our hearts were in mourning. Maury Lee Carmody had some idea of what we had lost, having seen us in our home, lionized by friends and neighbors, crowds in the bazaar parting at our approach like water lilies before a majestically gliding swan.

In the early eighties, Jackson Heights seemed to us a ruthful city of refuge for the exiled and the displaced. You would come and sit on my desk while I graded papers. I can still see the way your silky floral nightgown bloomed over your breasts, your thighs splurging across the edge of the desk. Gullu was born within a year of our coming here; she was our down payment, so to speak, for a plot in Jackson Heights, our votive offering to its beneficent spirit, its *lares* and *penates*.

In its narrow streets you could still smell sweat-soiled, turn-of-the-century overalls, catch the drift of conversation in older tongues, the stealthy murmur of workers returning from the night shift, toilers slouching at dawn to the subway stop. The momentum generated by past labors was like wind behind the new comers.

We watched Gullu grow, take to the ways of Jackson Heights, free spirited and vivacious. She was our guide to its history, the native speaker who brought into our home its secrets, moulding us to its ways. We were housebroken to America by our daughter; all its rhythms and beats rippled across her tiny body when she was a little girl. She was the uncrowned Princess of Jackson Heights. All her friends called her that. Kanti Chitral, Durbar's Jesse and Natthuram's Yamini too were born here, but it was our Gullu who was the cynosure of KC Way, its homecoming queen.

Gullu was of Jackson Heights as no other offspring in the immigrant family was. You might think it quaint, a father's loving fantasy, but after she was born, the trade in the neighborhood boomed; Indian and Pakistani merchants extended their reach on 73rd Avenue all the way to 76th Street. They came here in droves, as if answering a courtly summons, a royal decree. From India, Pakistan and Bangladesh, they came. Once again, it was like living in the undivided India of pre-Partition days. When it came to daydreaming, we Amolinis could teach a thing or two to Walter Mitty.

There was something operatic about the place even then. Sitting by the window in the Peacock Diner, enjoying the chiaroscuro of light and shadow in early spring, I used to fancy you only required a lorgnette to see a Gypsy carnival in progress as in the sunny streets of Carmen's Seville or watch the entire street well up like the elder Bruegel's canvas, teeming with a myriad little pig-in-the-bag deals and gambolings in progress all across the square. Like a multilimbed deity, Little India grew several arms, expanded its girth, and was soon dense with fabrics of silk and brocade. Here in this remote corner of New York, beyond the long shadow of Manhattan, Jackson Heights blossomed into a thriving, bustling town, a *sawai*, superior, Inderpur.

And you, my dear Shabnam, were part and parcel of that great experiment.

❧ 2 ❧

The Empire made geography obsolete. My cultural foundations were not ethnic or provincial like that of many subcontinental traders. My ruins were eclectic and stretched from Stonehenge to Turandot's Forbidden City; the dust of history's conquerors and vanquished lay incestuously mixed in our family graveyard.

My tale must unfold in whispers, like a tongue-tied ghost's, with long pauses of wounded silence, of someone who takes a tumble from the trapeze; the children laugh a bit uneasily and the horses sway to the band playing a sad tune. In the interest of larger truth, the really funny part of the story must await its turn in the queue, till its number is called. In the meantime, the show must go on, regardless.

Jackson Heights.

At first I thought, how could we possibly spend the rest of our lives in this cauldron of commerce? These traders lived along narrow, terraced ridges of caste and community and seldom strayed as far as Manhattan, except to catch coaches from Port Authority Bus Terminal to Edison, New Jersey, or some other ethnic neighborhood. Untouched by the mystique of 42nd Street, their cardiganed women sleepwalked under theatre marquees, like so many Lady Macbeths. Their bodies were here, their souls under the tropics, and their social give-and-take a secret handshake.

At a glance, Jackson Heights was not the refuge one had dreamt of standing for hours, sweating under a *sola* in a long queue outside the American consulate in Bombay, waiting for a visa. Not a good bargain, especially when one's hometown was famous for its elegant palaces, jousting elephants, public gardens, libraries and museums, not to mention nautch girls, agile mongoose and vendors of colorful balls of crushed ice.

Underlying the bazaar bustle of Jackson Heights was the general sobriety of its shop fronts; its work-a-day interiors reflected the stout practicality of earlier immigrants. Carrying on business in quaintly formal English, the newcomers displayed a touching eagerness to please their customers, but beyond exchanging a few social pleasantries there was nothing much one could say to them. Some of them were given to chewing betel nut, clearing their throats with loud harrumphs, often interrupting a sales pitch to growl in their native tongue at an erring assistant, or chortle over some topical in-joke shared with bargain hunters from their home countries. At first you and I joined in the laughter for old time's sake but we felt pretty stupid.

There wasn't a decent bookstore in sight for miles. College-educated Nambiar was an exception, but he mostly stocked pamphlets containing arcane religious commentaries, almanacs and spiritual guides. Little India packed the Tivoli for weekend entertainment, swooning over febrile romances from Bollywood. Returning from Kingman College, I made straight for home, barely looking at any of those worthies toiling away behind their counters, unwinding reams of textile before customers, or meticulously returning small change to shoppers in groceries, dreaming of the day when they would play host to their entire ancestral town in India, at their daughter's wedding.

To me Jackson Heights was a transit camp, where an asylum seeker might bide his time, pending a move to a salubrious environs, with urbane and informed neighbors, although the turnover in spouse trade was bound to be brisk in such places. According to family legend, after a dust-tormented journey in 1593, my Persian ancestors had taken shelter for a few days at a dung-littered caravanserai on the outskirts of the Khyber Pass, before their final trek on camel back to imperial Agra.

Only a cynic would call my attitude to the traders condescending.

Still, I must confess there was none of that love-thy-neighbor-as-thyself in the way I conducted myself; when accompanied by Maury Lee, I started dropping in at the Peacock Diner for a spot of mango *lassi*. The diner was a neutral place where one could be under the same roof with the locals and not be obliged to socialize with them.

In Jackson Heights everyone seemed to know everything about everybody. Later, when I made friends with Bookstore-Nambiar, Thakorji and Badé Miyan, I was astonished to find how much they knew about you and me. They had almost every detail down pat, not just where we came from and where I worked but all about our extended family, which included some pretty colorful characters, including an uncle who was in the habit of riding his charger up the winding staircase to his master bedroom. Indians respect teachers almost universally, but the fact that I taught English at Kingman College made me special in their eyes. I was one of them, but also like the *goras*, as they called white Americans who scrubbed their bottoms with paper instead of water.

In Inderpur, our Munshi dealt with the butcher, the baker and the candlestick maker. Ammeejan prepared the list of things she wanted and Munshiji placed orders on her behalf. Groceries were delivered at home; the barber, the tailor, the cobbler and the *dhobi* regularly visited our place to attend to our various needs. I lived in the *kothi* located in the old part of Inderpur, but as the son and heir to Nawabsahib's family I was always cocooned in a small inviolate space, out of bounds to the lesser breed. On the cobbled streets, people would walk around me as though I were a statue ring-fenced in impenetrable respectability. This rubbing shoulders with the ragtag and bobtail was a novel experience for me. Which is not to say that we lived in an ivory tower. Far from it. Though a princess by birth, my grandmother had trained as an emergency nurse and helped her husband modernize the government hospital, of which he was the chief medical officer. It was a time of great nationalist fervor in India, and the independent-minded young maharaja of Inderpur provided shelter to freedom fighters on the run from the British, who charged him diamond studded necklaces for looking the other way.

Days passed swiftly at Kingman College, teaching and attending meetings of various committees; but in the desolation of the nights, Inderpur, my lost city behind the hills, flashed back, penetrating my lids, forcing open clogged portals.

And somewhere along the railway tracks, gradually petering out under lush monsoon greenery, rose the shrill, massive head of a dark, malignant locomotive flooding my sleep with its milk of magnesia light.

$ 3 $

I never found out where the subway mendicant went when the Korean store closed for the night. I looked for him among the few slow-moving silent figures who occasionally came out from the far reaches of Jackson Heights. I imagined them to be Holocaust survivors or victims of state-sponsored terrorism in their former lands, whose rib cages, as depicted in *Life* magazine, resembled pot-bellied wicker coops in which Inderpur's poor stored their chickens at night. They still carried the singed look of those plucked from a burning pyre, but when they smiled, life surged back in their eyes like a lighthouse beam breaking through fog. I thought living in proximity to such consummate relocation experts might be instructive; some of their survival skills were bound to rub off on me. Sometimes I followed them as they moved with unseeing eyes, without bumping into anyone. I was like a boat run aground, deck still intact but with a fractured keel rotting in the mud below. I lacked their great silence; an inner radiance steered them as they glided through the bustling streets, lateen sails passing smoothly between pier heads.

The following year, when members of the Jackson Heights Conservation Committee served Natthuram of Kohinoor Jewelers a legal notice for altering his shop front without seeking prior permission, I allowed myself to be drafted in his defense team. Rescuing underdogs was a family tradition with the Amolinis.

Where old Natthuram came from, shop fronts could be painted incandescent purple without inviting official censure. Jit Singh, the head waiter at the diner, told me how Natthuram, with his bare-bones

English, was being hounded by the conservation zealots. I was urged to intercede.

At first I didn't see why I should get involved in what was obviously an open-and-shut case. Besides, I had seen Natthuram's round figure waddling along KC Way in an ill-fitting blue safari suit, a gold chain bouncing on his hairy chest. He reminded me of the nouveau riche businessmen-turned-politicians who had lately taken over the once elegant Inderpur Club with its wainscoted Men's Bar, its quiet Edwardian décor, and reduced it to a roisterous caravanserai, upsetting the old-time waiters by their loutish behavior. In other words, he was hardly the stuff victims of unjust persecution are made of.

But you urged me to help him for the sake of little Yamini, the jeweler's youngest child, who had attached herself to our Gullu and followed her everywhere. It was difficult for the likes of Natthuram to make a transition from rural India to urban America. 'Any yokel from Texas,' you said, 'had an advantage over them, when it came to making adjustments required by the city that never slept.'

You admired our neighbors' skimping ways, shared their craving for familiar food, which brought us together under one roof at the Peacock Diner. Our lives and theirs had so far run along different tracks, but our palates watered at the whiff of the same curry powder.

People saw us as lovers in exile and opened their homes to us. We brought romance into the drab lives of Rehana Qureshi and Bookstore-Nambiar. Every time Gullu came down with flu or fever, the Qureshis rushed to our aid like overanxious grandparents. On her birthday came sumptuous trayfulls of sweets from Badé Miyan's Karachi Halwa, and Bookstore-Nambiar made a special trip to Manhattan for illustrated children's classics. Eventually, my quest for a culturally compatible place was quietly abandoned.

The Jackson Heights Conservation Committee, or HCC, was made up mostly of retirees who gave me a patient hearing with grave avuncular faces.

'All right, Professor,' said the chairperson, 'shoot. How are we to interpret this act of your countryman's?'

I coughed politely and said, 'Not as a deliberate thumbing of nose at local convention but as an inability to see an inch beyond his nose. In our ancient land,' I told him, 'a mere hundred-year-old building claiming antiquity is viewed as an upstart, a schoolboy wearing a false mustache and beard. History has to be a toothless old crone, like the cat Deuteronomy tottering with palsy, to command attention from a casual passerby.'

Men like Natthuram, I said, are simply not used to consulting anyone before they decide to build an extension to their establishment. Their kind make little distinction between public and private spaces: then one fine day they take the oath of allegiance and promise to defend the US Constitution. They return from the ceremony waving a tiny American flag but don't know what to do with it.

My tone was of compassionate irony as I explained that in a typical old Indian township, jewelers or goldsmiths would have a street of their own, just as other sections of town would be set aside for blacksmiths, carpenters and cobblers, respectively. Such, anyway, was the street map of Inderpur. What was forbidden practice on one street was an endearing foible on another.

Save for one rather fiery member of the HCC, a spinster of limited social awareness called Margery Blackwell, everyone agreed to send Natthuram away with a flea in his ear.

The recalcitrant Marge resigned in protest, and from then on, I became a sort of cultural ambassador to the Indian community in Jackson Heights. I felt a slight twinge of guilt for speaking patronizingly about my compatriots. Even though roughneck strangers in Inderpur had rubbed my nose in the mud, the feeling of being set apart from the rest was still there. All the scorn and derision Prince Dicky and my ancestors felt for the trading classes had perhaps filtered down into our consciousness and the near-death experience in the wild streets of Inderpur, which had left me feeling like 'one of the ruins that Cromwell knocked about a bit', as Marie Lloyd used to sing, had done little to wipe out the sense of being special, the chosen one.

Perhaps some such sense of belonging to an exclusive club of delicately nurtured artists and writers, grossly misunderstood by the *hoi polloi,* had later prompted me to dismiss charges of blasphemy against *The Satanic Verses.*

It was strange to come back to Jackson Heights and hear the various accents of home after spending mornings and afternoon in the rarefied atmosphere of Kingman College. Everywhere, India was being enacted as if it were a script specially written for the benefit of Manhattan. A sense of an on-going pageant, a colorful spectacle, attached itself to the sounds and gestures of people behind the counters. At every step, one came face to face with India distilled and packaged; familiar historical sites stared down from posters and brochures, touting our five-thousand-year past.

Ownership of such antiquity created an illusion of untold riches and splendor. From busboys at the Peacock Diner to jewelers, grocers and haberdashers, everyone got into the habit of performing the Indian dance for the benefit of visitors. With our songs, our tales, life styles and fads we turned our corner of New York into a little theme park. It was hard to resist this ersatz India of Jackson Heights, while the real thing wobbled and convulsed.

Sweetheart, do you remember how after that Natthuram affair, every time we entered the Peacock Diner we were greeted with a respectful buzz? Maury Lee said it reminded him of the scene in *Casablanca* where Ingrid Bergman and Paul Henried walk into Rick's Café Américain for the first time. Indeed, with your rose-petal complexion and body draped in that flowing white chiffon sari, you looked like a maharani of times gone by, caught on the steps of Casino Monte Carlo by a society photographer.

I know you are amused every time the head waiter, Jit Singh, comes to our table and fusses over me. You can't wait to get home and mimic his pompous manner.

'Professor Sahib, your health condition seems so-so today. You are not eating your vindaloo.'

I love the way you laugh when I put on a melancholy Hamlet expression and say to Jit, 'I have of late—but wherefore I know not—lost all my mirth.'

The poor man doesn't understand what's what, and words of concern come tumbling down his areca-stained lips. Soon I put him out of his misery.

'No, I am fine. I am not very hungry. May I have some coffee now?'

My dear wife forgets that Jitendra Singh is from Fatia Bad, famous all over central India for its *gulab jamun* packed in earthenware bowls. A gentleman farmer turned waiter through the vagaries of what our young colleague Reeny Babukhan calls Indian 'diaspora', the head waiter, with his open, grey-templed, sharp-eyed look and sword-cut mustache is the iconic face of feudal India. He marches off to get coffee instead of ordering one of the underlings to serve it. While I am apt to dress up distress in the Bard's full-flavored lingo, Jit's English sounds like rain falling over a tin roof as he translates directly from Hindi, sending you into peals of quite unladylike laughter. It has to be said though, that old Jit does not squander his courtesies on all Toms, Dicks and Harrys who have clawed their way into Jackson Heights on forged documents for 'making moneys by hooks and crooks'.

You of all people should know that Jit's expansiveness owes something to my status back home as a *nawabzada*, scion of a *khandan* Muslim princely caste, from the state of Pacheesghar. As a Bombay girl, you have never understood the courtly ways of Inderpur. Perhaps you are right in thinking that Jit and I, at our 'arcane little tableau', are like some 'seedy members of the Russian aristocracy in their enforced exile in Paris after the Revolution'. You must remember that Jit belongs to an ancient Hindu clan of Rajput *thakurs*, and his over-elegant courtesy to yours truly implies fealty to a fellow blue blood.

All around us Indian American families are tucking into vindaloo and butter chicken. Each of them wears a different face, a distinct smell, yet they all trail the same loam-covered roots wrenched from distant soils. Some smell of curry steaming out of terrace houses in the north of England, of aromatic restaurants from New Zealand to New Jersey, of grimy uniforms at gas stations, musty taxicabs, seedy no-questions-asked motels in Texas. Then there are those who set up shops in Jackson Heights.

'What do they smell like?' you ask.

'Like Bombay Duck.'

Those were Marge Blackwell's words. You remember?

It's all behind us now, thank goodness; but let me tell you, I found it easier to persuade the HCC to drop the charges against Natthuram than to pacify our own lot.

The poor misguided Blackwell woman was thinking of Bombay of the congested suburbs, like Andheri with its open drains, not the sleek and gleaming commercial sections of Nariman Point or Marine Drive, where your parents lived in a luxurious ultramodern flat.

As you said, all in all it was an unfortunate misunderstanding. But remember how miffed some of our Indian friends were? Do that impersonation of Chitral.

'But why for, when we are talking of New York, we are having Manhattan in mind, not Harlem? But here everyone is thinking Bombay means Bhendi Bazaar.'

I suppose your talent for mimicry owes something to your being born under the sign of Bombay Talkies.

You said Mr Chitral could not abandon Bombay fast enough, and managed to build a fortune selling saris on the backs of poor relatives. They were made to slave for room and board without wages or health insurance.

Luckily for us Mr Chitral's is not the only face of immigration in Jackson Heights.

Bookstore-Nambiar, who is from Kerala, specializes in spiritual topics and stocks cassettes of Hindu religious songs, has only a tourist's knowledge of Bombay; yet how upset he was by that woman's jibe! Your Bookstore-Nambiar-on-the-warpath impression, in that Bollywoodish South Indian accent, rolling your eyes and puffing your cheeks, always has Gullu in stitches.

'Have you seen our Bombay, eh, have you seen Rajabai Tower, Victoria Terminus, Taj Mahal Hotel eh, eh? I am afraid, Mrs Blackwell, you won't be able to afford a room even for a night at the Taj Intercontinental, if I may say so.'

I am sure our Gullu has inherited her talent for mimicry from you.

Looking at the portrait of astronaut Chawla you ask, 'Where does she fit in?' To her, the entire planet beckoned like home as she peered down from deep space.

'When you look at the stars and the galaxy,' the astronaut said, 'you feel that you are not just from any particular piece of land, but from the solar system.'

The future skywalker would have been no more than a tiny wisp of a girl in pigtails somewhere in rural Punjab when we were married. Fast-forward thirty-five years and her heroic saga hovers over my travel-soiled narrative like a resplendent spaceship over a battered jalopy on a country road.

❧ 5 ❧

At home, gravediggers were busy on both sides of the border. Self-induced amnesia in Pakistan occluded the five-thousand-year-old pre-Islamic heritage of Mohenjo-daro, which traded with ancient Sumer, and crabbed archaeology in India accused the exquisite Taj of standing on the grave of an ancient Hindu temple.

There was embarrassed silence in Little India.

The American melting pot had leaked steadily into its consciousness.

Thakorji of Draupadi Saris, Qureshi Chacha of Dhaka Food Court, Bookstore-Nambiar, attorney Durbar Singh, Badé Miyan—alias Abdul Latif of Karachi Halwa—and Uncle Edulji of Mandalay were among its founding fathers. As a group, they presented a chiseled Mount Rushmore face to the world outside.

I felt relieved and insulated from all that madness at home. I'd let go of Inderpur and pole-vaulted into the unknown. You followed me, as a faithful Indian wife should. New World, they called this place, and true to its name, it has not been without a few surprises. England resembled to a tee its holographic image projected by Phyllis and Tilly at the Palace School in Inderpur. As soon as I got off the ferry at Dover in the early sixties, it had settled around me comfortably like a Savile Row suit.

I wasn't prepared for this sky-filling parallax of New York. In old Hollywood movies, ships are always docking at the piers, followed by a close-up of Cary Grant boarding a taxi. Romantic plot rather than the physical geography dictates the sequence, and in the next scene, he is on top of the Empire State Building looking for Deborah Kerr, who doesn't show up because she was crippled by an accident.

Remember how we panicked when we emerged at JFK after collecting our baggage and couldn't find Maury Lee? Even Immy was nervous, despite his nonchalant all-knowing air. When we finally spotted our friend we simply collapsed into his arms.

It rained buckets on that 4th of July, patriotism was in the air. The Star-Spangled Banner fluttering from tops of modest looking homes baffled us. In crotchety old India, we see the tricolor adorning a building and assume it must harbor some government office choking under piles of dusty files.

Immy, whose eyes had glowed with déjà vu in Manhattan, looked a bit dazed by the firework display in the sky at night. He remained glued to the window of our hotel, seemed wary as if it had just sunk in, that he was really in America and had to keep his room neat and tidy, make a good impression on the natives. And we, we were a bit sheepish and let Maury Lee shepherd us through the exacting geometry of Manhattan.

At first we were quite frankly ill at ease, felt lost in the constant underground hum and clatter of the subway, the interminable verticality of the skyscrapers against the constant flow of traffic, and everywhere the glass with its bewildering lack of transparency. Coming to Jackson Heights was a relief.

Immy had, by age twelve, soaked up much American history and popular culture through comics such as *Peanuts* and *Superman*, repeated viewings of Hollywood Westerns, and frequent visits to the US Information Library in Inderpur. It was so funny and touching to hear him recite the Gettysburg Address, when the punctilious immigration officer at JFK finally stamped our passports. You were afraid that if we were not waived in immediately, Immy might overdo the returning prodigal by treating the officer to some forensic exchange from *Gun Fight at the O.K. Corral* or *The Man from Laramie*. His mastery of American slang and crew cut owed something to Maury Lee's fieldwork in Inderpur.

That first day in America has stuck in my mind like a slightly askew picture frame on a blank wall and every effort to straighten it has merely resulted in another tilt. Even when the routines of life were well established, and Immy's slang grew wildly abstruse and his accent twangy, something held me back. I would break out in cold sweat and my eyes would snap open seconds before a hideous smile faded away slowly.

Jackson Heights put its arms around us reassuringly. I knew that ghosts haunting the ramparts of Inderpur would not be able to get past the immigration desks at JFK. For the first time in many months, I felt safe. No more hallucinatory daggers. The earth stretched and seemed roomier, the horizon drew back, and I could breathe freely at last. You smiled in your sleep.

Once I got over my squeamishness about money-grubbing traders, Jackson Heights seemed a bracing, sunrise sort of place. The sheer energy released by immigrants poised hopefully on the brink of a new prosperity was infectious. Stepping outside was not exactly a 'Hey nonny nonny and a merry tra la' experience; still, the bored-tourist-at-a-loss feeling I had earlier completely disappeared within a year of our residence here.

Maury Lee had always been a true insider; his parents' penny-pinching life had earned them a comfortable retirement in Florida, without bartering their home in Jackson Heights for hard cash.

To us, Maury Lee's wife Judy must always remain a mystery woman. A few days before she returned from fieldwork, we came upon this old heap with its Tudor façade. Its location in the English Garden section of Jackson Heights seemed to us more than a happy coincidence. In the kitchen I could smell a steaming cup of tea and a plate piled up with hot buttered toast. Those twin gables gave the house an aura of hooded sanctuary. It wasn't a 'walk-up apartment', as Maury Lee put it, but then Bayside, where Kingman sprawled along the lengthy shore-front, was only a fifteen-minute ride.

There was no one in our family who had been to America, most of the Amolinis having been Oxbridge types, but our Immy's first words out of the cradle had a distinctly Yankee accent. Even as a baby, Immy had that hot-dog smile with a French-fry burp, so to speak.

During Maury Lee's stay in Inderpur, the right wing Mafia's threat to our well being had not risen beyond the dogs-barking-caravan-passing stage. But later, when that tin-pot despot Bulchand, with every rag in town in his pocket, accused me of being a Pakistani spy, we were not amused. We Amolinis are not averse to gallows humor, but at a proper time and place.

That bit of mudslinging killed my Ammeejan. I can never forget the way her face crumpled when she heard the slanderous report from our cook. My only crime was joining a protest march organized by our friend Lepakshi and her husband against the local police, who terrorized the tribals for sport or off-duty entertainment.

For a hundred and fifty years before Dicky's warlike clan put us out to pasture, we Amolinis had been the rulers of Inderpur. While we emasculated ourselves writing verses about roses and beautiful women whose faces were like the 'moon of the fourteenth night', his marauding forbears trained to scale fortresses and joust. Relieved of administrative chores, we grew flabby and effete, but never ceased to think of Inderpur as anything other than our bailiwick. The spying charge was an insult to my childhood, to the games of street cricket, to smoking of beedis with neighborhood urchins, and above all, to the mouldering graves of my ancestors.

Abbajan had already succumbed prematurely to cardiac arrest before I went to England.

You gave me courage to fight back, and I stuck it out for two more years. Then something happened, something that was like a trapeze artist tumbling into a laughing-stock moment.

There was a communal riot in town and no news of your husband. You rang the English Department but the phone was dead. Out on the cobbled pathways of the Kasbah, you heard the police patrol telling people to keep indoors. Later that evening, Lepakshi telephoned to say

I was staying at their bungalow on the campus; it was dangerous for me to try and get home until curfew was lifted. Two days later, when her husband drove me over, you caught sight of my face in the blinding light of the sun. I tried to smile but my eyes wouldn't let me; they were blank like a halal goat's. You didn't ask any questions; just bent over me like a nursing mother.

Instead of opening the old padlocked family armory and selecting a weapon of choice to blast Bulchand's head off, I lay there like a circus clown thrashing about in the safety net, wondering how the Persian architect who was allegedly buried alive by Emperor Shahajehan to prevent him from replicating the beauty of the Taj, faced the last brick hammered into place. Next, my thoughts wandered off to Verdi's Rhadames and Aida bricked up in a tomb in Egypt for defying tyranny, and Puccini's Tosca hurling herself over the castle wall rather than be captured. Stuff of legend and opera.

A city was dying, a civilization was ending, and all I was left with by way of sustenance was a pair of wax pomegranates. When faced with a real hard choice in life, I flinched and ran, panicking at the realization that such esoteric knowledge carefully cultivated at Cambridge had become fake, irrelevant as an umpire at a brawling game of street cricket. Nowhere in the world had men of good will been reduced to such a freakish sideshow by wily thugs masquerading as politicians.

It was your idea that I should write to my Cambridge contemporary Miriam Shapiro. Save for exchanging New Year's cards, I hadn't really kept up with Miriam, who had been at Newnham with Ann during my Cambridge years. You held no grudge against Ann. Instead you said, 'Think what will happen if you don't get out. You would be just one more ghost among many if you allow yourself to be destroyed by men like Bulchand. He owns Inderpur now, not your friend Dicky. So set aside your fine misgivings and write to this Miriam.'

Maury Lee says that as soon as he led me to President Amanda Carmichael's office, she and I were cooing at each other like birds of a feather. 'I had no idea,' he said 'that you were such a hotshot opera buff.' How was he to know that Phyllis Tillinghast, our matron in Inderpur, had plied us with generous doses of Renata Tebaldi's arias, along with Gee's linctus in the school infirmary? Here in America, Verdi and Puccini were *personae grata* again, and I was back on the swinging platforms high up in the air.

There was a Met poster of Leontyne Price as Aida in her office, and soon the president was lamenting her dear husband's passing away. She had two tickets for a daring new version of *The Marriage of Figaro*. At the time, I had not heard of Stefanie Izzo, whose Susanna proved to be absolutely enchanting in the Brooklyn Repertory Opera's production that evening, but as soon as Amanda Carmichael opened her handbag and dangled those tickets before me, I gallantly declared, 'Madam, I would be more than happy to accompany you.'

Then sometime in the late eighties, *The Satanic Verses* flew in to Jackson Heights like a bird of ill omen.

❧ 6 ☙

Sometimes at dusk I catch sight of those slow silent men moving through the crowds, listing gracefully away like Venetian galleys from small flotillas of shoppers. Their stillness, a granary seen through a glass darkly by the hungry, their fragile smile the only clue to the riches stored within.

Those of us who live by the word often find ourselves barred from that enormous silence.

'This isn't the first time your literary brain teaser has backfired,' you said. 'An old-school type like Mr Farooqui was bound to think your tone insulting.'

I had not meant to hurt Mr Farooqui's feelings. He was a community leader from Brooklyn dressed in a traditional black buttoned-up *sherwani* and a green skull cap. He wore a patch over his right eye; his yellow-flecked, bellicose left eye never blinked once during the whole interview.

The local TV channel had invited him to provide a layman's perspective on *The Satanic Verses*. I naturally assumed that I was there to represent the teaching fraternity, a community of cultivated minds, a brotherhood of pen pushers and readers between the lines. Besides, I honestly felt that politics. rather than common sense, drove the crowd clamoring for a ban on the book.

So when the question came up whether I shared Mr Farooqui's opinion about the author being an apostate I said, 'Actually, he is simply a brilliant writer who unfortunately finds himself like a stricken bird at the mercy of small people.'

Call it an ivory tower syndrome, but somewhere at the back of my mind was a poem of Baudelaire's about the artist as an albatross, held captive by a belligerent crowd.

A misspoken word and suddenly I had found myself pitch-forked into a duel with a grim-faced adversary. Indeed, when the discussion was over, Farooqui had simply turned his back and hurried out of the studio like a miffed pirate of Penzance.

Prompted by you I wrote him a letter of apology, which brought a barely cordial reply.

Jackson Heights is not a reading community, and I had not reckoned with the capacity of Farooqui to shoehorn an extra bit of malice into innocent words. If I thought my brush with the Muslim leader was like a minor accident on the loop line of a toy train, a storm in a teacup vaguely threatening the tranquillity of distant shores, I couldn't have been more mistaken. My ears, always nervously cocked to great reckonings in little rooms, once again picked up the sound of another shipwreck.

In this alien setting, under milk white sheets, I had hoped to outlive that moment when Inderpur had turned on me like a whelped tigress and tried to devour me. I thought here no one would notice my crimped skin, so carefully had I camouflaged the scar.

By then Jackson Heights was well settled in our eyes and minds and even perhaps in our hearts; yet my sense of exile had not fully cauter-ized. Emotionally you were better prepared for such a sudden and wrenching move.

You must know by now that without you I would be lost like a dead Egyptian waking alone in an empty pyramid.

❦ 7 ❦

Ramadan, the month when eternal time redeems the present, was upon us.

Half awake one morning, I sensed an unusual bustle of activity in the house, save for the kitchen, where no kettle whistled nor could be heard the usual tintinnabulation of crockery. Dying for a cup of tea, I entered the dining room and found it empty. You were closeted in your room with Rehana Qureshi and came out for a moment to announce that no tea or breakfast would be served from that day on; you had decided to join the Qureshis and Badé Miyan's extended family in abstaining from food and water from dawn till dusk. This was to be a mega fasting for the entire duration of Ramadan; I would have to eat out, since our kitchen would be closed until nightfall. Behind you, I could see the snickering Rehana peering at me with her round bovine eyes.

Without my morning tea I am barely awake and thought I had stumbled into an absurd, subterranean nightmare, where bellicose strangers sitting at the table nonchalantly devour your breakfast.

I had forgotten that although you had grown up in Bombay's ultra-modern environment, at home your family did observe Ramadan and the festivals of Eid.

I was not going to stand and be lectured by you or anyone while perishing slowly of tea deprivation, so I found an old Earl Gray bag in a kitchen drawer and made myself a cuppa in the microwave oven. It was a tepid imitation of the real thing, but it revived me enough to try and grasp the gravity of the situation facing me.

Could your decision to resume fasting be a silent act of defiance for the way I had dismissed Farooqui's charge of blasphemy aimed at *The Satanic Verses*? It seemed too far-fetched that you would subject our entire household to monastic abstinence over a book you had not even bothered to read.

Reeny fasted during Ramadan because she was irreligious to the point of being religious. Hers was a political gesture; she would enter the cafeteria at Kingman to talk to a colleague and when invited to have a cup of coffee, she would let it be known, with elaborate gestures of renunciation, that she couldn't ingest any food or drink during the day. In the month of Ramadan, Dr Babukhan became a pious Muslim. Toothless Iqbal Miyan, our gatekeeper in Inderpur, would have cackled loudly and said, 'After polishing off over one hundred mice, Miss Kitty-cat is now headed for Hadj.'

It was pure political theatre, but you, my dear Shabnam, were incapable of empty gestures. Had someone drawn back the curtain on a long-put-on-hold spiritual yearning? Was it some ominous bird from the past returned to its nest after a long migratory night? Or was it something that was hastily buried to appease me, some silent sacrifice required of an Indian bride to bend her will to her husband's whim, now clamoring for exhumation?

Not even during the darkest hour in Inderpur did I feel so starkly abandoned. You told me not to fuss.

'I am only doing it,' you said, 'for those simple folk whose cases I handle so that they won't think I am some sort of a freak. It helps build confidence with our Muslim clients. We exchange recipes, and they advise me on what I should cook at night after each day's fasting. Don't tell Durbar though; like you, he thinks all these rituals are meaningless.'

But my anxiety grew day by day. One day I telephoned Immy.

'I don't understand it,' I said. 'What do you think has happened to your mum? All this deliberate starving by day and gorging on food at night. It doesn't make sense.'

'Dad, you worry too much,' he said. 'I am sure it's a passing fad. Mom is the least spiritual person I have ever known. Behind that pious exterior there is a thoroughly logical brain at work. She is one tough cookie inside. You are the softy really. So relax. It's all this hobnobbing with Mrs Badé Miyan and other *bibi* types that's probably got her hooked.'

Most Muslim shops closed early and folks repaired in small clusters to the white and green Moti Masjid. In the opposite direction, Hindu women in colorful saris, glittering with jewelry, floated like blooms of mist towards Thakorji's brownstone, where a vast hall on the ground floor had been converted into a communal space for the Ganesha Festival. These overlapping festivals, which in Indian cities tended to spark off communal riots, seemed to bind Hindu and Muslim families of Jackson Heights in an expansive fellow feeling.

I had worked so hard for such an alliance, but now, ironically, found myself at odds with it, since in a grotesque reprise of 1857, instead of the British, a book of deferrals and masks seemed to emerge as their common enemy. It would require the balancing skill of a butterfly on the tip of a mud hill to defend the writer.

There was purring camaraderie between Hindus and Muslims during those snuggling days of festivity. Jackson Heights at its best was rather like one of those luxury cruise ships, smoothly sailing under the stars, with light shimmering through portholes, a place of laughter and harmony, where good neighborliness meant a gift-food basket left on your doorstep.

Only Maury Lee was fidgety. There were moments when KC Way looked like a Bollywood set of his Inderpur days, a menacingly quiet street under dim lamplight across which flitted villainous furtive figures with bloodshot eyes, head covered in red bandanas. For a self-described 'cool guy', his tone was uncharacteristically jejune; his words dripped menace, when one afternoon he accosted me outside my office at Kingman.

'I smell something noxious leaking from Chitral's mangy den,' he whispered.

Conspiratorial nudgings had lingered on the tail end of his eye, and so on. Maury Lee assumed I needed some vintage prodding of the sort the lean and hungry Cassius administers to the dithering Brutus to jog him into action. He went to work on me. He declared that Cambridge had trained me to be 'a toreador of thought', adept at executing subtle moves in the seminar room, which were utterly useless when faced with madly charging bulls of the Pamplona breed.

Toreador of thought!

I rather liked the Carmen-like tartness of that phrase.

I recalled that every time he visited our *kothi* in Inderpur he would stare in astonishment at the small bust of my Cambridge mentor, Dr Leavis, sitting on the desk in my study. To him it smacked of idolatry, worship of a graven image, all the more surprising in an emancipated Muslim's home.

You often sided with Maury Lee, and I wasn't surprised when you said, 'Better watch out for that Chitral. His chums are spreading an ugly rumor that Ghaseetkhan, the halal butcher of Broadway Crescent, is collecting money for the guerrillas fighting in Kashmir.'

I said there were bound to be some malodorous specimens like Chitral in every immigrant community.

To me the Hindu Muslim compact in Jackson Heights was a renewable historical project; to you it was a castle in the air.

I desperately needed to believe in my own miracle—not someone walking over water, but someone bouncing on the moon planting flags. Sometimes a few of them failed to bounce back to earth, like astronaut Chawla, and were gathered prematurely 'into the artifice of eternity'. Nevertheless, they were real. We could touch them, walked streets named after them.

Besides, your fasting was eating me away from inside. I should have thought that after nearly three decades with me, you would have learnt to shine the light of intellect on all problems of life. This returning to the bosom of faith, even as a gesture of solidarity with your clients, felt like the betrayal of our marriage vows. Reeny's fasting was calculated to boost support among students during her bid for tenure. College boys and girls are taken in by any stunt calculated to bolster a person's ethnic profile. It appeals to their sense of mystery and romance.

For the first time, Reeny seemed unwilling to squeeze a personal triumph out of the public feuding over *The Satanic Verses*. Or so I thought. There was a catch. As Maury Lee found out, the book provided much needed ammunition to advance her professional career. She had already written two articles defending, in Lacanian terms, the book's 'syntactic excess over the semantic'.

'I am what you might call only a part-time Muslim, because I drink and eat pork,' she would daringly declare to an audience mesmerized by her scintillating small talk.

The so-called evidence against Ghaseetkhan was at best purely circumstantial, mere suppositions, and hearsay.

You eyed me sternly like a school marm across the dinner table and said, 'I am surprised, that after what happened to you in Inderpur, you still have that sweet belief in people's inner goodness.'

Why did I cling to the worn tapestry of 1857 so desperately? Because in the Inderpur of my childhood it had a compelling aura. You had grown up in Bombay, perhaps the most London-haunted city outside anything Dickens had dreamt of.

Following the partition of India in 1947, when Hindus and Muslims in the north fell on each other as though competing for an Olympic gold medal in human slaughter, neighborhood bonds in Inderpur proved to be so strong that not a single Muslim family felt the need to seek police protection.

Memory of that event was well worth the gamble. Perhaps, behind every winning number there's a quixotic lotto addict.

Thakorji, Badé Miyan and Qureshi did not deliberately set about to retrofit Jackson Heights to that elusive compact of 1857; shrewd businessmen living in the crucible of exile, they had lots of ready-made face-saving devices up their sleeves.

You feared that I might fall into the old trap that had led me to venture out alone during communal riots in Inderpur, like the sheriff in Immy's favorite Western *High Noon*. You thought this witless urge of an outsider to fit in with the crowd, a Cambridge-bred fantasy of rationalism, fixation with historical accounts of ideal brotherhood transcending man-made artificial divisions, was no more than tilting at the mill.

For centuries, my ancestors had striven to put Inderpur on the map of India—paved its roads, helped build its ramparts, promoted its arts, till it won renown as a cultural capital of the province.

Perhaps its descent into a carrion city under fascist occupation had deranged me. I was like a Parisian shamed by the sight of Nazis marching down the Champs Elysées, looking for any means to restore its past splendor.

Every significant moment in history splinters as time goes by; the mind cannot confront it as a whole. Memory has to pick up the pieces bit by bit, and sometimes a crucial segment is missed. I failed to notice that some important markers and signposts had vanished from the otherwise edifying narrative of 1857.

In the autumn of 1989, *The Satanic Verses* landed in Jackson Heights and splurged like Gulliver across Lilliput, while boggle-eyed locals pelted brickbats at the thing.

For the first time since we were married, I wasn't sure of your complete support.

The kindly wizened faces of Qureshi Chacha and Badé Miyan of Karachi Halwa were frigid with reproof. My old habit of fashioning hideous masks from history's missteps and wrong turns made me jump at the slightest scrabble at the door.

Once I followed for a mile an old man who had the burnt-offering look of a genocide survivor. I assumed he had witnessed the burning of churches and synagogues, the smashing of glass windows. He might be an escapee from a *shtetl* before it went up in smoke, or a petrified onlooker, from behind closed doors, to the Nazis burning copies of Thomas Mann's books in Berlin on 10 May 1933. I thought these men were veterans who had 'foresuffered it all', and knew that 'Where books are burned,' as Heine said, 'human beings are destined to be burned.'

When I caught up with the old man, I realized my mistake. He looked up, gave me a doltish smile, and kept walking. Perhaps he was only a drunk going home from a bar to a bitter impecunious wife. Perhaps there was nothing to distinguish fugitives of injustice from ordinary men and women. Some of them might even look like prosperous bankers. My imagination had attributed a long suffering past to a grubby old clown who had fallen by the wayside.

His smile told me nothing I didn't already know.

Meanwhile back in India, horse trading for Muslim votes led to the banning of the book. This act of political chicanery was a signal to consign copies of *The Satanic Verses* to an open fire.

﹏ 8 ﹏

A book of elusive meanings was being dragged through the lanes like a political effigy. Rain falling on a graveyard best described my mood. Unable, in all honesty, to badmouth the young author, I was paralyzed.

Thakorji stepped forward at that murky moment to suggest a viable alternative to book burning. I had great admiration for that tall, silent, clean-shaven man with a smile that reached out to you the moment you entered his shop. His silences were an invitation for others to speak; in loquacious Jackson Heights he was the ear.

When Kanti came home that night with Susan, you lovingly fed him chicken biryani and caramel custard. You had lavished maternal affection on him for almost ten years. From hosting birthday parties and monitoring his school records to helping him with his math, you had done everything—short of breast-feeding—that a real mother would have done for that sad enigmatic boy. Such prolonged intimacy had wiped out the sense of surrogacy, and for him our apartment had become the home he would first return to from a long odyssey.

At one point that evening, his deep-rooted Hindu squeamishness wouldn't allow him to accept the glass of water offered by Susan. He was choking and gagging after swallowing something the wrong way. You gently thumped his back till his eyes stopped watering. It was your tact that transformed what was an embarrassing moment into a little sociological joke. Your newfound faith had not curbed your fondness for that son of Hindu parents.

After the pair left I said, 'Susan must have felt snubbed; it was such a tender gesture, holding a glass to her boyfriend's lips.'

'Why should she?' you said from the kitchen. 'Everyone is not like you. Susan knows that there are certain connections made in your childhood that are never broken.'

Even though your voice betrayed no emotion, you spoke with such certainty that I was left groping for an answer. I felt outwitted and rebuked. It was disconcerting watching this new you stacking dishes, pushing loose strands of hair with the back of your hand. I don't know what possessed me, but I wanted to crush you in my arms and kiss that lovely, modeled neck of yours, but you looked peeved and elbowed me away.

I had presentiments of some dire loss. I remembered how butterflies, released by my childish fingers, would leave whorls of yellow and persimmon. The purlicue of thumb and forefinger used to make wings on a white sheet of paper. Empty handed, I watched the water fizz and gurgle down the drain when you turned off the faucet. Somehow I knew that my finger tips would no longer feel the yielding texture of those wings. From the radio wafted the pensive 'Chorus of the Hebrew Slaves' from Verdi's *Nabucco*.

Thakorji, Qureshi and Badé Miyan of Karachi Halwa went from door-to-door to wish Muslim families happiness on Eid al-Fitr, and also to invite them to an informal get-together the next day to discuss possible alternatives to book burning. I thought an appeal to moderate Muslims like Qureshi and Badé Miyan, highlighting the rational elements in the Islamic tradition of Moorish Cordoba might do the trick. It shows how blind I was to the realities on the ground. I should have realized that if Moorish Cordoba had turned up on a lonely road and tried to thumb a ride from them, they wouldn't have stopped to pick it up.

Every dozen or so years, the Hindu Navaratri Festival and Ramadan coincide during September and October, and the large hall at Thakorji's own old brownstone is temporarily converted into a shrine. During the just-concluded Ganesha Festival, the red and gold, pot-bellied deity, smothered in flowers, had reclined there on a canopied throne, with a benign elephant face, eyes crinkling in a private-joke smile.

Thakorji's choice for a neutral venue fell on the community hall of the local Baptist Church. Rev. Stilwell, under whose ministration the congregation had grown from all-white to multiethnic, agreed to preside. The pastor welcomed everybody from the podium and Bookstore-Nambiar set the tone for the evening's proceedings.

The Kerala Brahmin began by speaking about his Muslim neighbors in Cochin, with whom his family had lived peaceably for centuries. He talked of one particular friend who had taken him home when Nambiar's own mother was dying.

'My friend's mother is giving me food first, before giving food to her own son. For one week, she is procuring vegetarian food from a Hindu restaurant,' Nambiar recalled with tears in his eyes.

'I am absolutely certain that the aforementioned book will be making my Amma, not my real mother, but better than real mother Umrao Bano of Cochin, very unhappy and anything making her unhappy will be making me unhappy here,' he said pounding his chest, beneath which pulsed one heck of a good heart.

Thakorji had shrewdly judged that those assembled were most eager to hear the learned Professor Sahib's views on the book.

As I ascended the podium, I caught a glimpse of you sitting at the back of the hall with Maury Lee. You looked like a director who knows, on the opening night of an underrehearsed *Don Giovanni*, that the lead tenor has a nasty cold and is likely to sneeze in Zerlina's upturned face during '*La ci darem la mano*', possibly the most romantic duet in all opera. Even at that distance I could feel the intensity of your gaze.

I began by reminding the audience of the liberal Andalusian Arab culture and cutting-edge scholars like Al Baradi and Avicenna, who held the opinion that the Holy Koran allowed room for debate. The next moment I saw Maury Lee whisper something to you and knew instinctively that I was barking up the wrong tree.

Later he said, 'I am glad you realized that you were not talking to a bunch of bright kids at Kingman. These dudes wouldn't know the difference between the Alhambra and a kitchen garden.'

I could see Ghaseetkhan the halal butcher rolling his eyes and whispering to Hussein, the taxi driver sitting behind him. My ears had caught a swift murmur and bored sighs pass across the hall, and old Thakorji had to raise his hand to appeal for patience. You looked tense and sat there, eyes closed, head lowered, as if waiting for a grenade to explode.

Somehow Bookstore-Nambiar's reference to his surrogate Amma had clicked into collective cultural memory, whereas my opening remarks had produced only yawns and blank stares.

To be quite honest, Bookstore-Nambiar's words had taken me back to my own childhood, when every Friday, Ammeejan distributed alms to fakirs lining up the road to Hira Masjid that went past our *kothi*. Even as I spoke, I felt uncertain about how she would have reacted to *The Satanic Verses*. Would she have been able to separate fact from fiction?

I proceeded cautiously.

'I was brought up to be a free thinker as much as anybody, but if I were aware that some comments in the book would hurt my own mother, my dear Ammeejan, who far from being a zealot, nevertheless had faith in the holiness of the human spirit, I would have certainly not allowed the moving finger that writes to move on.'

I paused with a grateful nod to old Omar Khayyám.

'We tend to forget,' I pressed on, 'that religion also exists outside us in a cultural space, of praying together when one's child is sick or wounded.'

I was thinking of the time when I had walked into Gullu's bedroom to find Rehana Qureshi and you kneeling down in a silent prayer to Allah when our girl lay delirious with fever.

Muslim, Hindu and Christian heads were nodding in unison as I spoke.

Unknown to us, sometimes our metaphors can sweep away from our mind's barn the last remaining straws of discord. I was relieved that I had made my case without blanking out or fudging the issue, and best of all, without persiflage. I might have indulged in some breezy, after-dinner shop talk about Dr Leavis's eccentric walking companion Wittgenstein, who used to say belief in god was like kissing the picture of an absent beloved. But your eyes, trained on me with fierce ardor, reined me in, and I heard myself saying, 'For me, religion is the glow on the face of my mother, not the fierce hatred that reddens the eye of a fanatic.'

Here was an opportunity to make a pitch for the big picture, for giving a leg up to my pet project, the compact—the compact of 1857.

'Only lately have I realized that religion is about forging solid identities in the midst of this fast changing world. To move from the bosom of one civilization—that is, India, Pakistan or Bangladesh—and to be thrown in the midst of a whole range of different nationalities as here in our own Jackson Heights, forces us back into the familiar mental space of our people.'

I felt the power of my own words. A hush descended on the Baptist Community Center. Your eyes moistened with tears of relief as you gave me a thumbs up sign. Rev. Stilwell beamed with pleasure. Only a few incendiary types, who had been looking forward to indulge their pyromania, looked a bit disappointed.

As we walked along KC Way, hand in hand with 'an independent air', I really felt like the man who broke the bank at Monte Carlo.

Peace had returned to Jackson Heights after weeks of discord and our step was jaunty. *The Satanic Verses* moved from inflammable streets to college seminars, and once more checkout counters pinged, merrily scanning bar-coded merchandise. Everyone was relieved that Little India had not cut its comely nose to spite its exotic face. Our display of public affection amused Immy—he hadn't seen us being so cuddlesome since he was a boy—but Gullu said she felt like the girl in a TV commercial who comes home with a school friend to find Mom dressed as a sexy French maid in gathered skirt and serving cap, sitting on Dad's lap, spooning Yoplait into his amorous mouth. Oscar Wilde called it washing one's clean linen in public. We didn't mind. No one turned around and stared when couples strolled down Fifth Avenue holding hands, but straight-laced Jackson Heights did raise a few eyebrows.

As soon as we emerged from the diner, where Jit Singh had buzzed over us like a doting bumblebee, Bookstore-Nambiar joined us, beaming and hailing everyone in sight on KC Way. Even Natthuram's two sons waved from Kohinoor. Their old man was no doubt in the special room at the back of the store, flogging his precious *navratna* (nine rubies) necklace to some NRI lady of means. Chitral pretended not to notice us, although there were no customers in his Sari Palace. We stepped into Mandalay to see Mr Edulji and check how the restless Kanti was settling down to his new job. Business had been slow, even when the old man's wife was alive.

Edulji was at the piano entertaining Officer Haggerty, who listened rapturously as the old Parsi played 'Glocca Morra'.

How are things in Glocca Morra?

Is that little brook still leaping there?

Everyone in Jackson Heights knew Haggerty had a soft corner for Edulji. Perhaps that's why Mandalay had never been burgled.

There was something childlike about the old Parsi, an innocence born of faith in personal neatness. The perfectly knotted tie, the immaculate white shirt tucked properly into a pair of flannel trousers, the gleaming cuff links, the polished shoes and the well-groomed hair brushed back with not a strand out of place were to him the infallible insignia of world order. Tilly was like that. Even at the beginning of summer, when he entered the class, he had the fresh look of someone who had just stepped out of the shower.

Edulji's eighty-nine-year-old face was smooth as porcelain, his neck was wrinkle free and the slightly distended belly a testimony to good Parsi food—apricot chicken, *dhansak*, rice pilaf, *dhal* and fried fish served with a dash of vinegar by a doting mother back in Poona and, after coming to the US, by his loving wife. She had been carried away by a stroke in 1985. Even though alone and widowed, there was nothing slovenly about Edulji; all of Jackson Heights could set its watch by his standard time.

Kanti and Susan were busy attending to customers. Haggerty's eyes lighted up as you kissed Uncle Edujli's cheek. Though classically trained, the old Parsi had a bunch of popular melodies up his sleeve. Whenever we heard the keys churning out, 'O Sole Mio', or 'I'll change my name from Johnny to Giovanni', we were certain Officer Bartiromo had stepped in for a few minutes.

Meanwhile, Haggerty's watchful eyes had spotted a youth gang slouching around the corner of KC Way and 73rd Avenue, where they were invisible from Mandalay. Thakorji's Draupadi stretched across almost half a block. Named after the polyandrous wife of the Mahabharata warriors who could not be stripped, because Lord Krishna kept wrapping her in a sari of unending length, *Draupadi* evoked the old-world charm of medieval India, of merchant princes to whom maharajas and nawabs were beholden for generous loans when their own governments faced bankruptcy.

For the gang, *Draupadi* would be just another cash register to be cracked open later that night with a crowbar. We watched with bated breath as Haggerty, tapping his distended belly and narrowing his eyes like Clint Eastwood, walked slowly over to the gang. The mean looking lads scattered like mice because they knew from past experience that it wouldn't do to tangle with the Big Guy. Only a couple of teenagers, too scared to run, had to bear the brunt of Haggerty's tongue lashing, which never varied in its content.

'Man, look at the East Asians, they have only been here ten years. I remember there was only old Qureshi's grocery back in the seventies when I was a rookie cop, and this was my beat. You slobs are nothing but trouble.'

At least a quarter of the population in Jackson Heights carried the stigma of illegality. Officer Haggerty knew who they were, but as a great-grandson of potato-famine-scarred Irish immigrants, he looked the other way, as long as they didn't screw up.

The middle-aged American couple from Texas, shopping for a suitable present for their Indian doctor in Houston, asked you what you thought of the marble Buddha with a Burmese face that had caught their fancy. But you recommended the compact wooden cabinet from Rajasthan with religious paintings that was on display. It contained several folding panels, depicting in serial form some mythical episodes painted in fetching rustic colors. You sounded so knowledgeable that the Texan's wife asked you if you were a Brahmin. You smiled enigmatically and said, 'Sort of.'

I was so glad you did not mind their mistaking you for a Hindu. How could you, with Bookstore-Nambiar's words still ringing in your ears?

❧ 10 ❧

It was you who first noticed that our Maury Lee, usually so articulate, got tongue-tied in the presence of Reeny Babukan. The poor chap had fallen head over heels for that minx. We never got to know his wife Judy properly. Barely a month after our arrival, she returned from her fieldwork in Nevada, and was off again, this time to California. We simply assumed her visit home was cut short by some follow-up research project, but a year later, when there was no sign of his wife—a large intense redhead with dimpled cheeks and a back-of-the-throat-gurgle of a laugh—Maury Lee confided in you that Judy was never coming back.

In the meantime, his academic interests had shifted from anthropology to film studies, which he team-taught with Reeny. If you needed help to get through a dismal rainy day, you could sit in their class and hear the two of them hold forth on the separation of scenario and image, or mental space and time sequence, in *The Postman Always Rings Twice* and *Double Indemnity*. Maury Lee had an intuitive grasp of film noir of the forties, where the stifling claustrophobic inner world of Lana Turner and Barbara Stanwyck propelled them towards some fatal inevitability, carrying John Garfield and Fred MacMurray with the wash.

An outgoing gregarious man in the prime of his life, Maury Lee had been at a loose end for almost two years when Reeny joined the Kingman faculty. Like a real-life femme fatale, she had proceeded to colonize his mental space with a single-mindedness that would have stirred up the combined envy of Turner and Stanwyck.

Immy's wife Sally, who taught at this very expensive ultramodern school in Manhattan, where nippers aspiring to enroll had to possess almost encyclopedic knowledge, had convinced Gullu that without a pilgrimage to the Grand Canyon she would never be a true American.

'Every American child must visit the Lincoln Memorial in DC and the Grand Canyon, where the soul of America lives,' Sally claimed.

It's not as if Gullu, who had just turned fourteen, had developed formidable powers of persuasion, but her slightest wish had been our command ever since she was a little baby. Gullu wanted to see the Grand Canyon, and off we went. Immy paid for the trip, of course, and when we returned after visiting Yosemite and Yellowstone Park, in addition to the Grand Canyon, Kingman had acquired its very own expert in postcolonial studies by the name of Dr Nasreen Babukhan. Almost the first thing Maury Lee said as he drove us back from La Guardia was, 'Wait till you see her. She is really something. So articulate, intelligent and also stunning to look at. Quite a change from our present chick pool.'

Ordinarily, I should have welcomed the appointment of someone whose name signified an origin in our corner of the world. But the few so-called specialists in postcolonial and other fringe studies I had met had been full of sound and fury, signifying nothing. Listening to Maury Lee's infatuated patter, I had a strange foreboding.

'This Babukhan,' I said to myself, 'sounds like bad news.'

Maury Lee had seen our old *kothi* in the Kasbah, where my ancestors had lived ever since their sojourn from Persia in the sixteenth century. The cobbled streets, the hooded houses with wrought-iron balconies, the hunched-forward, whispering crones and the old retainers padding by silently in the inner courtyard had reminded him of *The Thief of Bagdad* with Douglas Fairbanks. Maury Lee was apt to classify people according to Hollywood genotypes and was, at the moment of Reeny's coming to land on the manicured lawns of Kingman, somewhat vulnerable to women of oriental stripe.

He had dined under chandeliers on *haleem* and *khubani ka meetha*, while Ammeejan urged him to second helpings.

After a major break with family tradition of marrying first cousins, when my grandfather chose for his wife a free-thinking woman educated in a Swiss convent, the House of Amolini had gained even greater distinction, for the bride belonged to a family of emirs at the Nizam of Hyderabad's court. Under her ministrations, our *kothi*, outwardly so very Indian with its domes, arches and rotund structure, had undergone refurbishment, so that the interiors recalled comfortable English manors, with bearded ancestors staring down portrait galleries and a large wainscoted drawing room with Edwardian furniture. Authentic Ming vases lined the corridors.

The Amolinis didn't live in what is called an upscale neighborhood, but there was always an invisible moat around them, which no trespassers were allowed to cross. Our womenfolk, however well educated—one lipstick-wielding aunt with bobbed hair and sleeveless blouses was a chain smoker—were never to be seen walking down the street. Coming and going, they were glimpsed fleetingly through windows of cars or carriages.

Maury Lee had little understanding of the finer points of Indian aristocracy, where every gesture, every rhetorical flourish carried a nuanced meaning decipherable only by those to the manner born. The hint of intellectual sophistication in her expression had misled Maury Lee into thinking that Reeny was a class act.

The founder of Kingman had attended St John's College, Cambridge, at the turn of the century and created a passable replica of the original in Victorian Gothic, with an ornate Bridge of Sighs slung over a little brook that gurgled between the main building and the playing fields. Even so, I was regarded by many of my colleagues as a folklore character, an Alistair Cooke figure introducing *Masterpiece Theatre*. Chicago-born Reeny had no use for that sort of arcane bourgeois entertainment.

One day you said to me, 'It may be a woman's intuition, but every time the name Reeny Babukhan crops up in conversation our Maury Lee's face twitches and his nostrils quiver like a bunny rabbit's.'

I expect it was that strong whiff of latent feline sexuality—that her tightly packaged compact body, prominent cheekbones and lush mouth exuded—that made Maury Lee follow her around with his tongue hanging out.

You were more charitable, found Maury Lee's school boyish yearning for Reeny endearing. You warned me not to make snide remarks about her in his presence.

'The poor man is torn between his loyalty to you and his admiration for her,' you said.

In the absence of Maury Lee's nearest kin, you came to represent for him a sort of family elder, whose approval lent a certain decorum to what was, at that point, a clear case of sottish giddiness resulting from enforced abstinence. At one stage, his infatuation took a deadly turn; his sturdy Yankee machismo developed a bleary-eyed swagger in unconscious imitation of a certain type of hyperventilating Bollywood idol of recent times. Of all people, he began to confide in Robby Franz, our music man, who was known as 'blabber mouth' to his colleagues. The latest issue of the alumni broadsheet *Chronicles of Kingman* archly hinted at the possibility of wedding bells peeling out of the Faculty Club.

I considered Babukhan's brand of 'identity politics' pernicious because it compelled students to embrace a narrow race- and gender-based course of action for social change. In her scheme of things, Shakespeare was required to prove his liberal credentials, like someone running for a political office. Only the other day in my class Joseph Eagleton, who is black, insisted on drawing untenable parallels between Othello's tragic downfall and the O.J. Simpson trial of a few years before. The play, he said, revealed the same kind of deeply entrenched white racism which hounded the former football player. Through such guerrilla tactics, Reeny appeared to be engaging me in a sly protracted war by proxy.

Well, Maury Lee had to learn the hard way what stuff his siren was made of. You couldn't help laughing when he barged in on us late one night last April looking terribly overwrought. It seems Reeny had proceeded to deconstruct the menu as soon as they had sat down to eat at an Indian Restaurant on Lexington Avenue. Poor man had obviously hoped to loosen more than her taste buds by plying her with succulent Mughlai dishes. What he didn't know was that Reeny hated fusion cooking. I wish I could have seen his face when she declared that the tandoori salmon he had ordered for her tasted like a rubber ducky.

Maury Lee was flabbergasted.

'This particular fish is not native to the North-West Frontier, the real home of tandoori cuisine,' she told him.

According to Reeny, the right method was to cook the meat slowly over charcoal, which sent up billows of steam from the dripping yogurt, giving it that peculiar smoky taste which the oven-cooked salmon decidedly lacked. The original ethnicity of the tandoor way of cooking was ruthlessly modified, she asserted, to suit Western palates.

Even the lovesick Maury Lee thought she was mad.

I don't know why you should have been surprised when Reeny blamed me for Maury Lee's shortcomings. Provoked by her outrageous conduct in the restaurant he had blurted out, 'My friend Siri is right. You are programmed like a mechanical doll to utter theoretical claptrap at a drop of a hat.'

The vixen retorted, it was the 'Panopticon' speaking through him.

'By the way,' you asked me, 'what is a Panopticon?'

'I believe it's Foucault's metaphor for invisible tyranny,' I explained. 'A series of circular cells, with a watchtower at the center, from which the gaze of power is trained on the inmates.'

Reeny pushed away the salmon, declaring, 'Professor Amolini is a tower dressed in tweeds.'

You had still not come under her spell and considered that remark to be utterly rude. But I laughed loudly and said at least the little hussy had a wicked sense of humor.

Reeny had obviously continued to regard the salmon with deep loathing.

'So snatching her plate, I shoveled a huge morsel into my mouth,' Maury Lee said with a victorious smile.

Reeny's reaction was predictable. She laughed sarcastically and said she didn't blame him for reacting so violently.

'It's not you who do not like to be contradicted by a woman. It's the center to which you belong,'

Maury Lee said he nearly choked on the salmon and shouted, 'You keep saying that, but I belong to no goddamn center.'

His hackles had been raised, and the chatter at the other tables was cut short, amused glances flashing in their direction.

'Yes you do,' Reeny asserted. 'That's why you want to call the shots. You think anyone who lives on the margins is, by definition, mad and irrational.'

'You are not irrational,' Maury Lee said. 'No siree Bob. You are so goddamn rational that you can turn an ordinary remark into an occasion for a graduate seminar.'

You thought it was unfair that Reeny should have dragged me into what was essentially a lovers' tiff.

There were no decadent nawabs in her family, Reeny said. Her grandfather was a simple jute farmer from Chittagong. Her dad didn't attend Cambridge but studied chemistry at Dhaka University, before migrating to America.

'Yet my dad thinks he is always right on everything, just like your friend Siri.' Reeny said.

By the time you served him coffee, he had calmed down enough to wonder if Reeny was enacting some sort of revenge fantasy against men who reminded her of her dad.

'Is there a sadder subtext of familial oppression behind Reeny's peskiness?' he muttered, anxiously staring at his coffee.

'Subtext of oppression, my foot,' I snapped back. 'Look out, old chap. You are even beginning to sound like her.'

'Who am I kidding?' Maury Lee laughed. 'She has got me pinned down under her gaze all right.'

The poor man was quite frazzled by that psychosexual stichomythia.

'It was like being trapped with Ethel Merman in a duet, "Anything you can say I can say better".'

I should have thought because we have been on such cordial terms with the Qureshis and Nambiars you would be offended when Reeny dismissed them as, 'turmeric covered *desis*, forever thumbing their dog-eared past like a farmer's almanac'.

Lately, she had been returning to Kingman after every MLA conference, armed with an amped-up theoretical spiel of staggering abstraction and blinding opacity, to bludgeon anyone who thought it was all gobbledygook.

I didn't notice the change in your language from piquant Inderpur-Club slang to bristling feminist jargon.

What if we had never left Inderpur? By the time that ancient city of ours felt the winds of change blowing through its old gullies and snickelways, you would have been too set in your ways, too comfortable with life that flowed gently like the artificial brooks our ancestors built to feed their *hamam* baths.

Here in America, nothing seems permanent, and marriages are an investment against future ruptures, fetching handsome returns in alimony.

Jackson Heights alone would not have changed you. Look at all the other wives in this place. They get bloated, and by the time they reach middle age their eyes disappear behind rolls of fat.

Like a forest fire ignited by the accidental rubbing of two branches, some dormant mutinous impulse flared up inside you. I thought your enrolling in law school was a temporary whim, a passing fancy. I was secretly pleased that instead of getting a face-lift, you wanted to strengthen your intellectual muscles. I should have paused to ask 'Why law school?' You had a degree in child psychology.

Somehow I never expected you to qualify, thought that the rough and tumble of law school would wear you down, and once again you would revert to being the elegant and graceful hostess you were, organizing charity functions at Inderpur Club.

Law school peeled off some of that old *khandani* veneer, that cultivated *adab*, or self-effacement, acquired after years of training behind exquisite *zarokhas* overlooking private courtyards. Jackson Heights thrust you to the frontline, especially after our friend Durbar invited you to join his law firm. He had problems getting through to immigrant wives who spoke little English.

While I was busy grooming young minds, serving juicy nuggets of poetry to students, pretending that Kingman was somehow special like Cambridge, you were being trained in hand-to-hand combat, rescuing women from the clutches of abusive husbands, something that came in pretty handy later when you showed me the door.

So gradual was your transformation that at first I hardly noticed it. The rescue of young Kanti Chitral, in his senior year at Kingman, from potential incarceration for robbing a tourist in Manhattan, had seemed, at the time, like a minor tactical victory; one could hardly call it an unprecedented courtroom triumph comparable to Portia's in *The Merchant of Venice*.

The lad was our Gullu's friend, and you developed for him a sort of second-son affection. Our Immy had fled the nest and set himself up as an investment banker while barely out of college. His evolution from precocious teenager to a worldly-wise player of stocks and bonds at the cutting edge of high finance had left us feeling a little cowed. We had watched, with a mixture of pride and alarm, his breathtakingly rapid progress from fledgling entrepreneur to one of the movers and shakers of Wall Street. There was nothing in our bloodlines that pointed to such an astounding financial wizardry. My ancestors had gone on from serving as provincial governors to the Mughal emperor in Delhi to independent rulers, and after being upstaged and supplanted by Dicky's people, settled down to a life of leisurely nobility in Inderpur.

I remember saying, half in jest, it was your genes that must have sent Immy prospecting for this tycoonhood. Your people had prospered, providing building material and hardware to the British who'd transformed most of South Bombay into an uncanny replica of London's West End.

Twelve years her senior, Immy was more like a junior uncle to Gullu. He was always first to pick her up before either of us could and stick a bandaid where she had bruised herself while playing. There was none of that sibling rivalry we hear so much about these days. I think we let Kanti fill the ambiguous space created by the difference in age between our two offspring. Gullu needed a sibling closer to her in age and we a teenage boy who had not prematurely outgrown our psychic need for parenthood.

So we sort of adopted Kanti after his father remarried. The lad was in mourning for his mother; he never let go of her. His pining for her somehow infected me, increasing my longing for Ammeejan. The memory of her pale wrinkled face kept me awake at night.

To us Kanti talked freely about his mother, the way she used to follow him from the kitchen to the front door and wait till he safely boarded the school bus. When he returned at three in the afternoon she would still be at the door, as if she hadn't moved at all.

Kanti had one precious possession, a torn piece of sari bearing scorch marks. The rest of the burnt remains of that garment had been sent to the forensic lab after the mishap with the stove which had taken her life. But nothing had been found to incriminate Chitral. He maintained that it was an accident.

'No accident,' cried Kanti's aunt and uncle, who had come over from India almost fifteen days after her body had been cremated. She had been an experienced cook, careful to the extreme, never allowing her baby son to wander too close to the cooking range. Chitral maintained that her *pallav* had fallen on the range while her back was turned to pick up a piece of cucumber. The sari had become a sheet of flame, gobbling up her flesh. Kanti was away at school at the time.

Long after his hapless uncle and aunt returned to India, tongues had continued to wag in Jackson Heights.

You had got into the habit of playing aunty-big-heart to various unfortunate souls, and I have to admit that Kanti's story was compelling, almost Dickensian one might say, with a destitute boy at its center asking for more bread. Only at the time, I had not foreseen that from a childhood playmate of our daughter and a pleasant diversion for you—a sort of spare-time hobby like amateur photography—he would come to have a viselike grip on our life.

He was by no means a malignant spider, lying inert somewhere in the netting, waiting for the right moment to strike—some teenage Rasputin in the making, casting a hypnotic spell on a needy patroness.

By himself, he was no more than what Jackson Heights calls a 'confused *desi*' looking for his dead mother; but he certainly stirred in you some oblique embryonal force of the kind that makes perfectly respectable women snatch strangers' babies from their carriages left outside department stores. I suspect you leaned more toward Bookstore-Nambiar's surrogate mother of his Cochin days rather than some calculating *frau* driven by morbid fantasies of unfulfilled motherhood. But then I am pretty sure that Bookstore-Nambiar's neighborhood Amma would have grabbed the nearest broomstick and given him a chase round the coconut palms of Kerala, if he had committed some serious breach of conduct.

Chitral replenished his marriage bed with a brand-new wife; his excuse was that Kanti needed looking after while he attended to business. We could see that the lad seethed with anguish. Kanti complained that dinner at his place was like a séance, where ghosts of mustachioed ancestors in red *puggrees* popped up every now and then to chide and chastise him for contradicting his opinionated father.

He spent almost all his spare time with Gullu, playing Monopoly and listening to rock music on her boom box. You willingly, and I somewhat reluctantly, became his proxy parents.

But there was a selfish streak in Kanti, and he often resorted to dissimulation when caught on the wrong foot. His sense of entitlement did not vanish after he abandoned Chitral's house; he used it as a ploy for getting a foot in the door.

At the midterm faculty meeting before spring break, the dean told us that Kanti Chitral was about to be dismissed. He had not been seen on the campus since the end of January.

Where was Kanti?

You went ballistic, kept repeating, 'I knew it, I knew it,' like a doleful voice coming over the mountains, whose prophesy of an impeding catastrophe had been fulfilled. When you slumped into your bed and buried your face in the pillow, I realized that, as Astronaut Chawla might have said, 'we had a problem on hand', if flames on entering the earth's atmosphere had not suddenly engulfed her.

'That poor boy. God knows if he is still alive or dead,' you said to the blank wall. Then you suddenly became frantic, rang Bookstore-Nambiar to find out from Kanti's father what had caused his son to abandon home in the middle of the night.

Chitral, who had by now developed the style and brusque manner of the head of state of a starving Third World country with a nuclear weapon in his kitty, told Bookstore-Nambiar to mind his own business; it was a purely domestic matter. He said Begumsahiba, meaning you, had spoiled his son and filled his mind with progressive mumbo jumbo. The boy had insulted his stepmother, called her a bitch, and walked out in a huff when Chitral tried to intervene. He was setting a bad example to his five-year-old son, who had picked up some foul language from Kanti.

But you wouldn't take the hint and back off. Oh no, you simply fired back, and even though you had never met Kanti's stepmother, you called her 'an ill-bred, foul-mouthed woman who had crawled out of some remote Indian countryside'. The obscene size of the woman's dowry, you told Reeny, had trumped the aspirations of several potential young brides, whose parents were eager to marry them off to a middle-aged balding roué like Chitral.

I was staggered; I had never heard words cascading down your mouth. You went berserk with your denunciation of a man with whom we had barely been on speaking terms; it made me uneasy. 'Who is this brawling woman?' I said. 'I don't recognize her.'

Nothing puts you on the fast track to assimilation than good, old-fashioned bumming in America. Kanti went missing for five weeks. He knew how much you cared for his well-being, yet he never bothered to ring you even once. When you received a phone call from the police precinct in Manhattan and were told that Kanti had been arrested for trying to steal a French tourist's handbag, right away you flew to his rescue and bailed him out.

For the first two weeks, Kanti had managed to survive by wielding his squeegee around 42nd Street. He was quite familiar with Port Authority bus station from earlier trips to his cousins in Edison, New Jersey. Tentatively, he began to hustle newly minted Indian or Pakistani immigrants. They were easy to spot, he said, by their goofy looks, huddled in corners while commuters brushed past them on Eighth Avenue.

I am not saying the lad didn't deserve our sympathy. But you need not have been so gleeful in applauding his tactics. It was bad enough that Gullu should have been so easily amused by his stories.

With Indians, Kanti spoke Gujarati or Punjabi which he had picked up a smattering of from neighbors in Jackson Heights. He greeted Pakistanis in the few standard sentences in chaste Urdu he had acquired from long exposure to what are called Bollywood Zenana movies, about upper-class Muslim families, set in Old Delhi or Lucknow.

'I avoided Bangladeshis,' he admitted, 'because I knew my Bengali accent wouldn't pass muster.'

Sidling up to Japanese or European tourists streaming out of the

Whitney or Guggenheim he would say, 'Excuse me, but could you possibly donate a dollar for my brother? He needs an operation for his failing kidney.'

He would put on what he thought was an Indian accent. He would say, 'I am liking you very much. You reminding me of my brother.'

He showed us that kitsch picture of Krishna frolicking with milk-maids that he carried in his pocket. He would waggle his head sideways like Indians, saying, 'Krishna is blessing you from bottom of his heart.'

'Technically, I never begged,' he claimed. That's how he avoided getting arrested.

I have to confess that I was intrigued by Kanti's account of how he survived for five weeks on the marauding streets on bits and scraps.

Ultimately, what view of life was Kanti advancing through his many impersonations? Dicky and I had our identities carved across our bodies; they could become defunct like unrenewed passports, but we could never take on new ones as if they were something replaceable, like toothpaste or a light bulb.

I marveled at Kanti's ability to wear so many different masks at such a young age; he seemed to follow the American vaudeville comic and quick-change artist who entertained crowds hungry for make-believe. The Bahurupia, literally 'man of many faces' of Indian folk theatre, used camouflage to escape a ruthless tyrant. In neither case was there a sense of intentional trick or treachery. I was uneasy with Kanti's many disguises, donned and discarded on the spur of the moment. His facility with masks had a hint of the wolf in sheep's clothing.

He gave our address at the precinct, and you persuaded the French-woman to drop the charges by appealing to her maternal instinct. You told her that Kanti had been much abused by his own father and step-mother. The French tourist, who listened with increasing fascination to your '*alliance française*' voice, relented and dropped the charges when she learnt that snatching her handbag was the first recorded offense com-mitted by the lad, who wanted to buy a birthday present for his girlfriend, Susan. It made the tourist's romantic heart quiver. So moved was she that it was your 'reproving stare', as you told me, that made 'Kanti flinch and withdraw his empty hand', when the moist-eyed Frenchie opened her bag and offered him a ten-dollar bill.

You were so convinced that Kanti's lackluster academic performance was due to his constant harassment by the stepmother, who made him babysit her 'spoiled brat', that I reluctantly made an urgent plea for his reinstatement. Ready to cross swords with every real or imaginary power broker, Reeny was taken in by Kanti's dramatic tales of survival and gave him a passing grade, despite his prolonged absences from her class.

Kingman specialized in recycling damaged goods, often with gratifying results. Once in a while, however, society repatriated some of our hurriedly patched-up specimens who had the unfortunate tendency to revert to type and required a brain transplant or a straight jacket, at the very least.

You thought Edulji could use a pair of younger hands at Mandalay. Susan went along with Kanti to lend him moral support when the old man interviewed him for the job. In Edulji's opinion, she had greater aptitude for the job, but you suggested a compromise, and both of them were employed to work as a team.

❦ 12 ❦

Children's lives do not run along designated tracks like trains, as you and I were to find out. Not long after Kanti's safe return to Jackson Heights, our Gullu and Durbar's son Jesse were to fritter away their freedom by warping suddenly into ethnic avatars, she with a *hijab* and he a turban.

First came the turban. Frankly, I had a good laugh at Durbar's quaking and spluttering over the sudden sprouting of a turban on his son's pate, particularly after an adolescence speckled with a phosphorescent Mohawk crest and piercing of the more tender parts of his anatomy.

When you said one day in spring, 'Try and come back a little early this evening; the Singh's are dining with us tonight,' I thought nothing of it. We had them over at least once a month, and as Maury Lee used to say, the Amolinis and the Singhs got on like a house on fire. Little did I know that what was billed as an evening with friends would flounder into something akin to a dark night of the soul.

It was quite touching the way Durbar treated you like a sister, called you Didi. Your way of addressing him, as 'Boss Bhaiyya' was equally charming. We had more in common with the Singhs than the rest of the folks in Jackson Heights, barring Maury Lee, of course.

Both Durbar and Matilda were products of Sikh–Mexican marital alliances at the turn of the last century, with one foot in their ancestral Punjabi and Latino cultures and the other planted in rural Californian soil. He was clean shaven and elegant to his finely manicured fingertips. Occasionally, Matilda, who was a pediatrician, wore a fetching black lace mantilla, which enhanced the pallor of her smooth olive skin. In that outfit, Maury Lee said, 'she was a dead ringer for Lupe Velez', the Latina actress of the sixties.

Trust Maury Lee to salvage old forgotten Hollywood stars from obscurity by casting them in modern-day, real-life drama. He was not invited that evening because the Singhs were having some problem with their only son, which they wanted to share only with the two us. Their Jesse used to follow our Immy everywhere. When Immy went to Cornell, Jesse fell in with a bunch of leather-jacketed lads with yellow teeth and fast bikes. Officer Haggerty told Durbar to act quickly and send his son to a boarding school before he got inducted into gangland.

When Immy returned that Christmas, he tactfully steered Jesse in the direction of Brooks Brothers and a Yale crew cut. We flagged young Jaspal (Jesse) Singh, cleaned and spruced up, off to California, where his ancestors on both sides had toiled hard in the early dog days of immigration and emerged as prosperous farmers and landowners. The last we heard, Jesse was planning to write his senior thesis on the so-called 'Mexidoo' families such as his parents belonged to. What happened to him at Stanford was anybody's guess.

Judging from the state the usually unflappable Durbar was in that evening, it was something pretty dire. You were really concerned because there were dark circles under Durbar's large brown eyes and the serene Matilda was having a hard time fighting back her tears.

During his teenage years, Jesse used to speak in short bursts of rhyming couplets, hands sawing the air as he shuffled along. You remember how once, when we stopped to chat with the Singhs on KC Way, Jesse stood by them throbbing and swaying, his hands moving in rapper fashion. His way of addressing his parents' friends was a hoot.

'Great to meet you man.'

'Daddy-o sure digs you.'

'So does this here mamma doll o' mine.'

Instantly, Immy was asked to launch a 'Bring Our Jesse Back' operation. Under Immy's tutelage, Jesse traded his dreadlocks, piercings and black leather jacket for the scrubbed look of an Ivy Leaguer. Durbar and Matilda couldn't thank us enough for rescuing their son from the clutches of those hoods.

But Jesse had returned from Stanford with his head sheathed in a traditional Sikh turban, and his father had simply gone off the trolley.

'I would have been less horrified,' Durbar said in a voice choking with emotion, 'if our son had taken my brand-new Mercedes for a joy ride and brought it back looking like a giant accordion, after a smash up with a tractor trailer truck.'

It was obvious that Jesse's turban had touched a raw nerve; the old boy was all of a twitter. Everyone knew how much Durbar loved his Mercedes, took it for a wash and wax once a week at the automatic car wash service in Jamaica, and had it vacuum cleaned at the local garage every third day.

You were very good with him. Matilda had told you on the phone that Durbar had barely nibbled at his food for the past two days. You took a day off to toil in the kitchen to cook his favorite lobster masala and *ras meethi sevai*. Your suggestion that we should eat first and then talk about the turban was a stroke of genius. By the time Durbar had spooned up the last bit of that delicious vermicelli, almond, pistachios, slashed cashew and milk dessert, he had calmed down enough to smile weakly and ask for a second helping.

Outside all was quiet now. Jackson Heights was shutting down for the night as Durbar sipped his coffee. Checkout counters that rang constantly with the sound of money passing hands were silent, the E train made sullen noises overhead, sari-clad dummies in dim-lit interiors stopped vying with each other for attention, necklaces glittered in their velveteen cushions, astronaut Chawla smiled like a tired angel from her perch in the Peacock Diner, and outside, a steady rain deepened the gloom as Durbar spoke.

Matilda had regained her composure and filled in the gaps whenever Durbar paused to sip his coffee. Meticulously, he began to reconstruct the scene in the courtroom where Jesse had staged a dramatic entrance with a turban. By the time he got to the climax, Durbar was smiling at the recollection of his own bumbling reaction to it.

'Surprise is not the word for it,' Durbar said as he paused to collect his thoughts. 'Tilda was busy at the hospital, so Jesse headed straight for the court. I was summing up my defense of Cedric James of Jackson Heights, formerly of Puerto Rico, whose green card was imperiled by his being busted by the police on a drunk-driving charge. When out of the blue I see some guy, head smartly wrapped in a blue and gold turban, face covered in whiskers, grinning at me like a baboon.'

Durbar's face was animated and Matilda was giggling almost hysterically, I thought. I didn't know what to make of it. But you had gauged Singh's mood correctly and freely joined in the revelry.

Durbar was saying, 'There I am, serenading the jury, my voice charged with emotion, observing the anxious-looking blue-collar faces of the jurors twitching in sympathy for old Cedric James, and suddenly I sense from the way Kirby Smith, the judge, frowns that something is wrong. Following the judge's gaze, I see the door in the rear being pushed open and a muscular party in a tweed jacket, head covered in a turban, is tip-toeing in and taking a seat on one of the back benches. When this Sikh guy waves to me, his smile rings a few bells, but I cannot tell for the life of me who it is. I am completely—what's that word you Brits use when you get tongue-tied?'

'Perplexed?'

Durbar shook his head.

'Flummoxed?' I said.

'That's it. I am flummoxed and speechless until old Kirby Smith growls, "Please proceed Mr Singh. We haven't got the whole day, you know."'

While Durbar summed up his case for not convicting Cedric, his mind fluttered around that turbaned face like a humming bird at a near-empty bird feeder. The judge adjourned the case for lunch, and the guards led Cedric out; but while Durbar was putting the case papers back into his briefcase and talking to his assistant Imelda Lopez, he found himself smothered in a bear hug. It was the muscular turbaned guy who was beaming at him, hollering 'Sat Sri Akal'.

'Then it hits me,' Durbar said, 'that the face beneath the turban belongs to my son.'

Within a matter of months, Stanford had transformed this clean-shaven, ex-punk-rock fan with the flaming crest of a few years before into a proudly glowing specimen of young Sikh manhood.

'And the funny thing is,' Durbar said, his face reassuming that hang-dog expression, 'Jesse didn't seem the least bit self-conscious.'

The fastidious Armani-suited Durbar Singh, who had always been clean-shaven and shared our ultrasecular views, was plunged once again into where-did-we-go-wrong kind of head shaking, lump-in-the-throat self-recrimination. Suddenly, a genie had popped out of the bottle.

The following day, during a stormy session at home, Jesse had argued that his turban was not just an empty appendage. It filled a vacuum in his head. Matilda thought her son seemed to be quoting one of his professors at Stanford when he told them, 'We are more than cells, synapses and sex drives. We are amazing, mysterious creatures, forever in search of something greater than ourselves.'

Matilda's voice shook slightly. 'My boy had a dreamy faraway look as he uttered those words.'

'That's right,' Durbar agreed. 'He did not sound like a fanatic, that's for sure. All the same, it was a shock. I need time, lots of time, to get used to it.'

I happened to look at your face at the time. You were in a trance and seemed glued to the chair when our guests got up to go.

Durbar and I slogged a burden of history far heavier than our American colleagues carried in their two-hundred-year tote bag. At one stroke, his son had put the clock back by half a century, when members of his clan in India ruled by the inexorable logic of vendettas, had transformed the five major arteries of the Punjab into rivers of blood to celebrate their independence from the British.

That night, long after the Singhs were gone, I found you asleep in bed, hands clasped between your drawn up knees. Something was amiss; there was a fleeting, almost childlike sadness on your face. Even now, after three decades into our marriage, the sight of your disheveled face and swollen eyelids stir in me a sort of carnal tenderness.

Gently I disengaged your hands and held them to my lips. You snuggled close to me without opening your eyes and whispered, 'That was so moving and beautiful, what Jesse said. "We are amazing and mysterious creatures, forever in search of something greater than ourselves."

I thought nothing of it at the time. Words that captured the evanescent, like the fading trail of a jetliner in a clear blue sky, always sent you into a reverie. For a while, everything—your family, your furniture, pots and pans in the kitchen, bookshelves, picture frames and flowers in vases—revolved in slow motion and disappeared into the shadows. You were lost to the world, so to speak, but you never cried. There was a smile in your unseeing eyes, but no tears. That evening, something inside you was uncaged, and the dewy glisten in your eyes mirrored its slowly vanishing flight path.

You had come down from Bombay to visit your aunt, Begumsahiba Bilkis Alladin, when we first met. Apparently she had told Ammeejan that I would forget Ann the moment I saw you. Madam Alladin, as cosmopolitan Inderpur knew her, hosted a literary soirée once a month at her palatial villa on the hillside outside Inderpur. That June, I was invited to introduce *The Waste Land* to her guests. The scrumptious spread at Madam Alladin's tea enticed many old timers, whose library shelves were adorned with cloth-bound editions of Sir Walter Scott, Dickens, G. A. Henty, Rider Haggard, and Kipling. Even Browning was too radical for their taste. After partaking of her 'humble repast', as Madam Alladin described her scones and clotted cream—'not quite Devon you know'—chocolate cake, and Shami kebab, when we assembled in her great hall, I immediately spotted you at the back sitting between Aunty Bilkis and Ammeejan.

About fifteen minutes into the session, after I had briefly explained the use of myth and symbol in Eliot's poetry to the well-behaved but generally clueless audience, when I began reading the opening lines of *The Waste Land*, the lights went out suddenly. Madam Alladin's faithful old retainers scurried about to find candles, fumbling and crashing on furniture in the dark. Without waiting any longer, I decided to recite the rest from memory, pausing to comment on the many literary and cultural allusions embedded in the poem, including the lyrical snippet from Wagner's *Tristan and Isolde*. My attempt to sing it wasn't as successful as the dialogue of the cockney women in the pub scene.

The applause at the end was deafening; the old timers, who had never strayed beyond Tennyson, looked a bit dazed by the amount of erudition Eliot packs in the poem. Then, in the flickering candlelight, you shimmered out of the darkness like the Hyacinth girl, and thanked me for what you said was 'the most enchanting evening' of your life.

On our way home, when Ammeejan asked me what I thought of 'Bilkis's smart young niece from Bombay', I feigned nonchalance; but that night I couldn't get you out of my mind. For the first time since my return from England, Ann's ghost had loosened its stranglehold on my sleep.

Ann and I had decided to wait at least for a year before getting married. The usual argument, 'if your love is true it won't fade away within a year', that sort of thing. I was convinced that taking Ann with me to Inderpur would be ruinous to her career. She had just been selected to play the younger sister of the lead in a BBC serial set in the eighteenth century, with carriages rolling down cobbled streets, tea on the lawn, and ladies in bonnets, the sort of stuff we still watch every Sunday on *Masterpiece Theatre*.

In those days, when it took nearly an hour to get a long-distance connection from Cambridge to Inderpur—I could talk to Ammeejan only once a year, on her birthday—and air travel was still rare, Inderpur would have been too drastic a change for Ann. Every August, when we went to Paris, where Ann held a temporary job as a translator at the Bibliothèque Nationale, we would trudge all the way to Gare du Nord just to get a copy of the *Guardian*. That was the way she kept abreast of what was on the boards in Drury Lane or Haymarket.

Inderpur was modern and cosmopolitan but had little to offer by way of evening's entertainment, and a college performance of *Arms and the Man* or *Julius Caesar* once a year was a poor substitute for anything on the marquees of Shaftsbury Avenue. And there was nothing remotely like Covent Garden, even in Bombay, except the old Opera House in Girgaum, which screened Bollywood hits. Ann's dad had a point, and we decided to wait till she had finished shooting the series.

To cut a long story short, Ann landed another part, this time in a film that would take her to Kenya. I could tell from her letter she was torn between Inderpur and Kenya, and I wrote back to say she should go to Nairobi.

Your tantalizing face, clear alabaster skin, luminous eyes and full figure, around which your chiffon sari hung in delicately sculptured folds, made even the magisterial T.S. Eliot seem like a jolly old codger every time my mind wandered back to that evening at Aunt Bilkis's place. Despite the difference in age—you were nearly six years younger—I was smitten. The whole of Inderpur seemed to be under your spell. Not since Dicky's mother had arrived as a young maharani thirty years before had the town seen such loveliness, and I had rarely met an Indian girl who had your sparkle and ready wit.

Ann's career was soaring when she fell asleep at the wheel of her Mini on M-1 and crashed into a tree. Her neck was broken and she died. I was shattered and spent hours staring at the wall and causing Ammeejan a lot of distress. Over and over I read the last card Ann had sent with the picture of Lake Windermere till I knew the text by heart. Her note at the back was telegraphic.

> 'Off to Rydal Hall. Don't want to go. Wouldn't be the
> same without you. Geoff and Pam insist. Too fazed
> out after hectic shooting schedule to argue.'

In those hurriedly scribbled words danced mocking demons. Ann going to London to act in television serials was one thing, but to Rydal Waters? Why should I have imagined that her commitment to me had been so total that there would be no place in her life for simple relaxation with a few friends?

The whole Lake District rose before me, aslant like a landscape glimpsed from a banking aircraft breaking through cloud cover. Ann and I walking hand in hand from Dungeon Ghyll to our favorite picnic spots—Little Langdale and Hawks Head, where Wordsworth went to school. The movement of her salmon pink, blue-veined calves below the hem of her tartan skirt always stirred in me waves of desire. This was England of my fantasy come true. Poetry by the hearth and the Flemings (Wordsworth's patrons) looking down from the wainscot.

After letting me mourn quietly for a year, Ammeejan asked me to reconsider my resolve not to look at another woman. The only wish she had left was to see a grandchild in the family before she joined Abbajan, who had departed even before I went to Cambridge.

I kept reminding myself that I was marrying you for the sake of Ammeejan. At the risk of alienating you, I decided to make a full confession about my life with Ann when I came to Bombay to meet your parents and finalize the wedding plans. I knew I had made the right choice; I could sense absolutely no ill will towards Ann from any of you. You even praised her looks when I took out from my wallet the photograph showing Ann and me holding hands and smiling into the camera. It was taken during our last outing together at Grasmere.

There were tears in your eyes when I told you about the circumstances of her death in a totally avoidable accident. We were married within six months. There was only one hitch. I wanted a civil marriage, whereas your mother insisted on a traditional Muslim wedding. Finally, at a very private ceremony, but in the presence of an eminent and enormously bearded *kazi*, and my Ammeejan, and a couple of your aunts and uncles, we were married in Matheran. All around us were green mountains and valleys with waterlogged paddy fields.

From the day we returned to Inderpur, we were the most 'observed of all observers'. It was an era when the common man, who wanted his princely folk to look like storybook figures, did not resent our standing out of the crowd.

The aura of Nehru still hung around us; our generation was remaking India. In those days, the US was not the chosen destination for ambitious young men. The best of us went to England and then returned to our cities and towns to refashion them. We were the new generation reshaping India as Nehru had dreamed of. The routines were well established for young married couples like us. One returned from one's varsity in England with a degree, married a pretty convent-trained English-speaking girl, and spent days at the local college teaching Shakespeare and Milton. Evenings saw us at the club: billiards for me, bridge or rummy for you with the *zenana* ladies, and once-a-month dinner at the local chapter of the Oxford and Cambridge Society, where we drank imported claret or port, while occasionally dashing off to Bombay or Delhi to attend seminars arranged by the British Council or US Educational Foundation in New Delhi.

Then Inderpur turned sour on us and forced us into exile. Those early years in Jackson Heights, when Gullu was growing up and Immy was still looking for something that would suit his amazing talent for making money, were truly banner years. I like that expression, which is so American and has such a celebratory ring. In many ways the Yanks are like us, always marching and waving banners on Veterans Day, Columbus Day, or St Patrick's Day. Not to be outdone, and always ready to beat the natives at their game, we Indians of Jackson Heights have taken to marching down Fifth Avenue on 26 January, our Republic Day.

Here in America, while struggling to adjust, we had worked like a team. But very slowly and imperceptibly, you changed during the intervening years. You did not argue, but your way of showing disagreement was to lapse into bemused silence, as though you were listening to some cuckoo clock within.

Not until much later, when I was cooling my heels at Maury Lee's brother's place in Vermont, I realized that living with me could not have been a picnic for you. There must have been moments in our life together in Inderpur when you must have asked yourself, 'Am I married to a man or to *Brewer's Dictionary of Phrase and Fable*?'

If Reeny was a mortician filleting all the vital organs from a living moment before wrapping it in the mummy cloth of theory, I was given to invoking Shakespearean ghosts and goblins at the slightest skid on the banana skin of life. As you once put it, I would stir-fry a TV dinner where simple microwaving was called for. Living with me must have been really like being incarcerated in a whispering gallery.

Your siding with Farooqui was the first sign that your thoughts and mine did not chime as in the old days. Generally, you said very little, but there was that helpless nun-like expression in your eyes, as if you were thinking 'How can I get him to stay and listen to what I say?'

At first, your highly charged, emotional reaction to Jesse's remark about religion intrigued and even amused me. To swoon over beautiful thoughts from someone of the stature of Ghalib is one thing. But more often than not you were drawn to the beauty of mere sound, even when the sense behind it remained vague or unrealized.

I know, I know. You'd say, 'There you go again, pontificating as usual.'

What had caught your attention in Jesse's words was some echo of your own quest. And that frightened me because I felt you were separating yourself from me in some fundamental way. You were always articulate, but in Inderpur your wit was deployed to provide cover for me while I went after a hidden enemy, like Bulchand.

But, my dear girl, in this tug of war between those who, like Farooqui, want to take the world back to the Middle Ages and those who want to move it forward; we have to be with the vanguard.

Every trip back to India, you not only saw old friends and family, but you also met your old self—docile, gracious, and above all, gentle. And you were appalled. Ironically, you had to go back to the scenes of your past to find out how much Jackson Heights had changed you.

'In India I had no life of my own, no sense of purpose. Now even Lepakshi looks up to me,' you said.

Gullu and you kept buying me all these broad, expensive, silken ties for my birthday. When things were falling apart we needed to hang on to—pardon the pun—some of our old ties. They offered a much better option than those strident slogans Reeny invented, which lost their flavor, like bubble gum, after repeated chewing.

Sometime I ask myself, where did I go wrong? Often I would try to conjure up a sort of police lineup of my many selves invented by Reeny, ranging from oriental despot, *éminence grise*, lantern-jawed imperial *bwana*, and above all, a creepy water spider out of George MacDonald Fraser's *Flashman* tales—wielding my power in varied disguises, but quite honestly I could not detect any likeness.

I will grant that in Inderpur you had no separate history of your own. But neither did I. I thought we were both makers of our history. Granted, when women in Jackson Heights needed someone to help them deal with an abusive husband, they reached out to you. That must have made you feel important, to be 'significant' minus the tag 'other', attached to it.

I didn't mind that a bit.

You remember that old song, *Love and marriage go together like a horse and carriage.* Nothing significant is lost in translation when juxtaposed with our Inderpur version which goes, '*Jab Miyan Bibi Raji to Kya Karega Kazi.*' Or, as Shakespeare put it, 'Let me not . . .'

But hush . . .

Let me not to our marriage of two minds 'admit' any more impediments.

❧ 14 ❧

One flight, one uprooting was all I could cope with in one lifetime.

Our Gullu used to be so reluctant to leave her friends, especially Natthuram's Yamini and Kanti, and go to Inderpur with you. But in high school she discovered India, began to pack her bags at Thanksgiving, and in December, you two would be off like migratory birds returning to their sanctuary.

Who was I to complain? I couldn't get it out of my system either, but I had no desire left to face this new Inderpur. According to Dicky, the city had been taken over by a ruthless Mafia. I was afraid to go back. I could barely adjust to this new self-sufficient you; I simply could not imagine the horrors of getting lost in my own town, to ask for directions to old sights where I could go blindfolded, to feel as Dicky wrote, 'like an intruder in my old backyard'.

In our flat in Jackson Heights, we recreated some of the ambience of our *kothi*. The last time you were in Inderpur, you rescued from gathering dust that small settee with upholstered seat and scrolled armrest from Ammeejan's bedroom. Every time I looked at it, I saw her reclining on it, reading a book or giving instructions to the cook or playing solitaire when Immy was away at school. Sometime I would come home to find her listening to Noorjehan, her favorite singer, whom she never forgave for moving to Pakistan after Partition.

The partition of India was a touchy subject on both sides of the border. Unlike the Holocaust, it was hushed up like a dirty family secret, left to moulder like the mad woman in the attic. Once in a while, you heard its insane laughter in the night, but by daybreak it was gone, a mere bad dream. The many ways of disposing of the Jews invented by the Germans were recorded, their taxonomy well documented and scrupulously published, the victims memorialized in art and literature. Auschwitz and Treblinka still stare out of black-and-white film clips with their pockmarked half-eaten faces. Not so with the victims of Partition, though the five rivers of the Punjab were still connected like arteries on a partially severed limb. Their memory awaited a Maya Lin.

My most cherished picture was Ammeejan and you sitting side by side on that settee, gossiping and laughing at some joke at my expense. 'You two are thick as thieves,' I used to say. I overheard you talking to her friends, the ladies of her bridge club who came to visit us a few days after she passed away. You told them that your own mother had not loved you as much as Ammeejan. Of all her friends, Mrs Gupta, who was closest to her, put her arm around you and said, 'Beta, what can I say, you were the daughter she never had.'

That settee was our only link to Inderpur.

I wish I could say the same about the other things you salvaged from the *kothi*. We didn't want to clutter our flat with all those old brass hookahs, silverplated *attardanis*, brocaded ceremonial clothes, and other incunabula of an earlier civilization in which ancient remedies were preserved in exquisite Persian calligraphy. Any old relic was not automatically granted the status of an objet d'art, so we donated them to Susan. It broke my heart to see those gracious heirlooms and the five leather-bound volumes from my grandfather's library, with gold lettering on their still upright spine, on a shelf at Mandalay, waiting to catch the eye of some up-market interior decorator engaged by a rich New Yorker. A customer snapped it up the following week, but I refused to accept the money it fetched.

Susan had a way of being intimate with antiquity without an appraiser's precise knowledge of dates and provenance. Kanti's cultural background gave him easy access to the booming trade in Indian art and craft, but he was apt to mistake artificially induced patina for something time-honored. Mandalay always had a sort of musty, Raj-time décor of old British establishments in Bombay. Susan redesigned the lighting in the place and highlighted the rare objects in the shop to distinguish them from the folksy sort. The childless Parsi widower who never quite warmed to Kanti—he was trained to sort fake from genuine—grew very fond of Susan. Bargain hunters were awed into paying the price Susan put on the tag when they found themselves talking to a man who looked like a biblical prophet and addressed them in impeccable West End diction.

But Kanti's old habit of biting the hand that fed him cost him his job. There were a few tiny red flags fluttering at the dark edges of my sleep when Edulji insisted on Susan coming on board with Kanti, but I had missed the meaning, failed to connect all the dots.

The old man accused him of dipping into the cash register and fired him. Kanti pleaded not guilty, but nothing Susan said in defense of her young man would make Edulji change his mind. The upright old Parsi had plenty of life left in him and resented anyone who thought he was ready for the knacker's yard and wouldn't mind being stripped of a few working parts.

Taking wrong-turns along the silk road of life didn't seem to faze Kanti because you were always there to set things right.

Edulji adored you and wished to spare you the details. He told me that for Susan's sake he had looked the other way; once, in her absence, Kanti had tried to fleece an old client by switching price tags. The man had paid up but alerted Edulji to the lad's sleight of hand.

Kanti, who had your number, put on that hangdog expression and turned on the waterworks. I suspect even you were not taken in by his act of Poor Little Misunderstood Pinocchio, but you didn't call his bluff either.

You used to chastise Immy for using swear words picked up from children in the Kasbah or when you caught him smoking beedis with them on the sly; but Kanti, who seems to be arrested at the mirror stage—when, as Reeny's Lacan claims, a child still thinks he is an extension of his mother—barely elicits a tut-tut from you.

Your asking Durbar to secure him a job at Tivoli Cinema was an act of sheer folly, even to those of us who were, by now, used to your playing the woman for all seasons in Kanti's Bollywood fantasy. Putting him in charge of the box office with all that cash pouring in had all the ingredients of a comic plot with a tragic twist at the end.

I didn't wish to sound curmudgeonly, but a job selling almanacs under Bookstore-Nambiar's watchful eye would have been safer. I hoped I was wrong, for Susan's sake, but going by the lad's track record, this new venture had disaster written all over it.

The owners of Tivoli were a sullen looking lot with poker faces and fat gold watches on fleshy plump hands. You should have seen Jit's face when they noisily entered the diner and bawled at the poor waiters if they were not served immediately.

The Tivoli was not in it for vending Indian high culture; for that you needed to be a member of Kingman Film Society, of which Maury Lee was honorary president. This spring, the semester kicked off with the *Apu Trilogy*, although my personal favorite in the retrospective was *Shetrunj Ke Khilari* or *The Chess Players*, set, as Ray fans remember, in the nineteenth-century kingdom of Oudh in North India, on the eve of what the British called the Sepoy Mutiny, and we our First War of Independence.

Only a few Jackson Heights residents had seen all of Ray's movies. The rest of them got high on the cardamom-laced masala tea doled out by Bollywood. Kanti stopped screening those low-budget, socially relevant films that came along from Bombay every once in a while, in favor of sleek blockbusters with thin plotlines and a lot of gratuitous violence. His aim was to keep making hefty profits for his employers, who wore dark glasses and sported khaki safari suits, like big game hunters, to set them apart from other immigrants. Originally from the subcontinent, they had come to the United States by way of Kenya, where their ancestors had run *dukah*s in the bush.

Perhaps Reeny Babukhan was right in her assertion that Little India was a schizophrenic place, like the double bill at Tivoli, where every weekend Bollywood went bumper-to-bumper with B-grade Hollywood, and the lovebirds that used to prance around palm trees along the Arabian Sea now whooped it up disco-style against locales stretching from the Brooklyn Bridge to Mount Fuji. No refund was allowed if the sexy Bollywood poster with a Hollywood cachet fooled some dating couple. They could either sink back and play snuggle-bunnies or give themselves up to nearly three hours of a steamy car wash of song and dance.

Reeny also thought Indians were hardwired by nature to cringe and crawl before those of high birth and to bully the lowly. She had probably picked it up from some book. Although in her mid-thirties and well past her graduate-student days, Reeny retained a touching faith in canned scholarship that answered all of life's questions. A bit of Marx, a dash of Nietzsche, a teaspoonful of Freud and Voilà! a glittering sound bite that summed up the meaning of existence.

Strictly speaking, Reeny was not an official resident of Jackson Heights, but because of her growing association with you, she was now an active member—or should I say pain in the hindquarters—of the Asian Women's Association. Granted, it was occasionally necessary to impress upon an irascible trader that wife beating was considered a blood sport in America, forbidden by law, and, at least in Chitral's case, there was circumstantial evidence of wife burning; but was it necessary, as Maury Lee said, for Reeny, Matilda, and you to swoop down on some erring husband like Charlie's Angels every time he chucked around a few plates or kicked down the bedroom door? In the old days, many such cases had been quietly disposed off by elders in the community, to the mutual satisfaction of husband and wife.

Once in a blue moon you used to take Gullu to see a Hindi film 'to get her acquainted with Indian culture,' although the fare served at Tivoli was at best pedestrian and at worst positively vulgar, with grown men flinging their arms and legs around in a hideous parody of Michael Jackson. You are too intelligent not to be bored by such tasteless displays of juvenile behavior from so-called veteran actors. By the way, your defense of that simulated epicene hetaerae, as a celebration of the vivacious spirit of Indian culture was pure balderdash.

I remember how you cried at the end of *Shetrunj Ke Khilari* when we first saw it all those years ago in Inderpur. Last week, you kept nodding your head dutifully when, during the post-screening discussion organized by Maury Lee, Reeny dismissed it as sentimental harking back to feudal India. You knew that of all the Ray classics it had been my favorite for years, yet you spent a good twenty minutes listening to Reeny's tirade while I waited in our car. I dare say she had a field day demolishing *Shetrunj Ke Khilari* with her pseudo-Marxist chatter.

Two different Indias were taking shape in Jackson Heights. No need to stress which version stank.

Fortunately we still had Mandalay. With some input from me, Susan got rid of the clutter generated by Kanti, particularly those faux marble, garishly painted miniature replicas of the Taj Mahal and the mass-produced figurines of the androgynous Shiva. By carefully choosing her material, Susan gradually transformed Mandalay into something like the Shield of Achilles, with different regions of India represented through genuine folk art and handicraft items, such as table mats, bed sheets and brassware, along with a few well-chosen pieces of genuine antiques acquired from old Parsi homes of Edulji's relatives in Bombay. For the IT generation, Mandalay was the place to shop for an eye-catching artifact or a piece of ethnic chic to primp up a living-room corner of their condos as a nod to the old country.

The only other person who remained untouched by all these changes was that solitary middle-aged Indian gent in his threadbare green cardigan, who seemed to be nailed to a wooden crate outside the Korean convenience store in the subway entrance. He was not a trader, but he let his head droop in a polite nod when we passed him.

In those early halcyon days in Jackson Heights we would stop every now and then at some shop to admire a recent Indian import, like a pair of gardeners trying to recover the taste of extinct fruit by studying their coloration in a still-life painting.

But you seemed bored with antiquity; you had learnt to live in the here and now.

The other day when Gullu came down for the weekend, I heard you say in the kitchen, 'Go tell Nawahsahib dinner is ready.'

When Gullu came to fetch me, she was grinning like a monkey. You thought your voice wouldn't be audible over the evening news, but I could hear every word clearly.

Arguing cases in the courtroom sharpened your wit, and I was proud of your work, but I could not let Reeny's lopsided and blinkered view of history demolish the Taj Mahal because it was built with slave labor.

It was Miriam Shapiro who first noticed the change in you and mentioned it to Maury Lee. I could tell something was afoot when Miriam looked at me searchingly every time we passed each other at Kingman, or stuck her head round the door of my office under the pretext of seeking my opinion on some student's performance that had already been discussed earlier at a meeting.

Maury Lee was less circumspect, and one day after a particularly tedious faculty meeting, when the new president had held forth for well over an hour, chuntering on about the need to build a more up-to-date gymnasium, Maury Lee accosted me in my office and came straight to the point.

'Are you and Shabnam having some trouble, mate,' he said in a fake British accent. He made the last word sound like 'might'.

'What makes you think that?' I asked warily.

'Well, for one thing, I have never known you to hang around here after a particularly mind-numbing faculty meeting like the one just ended. You would be out on the streets heading for home, bleating for your Darjeeling and Shabnam's *pakoras*.'

'Well if you must know, Shabnam is in court today. Exposing a bigamist with a wife and child back home, married to some local merchant's daughter. Something like that.'

'Come off it,' Maury Lee said. 'The light in your office is on practically every evening. I myself have seen you on the campus well past supper time.'

Tongues on the campus were wagging. The Indian and his loyal wife were having problems like everybody else. They might not split up, not yet anyway, but everything was certainly not tickety-boo with the Amolinis.

'Look Maury Lee,' I said, 'I honestly don't know what the problem is. You are right, our home is not at peace with itself. Something has begun to fester. I cannot fathom what. Nothing I can put my finger on. All I know is that we don't, that is Shabnam and I don't, seem to be on the same—"wavelength"—I believe is the expression. My receiver is not quite tuned to her megahertz or something. I am not putting it very well; what I am trying to say is that even Gullu is behaving strangely. There is a lot of whispering and giggling between mother and daughter from which I am excluded.'

Then I told him about the fight you had with our daughter-in-law the other evening over something trivial when we were at Immy's. Of all things, you accused poor Sally of cheating at cards.

'Can you believe it?' I said to Maury Lee. 'At cards. Sally is too much of a free spirit to worry about it, but I am scared stiff. May be it's a passing phase, midlife crisis and all that. I am told women get that way at a certain age, all moody and distracted.'

'But surely not the divine Shabnam. Are you sure you are not imagining things, buddy?' Maury Lee said.

'I wish I were, old chap. It's like this; let us say we are walking down KC Way, and if Thakorji or Bookstore-Nambiar comes out to chat with us, Shabnam just walks ahead without stopping to say hello. And what's more, she is now a regular patron of Tivoli Cinema.'

Maury Lee was astounded. He remembers you as you were in Inderpur.

The problem is I do too.

Book II

❧ 1 ❧

Maury Lee Carmody's Inderpur Journal

June 22, 1978

'I am knowing him since long,' the Bushshirt says, looking at the tall graceful man in his forties who has left his tweed jacket on his seat and is saying a final goodbye to his friends on the platform.

'His name is Siraj Amolini, he is professor at university,' the Bushshirt continues.

Amolini is lighter-skinned than most Indians I have met. A high Leslie Howard forehead, brown melancholy eyes.

'Yes, yes,' the Bushshirt proceeds, 'Professor Siraj is a good Muslim.'

I was to hear that expression repeated several times—uttered in dry patronizing tones at parties, flung as a clincher at the end of an argument, tipsily delivered in Men's Bar at the Club, droned like a mantra in servants' quarters, and intoned in Bollywoodish ululation in the bazaar. However divided Inderpur might have been on the issue of the big dam on the river lapping its eastern flank, it was united in its belief that Siraj Amolini was a good Muslim.

Inderpur was like an exotic butterfly frozen in the amber of time. Hurriedly yoked together at the time of Indian independence, from the tattered remains of an old princely kingdom and a dark craggy tribal land, sitting on an unlimited supply of manganese ore, Pacheesgarh, of which Inderpur was state capital, had managed to spawn a cutthroat culture that would have prompted the Borgias to let off an appreciative whistle.

Some of the most colorful characters who made up that mosaic appear in neutral roles of 'informers' in the journal I kept during my fieldwork. There was this socialist oddball in a white bushshirt I first met on the train to Inderpur. What he did to the Queen's English could only be described as the Empire snarling back.

In post-Vietnam seventies, young idealistic kids like yours truly, who wanted to make a difference, were a dime a dozen. Even after my brother Steve returned from Vietnam with that open-mouthed, fixed stare of a dead haddock and disappeared into the wilds of Vermont, I still held the geeky notion that travel brought you truckloads of maturity. If there was one thing any quack could prescribe for me in those days and still be my friend it was maturity. And the most favored way of stocking up on it was to head right back to yet another god-forsaken region as a Peace Corps volunteer, cutting a rug with the locals and getting high on their snake juice. In return, you were supposed to give them demos on hygiene, such as how to wash their hands after taking a crap, and how to always drink boiled water. In those days, I certainly acted like one of those suckers who believed rubbing noses with some unwashed dude in a drought-prone corner of the world was the way to find out who you were.

There were some scholarly underpinnings that propped up the choices I made. In those pre-globetrotterer days, cultural anthropology seemed like a cool choice. What ultimately tipped the scale in favor of anthropology was a cockfight. Not just any cockfight, mind you, with guys in sombreros hopping on their haunches, and goading a mean-looking fowl to attack its clucking rival in a dusty courtyard south of the border. No sir, these cocks had pedigree—breeding—stretching back to the beginning of time. According to Clifford Geertz, they were aristocrats of the highest caste, and witnessing this classy cockfight on the Indonesian Island of Bali was like watching Laurence Olivier perform *King Lear*.

This might sound corny, but I owed my tenure to the rank and file of Balinese poultry. Those intrepid bantams wielded their magic from the day I started teaching Social Anthropology 101 at Kingman, earning for me the Best Teacher of the Year Award three times in a row. As the man said, if you knew how to untangle its various strands, that cock-fight was more than a blood sport. It represented the entire evolution of Balinese caste structure over the centuries.

On the other hand, what pulled me in the direction of Inderpur was a dog-eared copy of *Kanthapura*, an Indian novella Steve had picked up at a used bookstore in Greenwich Village. Its well-thumbed, curry-stained pages gave off a strong whiff of cannabis and hemp, indicating a bookworm precursor in search of meaning. If books can seduce, this one was a slam-dunk, set in this fantastic little Indian town on the banks of a holy river and watched over by a patron goddess perched on a nearby hilltop. From start to finish, it detailed an alternative lifestyle of such extraordinary deceleration, that a turtle might get a ticket for speeding. Also my CV needed some bolstering in the form of articles in learned journals, because a doctorate from NYU and a back-up course I taught in film noir of the forties were not enough to clinch tenure at Kingman. I managed to get an NEH Grant, hitched my wagon to the Center for Tribal Welfare in Inderpur, and caught an Air India flight to Bombay.

Inderpur Express is ready to depart Bombay's Victoria Terminus. Arabesques of light and shadows under its vaulted ceiling. The train pulls out of station under billboards of hairy stars and starlets with oversized bosoms. I figure every escape is the start of a new jail term.

A first-class carriage with four bunks. Across the aisle is the Bushshirt, next to me is Professor Siraj Amolini, and sitting on the far side of the bunk from the Bushshirt is this swami guy, layers of jiggly flesh billowing down from chin to gut And there crouched by the window am I, being silently spied on by the swami and getting the willies.

Then a row of bare bottoms appears along the embankment outside our car, and the Bushshirt suddenly turns towards me like a veteran of a Balinese cockfight about to tear into its rival.

'You is shocked,' the Bushshirt says tapping my knee.

'No, no,' I reply, blowing my nose to cover my embarrassment. 'It's perfectly all right if the poor dudes have no facilities at home.'

'It is real shame, I telling you, it is real shame. And who is to blame?' the Bushshirt asks and taps my knee even harder. His eyes bulge fiercely. 'Govern-ment. Let independence come, they said. Independence come and gone. But what has happen? Peoples, peoples is still shitting in the open air.'

I hear a warning cough from my neighbor. I am thinking, this professor guy has little use for men like the Bushshirt, who let the country down before strangers.

'Surely,' the prof says in his British accent, 'you cannot blame the government for this outrageous exhibition. If these illiterate folk refuse to change their ways, no government can help them. Even our aborigines in the forest have a better civic sense than these city types, who spend all their savings on transistor radios and low-grade films instead of building themselves decent facilities.'

'But why for is Govern-ment not giving subsidies to build latrines?' the Bushshirt demands. 'Govern-ment only building atom bombs and making riots. Making Hindu Muslim fight, fight, fight.' He bangs his right fist in the open palm of his left hand three times.

'Don't be silly,' Amolini says. 'The poor are all over the country. They must learn to fend for themselves instead of rioting and destroying public property.'

'But Govern-ment make them fight. Divide and rule just like the British.'

Amolini clears his throat and says, 'I believe our friend here is alluding to the rumor that the recent communal riots in Inderpur were sponsored by the governing coalition. But it's criminals and vandals who start these riots. Then the poor join in the fray. Start looting shops.'

'No, no,' the Bushshirt says, 'poor Hindu and Muslim living together. There is no Hindu or Muslim. Only poor. See, see how Hindu and Muslim all shitting together? No fighting.'

I have this impulse to laugh real loud; the noise the Bushshirt makes wakes the fat swami. He rubs his eyes and farts.

At the next station a large mob gathers outside our carriage. One guy hands the holy man a fat garland of jasmine and marigolds. This charade is repeated at almost every stop. Once the holy man comes back with a large box packed with thick gobs of sweets.

'The real sages is living in forests and eating only fruit. This swami traveling first class and eating sweets,' the Bushshirt says.

'We are old friends,' the professor says to the Bushshirt. 'You wouldn't mind my saying this. You claim to be a socialist, and yet you travel first class.'

'Important meeting in Inderpur tomorrow. No reservation in third-class sleeper available,' the Bushshirt says, groping for a suitable answer. He is spared further embarrassment as the bearer brings us our evening meal.

Amolini and I tackle our roast chicken as best we can; the Bushshirt slurps down his rice and curry. The holy guy consumes some more sweets, drinks water from a brass pot, raises his left flank, and lets off a fart in sharp contralto. Fortunately, we had lost our battle to the unyielding fowl before the big bang.

At a wayside station, a train from the other direction rattles past, wriggles as it crosses tracks like a furious snake, and vanishes into the night. Somewhere in a lonely yard, a freight train emits a few dying gasps, then the driver kills its engine.

'Countries!' I think. 'What have I to do with countries? As some Greek dude said, "To set sail for somewhere is better than life."'

❧ 2 ❧

My memory of Inderpur has an attic-like quality covered with tangled webs, where characters and events criss-cross each other. I can still see the mute façades of buildings, but nothing else makes sense. Then someone moves, a street becomes avenues filled with scurrying silhouettes; Inderpur opens its Delhi Gate and Daulatabad Gate, its scooter-rickshaws rushing past yowling hawkers, and the same one-horned transcendental cow regulating traffic in the old market square. Occasionally, a woman squatting by heaps of lentils, cucumbers, and lady fingers arches her body forward gracefully to fill a customer's bag. Unseen by them, I watch the progress of an old couple steering their cart round knots of vendors. The sweets in the shops glow amber and green.

The old couple had come trotting up from a world I had never known. The man's head was lowered over his rickety ribcage, but the woman had looked straight at me, her eyes widening as if in recognition. It was a long face, high cheek-boned with dry, loose skin faded to dull yellow, like a palimpsest. Something strange had emanated from those old tired eyes. Perhaps the combination of jet lag and Dr Lepakshi's chatter about the enigmatic Golmal had spooked me. I was to hear that fading tinkle from the woman's anklets for days after I left Inderpur.

Doctor Lepakshi is at the Inderpur Road station to receive me on behalf of the Center for Adivasi Welfare, a Ford Foundation-sponsored outfit. The word 'Adivasis' means tribal or indigenous people. The station is roughly twelve miles from the city. She drives a battered Morris Minor. A telegenic woman, with almond- shaped brown eyes and full lips that in repose remain half open. Siraj is a good friend, and the doctor offers to drive him home after dropping me off at the guest house, which is on the way. I have corresponded with Dr Lepakshi's husband Dr Saradhi, who is an internationally known expert on Adivasi culture and is on the faculty at the University of Inderpur; but he is away in Australia at the moment. I sit next to her in the passenger seat, while Siraj snoozes at the back. Most Indian women in her age group I have seen in the US are wrapped in layers of clothing. This Lepakshi puts her magnificent figure on display. We pull out of the station courtyard scattering the swami's chanting devotees.

'Siri, the police made three arrests yesterday,' she says. 'Raided the Adivasi hamlet in the forest at night and took them away. Golmal told the press they were gambling. All bullshit.'

The doctor has a slight American accent, a hangover from the six years she spent at medical school in Chicago. The woman she calls Golmal is the local police chief.

'She's a bitch goddess and a tiger cat all rolled into one.'

I gather that Golmal is the police chief's nickname.

'It is Hindi for hanky-panky,' Dr Lepakshi explains. 'The crooks call her Hunterwali 'cause she always carries a riding crop with her. To her chuprasis *she is Madam Fut Fut 'cause she sputters around on her scooter. I call her Annie Get Your Gun.'*

I am curious. 'Why does she carry a crop if she drives a scooter?'

'It is really to ward off the pariahs who chase her scooter,' the prof says.

'We all know why she carries that crop,' Lepakshi says. 'It's rumored that she has to have it with her all the time. She never knows when she might need it. Every once in a while she locks herself in her office, takes off her uniform, and helps herself to ten lashes. Her constables count them for a wager.'

'I don't believe it; in the office?' I am baffled.

Siraj's voice is solemn like when he was talking to the Bushshirt on the train. 'When you've gotten to know our Lepakshi a little better, you'll find that she exaggerates a lot.'

I am to stay in the modest little red brick guest house where visiting research scholars are housed. I am told that the Adivasis were here long before Mohenjo-daro (5000 BCE) and predate the so-called Aryan conquest of India.

Blood-red curtains against blinding sunlight, a groaning cot for a bed, rust-coated shower head, toilet seat broken by guests who take a crap by squatting native style on their haunches, as witnessed from the train. Lobster-sized cockroaches; their breeding outstrips the most lethal pesticide. Breakfast is crisp toast, a bowl of leathery cornflakes splashing in watery milk, fried eggs swimming in oil. A dusky, well-stacked young woman with exquisite rows of white teeth does my room every day. Bold sign language leads me to believe she would do other things as well for a new sari every month.

July 3, 1978

Been here for over a week. Dr Saradhi is still away lecturing in Australia. Dr Lepakashi heads the Primary Health Center. The nursing staff is small but efficient. There is a compounder who dispenses medicine, and Mr Kapasia is the accountant. Next door is a Christian mission-run school. Yesterday, I met Father Yesudas, who doubles as school principal and priest at the local Thomist Church. The schoolhouse is an old dilapidated wooden building, which in the past was the Hunting Lodge of the local ruler.

The Padre is in his late sixties. An old English woman taught there for years before kicking the bucket a couple of years ago. A college kid called Chotta has been filling in for her. Chotta's dad works as a peon at the Health Center. His name is Mr Soni. Chotta is getting ready for college graduation. I don't much care for the Padre's mission to bring light to the tribals.

'This kinda stuff gives me the heebie-jeebbies,' Chotta says handing me a copy of The English Workbook for Non-native Speakers. *'Some of the exercises are really wacky. See ya,' he says and scoot*s.

July 29, 1978

First day at school. Smile at the kids. Hard boned co-ed bunch in well-pressed khaki uniforms. I write a sentence from the book on the board in large clear letters.

THE PRODUCTION OF PETROLEUM IN IRAN IS VERY LARGE. HOW MUCH PETROLEUM DOES INDIA _______________________?

86

'You there,' I say to a kid who is whispering to his neighbor. 'Do you know how to change your nouns to verbs?'

'You bet I do, baby,' the kid replies, hitching up his shorts.

'What did you say?'

'I said, "You bet I do, baby."'

I roll my eyes. Nervous smiles all around. Girls stare down at their books.

'You must not say "baby". Where did you pick that up?' I ask.

'In English film,' says the kid. 'Chotta teacher says to see English film to improve speech.'

'That's fine,' I explain. 'But it is not polite to use such expressions. Remember that,' I warn.

'Okey dokey,' says the kid.

'And don't say that either.' I rap the table with my knuckles. After that, no one volunteers to answer questions. I go to see the Padre. Tell him I am not cut out to be a teacher.

'Feel free to use any material that would suit you, son,' says the Padre.

He takes care of the syllabus prescribed by the board of education. Asks me to help kids converse in English. Shakes his head and says, 'Unlike the children of the upper crust, these get no practice in speech at home; parents are not literate. Kids do badly in interviews later on.'

'Or end up talking like Bonnie & Clyde,' I say, thinking of Chotta.

September 12 1978

Inderpur in the dusk unfolds like a gray, crowded lithograph of a medieval Tuscan township with domes, minarets and trees reduced to the size of their own tiny mock-ups when viewed from the top of the Hill of Devi. Looking up from the market square you see an old temple wrapped in a white marble shawl, leaning companionably on a mosque clinging to a steep ridge.

Lepakshi and her husband take me to Inderpur Club for dinner. The green of the eves and the ancient banyans set off the peculiar shade of tropical khaki of the club, squatting amidst clouds of bougainvillea. The entire front lawn seems to be dotted with policemen in uniform. A female officer in a crisp khaki uniform is in *charge. An athletic woman, she is a head taller than most of her men except for a mustachioed and burly inspector who scurries after the men like a herding sheepdog. Her upward glance makes her seem shy until you catch sight of the dark spot in her right eye. It rises from her lower eyelid, giving the impression of a twin pupil.*

Lepakshi makes a face and I know that I am in the presence of Golmal the police superintendent.

Lepakshi says, 'Hullo Ahilya, how is the law and order situation?'

'Everything is under control, thank you,' is the chilly reply. I notice that the black spot swimming up and down her right eye gives her face a menacing look. Her hair is tucked beneath her beret, and she carries a swagger stick with a shiny knob.

We head for the lounge where Siri and Shabnam are waiting for us. Shabnam moves with a quiet grace; she is there and not there. A blue chiffon sari and centuries of culture that set high value on self-effacement give her a sort of ethereal quality. Siri introduces me to his childhood friend, the Maharaja of Inderpur, last of a long line of royal actors, Digvijaysingh, 'Dicky' to old chums, now serving as a member of Parliament; a chandelier smoothly lights his bloated roué figure— swarthy moonface set on a loose-fleshed body, all rippled and swaddled in a Hawaiian shirt.

Then Bulchand, the state minister for finance, trots in accompanied by Golmal. He is one of the new breed of public figures, ruthlessly manipulative, his whole career set in terms of political skullduggery. The minister explains the presence of the police on the lawn outside. He is hosting a dinner for some dignitary from Delhi. Lepakshi, who has not bothered to get up, says,

'So you guys are going ahead with the dam?'

'Yes, we are. I know you object. But now that we have the mandate we must do what is best in the interest of the people.'

'Which people?' Siri demands sitting up. 'You make me sick. Aren't the Adivasis also people? Where will they go when their villages are flooded?'

'They will be provided for, believe me, Professor. Mr Tiwari has come down from Delhi to select the area for their rehabilitation. I am a good friend of the Adivasis and they know it.'

'I hope both Tiwari and you choke on your Mughlai chicken,' Lepakshi hisses

after him. There is a stunned silence. Bulchand turns around slowly. The fixed smile does not fade, but his tone is curt,

'Not possible, Doctor. We are both vegetarian.' Then he marches off with Golmal in tandem.

'That,' says Siraj, 'is the slimiest creature that ever walked the earth.'

'That may be, but unless you two back off, you will get us all in trouble,' Lepakshi's husband says. 'I am pretty sure he's after Dicky's seat in Parliament and is hoping to get into the cabinet at the Center. Look at all the fuss he is making over that minister from Delhi.'

'I am afraid Saradhi is right,' Dicky says getting up. 'Siri old man, how many times do I have to tell you not to blow your gasket in public? That there is a pit viper. His sting is deadly. As for you,' he said to Lepakshi, 'what can I say? I would hate to see your grant cut off suddenly. Old bully Bulchand won't hesitate to do that. We don't want to lose you, old girl. Be damned difficult to run the medical show without you. Well, I must join Bulchand and his gang of thugs at dinner. It won't do to snub his guest from Delhi.'

Two children who have strayed from their parents, a wide-eyed boy of three in a sailor suit, and a puff-cheeked little miss of five in pigtails with an observant eye, watch this grown-up prank. The boy is transfixed, his tiny hands locked adult-fashion at the back, eyes growing rounder.

The evening's entertainment is a preview of an Adivasi folk drama troupe that is preparing for a competition in Delhi. Bahurupia, the actor with many faces, plays a variety of roles. There is also a sort of bluebeard who announces the theme of each episode to the accompaniment of a single-stringed ektara. The bluebeard doubles as the government spokesman serving eviction notices to the Adivasis. He is in a cloth-of-gold turban, a long flowing green robe, churidars, *and red velvet shoes shaped like Viking ships. A beautiful girl, whom he addresses as Janaki, assists him on a harmonium.*

Tonight's performance, to be presented out on the lawn in the light of two oil-dripping torches, is called The Saga of the River People. *The ektara player accompanies the young woman as she sings a ballad, while a girlish boy enacts each scene in the form of a North Indian Kathak dance. He is the Bahurupia who sug-*

gests change in age and gender through skilful modulation of gesture, pausing only to tuck his pigtails under his velvet cap when not playing a girl and covering his shoulders with a pink muslin dupatta *when rendering a woman.*

The girl's voice rises in high soprano register, weaving a microtonal tracery of exotic sound, now elegiac, now percussive. The Bahurupia executes Kathak steps, managing to convey an underlying sense of foreboding through facial expressions and gestures. The music has a faintly classical tone color.

As the evening thickens into a dark moonless night, the Bahurupia becomes an Adivasi father transplanted to a barren land, then briefly a mother, then a childless widow forced into selling her flesh. Spinning filigreed lines from a small harmonium, the young girl breathes such life into her elegiac melody that the Bahurupia and the bluebeard all but vanish from sight. Such is the girl's grief at the loss of her beloved river that there is not a single dry eye that night. The song of the grieving Adivasi goes something like this:

> *The Oracle said 'Beware of the fork-tongued stranger.'*
> *Like lightening he blighted the speaking tree.*
> *Once the Earth and the Sky raised me*
> *The Sacred River washed me clean*
> *A blissful wind dried my tresses.*
> *Forlorn Moon, now who will brighten my temple walk?*
> *Where is the nest for my unhatched soul?*

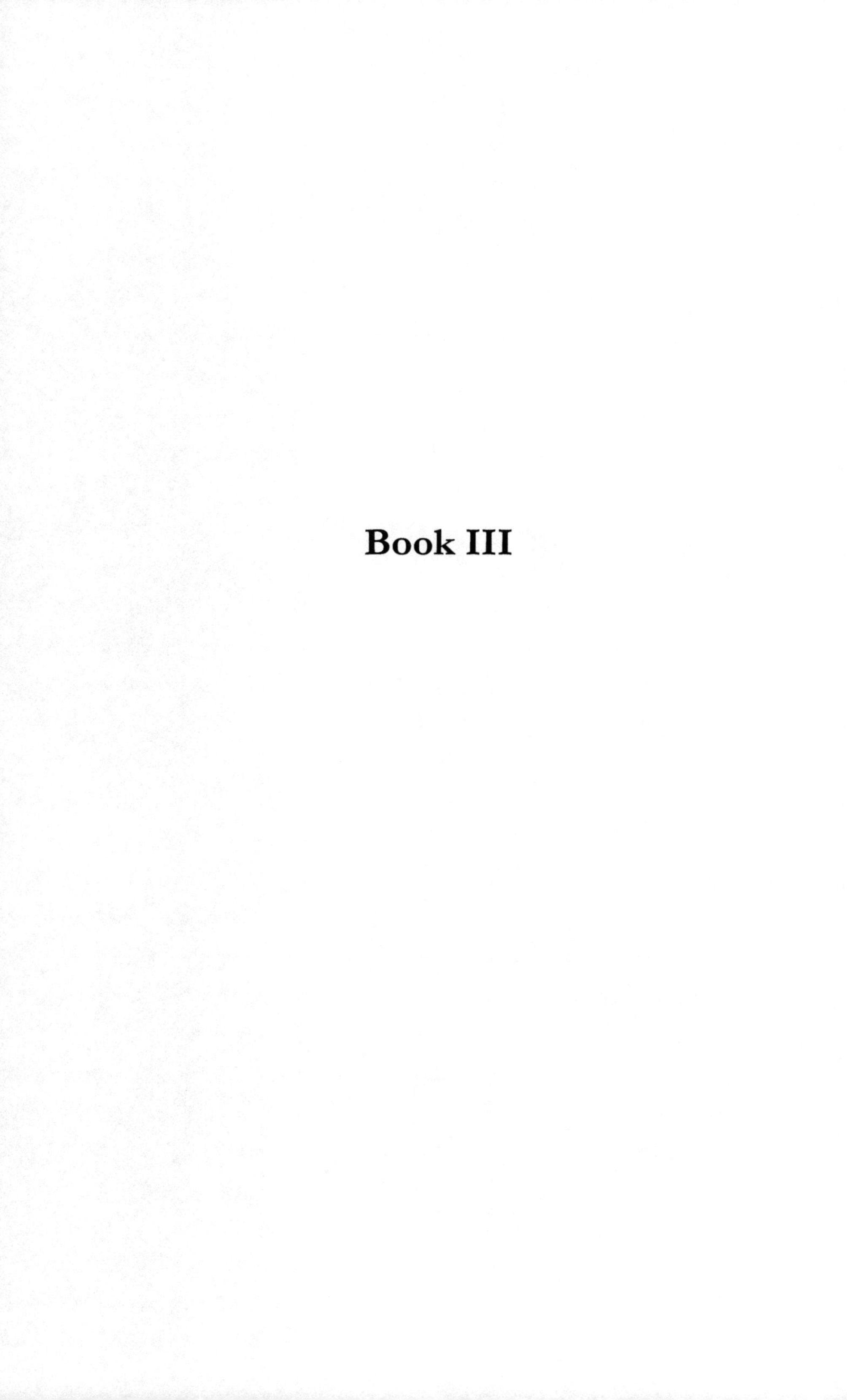

Book III

❧ 1 ❧

We leave our worldly possessions behind in our homeland but wherever we go, our history appears before us unexpectedly like Banquo's ghost with a blood-spattered face. That is why Durbar's response to the carnage of Partition—getting a hair cut and abjuring the iconic beard—though quite unspectacular, seems almost heroic when set against the larger scheme of things.

On the other hand, we arrive here more or less uncontaminated by American history, long after the scenery and vast façades of the Civil War have been rolled away. We have not shared their pains, their Pearl Harbors, Iwo Jimas, Koreas and Vietnams. We feel like onlookers, Johnny-come-latelys. Perhaps with some head-scratching we can tell where we were when President Kennedy was assassinated, but we watch with a sense of belatedness, the reruns of Walter Cronkite taking off his glasses in a gesture of profound despair after announcing the President's death.

England was familiar territory.

We were already briefed, so to speak; there was a compact with England that outlived the snapping of political ties in 1947. Wren and Martin, the watchdogs of the Queen's English, regulated the grammar of our lives. Bits and pieces of the Empire's geography and history were lodged inside us like live cartridges, so that the slightest pressure could trigger us to reciting Kipling's *If* or the brave words uttered by General Wolfe as he lay dying after taking Quebec. When the ferry from Calais docked at Dover, bluebirds fluttered above us as though scratched out from a decal sticker.

To Indians of my generation, America would always be a different kettle of fish, another ball game, so to speak. By the time you manage to get the hang of it, the rules of the game have changed, the ground beneath your feet shifts and you have the feeling of being washed ashore on a newly formed continental plate. Waking up, you feel like a clown in possession of a language that is no longer in use.

Take the word 'difference'. No single word in our time has caused more heartburn. As a tool for cutting a tyrant down to human size or giving your husband his marching orders, it has no equal. But it can also be misused to underscore your racial superiority, as Hitler did. There has to be a line drawn between its misuse by crackpot demagogues and its utility as a tool against deadbeat husbands. In the hand of Reeny and the growing number of her acolytes, it was beginning to gleam like a switchblade in a dark alley.

In this twisted new vocabulary, to 'differ' was to 'divide'.

Now don't get me wrong. I am not like one of those mealy-mouthed politicians in India who blame the British policy of divide and rule for the blood bath of Partition, as if our five-thousand-year civilization had suddenly been afflicted with amnesia or had gone AWOL, so that a bunch of shopkeepers, as Napoleon called the British, made us commit acts of unspeakable horrors.

Ding Dong Daddy from Dubuque was Maury Lee's nickname for Hackett, the new president of Kingman. And in Reeny Babukhan he found a perfect ally. During the argybargy over curricular reform, she began to visit our home frequently, ostensibly to win my support for purging the outmoded Kingman syllabus, top heavy with the weight of dead white males, and replacing it with multicultural honchos who sang in native tongues. She appealed to my patriotic duty as a 'Third World' academic to wrest our heritage from our colonial masters by toppling Shakespeare's statue from our mental traffic circle.

That was her mistake. I have always believed that in the academic racket such as ours, live and let live is the best policy. If someone wants to eat a crazy salad with their meat, as Yeats said about his muse Maud Gonne, I would say 'Please be my guest.' But Reeny didn't know when to stop, when to walk away with her winnings.

Having summarily got rid of our Great Books program, she then trained her 'gaze of power' on Shakespeare and blundered awkwardly into a Rosa Park moment. Ask the Bard to go back to the back of the bus and you are asking for trouble.

I stood firm, of course, with support from Miriam our chairperson and a few other like-minded colleagues.

That's when Reeny began to hatch her nefarious plan to establish a second front and start her recruitment drive right at the center of Jackson Heights, which to her was enemy territory at the time. What sweeter prize than building a spy network in the rival citadel at the height of a cold war?

You two formed what can only be described as the 'sisterhood of the traveling burqa', though neither of you went as far as donning one, thank goodness. Reeny would show up on Saturday evening when Gullu was home for the weekend, and the three of you chattered on in the kitchen cooking *pakoras*.

I wanted to join in the fun but something held me back.

You no longer waited for me to come home now, as you used to. You were too busy rescuing women from lubricious husbands who insisted on bedding them into the ground or squeezing them for a second round of dowry, which would bankrupt their parents. Lying next to you, I could sense your accumulated resentment against those goatish men getting diverted to me like a flight cleared for force-landing at the nearest airport.

I disappeared in the cavernous anonymity of Manhattan. Sometimes I stood for hours brooding over Mughal miniatures or South Indian temple art on loan from the British Museum. Sometimes I sat all by myself in a darkened cinema house without looking at the screen. I returned home late at night, long after Reeny had departed, and locked myself in my study.

These days I don't even call in sick, and it's all right with me if my face has gray patches where the shaver has missed stubble. Sometimes gripped with self-pity, I fancy that my face in repose still retains that haunted David Janssen look of the telly's *The Fugitive.*

Unlike our son Immy, I was too set in my ways when I arrived here to pick up speed immediately like the hybrid car. As soon as you turn the key in the ignition and hit the gas, it accelerates within seconds to sixty miles per hour. I was groomed to move in a leisurely fashion, with a Made-in-England, Wedgwood grace. I have never really felt quite comfortable in the rough-and-ready, coffee-mug culture of America, even after twenty long years. Let's face it, I am an anachronism. I am told my colleagues have been dining out for years, mimicking my taking of tea at the stroke of four in the afternoon, delicately holding the handle of the cup between thumb and index finger.

Dicky had kept me posted on the changes taking place in Inderpur—how ancient wrinkled towns were getting a makeover, how the building lobby was engaged in bleaching out all the skid marks of history with a McDonalds and a Domino's Pizza, set around the marble-tiled concourse of a mall. At the site of the dank and musty Mohan Talkies, where the show would start only when the palace Rolls Royce bringing Dicky and his school chums rolled in, its marquee depicting scenes from old Hollywood classics like *Casablanca, The Maltese Falcon* and the sumptuous *Gone With the Wind,* now stood a gleaming new IMAX, where Sylvester Stallone and Arnold Schwarzenegger routinely decimated whole squadrons of bad boys and hung them up to dry amidst the rubble of concrete buildings.

Our son took to his adopted land like a duck to water, preconditioned, as he was to its high-energy life style. Immy cannot be deposited in the neat box of 'like father, like son.' I am five-foot-ten, but he dwarfs me by several inches.

While still at college, Immy had shown signs of extraordinary financial wizardry and was the first to predict a sudden dip in the gadgetry trade when India unshackled its markets in the early nineties. Someone waved a magic wand in Delhi and here in Jackson Heights hundreds of electric shavers, cassette players, cordless phones, calculators, Casio keyboards and other gizmos disappeared overnight and were replaced by pendant necklaces, diamond bracelets, earrings in oriental settings, wedding rings and other things that glittered in the dark. As you observed, walking down KC Way was like being back in Inderpur. The place was now a mirror image of Bijli Chowk.

You were proud of Immy's rise in the world of finance at the relatively young age of twenty-eight. Your *behenji*s and *bibi*s had told you that Immy's Wall Street exploits were a staple around their dinner table. I looked askance at his hot pursuit of the American dream and was perhaps a trifle embarrassed by it. His lifestyle seemed to mock everything Dr Leavis had warned us about in his seminar room under the T Staircase at Downing College, Cambridge.

'An unexamined life is not worth living,' was Dr Leavis's Socratic principle. Immy had no time to examine or ponder anything; he was constantly hopping in and out of taxis. You were dazzled by your first born's gleaming new BMW, his three-bay garage, Colombian nannies for our grandchildren, and rich golf partners who smoked authentic Hawaiian cigars. You basked in the envy of clients whose boys had only managed to land petty jobs as salesman in haberdasheries.

Don't get me wrong. I didn't want Immy to be a teacher like me. To the question, 'What does your son do for a living?' I would have gladly replied, 'Oh he is a nuclear scientist or a neurosurgeon.' You must admit 'hedge-fund manager' or 'Wall Street trader' has a slightly musty odor of some dead rodent trapped in an air conditioner.

After their sixteenth-century trek from Persia to the Mughal court in Agra, the Amolini clan had produced a whole galaxy of creative people, who had distinguished themselves in different public-service enterprises. Our genes had evolved from satraps to zamindars, hakims to doctors, scribes to civil servants, *kotwals* to district magistrates, *mansabdars* to colonels in the Royal Inderpur Light Infantry and finally, as in my case, from *mujtabids*, or polyglot interpreters serving the East India Company, to English professors. In Immy, the Amolini strain had fanned out in an entirely new direction. He was a mutant, who, save for his last name, had retained practically no links with his venerable past.

When he was barely twenty, Immy gained fame as a wunderkind of high finance, spending summer breaks in Manhattan as assistant to Miriam's husband, Joe Shapiro. Joe had carved his way up to the top of his investment banking firm, and then splintered into a day trader, consolidating his status as a smart operator, but one who always played by the book.

Last week at Joe's place, while Miriam, Maury Lee, Sally and you played bridge, and Gullu, Kanti and Susan watched the video of *Au Revoir Les Enfants*, the Louis Malle classic about the hounding out by Nazis of a Jewish boy sheltered by a Catholic school in Paris, Immy and Joe tried to explain to me how the hedge fund racket worked. But soon they threw up their hands and went to the kitchen to get their beers.

Immy bought two luxurious houses on the rim of a picturesque town encircling a lake in New Jersey. He wanted us to move into the one next door, but for once you supported me in declining our son's offer. Your law practice in Jackson Heights was going full tilt, and I wanted to avoid the long commute from Greenwood Lake, New Jersey, to Kingman.

❧ 2 ☙

There was a myth in Jackson Heights that we Indians were somehow more civilized than the rest. We were not only smarter and better educated, practically owned Silicon Valley, but above all we had no Mafia of our own like the Chinese, the Vietnamese and the Russians, with their very own Odessas on American soil. The closest approximation to a godfather figure we had was Mr Sampat, who lived in a big fortress of a house in nearby Forest Hills. The question was, could we enter him for the 'International Godfathers Championship Derby'? Did he have what it takes?

Mr Sampat did not resemble your typical Mafia don. He was shriveled and creased, and looked rather like the painted effigy of an Indian politician, skeletal frame rattling under loose-fitting jodhpurs. One assumed a Mafia don to be a flinty-eyed, hatchet-faced man of generous girth, lolling on a sofa in a split-screen TV image, balancing a pole dancer in one hand and a cell phone in the other, while under a thin shaving of a moon in the parallel frame, his sidekick heaved a corpse into a lonely creek, to a tempestuous Scriabin-like score.

Mr Sampat might look like something the cat dragged in, but some of your new clients had admitted to paying his henchman in India huge sums of money for fake visas to get into the US. They now faced deportation, but there was no way of linking Sampat to the scam.

I was naturally worried. Compelling deadbeat Indian or Pakistani dads to cough up child support was one thing; tangling with a ruthless hard-boiled ruffian like Sampat was quite another.

Your growing reputation as a feisty attorney was leading you into dangerous waters, and I was beginning to have nightmares in which law officers were fishing you out of remote tributaries of the Hudson. Sampat was known to have got rid of his competition by resorting to Mafia-style intimidation. He had also acquired a number of gas stations across Upstate New York, where he employed convicted parolees. He always travelled in a car with tinted glass, and even at the height of summer he wore an oversized Humphrey Bogart trench coat and hat, nipping into Chitral's or Kanchan's house like a cat burglar.

Chitral himself fetched and carried drinks and *pakoras* so that no one knew what deadly conspiracies they were hatching in his attic. Only once, when he was young, his stepmother had sent Kanti to the attic with a platterful of *pakora*s. Sampat sat hunched, head lowered, peering into a leather suitcase, which he snapped shut as soon as Kanti appeared in the doorway. A pair of dead eyes stared out, but before the rest of the face came into focus, Chitral lunged for the plate to forestall his son's entry.

I sometimes wondered what made Kanti's father so cynical. Something more than a little malice seemed to propel him in the direction of almost vulgar acts of treachery. He took great care to please everybody, but an expression of unrelieved hatred darkened his brow whenever our paths crossed. What was behind that? Why was he always looking for a chance to create a rift between Hindus and Muslims on some pretext or the other?

I always thought him to be too self-regarding to harbor some dark memory of past suffering, or allow a satanic sense of injured merit build into a whirlwind of reckoning. There was nothing in him of the fearless avenger whose mission in life is to hunt down ex-Nazis hiding in the jungles of Paraguay, the fierce patriotism of a young kamikaze, or the innocent faith of the schoolgirl who blew up a British governor with a bomb in Calcutta during a prize distribution ceremony at her high school.

Chitral always had the stertorous look of a crocodile half buried in mud, waiting patiently for a buffalo at a watering hole. I should have thought that having disposed of one wife to make room for another even less likely to catch the eye of a neighborhood Romeo, he was the most perfect candidate for 'motiveless malignity' since Iago. Was he biding his time for a major goof up on the subcontinent, a gruesome lurch of a mob into unforeseen catastrophe that would get everybody frothing at the mouth and drive a permanent wedge between Hindus and Muslims?

Also, I could not see Chitral fondly urging his daughter-in-law-elect, Susan, to knock a silver cup filled with rice across the threshold of his residence with her dainty toe, as was customary in certain traditional families for Indian brides first entering their new homes.

I asked Kanti why his dad was so resentful, so full of rancor, spurning every gesture we made to bury our differences.

'Is it because he holds me responsible for your walking out of the house?' you asked Kanti.

'I don't think he really cares that much about me. I guess he simply loathes all Muslims, pardon my saying so,' Kanti said. 'I would have left home anyway; in fact he was quite relieved to have me out of the house. I think he would try to harm you whether you helped me or not. "They are our enemies, they are all alike, there are no good Muslims," he used to tell me when I was little and came here to play with Gullu. It's all because of what happened to him when he was very young. That one incident has made him bitter for life.'

The sad story unfolded slowly that evening. We had finished supper. There was complete silence as Kanti told us what happened to his dad.

'When he was a small boy of six in Sialkot, traveling with refugees to India, in August 1947, his teenage elder brother, that is my uncle Ratan Lal, whose photo hangs in our sitting room, had got off the truck to answer the call of nature, hoping to catch up with the slow-moving line of refugee trucks. But suddenly the convoy picked up speed. It was feared that my uncle was either killed by a group of Muslim refugees headed in the opposite direction or was dragged away and forcibly converted to Islam. My father never talks about it. I heard the story from my mother just before she died. One day my father beat me up mercilessly for something, I don't recall what. I was so angry that I wouldn't stop crying. That was when she told me about my lost uncle. She said that single incident in his childhood had drained him of all pity.'

Afterwards, when I was stacking dishes in the washer, you came and stood by me without saying anything. You looked as though somebody had walked over your grave.

'I am terrified,' you said. 'I just have this feeling that something ghastly is going to happen—that destruction of the mosque in Ayodhya is bound to have some serious repercussions here.'

I tried to reassure you that we of the Neighborhood Watch would be able to ride out this storm, as in the past.

'No, no,' you said, 'this is different; what they did last month to that mosque in India is much too serious. There is madness on both sides.'

Your diagnosis was that buried hatchets do not always stay buried; they can be farmed for a bloody harvest.

When news of the demolition of the old mosque hit Jackson Heights, the fissures between Hindus and Muslims, became a gaping chasm. I drew some comfort from the thought that, while sudden fear might disfigure older brows, boys of Kanti's generation did not seem unduly tense. His friends, whose parents included Muslims from India, Pakistan and Bangladesh, were not ready to 'rumble' simply because some miscreants in the old country had taken the law into their own hands. These boys were no jobless, knife-wielding desperadoes of *Westside Story*, I told myself, but up-and-coming entrepreneurs and professionals who did not want Jackson Heights to be turned into a no-man's-land, where old scores were settled with new blood.

You and I had seen Indian, Pakistani and Bangladeshi children grow up playing softball after school, drooling over doe-eyed Bollywood starlets and looking out for each other's sisters when some roughnecks tried to harass them. Unlike the older generation, they were not haunted by the bloodbath of Partition days. They were instinctively aware of their ethnic compatibility and knew how the Latino lads managed to fend off predatory gangsters by forging mutually beneficial alliances.

Our own Gullu was more concerned with civil rights violations in this country than some long-festering vendetta on the subcontinent.

You remember how when she was eleven, she'd come home one day, flung her school bag, and gone straight to her room? It was you who noticed that she had been crying. You thought she had had a fight with Yamini. When we both made her sit down and asked what was wrong, she said she had been crying for Lee.

You and I looked at each other not comprehending.

'Who is this Lee, darling? What did she do to you?' you asked.

Smiling though her tears, Gullu said, 'Lee is nobody, silly. I mean it's not a girl. I was crying for Robert E. Lee, the Civil War general.'

What had made our girl cry was Miss Pinkerton's description of General Lee's meeting with Grant in the McLean farmhouse in Virginia on 9 April 1865, where the terms of surrender were set without compromising the dignity of the vanquished.

On another occasion, Gullu had come home with a serious mature face. Our daughter was barely twelve when Miss Pinkerton's voice had faltered in class while trying to explain the reason for the internment of Japanese Americans by President Roosevelt during World War II. Gullu said her favorite history teacher had kept staring at the fan, and the class had avoided looking at Mitsuko Yamamoto when Miss Pinkerton tried to justify the bombing of Hiroshima.

Our lives were embedded in battles long ago; we never had that sort of visceral contact with America that Kanti, Gullu and Yamini did. So while the elders were closeted with their peers and talked in hushed tones about the demolished mosque, the back alleys of Jackson Heights continued to echo to the thuds of a softball hitting the bat.

But that night after Susan and Kanti had left, you were restless and kept moving in bed. I switched on the bedside lamp and asked what was bothering you. You stared at the ceiling for a long while, and said, 'Kanti's dad is only one side of the story,'

What do you mean?'

In hushed tones you recounted to me what Ghaseetkhan's wife had told you a few days before. Her husband, the halal butcher, had also been a casualty of the terrible carnage unleashed by Partition. He was the only survivor of a slaughtered family in a village near Amritsar. An old Hindu neighbor had sheltered him in his farmhouse, from where he could hear the screams of his parents and siblings being butchered by a frenzied mob. He was handed over to the police, who put him on a train to Pakistan.

The fang marks of those cobra days were still clearly visible on clenched fists on either side of the border.

❧ 3 ❧

The mosque episode polarized the two communities like stalactite and stalagmite. Reeny said, 'The trouble with you Indian Muslims is that you think you are superior to those of us who hail from Pakistan or Bangladesh.'

I thought Reeny was off again, spouting half-baked generalizations, as usual. But looking back, it did occur to me that when we first arrived here we were a bit slow to associate with families from Karachi or Dhaka. But that was because Bookstore-Nambiar and Jit Singh were the first two to go out of their way to befriend us.

Before your law practice brought you into closer contact with the *bibi* types, you didn't socialize with any of them. Having grown up in cosmopolitan Bombay in an English-speaking family, you had more in common with Matilda Singh than Rehana Qureshi.

Reeny said she wasn't talking about the two of us in particular. According to her, this feeling of cultural superiority was not confined to Hindus alone; even Muslim families from India shared it and made it a point to distinguish themselves from those from across the border with subtle hints, especially while speaking to the whites and the Latinos.

'With a wink and a nod,' Reeny said, 'you imply that, despite occasional flare-ups of communal violence in Indian cities and rampant political corruption, Muslims from India are, by and large, better educated and somehow more civilized than us, having reaped the benefits of a functioning democracy; while Pakistan, which has been mostly under military rule, and Bangladesh with its political instability, have remained frozen in a feudal limbo. This beguiling self-image,' Reeny went on, 'deludes you Indian Muslims into thinking that you are a notch or two above us Bangladeshis.'

Early attempts from certain quarters to exploit the tension around the demolished mosque in the city of Ayodhya did not catch fire immediately. Then gradually an icy wind started blowing through Jackson Heights, and Hindu and Muslim families stopped socializing. Women who used to go shopping together, men who carpooled during trips to Manhattan, avoided getting into small, enclosed spaces with each other. For a while, it felt as if Jackson Heights had reverted to the familiar Indian paradigm of an ancient, fear-gripped citadel huddled behind fortified gates, waiting for the barbarians.

Whether Reeny was right or wrong, the fact remains that the demolition of the mosque penetrated deep into a blood-is-thicker-than-water variety of kinship and resulted in a rapid bonding of Muslims from all the three subcontinental territories.

That was not all; our home saw some drastic changes in its lifestyle. You went and bought a clothbound copy of the Holy Koran and began reading a few *suras* every day before leaving for the office. A glossy print of the mosque at Karbala now hung above the mantelpiece, alongside the large portrait of my grandfather, Sir Shahnawaz Amolini in deep conversation with Mahatma Gandhi. The twelve-inch figure of the geisha, which had stood on a stand directly below the Mahatma, got shunted off to the far corner. Through the door of my study the busts of Shakespeare and Dr Leavis stared impassively. I felt that the middle ground, where give-a-little, take-a-little bargains were sealed was lost. Jackson Heights was full of ominous chatter, with springing paws closing in on faltering hooves.

A few days later, someone floated a rumor about a mischief maker distributing sweets to celebrate the demolition of the Babari Masjid, but Muslims of Jackson Heights dismissed it with genuine skepticism. All was not lost yet. Politicians in India routinely used such isolated acts of insanity to incite their followers to commit unspeakable atrocities.

106

For a brief moment, Jackson Heights hovered at the edge of a precipice; then it went into a huff, skulked, and remained painfully mute.

Fulsome greetings of the traditional sort gave place to curt nods and tight smiles when Muslims and Hindus met in public places. Hurt pride written on Muslim faces evoked a sense of collective guilt among Hindus, who tried not to aggravate the situation by a misplaced remark. Thakorji and Qureshi remained friends, but the frequency of their informal get-togethers dropped to an all-time low. A profound silence descended on Kalpana Chawla Way, and the buzz of conversation in the Peacock Diner, where people from both communities generally ate together, was tuned down to an awkward under-the-breath murmur at separate tables.

All the Muslims of Jackson Heights expected some gesture of solidarity from me. But I was suddenly overcome by a profound weariness and a crushing sense of futility of the sort Grant might have encountered on Lee's face in that Virginia farmhouse.

For years, across the length and breadth of India, city corporations had been routinely removing hundreds of mosques and temples from their old locations every day for the widening of roads. But the blind fury of the violence inflicted on the old monument was unprecedented. For me, places of worship—whether cathedrals, temples or mosques—had historical and architectural significance, nothing more.

But Ayodhya was special; it was where the compact between Hindus and Muslims was consecrated in 1857. The city where the demolished mosque once stood represented one of those rare shining moments of glory when Hindu sepoys had fought under the banner of Begum Hazrat Mahal, the Muslim princess who led a revolt against the East India Company for the unjust annexation of the Kingdom of Oudh. Similarly, Afghan troops had defended the Hindu Queen of Jhansi, till the last of them succumbed to the superior firepower of the British in 1857.

I tried to reason with you that the Ayodhya episode was like a perverse but inexorable balancing act of history, a sort of extratemporal tit-for-tat. You did not utter a word, but there was rage in your eyes, and your speechless face was like a death warrant. I could not take it anymore and fled to Manhattan, wandering among the tall buildings of glass and steel, preferring their stark neutrality to your reproving silence.

A claim of doubtful historicity had the mosque standing on the site of an ancient Hindu temple. Having burnt my fingers trying to defend *The Satanic Verses*, I balked at saying anything that might stoke fires instead of dousing them. I wanted to shout that, in the larger scheme of things, there needed to be a statute of limitation for redressing wrongs inflicted on one people by another at some remote point in history. What would be the legal temporal limit to restore the honor of a demolished shrine? How foolish it sounded, and yet how readily such sites became incubators of communal hatred.

Emperor Justinian's Hagia Sophia in Istanbul was converted into a mosque by the conquering Turks, and the Roman Pantheon into the Church of St. Maria and Martyrs by Pope Boniface IV. Fortunately, the main structures had not been demolished. I wanted to acknowledge that Istanbul and Rome deserved our thanks for merely serving eviction notices on old gods and leasing the premises to new ones.

Gandhi had a knack for dealing with such thorny issues without seeming to talk down to the masses. How did he do it, without ruffling the believers' feathers, without a word of reproof for their retreat into an 'eye for an eye' mind-set?

Oddly enough, it was in the US of the Roaring Twenties, when affluent Americans danced the Charleston and acted as though the good times would roll forever, that the pastor of the Community Church of New York, John Haynes Holmes, had called him 'Mahatma'—Great-Souled. Gandhi always found the right word, the telling phrase that lanced the tumescent boil and let out all poison.

But once again you had me at a disadvantage when you declared, 'In Inderpur we were always between a rock and a hard place.'

'What do you mean?'

'Well look, there were other minorities at the Club: There were the Parsis, the Christians and the Sikhs; none of them had to bend over backward to prove their loyalty to India. But even a perfectly honorable Muslim was forced to buy his patriotism in the flea market of secularism.'

I was taken aback. What you said was devastating. I did not 'buy' my ideas from a marketplace. I thought you knew that. But you had withdrawn into a silence so unforgiving that I could not reach you. It was as if you had kept parts of your life from me that others had more intimate knowledge of.

I know there are many in this world who find it hard to conceive that someone can be so completely untouched by claims of blood and lineage. Mistaking me for a Hindu, once a fellow passenger on a train had railed against Muslims all the way to Delhi. I could have easily silenced him by simply telling him who I was. On the other hand, I am terribly embarrassed, when some stranger's face suddenly lights up in a welcoming smile on discovering my Muslim parentage. I still remember feeling awkward when my Turkish friend Mustafa, surprised by the revelation of my Islamic roots, embraced me in a crowded Cambridge pub and planted a wet kiss on my cheeks. Accidental encounters in foreign lands between people with shared cultural history have their charm, but this explosion of loyalty to a stranger is like honking your horn very loudly to throw a one-finger salute to a fellow Porsche driver, or a leather-jacketed biker of the Harley-Davidson brotherhood going the other way.

Your taunt kept me awake that night. I tossed and turned and woke up next morning resolved to prove that you were totally mistaken. Mine was not what you called an empty 'pipe dream', some acquired taste for unfamiliar food like Sushi, or a flamboyant thesis on defiant secularism parroted by a callow teenager, some attention-seeking gimmick like Oscar Wilde's green carnation.

❧ 4 ☙

Blows raining down on the distant Ayodhya Mosque echoed deep in the heart of Jackson Heights. Trying to evade scornful looks of Muslim shoppers on KC Way, and barely concealed hurt in your eyes, I was reduced to hand-wringing silence. A low intensity war, with you registering mood swings ranging from clammy monsoon grey to presquall dolor, made me stay away from home. A glass curtain had descended between us, and you were just an unreachable shadowy figure in a spy film, waving from the other side of Checkpoint Charlie. Then with Durbar announcing his candidacy for a seat in the state senate, the sun came out in a flash, and like children being escorted by their art teacher to the Louvre, we ceased to squabble and formed an orderly line behind him.

Political elections in Inderpur had been a saturnalian affair, with partisan squawks filling the air from dawn to dusk. But Durbar launched his campaign on a relatively sombre note, though closer to the polling date, certain carnivalesque jollity began to run over the rim of Jackson Heights.

You had to step in to handle some of his pending court cases and were too busy to dwell on my 'chickening out'; the desecrated mosque receded backstage, making room for Durbar's senatorial bid.

Staking out the middle ground as a Sikh between Hindus and Muslims, Durbar on the stump emphasized the commonality of all immigrant experience. After all, the real business of Jackson Heights was business, and sending one of its own to Albany was a tribute to its enterprising spirit.

Several public offices, from the district attorney's to members of the city council, were up for grabs; but the granddaddy of all was the seat in the state senate. Jaime Suarez, the incumbent, was being given the boot by the Democratic machine. Immobilized by arthritis, Suarez had allowed some of his followers to misuse public funds for touting his past achievements on posters and brochures in preparation for the upcoming primaries in June and July. After much backroom head-scratching, and despite the fact that Asians did not make up more than twenty percent of the district, Durbar, who had served on the city council for just one term, emerged as the man of the moment.

Durbar asked me to accompany him during visits to his constituents. The only experience of the rough-and-tumble of electioneering I had was trying to rally votes in the Kasbah, to get Dicky elected to the Indian Parliament in the early seventies. That required nothing more than visiting near derelict hovels with Dicky. Those simple folks were awed by the mere sight at their doorstep of the ex-Prince of Inderpur with his pal Nawab Sirajuddin, as I was known in the Kasbah.

Jesse and Kanti rose to the occasion and disseminated Durbar's posters all across the Thirteenth Senatorial District, which, in addition to Jackson Heights, included Elmhurst and Forest Hills. Later in the campaign, when Durbar, flanked by Matilda and me, appeared on constituents' doorsteps, we were hailed with the unstinting zest of a hallelujah chorus.

Kanti's experience in the boon docks came in handy in forging grassroots alliances, wooing black as well as Latino voters. Little India mixed only selectively with Latinos and other ethnic groups. Nowhere was the unconscious racism of the Indian subcontinent more apparent than in the way African Americans were routinely referred to as 'Hubsies', a term that was roughly synonymous with the N word.

Doors of apartments, which harbored Matilda's grateful expectant mothers, flew open as soon as we stepped into their neighborhood. Having successfully induced difficult deliveries in scores of undernourished women, she had a lock on their votes. Durbar spoke feelingly at the rallies about his and Matilda's immigrant parents.

'Many of you may not know this,' Durbar told his listeners, 'but our folks did not arrive here by jet planes, crossing oceans in a day or two, but after a three-month-long cramped passage in the holds of ships, all the way from India. The ship on which they came over was no 'Love Boat' or luxury liner, with a swimming pool and well-appointed dining rooms, but of the same basic steerage kind which brought our Irish, Italian, Greek and Jewish immigrants to Ellis Island. My great-grandfather, his two brothers, and their sons landed on Angel Island in San Francisco Bay in 1902, huddled together in a converted barn without running water or electricity, and picked grapes, and hoed cotton, just like Mexican immigrants. Our folks had to put up with racial discrimination of the worst kind when, in 1913, the California Alien Land Law deprived them of legal rights to their own land. But just like your folks, mine had faith in America.'

I had never seen Durbar work a rally before. He certainly knew how to pluck the heartstrings of his listeners. I noticed that he had put away his smart Armani suit and was dressed in a white shirt with rolled up sleeves over denim jeans.

'You all know Dr Matilda Singh, my dear wife. How many of you know that she is only part Hispanic? She did not take my last name when she married me. Her maiden name was Singh. Her maternal great-grandmother was originally from Guadalupe. Because of restrictions on immigration, women from our ancestral land were not allowed to join their men who were already here, so our fathers looked around for family-oriented, hardworking partners and married Mexican women, overcoming racial and religious differences. That's true American-style assimilation for you. That is the real meaning of this, our melting pot, our USA, the greatest country on earth.'

Standing at the back of the crowd, I watched Durbar as he walked the crowd through his life's story. It was obvious to me that despite his anguished reaction to Jesse's turban, he was not averse to playing the Sikh card, 'all in the interest of a good cause', as he would say as a successful attorney. How astutely he harped, day after day, on the middle-ground Sikhism occupied between Hinduism and Islam.

Would I be able to do that?

I always dithered, like an over-earnest native who complicates a tourist's simple query about the way to the nearest post office by offering convoluted directions. I could not bring myself, with Durbar's self assurance, to tell my story. 'Good Muslim' is a certification that comes at a price.

Call it colossal insecurity or pure funk, but my last year in Inderpur was one of confusion and silent hysteria. The inability to get in touch with my younger self, breezing through the house at an incautious clip, that Cherry Orchard feeling of dispossession, sawed off my legs; the world moved on. I no longer felt my dead parents watching over me; in a ghostly diaspora they had abandoned the *kothi*. Not entitled to be in your own home is to be written out of its story.

As time went by, that cowering, sniveling persona of an exile lost its value as 'collateral' to stir wifely concern in you. Of course I never disclosed to anyone the full details of being held captive by a mob bent on destroying one's human capacity for shame. But even if I had told you everything, would it have made any difference? Over the years, its mystique as a life-altering event had evaporated; I found it difficult to keep that show on the road. I had the gestures but was too crabbed and closed in, and when given an opportunity to make a grand entrance, instead of a plaintive cadenza, what came out was the quack of Harpo Marx's horn.

Una furtiva lagrima, indeed.

I slipped and woke up a figure of fun. You no longer hovered around me like a bird by its plundered nest.

Durbar knew how to play the crowd, when to strike a solemn note, when to let the trumpet's clarion call rise above the oboe and bassoon. Again and again he stressed the basic humanitarian tenets of Hinduism and Islam from which Guru Nanak had forged a new harmony.

Turbanless and clean-shaven, this tall swarthy friend reminded me of the bronzed Argentinean polo player whom Dicky had invited to Inderpur to train his team. With the bilingual Dr, Matilda Singh by his side, Durbar would approach voters, wooing them with a perfectly pitched 'English or *Español*?' I suspect Durbar's born-again, Sikh-Mexican lilt proved more effective than any sound bite.

The toppled minarets of the ruined mosque still lingered painfully in collective memory, but the cheering at Durbar's rallies grew louder every day. There were warm smiles on the faces of Qureshi, and Badé Miyan of Karachi Halwa whenever I bumped into them on KC Way. On 7 November, the charismatic Sikh won the seat with a resounding lead over his GOP opponent.

Congratulatory telephone calls from Bill Clinton, and Senators Edward Kennedy and Chuck Schumer put the seal of approval on his victory. Hailed as the first Asian senator to the state legislature, Durbar, who was already one of the leading lights of the Asian community, became the guiding star of all of Jackson Heights.

$$\mathbf{5}$$

A sum of six thousand dollars was found to be missing when the bills were paid and the empty store, which had served as Durbar's campaign office, was vacated. Was it mislaid or siphoned off by one of the light-fingered staffers? No one could tell. The money, which was meant for snacks and soda for the young workers, had been contributed by Thakroji and Badé Miyan and was locked in a desk drawer by Jesse, who was in charge of disbursements. Mutual trust among Durbar's young staffers was taken as read.

Jesse suspected Kanti's hand in its disappearance but had no proof. Gullu's one attempt to link the vanished cash to Kanti was shot down by you with such withering contempt that she advised Jesse to let Durbar handle the mess. Lately, there had been a couple of instances when Kanti had borrowed money from her and conveniently forgotten to pay her back. She was still quite fond of him but knew that his growing gambling debts could force him to betray his friends. Flush with victory, Durbar was inclined to take the loss of money in his stride.

The long hours Kanti spent campaigning for Durbar cost him his job at Tivoli; the safari-suited cabal required absolute loyalty to their cash register. Susan's salary at Mandalay could not be stretched to support a jobless live-in partner.

Out of concern for Susan, I said nothing when you paid Kanti's car and medical insurance. May I say that you made quite a spectacle of yourself pestering poor Immy to find a new job for Kanti? It was irritating to see you fret and fume till Immy finally asked a friend who ran a motel in New Jersey to appoint Kanti as housekeeping manager. You nearly threw a fit when our son asked his friend to deposit the young man's salary directly into the couple's joint account.

With Kanti moving to New Jersey, you seized the chance to split the young couple permanently. One free-spirited American daughter-in-law was all you could manage. There had been a visible cooling of your ardor for Sally, a strapping blue-eyed blond who towered over you. By her side, Reeny looked like a schoolgirl striving to act like a woman of the world.

Sally's high-pitched silvery laugh mocked Reeny's attempt to browbeat everyone with her clanking jargon. Sparks flew around when those two accidentally came face-to-face in our house. Once Reeny claimed that the plight of a poor peasant's wife in the East lay beyond the grasp of a privileged white woman like Sally.

Our daughter-in-law listened politely then retorted, 'Who are you kidding, Reeny? I am not prepared to believe for a moment that you yourself have ever been within smelling distance of a single Bangladeshi peasant, man or woman.'

Sally's shrewd observation took the wind out of Dr Babukhan's sail, but it also rubbed you the wrong way. You complained to me later that Sally was disrespectful of Reeny, who had a doctorate and taught at Kingman.

Reeny and you were quick to criticize men who pulled rank but could not stand a younger woman outsmarting you and making you eat your words. The supine matriarch in you sat up and snorted.

The idea of American brides for Indian grooms makes immigrant parents jittery. It is unlikely to draw much applause, even from those who consider themselves well integrated and can render 'America the Beautiful' with fine gusto on 4 July. I can almost read your thoughts, when, with eyes narrowed, you look over your shoulder at our Sally. 'Do I really need another smarty-pants American daughter-in-law in the house? Why not settle for a nice Indian girl with an average IQ who'd serve him breakfast in bed?'

When the two of them came here to ask us what we thought of Kanti enrolling in the computer science program at Kingman, I made encouraging noises, although I was skeptical of his ability to finish the course.

But you resented Susan's 'hounding' of Kanti to get a better-paying job. That was rich coming from someone who never tired of flaunting our son Immy's wealth. As Immy put it in his Wall Street patois, 'In the traditionally bullish Indian marriage market, Kanti's stocks are down; he is not your typical bring-home-the-bacon kind of guy.' Add to that his wishy-washy attitude to marrying Susan and I would say the sooner they separated the better.

Your pampering of Kanti has gone beyond the pale of surrogate motherhood; it has acquired the adamancy of a mission. That worries me; I don't quite understand what to make of it. Remember how hard Lepakshi tried to give that misguided Chotta, the wonder boy of a poor family, a chance at a better life? The way she clothed him in Little Lord Fauntleroy designer dresses when he was a child used to amuse everybody. We all applauded when she paid his fees so that one day he would graduate and get a decent job. But he broke her heart in the end. Even at twenty he remained an adorable little Elephant Boy who thought he could talk to animals. Some mechanism that controlled the lateral movement of the mind was jammed in him. As old Iqbal Miyan used to say, 'splinting the broken spine of a kite wouldn't stop it from spinning in the sky. It will always flop down in a strong wind.'

The childless Lepakshi needed some precocious ward on whom she could project her motherhood. In your case, there is no such need. We ought to be focusing on what our Gullu has in store for us.

I feel that the old Shabnam is still there somewhere behind that recondite lawyer's façade. In repose, when sleep rinses off all the magisterial trappings, little spots of tenderness shyly creep back into your face. Sometimes, coming home late, when I find you dozing at your work-strewn desk, there is that moment when you look up and smile at me absentmindedly, and for a second-and-a-half my Hyacinth girl flickers in the dim light before being switched off, as if on cue, by a stagehand.

That tiny knowledge stops me from reading in your mentoring of

Kanti anything beyond a deep current of sympathy for a lonely boy thirsting for affection. But friends like Matilda and Durbar must wonder if you are not driven to balance your growing inner orthodoxy, a drift back into self-induced sectarianism, by this extravagant mothering of Kanti. Knowing you as I do, I simply cannot bring myself to say that the more Muslim you've become, the more indulgent you've grown of that Hindu lad.

The way you snap into a defensive posture every time Kanti is caught with a hand in the cookie jar is certainly getting to be robotic; you must accept that the little boy of ten years before, with his guileless laughter and taking ways, is gone forever. From being lovable, he has learned to play the lovable lad.

I see myself reflected in your blind gaze and it worries me. Giving yourself completely to others is like donating a vital organ to a needy patient. That way lies an arid desert of sadness if your sacrifice misfires. Besides, your playing Tinkerbell to his Peter Pan, doing the right thing for the wrong reason, wreaks havoc with your luminous reputation as defender of the innocent.

Jackson Heights came to depend upon Durbar for steering through legislation that would grant drivers' licenses to immigrants waiting for legal papers, Medicare, better police protection, school lunch programs, a ban on assault rifles and a whole lot of other bread-and-butter issues which generally got edited out on the senate floor. He was Joseph in Egypt to the down-and-out of Jackson Heights, and by the end of Clinton's second term, when voter antipathy was a real threat to his reelection as president, Durbar was sent back to Albany with an even greater majority.

The responsibility for running the law offices on a day-to-day basis fell to you after Jorge Vargas moved to his old law firm in Florida. 'Women are on the march in Jackson Heights,' Reeny declared gleefully. When Maury Lee confronted her with statistics indicating most women were still confined to home or were in low paying jobs, you and Matilda being the exception, she shrugged him off saying, 'Statistics are for the wonks. There has been a major paradigm shift here, Buster, and while the older women may still play second fiddle to men, they are not going to take any shit from them any more.' When aiming her sarcasm at real or imagined adversaries of the opposite sex, Reeny's language could swing from tortuous politesse to gang slang.

I suspect you thought my unwillingness to publicly condemn those who destroyed the mosque was viewed by Qureshi and Badé Miyan as betrayal of my Islamic heritage. In some circuitous way, your moving to another bedroom seemed like a punitive act, like ordering a child to go back to his room for misbehaving at the dinner table. But the reasons for my getting entangled almost half-wittedly, with our neighbor's Italo-Romanian wife Gabriella were far too complex. Gradual erosion of trust between us, rather than my male ego, bruised by a single act of rejection by you, probably set off a series of misjudgments, leading to what the self-righteous Reeny called my 'moral turpitude'.

Word on KC Way was that the learned professor had betrayed our ancient culture by behaving like a *gora* and was literally caught with his pants down. That explained why the demolished mosque did not make his stomach churn. He was a *nimak haram*, a betrayer of his own people.

With Reeny leading the charge, any attempt to rationalize my fall from grace was deemed unpatriotic, like flag burning. Almost the entire Jackson Heights acted as though you were a reigning monarch and I an egregiously disloyal courtier.

Following Durbar's departure to Albany, Muslim discontent about my so-called treachery over the demolished mosque resurfaced. It was very painful to see friends like Badé Miyan crossing to the other side of street to avoid being seen with me. While Durbar's emergence as a dynamic political leader was hailed by everyone, and Reeny served as the court of appeal for the younger generation, I was forced to spend long hours away from Jackson Heights in virtual hiding. No one taunted me on the streets, and Hindu friends like Thakorji and Bookstore-Nambiar received me with genuine warmth; but Qureshi's smile was like a catapult drawn taut to deliver a flinty rebuke.

According to you, my silence over the mosque episode was being widely interpreted by the Muslim community as an act of cowardly appeasement. You yourself told me repeatedly that my stoic approach was personally offensive to you and moved your bed to the room where you used to meet your clients. Unbeknownst to my Kingman colleagues, the Amolini marriage was unravelling, eventually landing me into Gabriella's bed.

In a last-ditch effort to win you over to my side, I sat down and wrote you a letter in which I pleaded with you to look at the situation from my point of view.

'The situation we face today is far more complicated than it appears,' I wrote. 'Everyone must step back and reflect on how and why that mute old monument was subjected to this terrible act of revenge. We must be patient because we cannot step into a supermarket and buy peace between communities. History proceeds in loops and eddies, often leading us back to square one, turning yesterday's victims into today's tyrants,' and so on.

But you laughed in my face and said I was pathetically out of touch with people of flesh and blood. You said there was an 'obscene imputation' (how you lawyers formalize invective) in my letter that such acts of desecration could be written off as sins of the fathers visited upon the sons.

To add further fuel to fire, Reeny, who normally avoided shopping in Jackson Heights, accepted Qureshi's invitation to address a peaceful Muslim rally. I stayed away from Jackson Heights, working late in my office at Kingman, but Reeny appeared at the rally, dressed, as Maury Lee reported, 'for the occasion' in a *salwar kameez*. She spoke feelingly about the poor masses in India who were being manipulated by both sides into fleeing to ethnic ghettos, while corrupt politicians grabbed their old neighborhoods at throwaway prices and sold them to rapacious real estate dealers.

'When it comes to corruption,' she declared, 'the difference between democratic India and autocratic Pakistan is so slight that only by juggling statistics can one determine which is worse.'

To Maury Lee, the rest of her talk seemed so heavily laced with Marxist jargon that only a handful of those present might have vaguely understood what was meant by terms like 'productivity', 'alienated labor', and so on. But the crowd listened because here was another professor speaking to them when their own man of learning was conspicuously absent.

'Our people do not understand,' Reeny said, 'that labor has never belonged to gods. When temples and mausoleums were built in the old days, it was thought to be a service rendered to gods. But even then, gods were not the real lords of labor. Kings and despots who built those shrines with slave labor were. And now politicians have become gods and watch from a safe distance as we fight and kill.'

This was serious stuff, and it bestowed unexpected respectability on raw and inchoate mob passion by being dressed in a pseudo-academic gown. Nothing like a few juicy bits of Karl Marx to garnish half truths before serving the stew to the under-informed.

Like Antonio, the sad Merchant of Venice, I had staked much intellectual capital on the far-flung argosies of European Enlightenment. I suddenly realized that my pound of flesh was forfeited to a shipwreck. I was no better or wiser than our school matron Mrs Tillinghast, for whom all of India was a classroom, filled with constipated pupils who needed to be regularly administered spoonfuls of scientific reason like cod-liver oil.

Miriam, reflecting on my peculiar dilemma, said I reminded her of German Jews of her grandfather's generation who, when confronted with murderous Nazi irrationality, were so numbed by the spectacle of their homeland turning into an abattoir that they simply went like lambs to their slaughter.

'You, my learned friend, are an anachronism,' Miriam said with a sad smile, 'a throwback to the times when reason was god.'

One evening when I was working late in my office at Kingman, I received an anonymous phone call from someone claiming to be a jihadist. He threatened, in what I took to be Brooklyn accent, to slit my throat with a butcher's knife if I did not make a public statement denouncing the attack on the mosque.

Of course I simply ignored it, but then the jihadist left the same message on your machine at home. As a lawyer, your immediate response was to report the matter to Durbar, who got the detectives at the 151st Precinct to trace the call to a pay phone in Manhattan. Fortunately, the would-be jihadist proved to be one of those wayward lads in need of attention: once he got wind of the police investigation, the calls stopped altogether.

You may well ask, how is it that Siraj Amolini, scion of an ancient Indo-Persian house, where men smoked the hookah and dallied away their time playing the game of chess in their attar-scented *harims*, as in Satyajit Ray's movie, reciting couplets penned by the court *shayars*, got so hooked on his Anglo teachers' brand of rationalism that without it he writhed like an addict?

Abbajan always used to say he was an Indian first and foremost. But that was in the fifties when Nehru still ruled the country from Delhi. By the time you and I left for the States in 1980, the communal virus had so deeply infected a large and vocal section of Inderpurians that the local rags routinely referred to our Kasbah as enemy territory. It was alleged that we flew the Pakistani flag from our rooftops when India lost a test match to the team from across the border.

‖ 7 ‖

Like a schoolboy with unfinished homework, tiptoeing sideways
along the wall to dodge his elders' eye, I had bypassed religion. I remember an old widowed great-aunt who lived all alone in her small
garret near the *kothi*. On certain festive occasions, like Bakri Eid, she
would chide Abbajan for not giving any religious training to me. After
one or two half-hearted attempts to transmit some basic information
about the Holy Koran through an impoverished but genial mullah who
regaled me and my cousin Murad with tales of the Arabian Nights, my
religious training ended rather abruptly when I was selected to be a
companion to Dicky, the crown prince of Inderpur, and went to live at
the villa in the grounds of the main palace. I really liked to hear the
mullah recite Koranic verses in his mellifluous voice; the solemn
rhythm of the *suras* was enchanting, but I was too young to engage with
abstruse commentary. The mullah was flattered that his recitation was
appreciated and did not report my lack of interest because he feared it
might reflect on his own ability to teach and cost him his job.

The vast chambers on the ground floor of the Italianate building
called Nazar Mahal served as school, and Major Tillinghast, the principal and English master, lived upstairs. Three other British masters
taught us math, history and geography. There, Dicky, the heir-
presumptive to the throne, and I, along with about twenty day-borders,
lost whatever connection we had with our own inherited faiths, singing
carols at Christmas with the wives and children of the masters. To this
day '*Adeste Fideles*' takes me back to that enchanted quadrangle of our
school when we were princes in that far off town. Every Christmas Eve

I try to catch *Once in David's Royal City* in live broadcast from King's College Chapel in Cambridge. Dicky and I never made real connection with any deity. Christ was little Tommy's and Johnny's god, not Dicky's or Siri's. Both of us grew up singing carols but believing neither in Christ nor our own gods.

On the other hand, all my life I have been haunted by lost cities. For all practical purposes, both Inderpur and Cambridge have become fleeting images of past splendor, like Samarkand or Istanbul, Dickens's London or Raskolnikov's St Petersburg. Both have moved with the times, but the older I get, the more difficult it is for me to give up their ghosts.

Sometime in the seventies, Cambridge colleges opened their portals to American tourists so that visitors could sort one medieval building from another. In my time, you simply knew which was which by following your nose from King's to Clare, and on to Caius. When the fugitive mood is upon me, I only have to close my eyes and those narrow, twisting, cobbled lanes flash before me, and spectral scholars egress like hooded figurines from the dark interior of one of those old Swiss clocks.

Maybe I am fixated on a fragile idyll of a lost time that can only be regained by a madeleine gone soggy in a cup of tea.

Once, I had to remind Maury Lee that a madeleine was not a cookie. We were in a restaurant in Manhattan where the menu boasted such standard British afternoon tea fare as scones with clotted cream, marmalade, as well as some choice continental treats. He had that disdainful 'who-cares-for-such-elitist-distinctions', look on his face. How typical, I thought. In their first act of rebellion, Americans dumped a lot of good tea into Boston Harbor, and their second break from the past came when they institutionalized dunking donuts.

Like some of those men serially marrying women who resemble their mothers, we old colonials are given to reinventing our past.

Somewhere in the background there was always Gandhi, whom my grandfather had accompanied during the Salt March, causing a lot of frenetic toing and froing of diplomatic pouches between the British

Resident's desk on the outskirts of Inderpur and the maharaja's secretariat. Then there was Dicky's father, the old Highness, who rode the same gold encrusted, caparisoned elephant in the Hindu Dussera and the Muslim Eid processions, reassuring each community that he was everybody's maharaja, although his family were Hindu.

Then there was Dr Leavis, who used to say, 'If you have read Shakespeare's *Lear* or *Coriolanus* properly, you don't haggle with a cabbie over taxi fare.' He didn't mean one should be improvident to the point of handing over one's wallet to the cabbie, with all the loose change and photographs of wife and children, not to mention driver's license and credit cards.

Though not a penny-pincher, the Bard himself was not a reckless spendthrift but a careful manager of his estate, as everyone who has heard of the second-best bed left to his wife, Ann Hathway, knows. But you can see why asking Shakespeare to empty his drawers and move out of Kingman with a cardboard box to a retirement home for laid-off authors, was to me like Lear's ungrateful daughters asking him to pack up and pitch a tent on the Heath.

That Pisgah vision of Cambridge, silver-grey as an etching, has gradually dimmed over the years. But I can still conjure up Dr Leavis's spare figure riding a bicycle, head thrown back, grey hair waving in the air, buttons of jacket undone. Like an illuminated traveling dot, he moves out of his house in Bulstrode Gardens, turns right on Madingley Road, then left on Queen's Road, left again along Garret Hostel Lane, reemerging on King's Parade to pass the Chapel. Then, like a shooting star, he streaks across Trumpington Street, bears left to reach the ornate gateway of Downing College with its Neo-classical buildings, where students await this man with a mind like a burning lamp.

Abandoning his bicycle, eyes brimming with mirth, he casually slips into his don's gown and marches towards his room under the T staircase in East Range.

Long after I left it behind me, Cambridge continued to make a special sound, segueing from note to note like the *The Magic Flute*.

Book IV

❧ 1 ☙

August 1, 1978

My room at the guest house has red-curtained windows for muting the blinding sunlight battering the glass. The curtains part to reveal the hazy blue cone of a hill which is the residence of Inderpur's patron Devi (goddess) rising sheer beyond the riverbed. The head bearer has got me hooked on 'bed tea', served every morning at six-thirty because 'gentlemen from foreign always have it'. As an experiment, I leave a ten-rupee bill for the dusky Adivasi woman with pointed breasts. When I return in the evening, she is lying in bed stark naked. It takes some frantic signs to get her dressed before someone comes in.

There is a soft knock on the flap door, and in steps a reedy man in his early forties with a happy toothy smile. He wears a striped shirt over a peon's khaki shorts. His name is Ramakant Soni. His son Chotta is in the final year of college. For some reason, Mr Soni doesn't wear a full uniform. The accountant Kapasia never tires of reminding him to do so, but that otherwise humble, gentle man defies every attempt to dress him like a peon.

He is a combination of custodian, janitor, member of the cleaning crew, mail-room assistant, messenger boy, and in my case, honorary personal secretary and mentor. From the very first day, Mr Soni adopted me. He not only runs errands for me, but also takes my laundry to the cleaners and cashes my paycheck. The last requires a Herculean effort. He has to stand in a line at the bank and receive a shiny metal token at one counter and cool his heels at another, while the check goes through a mind-boggling relay system from one clerkly desk to another, where it is subjected to fierce scrutiny to determine its legitimacy. It finally lands at the teller's counter, from where his name is hollered. The entire exercise takes almost an hour.

After one trial, I allow Mr Soni to tackle the system. Without his ministrations

I would be now several thousand rupees poorer in lapsed checks.

Mr Kapasia, the accountant, accosts me and says, 'No need to call him Mr Soni. In foreign that may be all right. Here it is no good. Only spoils the fourth-class servants.'

'Fourth class?' That was news to me.

'I didn't know there was a fourth class. Is it like the fourth caste you Hindus have? The untouchables or Harijans, as the Mahatma called them?'

'Fourth class is fourth class. Not untouchable. Otherwise we would not be drinking tea made by Mr Soni. No, peons and other servants are fourth class,' Kapasia explains patiently.

'I see. And are you first class?'

'No, you only are first class. You are teacher. I am staff, I am second class.'

'So that means if I belonged to the Harijan untouchable caste I'd still be first class by virtue of being a teacher.'

Kapasia looks stunned. He frowns, shakes his head, mutters something under his breath, and wipes his forehead with the loose end of his dhoti. Kapasia does that all the time. He closes his eyes, holds his nostrils, groping for the right answer.

'No sir, I mean yes, sir; but you see the situation would not arise, has not arisen here so far, thank god.'

'But it might arise mightn't it? The government wants to reserve higher posts for the Harijans, I am told.' I am not done with Kapasia yet.

There is ice in his voice when the old man says, 'Fortunately I am to retire next year. I won't be here when that happens.'

Meanwhile, my dependence on Mr Soni grows day by day. He can tackle the poker-faced men who lurk behind heavily barred windows at the post office in town, where they sell stamps and disdainfully receive parcels with the air of doing you an act of kindness you don't deserve. From his miserable salary, Mr Soni buys Cadbury's chocolates for the orphans at school. His 'emoluments', as Kapasia calls the monthly payment Mr Soni receives, would not pay my weekly autorickshaw fare.

August 22, 1078
Today Mr Soni arrives at school with a shorn head and sad-eyed smile.

'Son dead,' he says.

'What? When did he die? I saw him at school only three days ago. He was coming out of Father Yesudas's office.'

'Not real dead. He change religion secretly last year. I came to know only yesterday. Caste members say he convert to Christianity because he is in Mission School. For the caste he is dead.'

'How stupid of him. Whatever possessed him to convert?'

'He wants to go to America.'

'Yes, but he doesn't need to convert for that.'

'He thinks if he becomes Christian, the Mission will help him to reach America.'

'What a shame. It must be quite a blow to you.'

'Yes sir, that's why I shave head. Is our custom.'

'But why didn't you ask Dr Lepakshi to talk to him.'

I knew that Lepakshi and her husband had encouraged Chotta to enroll at the university and had paid his fees. He is to major in English. According to Siri, he is a B student, and if he works harder he might do better. But he is always spending money on fancy clothes. All his friends are from well-to-do families and he tries to keep up with them. Mr Soni's salary is not enough to satisfy his needs.

'Doctor Sahib kind but what can she do?'

'But that's not right, Mr Soni.'

'Krishna says happiness not in my fate.'

'Krishna is a bloody fool. What does he know?' Krishna was the young peon who worked for the principal alone.

'No. No, sir,' Mr Soni says, sticking out his tongue in horror, tweaking his ears with both hands, and rolling his eyes. 'Not our Krishna, sir. Lord Krishna.'

Then he recites something in Sanskrit, but unlike Kapasia, he does not close his eyes. I am impressed.

'Where did you learn Sanskrit?' 'At home, sir. We are Sonis. We are business caste, sir. Gold ornaments. When Morarji Desai was finance minister, he took away our gold. For economy purpose, he say. Good for the country but not good for Sonis, sir.'

So that's it. The guy is almost an aristocrat. You didn't need detailed knowledge of the Indian caste system to know that. He had lost his son but not his breeding.

$$\text{2}$$

October 7, 1978

In the afternoon I help in the Primary Health Center, which stands in the extended compound next to the school. It is a wooden building with large glass windows all around. The wood is honey brown, owing to the monsoon lashing it for three months. The window frames are painted almost cobalt blue; they glow in the dark. A huge banyan shelters one side of the building, and the rest is smothered in a bougainvillea bush of ferocious purple. There is a little garden in the front, and you can walk up to the building along a brick pathway.

The Center is equipped with a mobile van, and Surjit drives Lepakshi and her team to the tribal interior every Thursday. The van brings free medical help to the Adivasi community. The Center itself is heavily subsidized and offers low-cost treatment for malaria and other communicable diseases.

I have picked up a few skills and can administer an injection to immunize people against flu and typhoid. But my main project is to study the Adivasis in their natural habitat.

One Thursday we go deep inside the Adivasi territory where the Freegunjees are said to be active. They are Marxist guerrillas and are waging a covert war against the government for a state of their own. Under the present system, the Adivasis are no better than slaves to men like Bulchand, who have mining rights in their territory and have made huge profits selling manganese. With hefty contributions to his political party, Bulchand has managed to become the state minister for finance. After robbing the Adivasis of all their manganese, he has now been trying to evict them from their own lands so the dam can be built. It would provide hydroelectric power to industries owned by high-caste guys like him.

As we crawl towards the interior, the hamlets seem dustier and barren of life.

In sharp contrast to the villages under the Padre's supervision, here there is nothing like a road or an alley dividing the huts but narrow, crooked, and deeply rutted open spaces. Except for a solitary hillock rearing up now and then, the land is devoid of any arresting shapes. The fields by the road have been scraped flat by a lean harvest. Occasionally we pass a dark quilted figure of an Adivasi, his feet barely touching the ground, hurrying for his daily toil in the city.

After we have driven for nearly two hours, the barren land begins to undulate. Grey stunted trees with gnarled boles and thick dark leaves hum with drongos and starlings, and jungle fowl cower by the ridge. In a little clearing a couple of stately peacocks, like Dicky's liveried footmen, step out of the foliage into sunlight.

Despite jolts and stomach-contracting descents, I begin to enjoy the ride. A brace of monkeys scatters abruptly, executing stylized threats and displays, but one elderly simian watches us with grave courtesy.

A group of Adivasis carrying huge peacock fans in their hands, their faces painted ochre and white, come up to us. They greet Dr Lepakshi respectfully, but they seem to revere the Bushshirt, whom they address as Bapaji, Great Father. It is easy to see why. The Bushshirt has taken up their cause and has been fighting for their rights. The man apparently never sleeps. It seems last year, when the manufacturers of cricket bats came to cut down the ash trees, he organized a very effective protest. Each Adivasi family clung to a tree, and despite being beaten by the police, they would not let go. In the end, the manufacturers had to give in.

The Bushshirt is everywhere, receiving social workers at the railway station, finding them lodgings, and helping them make train connections for the return journey. His uninhibited screed fills the air as he points out to Lepakshi which family needs medical treatment that day.

My portable record player is playing Stayin' Alive, *the old Bee Gees classic.*

The Bushshirt reacts to that.

'This phoren music I am not liking. Is American capitalist music no?'

'Which music do you prefer?' I ask.

'I am liking Vodka Boatsong. When I am in Roossia I hear Vodka Boatsong. The Roosian people is singing the song on Volga River but they drinks Vodka when singing so I call it Vodka Boatsong. Like the Adivasis singing on *the river. But they are drinking toddy only.'*

Meanwhile Dr Lepakshi and her crew have set up their folding desk and chairs under an enormous banyan and are already busy examining their scrawny patients. The Bushshirt is agitated over the government's decision to shift the Adivasis to a barren piece of land in another part of the state. It is said that sixty-seven hamlets would be lost to the proposed reservoir.

It is wonderful to watch Lepakshi at work. Her forehead glistening with concentration, she takes a child by the hand and gently removes the scabs, drains the puss, and lets the nurse bandage the wound while the kids' parents watch, their eyes set deep in ravaged faces.

After she has finished with the children, she and the nurse make their rounds among expectant mothers in the hamlet.

Lepakshi tells me that the Adivasi family tree spreads its branches far and wide. 'A guy brings an old lady and tells you she is his mother; a few weeks later he brings another woman calling her mother. There is no caste system here.'

But she figures all that will change once that stupid dam sweeps them out of here and into the lap of civilization. I can see why Lepakshi is upset. For these folks, the river is not just another puddle of water with which to wipe their ass. Their past flows through it.

3

Mr Soni's son Chotta, educated by Father Yesudas at his school, dreamt of going to the US someday and becoming a marine. He had converted to Christianity in the hope of getting financial help from Father Yesudas's church, which had benefactors in the US. Mr Soni, under pressure from his own caste, was forced to disown him, though it broke that poor man's heart. He yearned to see his son's face, but he dared not take him back. He lived with his wife in a house on Goldsmiths Street in Inderpur. Every time I hear the term 'confused *desi*' in Jackson Heights, my mind invariably goes back to that very bizarre day in January 1979 when the meaning of the expression was shatteringly brought home to me.

Chotta's transition from his native, intensely traditional culture to half-digested western notions of straining after the impossible proved to be fatal. His confusion took one of the most perversely self-destructive forms. Yamini's clear-sighted act of self-emancipation was in sharp contrast to Chotta's mad urge to enhance his standing among his upper-caste friends.

Chotta was fixated on certain type of Bollywood remakes of Hollywood blockbusters in which macho stars with contoured bodies boldly walk into underworld dens and beat the crap out of leering dons and their beady-eyed cohorts. Garish posters depicting romancing couples from the latest hits adorned the walls of tailor shops and interiors of ramshackle autorickshaws. Rich and poor Inderpurians of a certain age lived in a constant movie-induced haze, where the unreal trumped the real and the air was full of vaguely rosy promises. Sudden windfalls beckoned those who acted purposefully, like the hero in the poster with his devil-may-care grin, balancing a swooning starlet on one muscular arm and knocking the stuffing out of the villain with the other.

One bright and sunny day, Chotta lowered himself into an aging lion's cage at the Inderpur Zoo. It happened soon after the new church was consecrated with all the pomp the small Syrian Christian Community in central India was able to muster.

The state government and the Padre had forged an unholy alliance, whereby the School for Adivasi Children received a handsome grant from the ministry of finance, then headed by Bulchand, and Yesudas in turn lobbied support for the dam among the tribals. I doubt if the Padre actually believed that the dam would bring in jobs and prosperity to the tribal areas. The Freegunjees considered the compensation offered by the government to those uprooted from their homes by the river totally inadequate, as I noted in the journal.

January 27, 1977

It's been barely two weeks since the new church was consecrated. Today it is once again in the news. I am having tea with the Padre in his office when the flap door swings open and a distraught Lepakshi rushes in.

'Father,' she screams, 'come at once. Poor Chotta has gone mad. He has locked himself up in Kesri's cage. I sent a chuprassi to fetch his parents as soon as I heard the news. They must be at the zoo already.'

'Who's Kesri?' I say getting up.

'Kesri is the old lion in the zoo, a part of Inderpur University's botanical gardens.'

Lepakshi, making sixty miles an hour, brought us to the botanical gardens within ten minutes. She explained to me that the university's zoology department had taken over the administration of Dickey's animals and exotic birds.

Unable to cope with the humiliation inflicted on him by some high-caste girl's parents who returned his letters to her unopened, Chotta plunged into depression and emerged from it with his wits completely impaired. He had apparently watched the movie Born Free *several times at the local cinema and decided to cast Kesri in the role of Elsa the lioness, with himself playing Adamson. He had also heard that those tribals who still lived in their thatch-roofed abodes in the forest were often able to talk to wild animals in a strange language made up of hoots and clucks. It was believed that leopards and wolves never carried away their livestock.*

A flustered Siri arrives in time to see Chotta lift the lion's tail with his stick to thunderous applause from the crowd, which he receives with a gracious salaam, flicking his right hand to them like Peter O'Toole in Lawrence of Arabia. *A cheetah stands aloof in the cage on the left, watching the crowd with a certain hauteur, its small aristocratic head raised disdainfully, while baboons in the cage opposite hurl themselves from bar to bar whooping at the jeering crowd. A resentful snarl from Kesri goes unnoticed in that carnival-like atmosphere. I can see from the way his tail curls up to swat a fly and a series of steady growls emanating from the slab that the lion is losing patience. Heaving himself up, the beast slouches to a corner at the back of the cage. The watchful leopard goes taut as a bow, and the baboons fall silent. Only Chotta preens himself, eyes dazzled by the shaft of some hideous fantasy. A giant wave of laughter sweeps through the crowd as someone sets off fire crackers. I can see the cart couple watching solemnly from some distance. Kesri moans, rubbing his muzzle with an enormous dusty paw.*

At that point, Chotta seems to be responding positively to the joint pleas of the Padre and Lepakshi. He moves towards the entrance and is halfway between the empty slab and the lion when, as the hushed crowd watches breathlessly, he pivots, and springing from the ground, straddles the lion. An ear-shattering roar shakes the bars of the cage violently, something drops from the tree with a wild shriek, and the next moment the beast pins Chotta to the ground with his forepaws after felling him with one swift powerful blow.

A shot rings out. The Padre flings himself on the constable who has fired. Poor Chotta loses his nerve at that point. A struggle ensues as the lion tries to hold its tormentor down, growling almost playfully now. Suddenly Chotta goes limp under the paws and the beast retreats slowly to the other side of the cage. With the constables' guns trained on the lion, the chowkidar *and his men pull Chotta out. There* is a brief stampede, and the crowd vanishes, save for a few stricken girls whimpering under a tree. Chotta is rushed to the hospital by the police but is pronounced dead on arrival. His neck has been broken during the struggle to escape.

Lepakshi parks her car under the giant banyan at the hospital and we wait for the postmortem to be over. Siri, who has preceded us to the hospital, comes up and says, 'Let us stay here with Soni; he might collapse any moment. He is shaking all over.'

'I don't want to go home ever again,' Lepakshi says, wearily resting her head on the wheel. 'It was a dumb, dumb thing to do. Poor kid. What a way to go. I always knew he was a bit crazy but not this crazy.'

'Sheer lunacy,' Siri says. 'At one point I thought the Padre would get him out. Chotta's mother will simply go out of her mind when she hears of this. I bet those wretched parents of that girl will be relieved now. Their daughter has been rescued from the clutches of a horrible Christian convert. Now she can marry some fat, double-chinned, green-card holder and live happily ever after.'

Tears begin to make furrows across Lepakshi's cheeks. Soon a flurry of sobs and hiccups shake her frame. Siri, who is leaning against the car, pulls out a hand-kerchief and gives it to her, but the tears keep coming.

'We should have never come to this dump,' Lepakshi whimpers. 'We were so happy in Chicago. My husband was almost due for tenure. I was finishing medical school, had an internship lined up in a good hospital. But no,' she pauses and wipes her eyes, 'he had to get back to his precious Adivasis. His life's work. Big deal.'

After the postmortem, the body is handed over to the Padre. We follow the ambulance to the churchyard. Poor Mr Soni, who has held his tears back, breaks down, and kneeling by Chotta's body, sobs bitterly, knocking his head on the ground.

'Memsahib,' cries Mr Soni, turning his tearful gaze to Lepakshi. 'Our Chotta is gone. You were his mother and father. Those church people killed our poor Chotta. I had warned him. We are small people. You should not forget that. Memsahib, you sent him to university, and see what happened.'

With tears streaming down her cheeks and groaning with extreme pain, Chotta's mother lowers herself to the ground and sits there rocking and caressing his face. Then she gets up, and leaning on Mr Soni's shoulder, moves toward the waiting *rickshaw. Suddenly she breaks away from him and dashes her head on the brick platform on which Chotta's body is placed by the ambulance staff. We all rush to her as she careens and slumps to the ground, blood gushing from her forehead.*

The Padre suggests that we go home and rest and come to the service in the morning. Chotta's body is conveyed to the church.

January15, 1979

Today at the school a deep sadness lingers across every face. Even as Chotta is being laid in his grave in the small cemetery behind the Padre's lodge, we hear the soft keening of Adivasi women who, despite their conversion, continue to mourn in the old tribal way. In that young death are forebodings of sickness and disorder at the heart of things.

I have attended several Catholic weddings and funerals in the States but have never been present at a Syrian Christian funeral. While we wait out on the lawn, the priest conducts some preliminary rituals in the church. Then we follow the Adivasi converts into the church. Some of Chotta's non-Christian relatives wait in a little cluster outside. The Syrian Christian service, conducted by Father Yesudas with great solemnity, turns our collective grief to quiet reflection. Inside the church it is dark. I sit with Siri and Lepakshi to the left of the aisle in the front row, behind the wooden railing.

The only light is from a tall brass lamp with several glowing wicks sputtering in a bowl filled with oil. On the stone altar behind the drawn curtains is the cross with the image of Christ in ivory. There below the altar lie the mauled aspirations of a young man for a better life. As the priest reads from the Bible, the spluttering brass lamp begins to take hold of his words. Then Father Yesudas makes the sign of the cross with some sacred oil on Chotta's face, intoning:

'This oil is poured out for everlasting life, with rest from toil, peace from warfare, and joy with the saints, in the name of the Father, the Son and the living Holy Spirit.'

On reaching the guest house, I feel as though my limbs have gone askew. I slump into one of the deck chairs in the garden. The bearer brings me a glass of milk when I tell him I do not want any food. Someone has begun to groan down the road.

Then a drumbeat follows, then another, first softly, tentatively, then ascending to a volley, crashing erratically like gunfire. As the drums fade, a mournful wail arises. Then a trumpet begins to tear into the night, and a chorus wafts across the breeze, half chanting, half chattering, and all the while in the background is that dirge slowly spreading across the starless sky. It is cut off as suddenly. For a minute or two the silence is unbearable.

This is Raja Rao's India, I think. Voices singing in the dark under the Hill of Kali. One soggy afternoon in Jackson Heights, I had read Kanthapura, *only to be ravished by its evocative witchery. Watching the little villages huddled together in the valleys beneath the Green Mountain ridges from a train on the way back from Steve's farm in Vermont, was the closest I had ever come to rural life.*

The chanting begins again, and a savage scream rips through the air, gradually dropping to another prolonged wail, which seems to move closer to where I sit. The bearer's beedi glows reddish in the dark. Never before have I heard anything so raw. This singing, if it is that, is one long gangrene of a song that confronts me death-like. There is no savoring it. The Native American drums are talking drums; they open your ears to the sound of buffalo hooves on the prairie and whispers in the trees. Here the trumpet's cacophony is filled with a sense of agony. To me it suggests no vital continuity between earth and dancing feet.

In the light of the Petromax lamp I can see little shoots of grass sprouting from the pots on the heads of Adivasi women in the procession. Families from the servants' quarters come traipsing out with pitchers and sprinkle water on the grass in the pots. Again and again the dirge rises above the drums, interrupted briefly while the chorus replies in short snatches.

'What are they singing?' I ask the head bearer.

'Adivasi women,' he replies, 'they praying for the soul of dead boy. When grass grow high in pot, his soul will rise to heaven.'

Then pausing here and there, he translates the song in that peculiar syncopating syntax I have got used to by now. Strangely, in this part of Inderpur, that watchful moonless night of death, Adivasi women await the birth of their god.

> *The ants they are dying*
>
> *Summer is our country.*

The cows' udders are empty
The lotus ponds are dry
Summer is our country.
The children do not sleep
The cocks don't crow at dawn
Summer is our country.

Slowly, as the procession winds its way back to the forest, the song fades into the night. 'Perhaps,' I think, getting up to go inside, 'perhaps Kanthapura is only a dirge, a sort of musical passing away of its own.'

BOOK V

❧ 1 ❧

The Festival of Navratri (nine nights) was about to conclude when the news of Yamini's disappearance ripped through Jackson Heights. For eight evenings, young women, their shapely palms dyed with intricately stippled floral designs in ochre and yellow, had been dancing in Thakorji's courtyard before the glowing image of the mother goddess under a yellow silk canopy. On the ninth and final night, Yamini, who always led the chorus of singers at the dance, did not show up.

On the following day, as Jackson Heights was gearing up to celebrate Dussera, the second most auspicious day in the Hindu calendar, Yamini's whereabouts, spiced with lurid rumors, began to hush private conversations. Some said she was abducted, others reported sightings at JFK or Port Authority bus station. Still others had her in Battery Park walking hand-in-hand with a white man of uncertain age.

The previous night, Natthuram's two sons had come looking for their sister, and not finding her at Thakorji's, had concluded that she had fled the coop to avoid being forcibly married to a man of her father's choice. You and I knew that she was under Reeny's protection in her flat in Flushing. Bit by bit the news of Yamini's sudden disappearance spread like wild fire, with flames of suspicion being fanned by dizzy speculation.

Natthu's choice for his only daughter's bridegroom had all the pong of a shady backroom deal, which set the young against the old in Jackson Heights. Gullu and her friends cried foul, but the opinion in the geriatric circle ranged from full-throated support (the bridegroom was something of a money bag), to 'none of our business, purely a domestic matter' sort of cop-out.

That his daughter might have an opinion of her own as to whom she should marry was to Natthuram as incomprehensible as the starving Parisians demanding bread were to Marie Antoinette. Unlike the unfortunate queen, he did not actually lose his head, but that, as they say, was only a question of semantics.

A few years before, girls like Yamini would have had no other recourse but to obey their parents, still bound to feudalistic codes of honor. No one was able to raise a finger to protect Jit Singh's Rajkumari when she was handed over like a gift package to her curry-slurping, toothpick-chewing husband.

You were still an untried, budding lawyer when she was married off to an older man from Jit Singh's clan. Poor Rajkumari was born in India, and despite having majored in art history and painting at Kingman, couldn't defy her parents. A fine promising talent, she had to pack up her paintbrushes and easel when her children began to arrive with what Gullu described as 'assembly-line regularity'. At thirty, she was a mother of four girls who were the pride and joy of Jit Singh's old age. Gullu was in high school then and never forgot Rajkumari's tear-stained face when she left for Texas with her husband.

Before she got into the limousine, Rajkumari stopped to hug Yamini and whispered that she should not let her parents highjack her dreams for the future. Gullu and you expected me to reason with Jit, but it was like trying to forestall a bird flying headlong into a windowpane.

The groom seemed to think his being almost seventeen years his wife's senior was his strongest suit, an additional qualification, like a veteran horse trainer's impressive record of Derby winners. The groom was much sought after, and though not even reasonably well-to-do, he claimed descent from some iconic warrior whom the clan worshipped as god.

You were really annoyed with me for not preventing Jit Singh from handing over his daughter to a man for whom a wife was just a breeding machine. But really, what could I have done? Jit had this self-image of an unbending Rajput. Having lost most of his own ancestral farmlands to Mrs Gandhi's reforms, which made it illegal to own more than fifty acres in his home state, all Jit Singh was left to pamper his ego and burnish his pride was his own family name. To a proud warrior it was the only compensation for having to eke out a living as a waiter in a foreign land.

Gullu didn't speak to me for two whole days, and I had this odd feeling that you were somehow laughing at me inside. For days afterward, you wore that odd, almost contemptuous, eyes-blank sort of smile. With hindsight, I see now that to you my refusal to intervene amounted to tacit support for Jit.

Of course I was very concerned and managed to have a quiet chat with the poor girl. After all, she had been one of our brightest pupils. I told her that only she could avert her fate by leaving home and taking up a job. You know what she told me? Jit Singh had threatened self-immolation if she did not consent to the match.

A flood of congratulatory letters and telephone calls from his clan members poured in every day. His people in India envied him for striking gold in the bridegroom market, and Jit actually carried with him a handwritten letter from a moth-eaten maharaja who endorsed the match. So absolute was his joy over what he considered to be a coup, so brightly did his eyes burn with clannish pride, that I could barely proceed beyond the throat-clearing stage.

You were able to mount the Save Yamini operation because the girl herself was determined to defy her parents. Rajkumari had willingly put her head on the chopping block, preempting any intervention. I am really sad to know that the poor girl, who already has four daughters, is under pressure from her mother-in-law to produce a male child or face the prospect of enforced abortion in India.

I couldn't recognize her when I saw her, gold-heavy, carrying an infant in one arm and a shopping bag in the other as she waddled behind her swaggering, chunky husband down 73rd Avenue. Her face had hardened; all tenderness in her eyes seemed to have been washed away by the labor of four back-to-back pregnancies. Given Jit Singh's one-track mind and his pathological fixation with racial purity, I could not have done much to prevent him from blighting Rajkumari's life.

But some pent-up storm had exploded in Yamini. Her female ancestors were probably forever relegated to the smoking *chullah* or forced to tonsure their heads when widowed in the prime of life. Those unfortunate women seemed to have become for her one clamoring chorus of furies.

Yamini had gone through several stages of social evolution and was well prepared to resist being married off to a father of two who simply wanted a green card. By moving to the States, the groom would not only win a nubile bedfellow but also lay the foundation for his children's college education.

'Uncle (Yamini called me 'Uncle' when she visited us at home), isn't some sort of chemistry expected in order to be convincing, even from actors paired as a make-believe screen couple? How could I spend a lifetime with someone who strains the logic of the "marriage plot" in Jane Austen? I remember laughing loudly at the pompous Mr Collins when you read that chapter where he goes down on one knee and proposes to Elizabeth Bennet in *Pride and Prejudice*. How then can I get hitched to this ridiculous creature, who is old enough to be my father? Why,' she said with a twinkle in her eye, 'it almost amounts to some kind of incest, doesn't it?'

Elizabeth Bennet had a sensible father who was more than a match for her flaky mother. 'Your mother will never see you again if you do not marry Mr Collins, and I will never see you again if you do,' the clearheaded Mr Bennet warns Lizzy.

I think the real turning point came, when Yamini saw you hand over a couple of letters addressed to Gullu which had arrived when she was still in Providence the week before Thanksgiving. Neither you nor I asked Gullu whom they were from.

'At my place,' Yamini said, 'Papaji would surely have opened the letters and read the contents without feeling the least bit embarrassed.'

As a child, Gullu had a separate bedroom, whereas Yamini slept in her mother's bed till she was almost twelve. She told Gullu that one night she was awakened by a violent rocking of the bed. The poor child had opened her eyes to find her father copulating with her mother.

Gullu told us that Yamini, seeing her Papaji sprawled over her mother, panting and breathing like a walrus, had vomited.

Apparently, while the girl crouched frightened under the bed, her Papaji rolled over, cursed her, and padded out of the room without bothering to cover his rump.

Let me say that, for once, I applauded Reeny when she provided temporary shelter to Yamini. That wretch Chitral tried but failed to make capital out of a story of a Hindu girl being abducted by two Muslim women on the eve of her engagement to a high-caste man. It is the sort of fissile material that blood-spattered communal riots are made of in India.

Qureshi urged me to rein you in; his exact words were, 'And who is Begumsahiba—meaning you—to tell Natthuram what is right for his daughter?' Qureshi always called you 'Shabnamji', but he used the more formal expression to stress that, as my wife, you should behave like a traditional compliant Begum. I had a quiet laugh. If he only he knew, I said to myself, if only our Qureshi Chacha knew.

The Bangladeshi grocer's fear that rumors about a Hindu girl being spirited away by a pair of Muslim women might trigger violence were not altogether unfounded. They possessed the potential for fueling a lethal communal riot that would make the storm over *The Satanic Verses* and the demolished mosque seem like a minor dustup.

Even those who were generally outside Chitral's sphere of influence had serious reservations about what to them was 'two nosey Muslim women leading a Hindu girl astray'. Only young faces, flushed with the exertion of dancing the *garba* before the mother goddess, looked blissfully happy over the outcome.

Natthuram's efforts to bundle off Yamini to India began to split the Jackson Heights community along generational rather than religious lines, once the unsavory details about the would-be-bridegroom's antecedents came into the public domain. The younger people cheered the defiant Yamini, while their parents commiserated with the jeweler.

I must say I was amazed to see that even after years spent away from their homeland, both Hindu and Muslim families favored arranged marriages. Badé Miyan argued that a highly qualified girl was difficult to match with men of substance, who generally lacked college degrees because of their early induction into hereditary businesses. Jackson Heights being a mostly trading community, a slightly shop-soiled husband of means was considered a real bargain. The Navartri Festival of 1992 proved to be a landmark event as the younger generation came of age.

With Immy away in New Jersey and Gullu mapping her future, which did not include either you or me, I felt some envy for Thakorji, who lived with his ever-expanding family in one big house with separate bedrooms but a common kitchen. It reminded me of our *kothi* in the old days, filled with aunts, uncles and cousins, several times removed, living under one roof. I was an only child of my parents but never felt alone in that vast building with its innumerable rooms, some of which remained padlocked forever.

❧ 2 ❧

When I declare that by mid-December I begin to feel nostalgic for Christmas time in India, my colleagues—with the exception of Maury Lee look at me in disbelief. Newspapers in the West routinely talk in binary terms about Hindu India and Muslim Pakistan. When told there are more Muslims in India than in Pakistan, the average man on the street shakes his head in disbelief. That any person who is not a practicing Christian would have memories of Christmases past in the subcontinent sounds bizarre to him. His surprise is complete when he is told that Jewish settlements along the east coast of India predate Christianity.

In the afternoons we played cricket in the toasty sun, with mild breezes bouncing off our faces. The masters only had their toddlers with them in Inderpur; the older children were away at school in England so that our lunch and tea breaks saw quite a spread on the pavilion lawn. We were pampered and spoiled by the masters' wives, who missed their boys and girls at Christmas. Bloated with Yorkshire pudding and cashew nuts, our fielding was lax, and we allowed simple catches to drop through butter fingers.

Something of that halcyon spirit used to enliven Diwali celebrations in Jackson Heights before the mosque episode split the community. Even the electronic gadgets in their display cases had an aura of exotic tropical fruit, with festive sale signs bursting out all over, touting low prices. Colorful buntings on groceries, *halal* restaurants, and confectionaries suggested that time in Jackson Heights was a *flaneur*.

Strict aesthetic standards enforced by the dreaded HCC prevented KC Way from pullulating like an oriental bazaar with pavements disappearing under overspill of merchandise. A blithesome spirit permeated every street and alley in Jackson Heights with booths and food stalls taking over the pavements. Indian women in gossamer saris and men with foreheads splattered with auspicious marks floated like flamingos in streaming lights. Friends formed little islands, choking all traffic in that log-jammed isthmus of humanity. It used to take the two of us hours to cover KC Way.

But now the ghost of that ruined mosque haunts the streets of Jackson Heights, and no longer do you see Muslim faces among the milling crowds; Qureshi and Bookstore-Nambiar do not stroll together, heads lowered in a tête-à-tête. A backlog of files at the office is your excuse for not joining me when I step out to greet Thakorji and his extended family. I watch from one corner a group of New Yorkers with serious abstracted faces clicking their cameras at everything and nothing.

Maury Lee joins me, followed by Bookstor-Nambiar and his wife. We have a quiet laugh when some visitors stop at food stalls, taking small nibbles gingerly, hoping that what they are about to bite into does not pack a wallop. Their mystified eyes seem to ask, 'Will my tongue stay in my mouth, if I push this samosa thing in or will it be decapitated, and fly around like a demented swallow?'

Among the visitors are lapsed hippies, veterans of the *dhabha* during their salad days in India. They look smug, flamboyantly urging some lethal looking *vindaloo* on their demurring friends. Hard-pressed taxi drivers and gas attendants from India mingle with the denim-clad IT crowd, the computer wizards who speak in their peculiar whittled tongue.

Just a few years back, Jackson Heights used to be transformed into Inderpur during the Festival of Lights—not the glitzy urban Inderpur of today but the one of my childhood— the civil, cosmopolitan city at the foot of the hill. Now the Muslims watch from their shops with unsmiling faces. Badé Miyan, with his bushy eyebrows, curled mustache and laughter crackling like a frying *jalebi*, is conspicuously absent.

Maury Lee walks with the knowing swagger of someone who has seen the original in Inderpur, of which Jackson Heights is a mere copy. The anthropologist in him takes over and like a tour guide, he offers a running commentary about the meaning of Diwali, highlighting its affinity with other harvest festivals like Halloween, its tantalizing imprecision that looks beyond the everyday sectarian boundaries.

Bookstore-Nambiar seems to have forewarned his wife not to put a question mark in the empty space by my side, normally reserved for you, and I am spared the embarrassment of explaining your absence. Edulji's old piano continues to tinkle but his grace notes are getting fainter.

How did we become such strangers?

I had not understood the full import of our odyssey, that a time would come when not only our children, but you too would sail away on a ship flying a different banner. Nothing in your body language, when we left Inderpur hand-in-hand, had warned me that one day your steps would quicken, leaving me stranded in a strange city.

If only you had sulked, thrown things around, kicked chairs out of the way, I could have lived with it. Used to streetwise servants of Bombay, sometimes you were a little impatient with Iqbal Miyan, our old gatekeeper in Inderpur, who could be longwinded explaining his tardiness in letting us in when we drove back from the club late at night. A tiny flame of resentment would flash in your eyes, but you would immediately douse it for my sake, because decrepit Iqbal Miyan had been with our family for over sixty years and was exempt from reproach.

Often I don't even hear you come in. You seem to be able to walk through walls, heading straight for the kitchen, getting dinner ready without any noise, chopping onions with dry eyes, no sound of pots and pans, and after an hour you emerge and say to the wall 'Dinner is served.' I miss being asked each evening what I should like to eat. Now we sit at the table like figures frozen in a tableau, with awkward silence between us. Not for us the mock bickering of married couples in soap operas, the fake sparring, the juvenile puns, and the non sequiturs with canned laughter of studio audiences, erupting intermittently in the background. What is truly amusing is the tremendous effort you put in to avoid looking at me. By now you have probably scanned every inch of our dining room ceiling like an avid tourist inside the Sistine Chapel.

Shouldn't remembrance of things past be a joint venture?

I have made peace with Immy's unseemly pursuit of wealth. I don't know what our Gullu is up to. I am quite reconciled to her going away to India to work for the poor—'like Uncle Maury Lee', she says before I can raise any objection. It's no use telling her that things have changed since his time in Inderpur.

Gullu thinks she is being funny when she calls herself an ABCD, American Born Confused Desi. I wonder if there is a suitable expression for a loving Indian wife who suddenly metamorphoses into a sphinx.

❧ 3 ❧

Ever since Judy's westward flight, Maury Lee had been our guest at every Thanksgiving. He found your turkey, stuffed with just a suggestion of Mughlai, irresistible. He was glad that, unlike Reeny, you did not have any hang-ups about fusion cooking. Everything from cranberry sauce to sweet potatoes had the flavor of our kitchen in Inderpur.

Like a witness suborned by the prosecution, our younger child turned up on that Thanksgiving Day in traditional Muslim garb. I didn't know how to respond. This is how a man must feel, I thought, finding himself in the dock. Something jagged came unstuck within me that day, and at night I dreamt that a bewigged judge was drumming his bench impatiently with a pianist's long tapering fingers.

Our son Immy was born in India, but Gullu was American to her fingertips. She didn't even have a smattering of Urdu, freely dated boys from various backgrounds, and was a vocal political placard waver on the Brown campus.

Miriam had just finished whispering to me that Hackett, the new president, was planning to hand the pink slip to some of the senior faculty, when we saw a strange young woman, face covered in a *hijab*, enter the apartment. Not until the veiled figure came into full view did everyone realize that it was the daughter of the house, the joy of our life, and not some neighborhood *bibi* come looking for you.

Despite my astonishment, I could not hold back an impulse to laugh. It was suppressed hysteria, of course. Gabriella laughed nervously, and her courteous English husband got up from his chair. There was something in Gullu's demeanor which held the rest of our guests back. They just sat there, attent and transfixed, like spectators at a play's climax, afraid to cough.

When you asked Gullu if she would help slice the turkey, our daughter took the knife and began to jab and cut the bird. Head wrapped tight in that white piece of cloth, she looked like a high priestess performing an ancient rite.

This *hijab* business, though quite a surprise to me and my friends, had apparently been building up for quite some time, judging from your resigned expression. I was in a state of shock. My eyes wandered aimlessly across the room looking for an answer.

In a framed photograph on the marble-topped table next to the telephone, my hero, Jawaharlal Nehru, was strolling with JFK on the White House lawn. In an adjoining glass cabinet, a small replica of the *Pieta* by Michelangelo sat by a porcelain pot-bellied Chinese merchant. A large print of the Karbala mosque now hung above the mantelpiece, from which had been booted out the comely ten-inch Geisha doll in her silken kimono, with a stylishly furled turquoise fan in her dainty hand. She now stood politely smiling on a teapoy by the door.

In my study there was a plaster-of-Paris bust of the Bard under a glass dome. The rest of our apartment was decked out with reproductions of Monet, Mughal and Rajput miniatures, and a replica of the wheel of time from the Sun Temple in Konarak. Our family heirloom, an exquisite Persian carpet, covered the living room floor. A *hijab*-clad woman in such an eclectic *mise-en-scène* was an anomaly.

What was most intriguing to everybody present was that you seemed to be in on it and appeared to be smiling inwardly at my stupefied expression. That was obvious from the way you hissed, 'Leave her alone, please,' when Miriam asked Gullu what impelled her to don a *hijab*. Miriam had no choice but to shut up and beat a hasty retreat from the table, murmuring something about calling her husband Joe, who was visiting his parents in Florida.

I wondered if you resented my closeness to Miriam. We shared many interests and were attuned to each other's intellectual and moral concerns. According to Maury Lee, the Kingman music man, Bobby Franz, thought something more than simple collegiality bound Miriam and me. Of course Bobby had a roving eye himself and held a jaundiced view of all friendships.

I had heard about Muslim families in England whose daughters had suddenly started asserting their ethnic identities by wearing a *hijab*. I remember a movie called *My Son the Fanatic*, where the eldest boy of the family becomes a follower of an ultraorthodox *mullah*. But most of those children belonged to parents who practiced religion; they were mosque-going Muslims. We had brought up our children to view all religions as though they were historical artifacts. We had welcomed Sally into our family with open arms.

I decided to have a little daddy–daughter chat with Gullu as soon as the guests left.

When I opened my mouth, a tremor passed through my body. 'Don't be cross,' I kept telling myself. 'I am sure this is just a momentary fad. We'll all have a jolly good laugh about it tomorrow.' The *hijab* must have really administered a piercing jab to some central nerve, because forgetting my earlier resolve to handle the situation calmly and tactfully, I let off a disconsolate groan.

'What have you done with my daughter Gulshan? My beautiful child with her glorious hair?' We had named her Gulshan (rose garden, in Persian) because when she was a baby, her skin was soft as petals of damask roses. My eyes prickled with anger. My little girl was about to step off a cliff, and I was unable to stop her going over. The nightmare was real, it was no hallucination. My child was vanishing before my very eyes. Amazing what a piece of translucent fabric can do to a face: erect a Wall of China between you and your child. An impenetrable barrier.

'Abbajan,' Gullu said.

'Who the hell is Abbajan?' I asked, pretending to look around.

'Now, Daddy, please don't take it like that. There is nothing wrong in asserting one's ethnic identity. Aunt Miriam often says how assimilated Jews began reasserting their Jewishness to show solidarity with the victims of the Holocaust. I am doing just that. Displaying my affinity with my Muslim brethren. What's wrong with that?'

'What's wrong with that? I'll tell you what's wrong with that. You are undoing all the work your mum and I did to make you into a modern forward-looking young woman, a rational being who would always be ruled by reason and not by some . . . some fanatical notions of exclusion.'

Immy walked in with Sally at that very moment and both did a double take.

'Oh my god,' Immy said in mock horror. 'We have a proper *begum sahib* visiting us, a goddamn Gulshan Bano.'

'What's the meaning of this prank,' Sally asked, helping herself to a snapple. She was from a family of nonbelievers and had never stepped into a church.

'No need for sarcasm. Every woman should wear a *hijab*. It is like a scarf, keeps you warm in winter,' Gullu told her.

'But you are a trained actress. How do you expect to land a part on Broadway? They are not doing *Kismet* anymore,' Sally said.

'Ha, ha, ha.' Gullu released an empty trailing laugh.

'But seriously, Gullu, isn't it a sign of your subjugation to patriarchy, or have you forgotten your basics of feminism?' Sally said.

'Not at all,' piped my clever girl. 'Individuality is just another word for pure selfishness. There is something to be said about group identity. I don't see why I cannot play a nurse in a *hijab* or an office secretary, or even an executive.'

'Or a penguin? That's what you look like. Like a waddling penguin,' Immy said.

'It's all semiotics,' Gullu said calmly in her best Brown alumna voice, her eyes brimming with mischief. 'Ask Abbajan why he wears a tie?'

'Don't call me that.'

Sally told me later that at one stage during the back and forth between Immy and Gullu I had turned red in the face and had a mad look in my eyes.

'Look, I have nothing against the word "Abbajan". We called our dad Abbajan. But we grew up calling our parents Abbajan and Ammeejan. You never did. And it is a bit melodramatic to start that sort of thing in this house.'

'Sorry, Dad,' Gullu said in a conciliatory tone. 'All I am saying is that, just because you wear a tie, no one would accuse you of being a lackey of the British Empire.'

By that time, Sally's calming presence had restored some civility in the room.

'What are you "signifying" with that head gear, which conceals your beautiful hair? Tell me that,' Sally said

'I am signifying that I am a Muslim.'

'You are an Indian,' I said.

'Indian Muslim,' said Gullu triumphantly.

'But you are also American,' Sally said. 'You were born here for Christ's sake. My Immy spent his childhood in India. The first air you breathed was American air.'

'Well, then I am an Indian American,' Gullu said checkmating her sister-in-law. 'It is because I am American that I feel free to make a statement. This *hijab* is a symbol of my privilege as a free American.'

'But once you cover your face up, you disappear behind reams of clothing. Where is the real you?' I said.

'Dad, don't exaggerate; reams of clothing, indeed,' Gullu said. 'I am an American. My language is American. My language tells me I can wear anything I please. Traditional women, the *bibi* types, wear a *hijab* because they have to. I am not under any such pressure. It's a free choice. Like the Amish and their hats.'

After she started wearing the *hijab*, a couple of traditional, bearded and intense-looking lads began to hover around Gullu. I knew that she was too high-spirited to enjoy the company of anyone who wanted her to play a secondary role. In the meantime, Christopher Jenkins, the boy she had been dating, stopped calling her.

Every weekend when Sally and Immy came to visit, they teased Gullu.

'Gullu?' Immy would say, pretending to look around for his sister.

'Yeah?'

'Oh there you are. I didn't see you. You look like the Cheshire cat with just the face.'

One day I came upon my children having an argument in the kitchen.

'What if, in some galaxy far far away, the *hijab* was part of standard uniform for all men and women,' Gullu was saying. 'Like characters on *Star Trek* going through a time warp and landing in some ancient city behind mountains.'

'If their uniforms were alike, how would you tell the difference between the sexes?' I retorted.

'What if the idea of difference doesn't exist on that galaxy? Difference may be purely an earthly construct.'

'Earthy,' I corrected.

'What?'

'Earthy construct, not earthly.'

'What's the difference?' said the little apple of my eye.

Immy treated his sister's *hijab* as a joke, a teenage gesture, like tongue piercing. But it hurt me to think that I would never see my daughter's beautiful hair again. It was as if she had shaved it off or contracted some wasting disease. Her face without the hair had an austerity, a severity that reminded me of an old *hijab*-clad aunt widowed in her youth, scuttling around her old lonely house in the Kasbah.

❧ 4 ☙

My life had come to a full stop in Jackson Heights. End of the line, 'We'll go no more a roving . . .' and that sort of thing, no bridges to burn. As to green grass on the other side, there was not even a hint. There *was* no other side, I thought. This was it. Period, as they say here in America.

Maury Lee and I sat at our usual place in the Peacock Diner; a grimy bandage creased my right temple. It had been a week since I had managed to wreck the new car, a brand new Cadillac given to me by Immy on my sixtieth birthday. Gullu's *hijab* wasn't the only thing that was weighing me down. After a heated argument at Kingman, I was driving home when I swerved to avoid hitting a truck that had suddenly stalled right in front of me. I went off the road and smashed the car into a telephone pole. I was lucky to escape with a few cuts and bruises, but as Immy said, the car was 'busted'.

'That bandage seems ready for the trash can,' Maury Lee said.

I did not respond.

'I don't mean to be rude,' Maury Lee said trying to cheer me up, 'but you look like a death-row inmate whose final appeal for reprieve has been turned down by the governor. Sometimes you Indo–Brits really overdo the stiff-upper-lip gig.'

'It hurts here when I try to laugh,' I said indicating the cut beneath my lower lip.

I noticed that Maury Lee's attention had been drawn to something on the street. Following his gaze, I saw Reeny Babukhan, her petite body was tightly wrapped in a black leather jacket, setting off her dark luminous eyes in a baby face. She halted abruptly at Kohinoor Jewelers, turned around, and signaled impatiently to a tall sallow woman in a billowy white chador.

I knew how the mere sight of Reeny could set Maury Lee's pulse racing.

'That old lady must be Reeny's aunt on a visit from Chittagong,' I said in a neutral voice.

The aunt's unhurried carriage and pale skin suggested some gracious mansion with carved wooden balconies and shady inner courtyards, where shopping was mostly done by saucy maids with coquettish smiles and transsexual, bazaar-wise errand boys.

'I don't want to sound rude,' I said, echoing Maury Lee's words from a few minutes before, 'but she has a big chip on her shoulder, your precious Reeny.' Reeny's sharp tongue had wagged at more than usual velocity last week at the meeting of the curriculum committee.

'Where does she get off calling me a Don Quixote?' I said.

'What? Who called you that?'

'That Nusreen bloody Babukhan.'

'Why?'

'Because I put a stopper to her nefarious scheme to banish Dickens and Jane Austen. Over my dead body,' I said. 'First it was the Great Books program. Now she wants to make Shakespeare optional for English majors. Where will it end?'

Maury Lee was unusually quiet. I could see that he wanted to change the subject.

'And the funny thing is we have so much in common,' I added in an olive-branch, no-hard feelings tone. 'That aunt of hers would have been perfectly at home in our old *kothi*, don't you think?'

Many a gourmet evening had Maury Lee spent at our *kothi* sampling a range of Mughlai cuisine, the likes of which would never grace any curry-stained menus of an Indian restaurant.

'Here comes Miriam,' Maury Lee said, smiling with relief.

Maury Lee had not seen Miriam since the fateful Thanksgiving supper at our place. Her twinkly blue eyes, which looked out of a ruddy, cheering stadium of a face, put everyone at ease. As a lonesome nursery warbler tip-toeing through the hushed household of an Auschwitz survivor, she had turned out to be a dynamic public speaker with a zest for backing lost causes. She understood the pain I felt over Gullu's *hijab*.

'Sorry, I am late' Miriam said, slumping in the chair opposite. 'This place needs a parking garage. I had to drive three-quarters of a mile to find a spot.' She smiled at Jit for filling her glass with mineral water.

'You are very, very welcome madam,' Jit Singh said with an elaborate bow when she thanked him.

Playing Nawab and Thakur in the presence of Miriam would be bad theatre, so I ordered another coffee. Having stalked out of the curriculum committee meeting last week, I was done with large gestures.

'You shouldn't have left so abruptly, Siri,' Miriam said. 'A straw poll after the meeting found us just one vote short for retaining Shakespeare as required reading for an English major.'

'I couldn't take it anymore. But you are right; I shouldn't have sneaked away with my tail between my legs.'

'There are those,' Miriam said to Maury Lee, 'who do not think that the world would "dissolve", leaving "not a rack behind", if the Bard were bumped from our syllabus. But for our Siri, that would be like the sacking of Rome by the barbarians.'

During a heated discussion, Reeny, the Third World crusader, had twitted me, saying that for an Indian, an Indian Muslim, a member of a despised minority, to pick up the gauntlet on behalf of the Empire's Bard was, to say the least, quite quixotic.

There was a stunned silence. After the dean adjourned the meeting, Reeny apologized to me immediately for getting carried away, but the damage was done.

'I have never seen Siri lose his temper before. It was awesome. You should have been there, Maury Lee,' Miriam said with a mischievous smile. 'He simply got up, stuffed his papers into his brief case, and left, muttering to himself like, like . . .'

'Like a broken Coriolanus,' I said, laughingly completing her sentence.

❧ 5 ❧

'The Bollywoodization of Inderpur hurts me most,' wrote Dicky in an unusually long letter. Apart from an occasional missive about the declining fortunes of his polo team in national ranking, Dicky's dispatches had been more like terse telegraphic chits delivered by *chokra* boys who ran brisk errands for the palace. My reports from early years of exile in the US , reinforced by home sickness, had not elicited more than a few well-meant but desultory notes from him, and finally we had settled to yearly exchanges of birthday cards.

This time, a rambling account typed by his secretary on the familiar Gagan Vihar Palace letterhead, landed on my desk. Perhaps it was my imagination, but I thought the envelope, embossed with the royal crest of Inderpur, gave off the cool damp scent of *khus tutties*, hung during hot summer months on ornate doors and windows of the palace *kutcherry*, with balconies of intricately wrought fretwork jutting over the inner courtyard. I saw again the derailed toy train on its broken tracks in the vast garden at the back, and the porticos and arched windows softly lit at night by colored lanterns.

'I am afraid our Inderpur has disappeared behind walls of feature-less concrete,' wrote Dicky. 'The Georgian bungalows of my grandfather's time, with their graceful green gables and red tiled roofs, have vanished without a trace; in their place are hideously garish shopping malls. All landmarks—stepwells, cenotaphs, office buildings in red brick or stucco, palatine villas with fountains and turrets, and domes have been demolished, everything touched with history snuffed out.'

Dicky's pain was palpable.

'Wherever I look there is a concrete wall, impassive, aloof. Not the sort of wall that ascends mountains, snakes through valleys and across ridges, but a blank, pitiless wall like the one that divided Berlin, an ugly barricade straight as a tyrant's decree. I feel like one of those ancient Greeks Tilly used to talk about, mourning for his ruined city.'

You were too busy to notice that I was troubled by Dicky's obituary of Inderpur. I urged you to read his letter, thinking that his words might rekindle memories of tea parties in the palace, with his pet ostriches snapping up pastries from our plates. But you barely glanced at it; the passing of our old town did not merit one backward glance. You might have been listening to an historical account about Pompeii being swallowed up by Vesuvius. To you that drabness and monotony of shopping malls, with the soulless IMAXes of the new Inderpur were all signs of progress. Besides, you were too busy trying to put that swindler Sampat and his demon spouse behind bars.

You sat for hours at your paper-strewn desk, head tilted to one side, eyes narrowed, scanning documents. I was apprehensive about your taking on a ruthless barracuda like Sampat, but you merely shrugged your shoulders and went on reading your case papers.

The Save Yamini operation had been a mere prelude to a series of battles won by you in the courtroom, culminating in your sensational victory against the 'Godfather in Jodhpurs', as the papers called Sampat during his trial. Instead of his usual Raymond Chandler, private-eye trench coat and felt hat, Sampat would arrive at the court flanked by his sniggering lawyers, dressed like a Bollywood caricature of a 'man of the people', whose buttoned-down exterior concealed a plethora of iniquities. His plan was to cast himself in the role of a misunderstood oriental gentleman of distinction, victimized by xenophobic American bureaucrats.

Against Sampat's dream team of high-powered lawyers, you started as an underdog; but once the trial moved from preliminary hearings towards its finale, and Sampat's conviction on charges of human trafficking and diamond smuggling seemed like a foregone conclusion, my chest became the size of a kettle drum with pride. I ask you to believe me that nary a smirk crossed my lips when the tabloids began to hail you as the 'Joan of Arc of Jackson Heights.'

I had never so much as glanced at the local TV channel before, but now I couldn't wait to turn it on as soon as I returned from college. At five-thirty every weekday, it aired a ten-minute segment highlighting the most dramatic courtroom moments of the day. To see Sampat squirm under your polite but shrewd questioning would have been gratifying any time, but, knowing that it was none other than my Hyacinth girl out there at the center of the packed court room putting a murderous criminal through his paces gave me the kind of thrill we used to feel when, coming from behind, the Palace School defeated the vastly superior Infantry Cricket Club with members who represented India in test matches.

Sampat's cocky, smooth-talking lawyers, who at first seemed quite confident that the charge of causing bodily injury to their daughter-in-law Maya would be dismissed by the judge, were beginning to wear the bedraggled look of embattled fowls at a cockfight in the Kasbah. Somehow you had ferreted out Sampat's well-guarded secret—smuggling diamonds into the United States from Sierra Leone. The man was practically an international thug.

When those watching from the gallery applauded and Judge Burrell looked up angrily, you just stood there calmly reading your notes. Your composure was in sharp contrast to the florid theatricality of that vulgar little man the Sampats had engaged to defend them. It was apparent from the scowl on Burrell's face that he couldn't stand the fatuous upstart, despite his formidable reputation as an expert in criminal jurisprudence.

In clear measured tones, you explained how Sampat had the diamonds set in cheap-looking trinkets before flying to India. The priceless stones were embedded in something that looked like costume jewelry so as not to attract attention, and once inside India, the roughly-hewn necklace or bracelet was dismantled and the stones hawked for millions of rupees on the open market in that 'jewelry-mad country'.

I quite liked that phrase; hoarding gold and diamonds had been our national pastime.

Maya led the police to the room at the back of the house where Sampat hid his loot. They found an exquisite secretary of uncanny workmanship, honeycombed with numerous secret panels.

Old Edulji was happy to oblige when you sought his help in opening the secret compartments. As if pecking his piano in a staccato interlude, his trembling fingers found the secret levers that threw open the panels, revealing several velvet pouches practically bursting with precious stones.

Sampat channelled the profits into real estate in cities like Bangalore and Hyderabad, boomtowns of IT enterprise. I think your equipoise and reluctance to play to the gallery made a big impact on the judge. I noticed that every time you spoke, he leaned forward and took notes on his pad, but assumed a bellicose posture when the defense lawyer Damato harangued your witnesses.

You demonstrated to the jury how ingeniously Sampat's suitcase, with its secret chambers for contraband objects, had been fashioned by Indian craftsmen, with long experience in the smugglers' trade.

By then it was obvious to everybody that Sampat and his wife led a double life. To the public, they presented an almost doltish profile, while deep inside their fortress-like house, with its chateau-style pitched roof, they ran an industrial-scale operation in blood diamonds. The cruel act of branding their daughter-in-law with a hot iron was the last black tile that completed the mosaic of a ghastly carnage.

Watching the faces of members of the jury on the TV screen when you led them through the scene of crime in the Cord Meyer section of Forest Hills, I could tell that the jig was up for the Sampats. Bit by bit, with incandescent clarity, you laid bare the details of the secret life of the Sampats.

The ghoulish couple, masquerading as philanthropists, had managed to keep their son's wife Maya caged like an exotic animal by impounding her passport. Since she did not eat meat, the young woman had been forced to subsist on bread and water, and when she was ill, she received no medical treatment but was forced to work in the kitchen.

'For three long miserable years,' you said in your summing up, 'no one suspected that poor friendless Maya was in the house.'

The Sampats kept their drivers on a tight leash. They lured illegal immigrants, promising sponsorship for a green card, but as soon as the men got restless, they were fired.

Earlier, during his cross examination, Damato had tried to confuse the driver who'd heard the young woman's heartrending screams as she came running down the staircase with her right arm swollen and blue like a stuffed eggplant.

The driver's testimony ultimately sealed the Sampats' fate, because it was he who had driven the hapless daughter-in-law to North Shore Hospital. No one was convinced by Sampat's fiction that the young woman had accidentally managed to brand herself while cooking.

I think your apportioning the blame equally between Sampat and his wife anchored the narrative in a cultural ethos. The girl Maya had been a 'paying guest' at the home of Sampat's sister in the eastern state of Bihar, and tutored her host's children while attending the Teacher's Training College at Patna University. The sister had persuaded the girl's parents to marry her off to Sampat's son, who had just come out of a drug rehabilitation center.

The girl's family was kept in the dark about their future son-in-law's history of drug abuse. He was flown to India, accompanied only by Mrs Sampat, for a fast-track wedding. Mrs Sampat had played the beguiling Indian mother, scouting for a sweet, well-brought-up bride for her precious son. She had no use, she said, for those ultramodern girls of immigrant parents in the US.

Maya's people had been completely taken in by Mrs Sampat's courteous ways during the simple wedding ceremony and were over the moon for contracting such a blessed alliance. Mrs Sampat had enticed Maya with a promise to enroll her in graduate school.

But the son's rehabilitation had been far from complete, and a few days after returning to the States, he'd reverted to his whimpering infantile self. Maya, who had been forcibly confined to home, was gradually transformed into a slave girl, yoked like a beast of burden to the unending process of nursing and cleaning up after a drug-addled husband who terrorized her when he was not completely stoned.

As you said in your summing up, 'To the Sampats, Maya was a sub-human creature, and when all the dots in her story are connected, what emerges is a tale of ruthless exploitation of the poor and helpless by the privileged few.'

For me, your concluding remarks echoed the stark simplicity of Yeats's words, 'The beggars have changed places, but the lash goes on.'

At the same time, I couldn't help remembering the living horror of seeing the three blind Adivasi faces, mutilated by Bulchand's police lackeys in Inderpur.

The Chitral–Kanchan–Natthu troika tried to paint you as an uppity Muslim woman after the blood of an innocent Hindu couple. But their own children were not convinced that Maya could have faked that eviscerated face and the eyes of a hunted deer staring at them from the newspapers. The Sampats tried to bribe the driver, and Chitral, as his emissary, carried the check to Salim Ali. The poor man even received death threats from hired goons.

But all efforts to break him failed. The Sampats were convicted and slapped with a five-year jail term and ordered to pay two million dollars to Maya by way of compensation.

That night of the verdict, I stood outside your bedroom for several minutes and knocked two or three times. But you were fast asleep and I tiptoed away; I was euphoric and could not sleep. Next morning, when you asked me to get Maya admitted to Kingman, I couldn't stop myself from kissing your eyes. You laughed heartily and said you wanted to act swiftly to secure Maya's freedom from a sham marriage. She had enough money now to build a decent house for her parents in Patna.

When Bookstore-Nambiar, the almanac-thumbing Brahmin said, 'An inauspicious lunar eclipse hanging over Jackson Heights has run its course, and the earth has reemerged fresh and clean,' I thought he was talking about us.

$$\approx 6 \approx$$

Your courtroom triumph banished the gloom that had spread through our lives. I began to feel that the worst was over and it was time to revive plans for our long-deferred trip to Naples and Rome. It would be our second honeymoon, and I found myself humming 'Santa Lucia' like a nostalgic Neapolitan returning home after a long voyage.

When I turned into the driveway at Kingman and headed for the parking lot, I saw Reeny Babukhan's red convertible in the spot which had been mine by convention. I had to go around to the back of the faculty parking lot on the far side and walk to my office in the rain. Reeny had thrown down the gauntlet and declared open war. The reason was simple.

You would remember she was appointed in my absence, when we took Gullu to the Grand Canyon after her high school graduation. Mine had been the only dissenting voice when we'd met to discuss Reeny's tenure. I know she is your friend, but how can I convince you that my objections were based on sound academic principles?

I honestly felt that Reeny's specialization was too narrow and did not serve our liberal arts curriculum well enough to warrant tenure. She often said, though not in my hearing that India was conquered by the Bible and Shakespeare, not by the British Redcoats. It was difficult to tell whether Reeny targeted certain writers because she genuinely thought them to be patriarchal straw bosses or because they happened to be my particular favorites. It wasn't just Dickens and Jane Austen, who in her reckoning were crypto-imperialists, but also Conrad.

That quisling Bobby Franz, our music man, tattled about my objection to granting her tenure. I was outvoted of course, and for the sake of departmental harmony, even Miriam had to go along with the rest, even though she shared some of my reservations about Reeny.

Babukhan's retaliatory moves were not confined to hogging my parking space that day. The following week she presented an extremely tendentious paper at the faculty forum. From the word go, it was sheer drivel. She claimed that Shakespeare had been instrumental in destroying indigenous literatures in undivided India. The British, she argued, used the Bard to measure the worth of Indian writers hailed as classics by the Germans and the French.

The real coup de grâce was her sharp attack on Cleopatra. The Egyptian queen, Reeny maintained, was an Asian woman doubly colonized, exploited by Roman warriors both politically and sexually. Then she proceeded to tear to shreds one of my favorite passages containing the Egyptian queen's eulogy to the dead Antony as a species of 'colonial ventriloquism'.

> O see, my women,
>
> The crown o'th' earth doth melt. My Lord!
>
> O, withered is the garland of the war,
>
> The soldier's pole is fallen. Young boys and girls
>
> Are level now with men. The odds is gone
>
> And nothing is left remarkable
>
> Beneath the visiting moon.

She recited the passage in an obsequious whine in what I assumed to be a silly, Valley-girl's voice, fluttering her eyelashes and simpering coquettishly.

'Why should an Egyptian woman, sexually colonized and derided as "tawny"—meaning black by the occupying force—pay lip service to the Roman ideal of militarism, especially when just before breathing his last, Antony doesn't even look at her but exults in "a Roman by a Roman slain"?'

To her the answer was obvious. The queen had internalized Roman discourse to a point where her own political identity was totally erased. Not only Cleopatra herself but also her language had been penetrated through and through by the 'phallogocentric logic' of imperialism.

You must understand that I was beside myself. As soon as the applause died down, I got up slowly and spoke, more in pain than in anger. I believe the only harsh expression I used was 'scholarly myopia', which prevented academics of Reeny's persuasion from responding to Shakespeare's insight into mature love that transcended the narrow politics of us and them by taking poetry to new levels of experience. What the Bard had fashioned out of this great moment of personal loss was an ambiguous elegy.

Frankly I can't understand why you are so taken with Reeny. She is not at all like you. I know we have had our problems, but you are alive to others' suffering. The way you flew to the defense of Maya is a case in point. But Reeny is just an emotionally crippled harridan who has obviously never known love of any kind. I feel sorry for Maury Lee. He has let his infatuation blind him to her inner void.

Reeny operates in a low-budget, hand-held camera situation and the images wobble. Her strictures against Shakespeare leave the picture sadly incomplete. The Bard offers a Grand Canyon view of life, where everyone and everything—the tiny shrub, the majestic ridges and the sheer cliffs—are accorded an equal status. That's why I was so thrilled when our Gullu was picked to play Perdita in a production of *The Winter's Tale* by the Department of Theatre Arts at Brown. She had gone to Providence to study political science but switched to theatre after she got selected for the acting class. Even you applauded her choice and encouraged her to become a professional actress. Everyone knew you wanted her to follow in your footsteps.

❧ 7 ❧

Daffodils
That come before the swallow dares, and take
The winds of March with beauty.

I don't even remember when I took your hand into mine in that darkened theatre. In the circle of light on the stage stood our Gullu, playing Perdita, the lost daughter of the king, speaking to young Prince Florizel, whom she would marry at the end of the play. You did not withdraw your hand till the statue of Hermione, the estranged wife and queen, stepped off the pedestal to be reunited with her daughter and contrite husband. In Shakespeare's last plays, families break up, and after a painful interlude, come together in a profoundly tender reunion.

Now in her new incarnation as a political activist our daughter seems to be irretrievably lost to us.

When Gullu sprang her *hijab* on us that Thanksgiving evening, she had just started making brief appearances in off-Broadway productions, playing Turkish, Albanian and Indian girls in plays embodying the immigrant experience of alienation and assimilation. You were delighted when her work was reviewed in the *New York Times*; and while the plays themselves received only lukewarm praise, her performances were hailed as promising. And now our girl seemed ready to throw away all that for what appeared to be a whim, initially, but was fast turning into an obsession.

Finally Gullu confided to you that her *hijab* created some unforeseen difficulties for her. It changed other people's perception of her in ways she had not bargained for. She is pale like us but has these sparkling greenish-gray eyes. She had bagged a variety of roles playing Spanish women—a Creole from the Caribbean and even Jewish girls.

'I don't see why they won't cast me as a professional—a doctor or a nurse or even a lawyer,' she complained to me.

You have to admit that Gullu's *hijab* was a self-inflicted wound. The first thing that happened was that Chris Jenkins, whom she had been dating against his parents' wishes, dropped her.

'Chris just chickened out,' she said. 'I mean literally. He couldn't take it.'

'Don't you think you are being unreasonable?' I said. 'The poor lad has difficulty keeping up with his born-again Christian parents, and you expect him to convert to your faith. He met you when you were out there with no religious tag attached to you.'

'But I am not religious, Daddy,' Gullu said. 'I don't want him to convert or anything like that. How many times do I have to tell you that I wear the *hijab* as a symbol of freedom? It gives my ethnicity a historical dimension.'

'Listen to me, young Gullu,' I said. 'Listen to me carefully; it doesn't work that way. You cannot separate your ethnicity from your religion. Believe me, it is very hard. I should know.'

'Oh yes you can. We live in an age of unprecedented political conflicts. How am I to distinguish myself from other girls who belong to mainstream culture? I am light-skinned enough to pass for an American, white American, I mean. I must have something that says I am American but also belong to another culture.'

It was no use arguing with her. The poor child had somehow convinced herself that the world would accept her interpretation of ethnicity sans religion.

I rang Chris to find out what exactly was going on. Chris said he had gone along with Gullu for nearly three months after she had started wearing the *hijab*. He obviously cared for her and understood the force of her argument, but he didn't see how he could sustain their relationship.

'Look, I don't want to hurt my parents. They never forced their religion on me. Now they fear that I am going to convert to Islam for Gullu's sake. They don't buy Gullu's argument that wearing her *hijab* doesn't mean that she has become a practicing Muslim.'

Chris began to miss their dates and finally faded away. Meanwhile, Maury Lee was brought into the picture to mediate between the two. He had always been fond of Gullu and wanted to help. He took Chris for a long walk, during which he argued Gullu's case; but he came away convinced that it was one of those impossible situations you read about where two sides are frozen behind their own sand piles.

'It's an impasse,' Maury Lee said, 'one of those "Hegelian whatchamacallits", where each one stakes a moral claim of absolute validity, like extra-virgin olive oil. In the Wild West they would have settled it with a shoot-out, both gunmen biting the dust at the same time. Though I must say, all things considered, I lean more towards Chris. He was left with no choice when Gullu refused to take off her *hijab* while auditioning for TV roles; he thought enough was enough.'

She did manage to get a couple of bit parts as a babysitter, but the *hijab* gave her a severe look and she never received another call. The network people were uncomfortable with the *hijab*; it was not good for business. When she auditioned for a nurse on a medical show called *Doctor Brainshaw*, the producer turned her down on the spot when she insisted on appearing on the show looking, as he put it, like a 'muhajababe'.

You took her case to the Civil Rights Administration, but the network lawyers pointed out that it was written in her contract in fine print that she would be willing to put on any sort of make up and wear dresses approved by the producer as suitable to the show. The suitability clause was a loophole she could not beat.

One day Gullu came to my office at Kingman when I was grading papers and without a word slumped down into a chair. When I looked up, I found that she had tears in her eyes. I knew something major had happened to get her crying like that.

I got up, made some tea, gave her a cup, and sat down. She accepted it like an obedient child, took a sip or two, and put down the cup. Her hands were trembling.

'Something terrible happened today. It made me feel cheap and soiled. I was walking down the street, and this horrible woman with henna-red hair and broken teeth stopped me and put her arm around me. I thought she had mistaken me for someone else. But she hadn't. Oh I feel so awful.' It turned out that the woman was a marriage broker for Indian and Pakistani Muslim boys and girls.

'She showed me a photograph of some guy with a mustache, and said she would like to arrange a meeting with him.' Then switching to a sub-continental accent, Gullu said, 'He is a nice boy, a homely Muslim boy. His father owns three gas stations. Is very, very rich. Good *khandan*, a rich and very respectable family of old *Zamindars*.' The actress in her had suddenly surfaced. She was laughing through her tears.

I could imagine the scene. I had not seen the woman, but Gullu's rendering of her was pitch-perfect. I could imagine how awkward it must have been for this freethinking American-born daughter of ours to be accosted by a traditional marriage broker.

When she decided to put on the *hijab*, you didn't seem unduly worried. But you too had not calculated all the ramifications, that it would change other people's perception of our daughter so drastically. The marriage broker had simply assumed that Gullu's return to the fold was complete and that this young girl of misguidedly secular Muslim parents had seen the light.

To Gullu it must have been a shocking revelation; her political act had attracted some unwarranted attention from unexpected quarters. This was America, and it was very humiliating to her personally that she was now deemed eligible to be bought and sold on the marriage market like Jit Singh's Rajkumari. I am sure the thought of our daughter turning into a biddable object in the eyes of strangers must have stopped you in your tracks. I remember how it upsets you when some parents advertise their daughter on the Internet, as though she were a stray kitten in need of shelter. The thought of our beautiful and fiercely intelligent daughter becoming a commodity to be traded on the bourse was repugnant to you. Who knows what horrors, such as honor killing, lay in wait for her?

One day I found you making coffee in the kitchen at two o'clock in the morning. You said you couldn't sleep because you kept seeing the woman with the red hair come swooping down upon our Gullu like a fearsome *dayan*.

But that was not the end of it, was it? You had to threaten Mirza Ali of Shalimar Laundry with legal action when his son Ibrahim began to make passes at Gullu. He was willing, he said, to ignore her past as the daughter of heretical parents, now that she had, as he believed, seen the light. Although he was born here and raised as an American lad, at home his intellect had been stunted by unrelenting orthodoxy. One day, Qureshi's Yusuf stopped Gullu on the road to hand out brochures and induct her into the Muslim Students' Welfare Association.

We were apprehensive when Gullu decided to attend the meeting and check out for herself what went on there. However, to our surprise, Gullu discovered that some boys were really very smart and spoke feelingly about how to improve the negative image of Islam in the United States. Gullu said they were not at all rabid, and some of them were from highly educated families.

Then what I had feared all along happened. At one such meeting, a boy called Yunus caught her attention. You said it wasn't such a bad thing after all. Gullu was well past the age when girls in India are married and have at least two to three children. You wanted me to find out more about the boy's background. I put it off as long as I could, until you literally began to nag me like Mrs Bennet. Oh how reluctantly I agreed. But I must confess, when I did meet Yunus, I was pleasantly surprised to find that he was a smart and thoughtful young man. Of course at the time, we had no idea that Yunus might one day return to

Pakistan after obtaining his degree.

Maury Lee and I were having tea and snacks in the diner when Gullu came in with a clean-cut boy with broad shoulders. He was finishing up his PhD in economics but spoke knowledgeably about Sufism and its message of love. He was tall and had long eyelashes shading large brown eyes. It was obvious to me that our Gullu was quite taken with him. 'Our Perdita has found her Florizel,' I said to myself. She kept flashing rapid glances at me to check for any possible signs of disapproval. Seeing that Yunus had passed muster with her dad, her eyes welled up with happiness.

After the young couple left, I turned to Maury Lee and said, 'Impressive young man, I think. Let's hope he is not the sort who'd marry a girl just for obtaining a green card.'

'No need to count the chickens before they are hatched. What makes you think Gullu will marry him?' Maury Lee said.

'I know my little girl. I have never seen her looking so bashful and shy. I feel it in my bones. She has fastened him to her soul "with hoops of steel".'

The next day, I gave my approval with cautious optimism; something good might yet come out of this *hijab* business, I thought.

Gullu and Yunus began to go out. He took a keen interest in theatre and often went with her to see experimental, off-Broadway productions.

One day Gullu phoned and asked me to meet her at the American Café at Rockefeller Plaza. The place was crowded with office-goers snatching a bite before heading home, but the rest were tourists, judging from their tote bags and cameras.

'Yunus has asked me to marry him,' Gullu said without much emotion.

'Well, congratulations. I am delighted, and your mom would be equally pleased to see you happily married,' I said.

'Oh, I am not worried about that, Dad. You two couldn't have been more supportive. The problem is that Yunus wants to return to his old job in Multan. At first he said his J visa required that he should go home and work for two years. But now he wants to return permanently. He is very attached to his old parents, and he wants to be useful to his community back home. His region has suffered economic neglect, and he wants to help in its development.'

'I take it that you want to go with him,' I said, trying to quell a sudden surge of panic at the thought of her leaving us.

'It's not Yunus I am worried about, but the rest of his family. I have had complete freedom here; you two have brought me up to be absolutely independent.'

'That's true, but more than that I think you have to consider Shabnam's situation,' I said, weighing my words carefully. 'She has never been separated from you. I shall manage somehow, but as you know, your mother would simply go to pieces. Immy too would be utterly miserable if you left. Have you thought of that?'

'Of course I have. What do you think,' Gullu said, ' because I wear a *hijab* I have not stopped loving Immy? And what about you? That car accident the other day was not an isolated event. The way you went off the road was really scary. Immy said you might have been killed.'

Gullu was openly crying now. I handed her my hankie and stared into my teacup. Then putting the cup down with trembling fingers I said, 'Well, if you go to Pakistan, your Mum and I would certainly be devastated. But that's the risk you must take if you really care for Yunus.'

I couldn't say more.

'It's the unknown that worries me,' Gullu said dabbing her eyes. 'I don't want to go with Yunus, marry him, and then leave if I can't get along with the rest of his family. My friend Ayesha married someone from Lahore, but she didn't last there for more than three years. As soon as her daughter was born, her husband's parents started badgering her to produce a boy. They are obsessed with sons in that part of the world. I am not criticizing them, but for them a son is a must; I don't want to end up like Rajkumari with a whole bunch of girls, hoping that next time it will be a boy.'

'I don't think Yunus would go along with his family. He doesn't seem to be hidebound,' I said. A ray of hope was breaking through the clouds of gloom. We won't lose our Gullu, after all.

'No, certainly not, but there will be tensions,' Gullu said, as if she were considering other alternatives to going away. 'He insists on our staying with the family. He simply cannot abandon his mother in her old age. In his culture it is simply not done. His friends and colleagues would not permit that.'

'Well, I don't know what to say,' I said almost cheerfully. 'Living with his mother might not be such a bad thing, after all. No one, not even Shabnam, could have induced me to abandon my Ammeejan in her old age. It's just the way things are in our part of the world, however westernized we may get. Anyway, whatever you decide, you know you can count on our support.' I left it at that. I thought it was time for our Gullu to decide what sort of future to opt for.

We waited with bated breath for the outcome, while Gullu tried hard to make Yunus change his mind. He did seem to reconsider his decision to return to Pakistan, but then he got word that his mother, whom he adored, was ill. He decided to go back, promising to return, but he never came back. Let us be frank: I was relieved and so were you. We made commiserating noises for Gullu's sake. Yunus wrote long beautiful letters describing life in Multan; Pakistan had changed in the last few years, there was political corruption as everywhere, but slowly the place was modernizing itself.

It was increasingly plain to me that Gullu simply couldn't see herself living in Multan for the rest of her life. She decided to visit him after he had settled down in his job, and I offered to pay the airfare. But you and I know that in those parts, a young girl traveling all alone to be with her man was bound to raise eyebrows in Yunus's clan. Ultimately, Gullu's plan to visit Multan fizzled away, and we breathed a sigh of relief at last. But it was a close shave, and when Chris Jenkins reappeared on the scene—having been convinced by Gullu that her *hijab* was a political, not a religious, symbol—we welcomed him back like a returning prodigal.

❧ 8 ❧

Before the sound of fanfare inaugurating Hackett's tenure as the new president subsided, he issued directives which overnight made Kingman sound like a car manufacturing plant in Detroit. It was when official memoranda were issued to the effect that students would henceforth be known and treated as 'customers' that I lashed out, to everybody's surprise.

I had never been known to take much interest in administrative matters and either graded papers during long boring faculty meetings or skimmed through the *New York Review of Books* in one corner. But that day I got up and delivered myself of a sort of Periclean oration, which, despite or because of its learned allusions, made Daniel Hackett feel like a Connecticut Yankee in King Arthur's Court. The man was left in no doubt that he had to embalm some of the senior faculty in a retirement plan. Reeny and a dyspeptic young reed of a man, an assistant professor of chemistry who tried to interrupt me, were booed into silence by the rest my colleagues, who had been equally outraged but dared not to speak up.

I realized my days at Kingman were numbered. It was clear to everybody that Hackett would not be held hostage by a bunch of 'geriatrics', when he had most of the trustees in his pocket. He had attended a crash course at Harvard on how to turn around financially strapped colleges, and the clock was ticking for some of us. Hackett found a natural ally in Nasreen Babukhan, who had the bounce to take old fuddy-duddies like me.

You acted as though my problems at Kingman were no concern of yours, and they belonged to some alien people on the evening news, in a remote, strife-torn landscape like East Timor or the mountain villages of Peru.

Once Gullu's expedition to Multan was postponed indefinitely, we entered a new ice age, with long silences at the dinner table, punctured only by the crackle of voices when the phone rang. This enigmatic you, with your Russian doll interior, made me feel like a castaway, a beach-comber returning home late to catch his forty winks. The world around me seemed to just sail away silently, leaving me stranded on a jetty.

All your creative energy was now diverted to keeping Kanti's nest warm while our home suffered from frequent power outages, so to speak. Don't tell me you had nothing to do with Maya ending up as his wife.

Kanti was having lunch with Gullu and Yamini at the diner when I saw him last month. He said it was his day off at the motel and he'd come back to catch up with the girls on all the gossip in Jackson Heights. Now I see that it was the newly munificent Maya on whom his sights were trained. He was merely using Gullu and Yamini to dig a subterranean passage to the secret horde, the two-million-dollar com-pensation that the judge had awarded Maya after granting her divorce from Anand Sampat.

To charm a bird off a tree might have been Kanti's god-given talent; still, I don't think Maya would have tied the knot with him so soon after her stint as the Bride of Frankenstein. His usual sales pitch—poor little misunderstood boy—would not have made her invest in Kanti's patent so heavily unless you had undertaken to provide a life-long warranty. Maya had come to look upon you as a substitute mother and would have jumped off a cliff if you'd asked her to.

This playing god with other people's lives has its funny side, but ultimately the joke is on you. I mean, what were you thinking when you pushed that young woman you had rescued from the clutches of rapa-cious in-laws into Chitral's cage?

I knew that for some reason you never liked Susan and were secretly pleased when Immy found a job for Kanti that tied him to his desk almost round the clock in a remote New Jersey town. You thought perhaps a thrifty girl from a humble Indian family would be more forgiving of Kanti's evasions and malingering. You didn't stop to reflect that it would drain Maya's energies completely to be hitched to a congenital slacker. What Kanti needed was a good dressing down, not a babysitter.

Gullu realized that Kanti was merely using her as an alibi to explain his presence in Jackson Heights, when he should have been toiling away at his motel desk. When she found out from Yamini that he'd been meeting Maya secretly in her dorm on the campus, she got worried. A few days later, when Maury Lee stepped into the campus center to see a student, he found Kanti and Maya having tea and snacks at a table. Maury Lee's trained eye caught them holding hands under the table. Till then, some of us didn't know that Maya was even aware of Kanti's existence.

Chitral Seth must be delighted, because your interventions—I should say meddling—had repatriated his errant son to his camp. Kanti has grown from an improvident lad into a mountebank who can sell the Taj Mahal to an oil-rich Sheikh. The chickens are coming home to roost. Given the boot from the motel for dereliction of duty, Kanti is once again at a loose end. The last we heard was that Chitral had offered him a business partnership, killing two birds with one stone. In his old age, he gets his son back and also a chance to help himself to his daughter-in-law's doubloons. If you think Kanti would be able to resist the prospect of inheriting his father's fortune after his death, you are sadly mistaken.

I wonder if you realize that there is practically no difference between the fraud perpetrated by Mrs Sampat in enticing Maya away from India and your letting Kanti slip a noose around her neck. I am sure such an assertion would horrify you. You see yourself not as a marriage facilitator with henna-red hair, but a one-woman 'rescue squad' of the unfortunate and destitute. But there is a fearful symmetry between your blindness to Kanti's failings and Mrs Sampat's deliberate cruelty, a kind of

186

redoubling and criss-crossing of tangled motives too difficult to unravel.

Know that I am not blaming you. What has driven a wedge between us is part of a much longer narrative of gropings in the dark and grasping the nettles. I allowed your silences to stretch till you practically disappeared behind them. I had no clue about their significance, thought it best to let you deal with issues that meant so much to you and so little to me. I showed total disregard for that mysterious pain you felt over the demolished mosque. It was a kind of betrayal; I had acted the great visionary when you needed just a sympathetic shoulder to lean on. I mistook your outward calm for the absence of the storm within. I failed to understand that the brittle quality of your language; its legalese neutrality was a cry for help. Our marriage was not a poorly executed alliance which had to be dissolved. A negotiated peace settlement shouldn't have been ruled out.

Now we are like most other couples that merely 'get along'. Most of my colleagues are on their second or third marriage. Those who are still in their first humiliate each other before friends or pointedly ignore questions addressed to them by their spouses. When we are with our friends, we do our snubbing in a civilized way; with a peculiarly Indian twist, we freeze into nonspeaking roles with meditative Buddha-like postures until it's time for us to go home.

It was when I was beginning to feel like a superannuated *dhow* left to rot on alien shores, after logging thousands of hours in the Persian Gulf, that I felt a sudden tug and saw Gabriella unmooring me for a new adventure on the high seas.

In the old days, I really was not much of an enthusiast for Rubenesque women. Because she worked hard at the bakery after Jimmy deserted her, in a few months her flesh got distributed evenly. A tall figure with a tapering Botticelli waist, glossy silken hair and flashing black eyes, she ripped through my fragile defenses. My aging body came alive like an orchestra at the start of the opera season.

While Gullu was going out with Yunus, occasionally you used to creep into our old four-poster, more for a cuddle and when I was aroused you did not turn away from me. Last month when I sneaked into yours, you flinched and got up as though bitten by a scorpion.

I just needed the feel of warm flesh by my side at night. I didn't go shopping for it or prowl around the campus like some of our colleagues. Heaven knows I used to lower my gaze or look away whenever Gabriella turned her appraising eyes at me. But after you renounced our bed, I found myself returning her look with a smile. At first I felt like an ass; that sort of romantic interlude was the stuff of a Mills and Boon romance novel.

In the beginning, Gabriella had been just a presence, more like a casual acquaintance who sets ticking again an old, damaged, ormolu clock by accidentally knocking it sideways. After President Amanda Carmichael retired and went to live with her sister in Florida, for a few days Gabriella and her husband, Jimmy Winterlake, drove me to the performances at the Met. I didn't see very well at night and readily accepted their offer of a lift.

Opera was like mother's milk to Gabriella. One day she turned up alone in their car to pick me up, eyes red from crying and hair disheveled like Lucia di Lammermoor in the mad scene. Gabriella's enormous eyes filled with tears as soon as I said, 'Where is Jimmy?' Large drops cascaded down as she drove through the dense evening traffic, took a wrong turn and we found ourselves headed towards Greenwich Village. By the time she realized her mistake it was too late to turn around and still reach Lincoln Center in time for that evening's performance of *Tosca*. Instead, we went to an Italian restaurant and there, under a large print of Castel St. Angelo in Rome, she told me that Jimmy had left her for another person—a man.

Initially we were just a pair of opera lovers sitting side by side, hands and knees in occasional clandestine contact in the darkened hall, during the time it took Tristan and Isolde to quaff the 'magical potion' prepared by her maid Brangäne, until the moment of their 'love death', when she breathes her last, shedding her soul in Wagner's attempt to bring the yearning of all lovers to one lyrical focal point.

Gradually, on our evenings out at the Met, Gabriella's smiles acquired a degree of comeliness, and her dresses grew tighter around her bosom. Was this really happening or was I imagining things? There came a time when our hands would go into a locking mode to the strains of 'Amami Alfredo' in the second act of *La Traviata*, as the sickly Violetta began to unpack her soul to the estranged Alfredo, and remained that way till the end.

One night during our ride back, after witnessing a particularly moving finale of *The Daughter of the Regiment*, with Marie's soulful plaint *When I was left all abandoned (Quando il destino mezzo stagiera)* still ringing in our ears, I found myself in a lift going up with Gabriella to her apartment. When the doors of the lift opened we were still coiled around each other like a pair of mating cobras.

Gabriella is a stylish woman, despite those rhinestones on her Coco Chanel T-shirt and blond extensions in her hair. She was, after all, raised in Milan with six older siblings on reports of fashion shows and is rather like a quilt made of the European Union, with bloodlines stretching back to Irish, Italian and Bavarian forbears, with a dash of Hungarian hemoglobin. I am a bit embarrassed when she wears green on St Patrick's Day and marches in the parade. But she is most alluring when she speaks only Italian on Columbus Day in a perfect Milanese accent. And anyone who has tasted her strudels and Bienenstich during Christmas would tell you what a superlative cook she is.

Your silences were gradually replaced by barbed-wire taunts. A few weeks earlier, a minor disagreement had resulted in your assertion that I did not care for you as in the old days. Even an innocent question such as 'Where is Gullu?' was met with a sardonic, 'As if you care.' What finally pushed me over the edge was when I asked you where my blue tie was and you replied with needless scorn, 'Why don't you look for it yourself? I am not your *nokrani*.'

That was the first mean remark ever to have escaped your mouth in our entire coexistence. As nasty retorts go, it was pretty standard stuff, but its novelty was corrosive. A few days later my appreciative remark, 'Thank God there are still some women who know how to cook a proper *biryani*,' resulted in my being hauled across burning coals by you, assisted by Gullu. Both of you ganged up against me. I was mercilessly twitted for implying that women were only good for making *biryani* for their lords and masters.

When I tried to calm you down and said I had always stood up for you and tried to shield you from the slightest harm imaginable, you simply walked out of the room muttering to yourself. Then you returned with the pudding and said something that still doesn't make any sense to me.

'You were protecting yourself in protecting me.'

The pudding was like ashes in my mouth. 'Now what does that mean?' That simple query of mine brought on a whole explosion of unsubstantiated charges.

'It means that you were protecting the person I was then.'

Your tirade had something rehearsed about it, possibly in the presence of your friend Reeny, judging from the bits of feminist theory sticking out from the explosive harangue like broken glass on the wall surrounding an ordinance factory.

Your exact words were, 'That person I was then was not I, but someone you had fashioned out of clay like a clever potter. I thought I had married a prince among men, a Sahabjada, but you turned out to be a prince of wantonness, self-regarding, riding roughshod on others' wishes. I have served as a one-woman audience to you far too long. Oh you do it so gently; it is such a delicate operation that no blood is spilt, but it hurts all the same.'

As if that wasn't enough, you went on to analyze our marriage like a social scientist. I could see that practicing law in Jackson Heights had given you a strong sense of personal worth, but the rest was all vintage

Reeny twaddle, particularly when you claimed that you simulated happiness in our marriage when in fact it was a form of bondage.

The voice sounded like yours but your face reflected uncertainty about its true meaning; you were trying to convince yourself.

'Here I make things happen,' you said. 'Do you understand that? Women in need reach out to me. I feel wanted here by a whole group of people. I am no longer a delicate chrysanthemum in your garden to be admired at the annual flower show. I can shape an existence according to my own desires. Jackson Heights has given me wings; I have rubbed shoulders with working girls on the E Train.'

I had stopped listening. You were almost hysterical, talking to yourself by rote. Your voice was like breakers crashing on a vessel run aground.

'I was afraid of water,' you said, 'although in Bombay there was water all around. Then one day in Nainital, a friend pushed me over the edge of a swimming pool, and I began to thrash but managed to stay afloat. I never knew how deep the pool was. Had I known that, I would have probably panicked. But my whole being was focused on staying afloat at any cost. In that brief moment, I'd learnt to swim. I think that's what happened to me when I came here. At first I was afraid to walk out alone without you— the Indian, with his wife walking a few feet behind him.'

Then you lapsed into silence. What were your thoughts then? Did you feel relief after giving vent to years of anger and frustration? I thought you looked a bit dazed by all that eloquence, as though you were still arguing a case in the courtroom. You might even have been a little contrite. Reeny had coached you well, but I am sure some of your charges against me, must have sounded hollow to you. Your sense of fair play must have kicked in at some point during your colloquy.

As for me it was the end of everything. I thought it best to leave you alone.

The expression in your eyes frightened me. It was madness. In Inderpur, you and I had been like gladiators handcuffed together for an epic battle. Now the shit was hitting the fan, as Maury Lee would put it. 'For a bald French guy,' he once said after a particularly fractious evening with Reeny, 'Foucault has single-handedly wrecked millions of happy marriages. Under that hairless pate, his brain has constantly raced toward new ideas until he made "madness" itself sound like a gift from the gods.'

❧ 9 ☙

From that point on, life turned into a long nightmare; I began to spend more and more time away from home. It was now obvious that you had assembled a whole arsenal of jibes, which you proceeded to employ with pinpoint accuracy. Oddly enough, my anger was dissipated by my grudging admiration for this new independent you. The remote and beautiful Shabnam who had set my heartstrings thrumming the moment I saw her forty years before was gone forever.

I was in thrall of this gorgeous diva whose passion for opera never withered, despite her unhappiness over a failed marriage, and whose body sang at every inadvertent touch of our elbows in the darkened auditorium. But Gabriella was more than just an enticing siren undulating before me like a flame; she could discourse on a whole range of serious issues with impressive facility. From her architect ex-husband Jimmy, she had picked up enough useful small talk about the relative merits of Frank Ghery's postmodern design for the Guggenheim at Bilbao and the soaring maritime splendor daringly envisioned by Jorn Utzon's Sydney Opera House. While still flushed with the exertions of lovemaking, she could not only expostulate with charming ease on Schopenhauer's influence on Wagner, or the mysterious power of Balinese shadow puppetry, but combining the aesthetic insights of Sir Kenneth Clark and the casual sophistication of Sister Wendy Beckett, hold forth with amazing facility on the nude in art.

Her life was almost immaculately free of premeditated spirituality. Her crossing herself after every profanity was merely a graceful gesture left over from her Catholic childhood in Milan. One could pass days and nights with her without feeling guilty to be alive, whereas every encounter with you ended in a duel of wits.

You had simply been my best friend, my talisman against the world. But now to come into your presence was like going before the Spanish Inquisition.

But what turned an essentially low-intensity border skirmish with occasional sniping into a full-scale war between us was the untimely death of Diana, Princess of Wales. Looking back, it seems utterly ridiculous that her accident in the Paris tunnel should have pushed us to the brink, me into betraying our marriage vows and you to file papers for divorce.

The sudden and unexpected public relations tornado that hit Buckingham Palace in the wake of the Princess's death wreaked greater damage to its august façade than was caused by the Luftwaffe during the Blitz. Our crisis had a distinctly manufactured air. The assassination of Archduke Ferdinand by a mad man might have started the First World War, but to suggest even a tenuous link between the crack in the House of Windsor and the collapse of our home is to attribute forest fires in California to solar flares. It was just too far-fetched and absurd. We were the saboteurs of our own happiness. Diana's death in the Paris tunnel merely took the lid off some subterranean seething in our marriage waiting to erupt.

There had been telltale signs of what was to come. However ridiculous it may sound now, I was genuinely upset when everyone under fifty in England lost their sense of proportion and made the Queen seem like a heartless matriarch. You must remember that the Royal House of Inderpur had had very cordial relations with the Windsors since Queen Victoria's time. In fact, the old Highness's father had named him Edward after the Prince of Wales. His full name was Maharaja Edward Surjit Singh, and everyone in Inderpur was heartbroken when his namesake abdicated the throne in the thirties. In both world wars the Inderpur Light Infantry had fought with great valor in defending the Empire. And my uncle Lieutenant Colonel Jehangir Amolini had lost his leg fighting the Japanese in Kohima.

These are ties one cannot easily forget. During all that snipping and badmouthing in the media, the Queen had comported herself with utmost dignity. She is not a heartless monarch. In fact I remember that, back in the sixties, when a small school in Wales was buried under a collapsed coal tip, the Queen had tears in her eyes while trying to console the bereaved parents.

But Gullu and you went simply berserk and called the Queen all sorts of names. I was naturally outraged by the falsehood and canard to which she was being subjected. I was sorry for the Princess of course and more especially for her two boys, and I admired her for campaigning to ban land mines. But by contrast, it seemed to me that her conduct in general was not consistent with her station in life. What forced me to retaliate was your labeling the Queen a tyrant.

Diana's reading habits and friendships had left much to be desired and took some shine off the public good she seemed capable of doing. The Queen had retained her composure in the face of tragedy and acted like a real monarch. To me, the difference between the Queen and the Princess was the same as between the old Highness of Inderpur, the enlightened ruler, and my own friend the profligate Dicky.

I still remember how utterly obtuse your response was. You said, 'Do you know that when you are angry the whole building trembles as though it had developed epilepsy?' An old lawyer's trick I suppose; when you run out of argument, just hit below the belt.

Of course I was not angry. I was merely trying to point out the flaws in your argument. That's what we poor teachers are trained to do. Raise an eyebrow when our students digress into subjective anecdotal speculation, instead of applying their minds rigorously to a text.

But then I was only one against you two—the mother-and-daughter firing squad.

'Of course you are angry Daddy,' Gullu said as if on cue. 'I can tell by the swollen vein on your forehead. I don't see why you have to work yourself up into a state over the Queen. What is she to you anyway? Have you ever thought that your devotion to the Queen may be a symptom of the problem you have with us?'

'What does that mean?' I demanded trying to introduce a modicum of reason in what was beginning to look like a kangaroo court.

'Nothing. Calm down,' you said.

But Gullu persisted. 'What Mom means but would not say is that your partiality to the Queen may be a source of some hidden reservoir of unexpressed despotism.'

That certainly made me lose my temper, especially when I saw Gullu grinning triumphantly like a chimpanzee. But I had had enough of it.

'Please don't patronize me with that Stanislavsky claptrap. Hidden reservoir of despotism, my foot,' I said.

You two beat a hasty retreat, but not before I caught you signaling Gullu with a cautionary glance to drop the argument.

These days Jackson Heights gives the impression of an uprooted civilization. From the elevated train, the place looks like a circus that has seen better days, trying to make a comeback. Returning late from the Met, I feel as though I am entering an empty stage, the audience gone home and the cleaning crew departed after locking up for the night. The sari-clad mannequins with their alabaster pallor and blind-stare, headless busts in jeweler shops are like an alphabet of some dead language. The ideal of beauty is pushed so far beyond its Indian *beau idéal* towards the elongated Caucasian model that the fabric on the dummies has the aspect of some accidental spillage, rather than a garment meant to cover the body.

The mannequins are another chimera. It is perhaps a subtle way of telling the locals that we are not very different from them. After all, Indians are Caucasians, albeit sunburnt brown ones. There was the story of an Indian family who had filed a suit in some court, claiming Aryan descent, and won the case, but with a caveat that they were to be known as 'Brown Caucasians.'

'Is this narcissism gone awry?' I wondered. 'Are we as a people congenitally doomed to exhibitionism?' Was Gandhi's loincloth a subtle dig at the native tendency to splash colors, rather than an object lesson in plain living and high thinking? Did colors compensate for some inner lack, some spiritual emptiness? The melting pot was beginning to look like a dyer's vat mixing different hues. If this was assimilation, then heaven help us.

Tilly used to say, 'If you are really someone to reckon with, people will take note as soon as you walk into a room. Colors are for the feeble of character, for milksops and poltroons.'

It was astonishing how selective we Indians were in taking from the West what suited our way of thinking. Was I being hidebound? Was I missing the central point about cultural assimilation?

I often thought of the young architect from a small town in North Gujarat who had arrived recently and set up a tiny one-room office on the top floor of a narrow building on 73rd Avenue. He had very little English when he got here, but within a year he'd picked up the lingo, with its phony chumminess. He chatted up prospective clients fluently in a language they could understand.

'Hullo, this is Sam Patel,' he would say, anglicizing his name, which was Sameer.

In a few crisp sentences he explained what he had to offer and described imaginary projects he had completed in Florida (which he had not yet visited). Then he quoted a price with hints of large discounts. He ended every conversation with 'Nice talking to you' and started dialing another number. Within a year he had managed to build up an impressive business in real estate.

Then there was Mrs Swaraj's daughter who belonged to a socially prominent Inderpur family, and who, after the death of her alcoholic husband, had migrated to the US late in life, marrying an enterprising widower with a motel in Queens. She had been a member of your bridge club and invited us for dinner at her husband's motel, where she cleaned toilets and made beds for the guests. While escorting us to our car, she urged you not to let anyone in Inderpur know that the daughter of a noble family was cleaning toilets in the US. I was not quite sure what sorts of adjustments were required of someone who had maids in Inderpur to run her bath and clean up afterwards. She had money back home and children by her first marriage. Why did she have to come here to clean toilets?

When old Mr Edulji died, the last remaining link with my past disappeared. I felt an acute sense of orphanage with the old man's passing.

The history that oversaw transition from Edulji's to my adulthood had an international cast. It was a blur of rapidly changing cinematic images: shots of an ill-tempered Hitler screeching into the mike; Chamberlain with his brolly, hapless evacuees at Dunkirk; German soldiers goose-stepping down the Champs-Elysées; Churchill's fat fingers giving the Victory sign; emaciated survivors at Auschwitz; the Big Three at Yalta; the mushroom cloud over Hiroshima; the Mahatma reclining on bolsters with Nehru; Stalin's heavy-duty mustache; and Kenyatta, with his fly whisk, being sworn in as president of Kenya in Nairobi. The Inderpur of my adolescence belonged to the whole world.'

New York glimpsed from Inderpur's Mohan Talkies was a dun-colored city, peopled by gum-chewing men in felt hats, double breasted suits, and corner-of-the-mouth menacing talk. In a film based on *The Heiress* by Henry James, Ralph Richardson's house with heavy wooden doors stood in Washington Square. His daughter was played by Olivia de Havilland deglamorized for the role. With her hair plastered down and gathered at the back in a bun, she waited inside, while on the other side, Montgomery Clift, the renegade fortune hunter, pounded on the door.

Maury Lee said I reminded him of the Woody Allen character whose Manhattan was like a grainy woodcut. It was something of a disappointment to learn from Maury Lee that the Kasbah scenes in *Casablanca* were shot on the back lot of Hollywood studios.

Mr Edulji's funeral briefly revived that old sense of belonging to a special neighborhood. For one brief moment, Jackson Heights came together as a community to share a common loss. Even those who didn't understand his music felt that something precious had been lost. KC Way would never be the same again. The stooped figure, pottering amidst his beautiful artifacts, was one of the common sights of Jackson Heights and his exit left a void. A familiar landmark had vanished from the street.

I was reminded of the time when the whole of Inderpur had mourned the death of the king, the old Highness, as everyone called him. Several thousand Muslims had joined the funeral procession of the Hindu king. When the cortege entered the Muslim majority Kasbah, women were inconsolable.

'Maharaj, who would take care of us now?' they had cried.

The people of Jackson Heights assembled for one last time to bid the old Parsi a fond farewell. He was a prince among men they said. Ezra Pound's lines from *Vecchi* suddenly flashed through my mind. 'They will come no more, / Those old men with beautiful manners.'

In India, the old emaciated body would have been transported to a tower of silence to serve as food for hungry birds. But when Susan asked the Zoroastrian Association of Greater New York for assistance, she was told that they would take care of the funeral arrangements and have the body cremated in the presence of their priest, since the ancient Dakhma-nashini mode of disposing of dead Parsis was not practical outside India.

Some of us old friends carried the mortal remains of Mr Edulji in a silent procession to the ambulance sent by the Parsis, which was tactfully parked about half a mile away to allow for a ceremonial 'last journey'. Looking like a flower shop at Christmas, Mandalay simply overflowed with bouquets and posies from local families, and Susan illuminated the emptiness of the reclining chair with two flanking candles.

Hindus, Muslims and Latinos marched side by side in the procession. I could hear Bookstore-Nambiar muttering something wise in Sanskrit to Badé Miyan of Karachi Halwa, whose lips framed a silent *'Insha Allah'* and *'Jazaakallah'*. Qureshi, who was ahead of me, sobbed openly like a child, although Islam forbids tears at funerals. Even Officer Bartiromo was seen dabbing his eyes, while his colleague Haggerty directed traffic with a brave Irish face.

I was surprised to see the hermit of the subway lobby walking stiffly like a statue behind the procession. It was a moot point whether the two old recluses were even aware of each other's existence. Were they part of some unknown *camarilla*, some in-group that met unbeknownst to Jackson Heights? Obviously there was some ineffable connection, a secret affinity that linked the slow-paced of this world, their ruminations traveling through the charged air like cross-pollinating butterflies.

The subway saint never asked for money. He just sat there looking grave and abstracted, with a 'mind-elsewhere' sort of look. He was such a familiar figure that despite his obvious destitution, were he to absent himself even for a day, commuters would find the emptiness oppressive. The expression 'hanger-on' didn't apply to him; he had adopted that spot like a wayside Indian deity and installed himself in it.

Yet his being there was so devoid of any sense of supplication that commuters did not even look in his direction anymore. He was part of the scenery, but uncategorizable. Neither beggar nor mendicant, he was treated as an extension of the Korean shop. Of it, and yet not of it.

Anywhere else he would have been questioned by the police. The Korean shopkeeper would have considered him a blot on his property, someone who brought down its value, an embarrassment. His Buddha-like serenity preempted any civic impulse to dislodge him. Besides, he was on neutral territory, as subway station lobbies tend to be, suspended between heaven and earth.

Maybe he reminded commuters of their own grandfathers sitting in some village on a *charpoy* sucking on a hookah. Maybe he kindled a sense of guilt in them for not providing care for the old party back home. Whatever the reason, all immigrants, not just Indians, came to think of him as an example of that famous Jackson Heights spirit of tolerance.

Lately I had begun to take a greater interest in the man. He never spoke, so there was no way of getting to know him. Half *sanyasi*, half *fakir*, he seemed to have reached a stage in life from where all conflicts were banished and no want, nothing, was left unfulfilled.

Book VI

❧ 1 ❧

'Am I imposing my white man's ideas on this culture?' I often asked myself in Inderpur. Anthropology had become its own worst enemy, deconstructing itself before anyone else could, with too many ifs and buts. Instead of a tribe with exotic customs, I had come upon a poor and oppressed community of Adivasis lost in the modern wilderness. Their only source of livelihood, the river, was snatched away from them. Before their very eyes, waves rising from the imprisoned river had drowned their hamlets and their whole history, and their past had disappeared. As far as you could see there was water, and blocking it were rock-solid concrete slabs piled on top of each other. Old men still recited their history, but there was no place they could point to where battles had been fought and won, where wild beasts had been speared and marriages celebrated.

The art of catching truth on the run, which was my job as a budding anthropologist, was turning out to be a murky business. The opposite of objective truth is 'ecstatic truth', ecstasy of intelligence, as if intelligence were slightly drunk, not completely blotto, so that it captured reality on the ground as seen from the skies by an astronaut. But in Inderpur, I always had this sense of being suspended between the sublime and the grotesque. I had a similar feeling during my study tour in Rome when stepping out of the Sistine Chapel and getting caught in the routine rhythms of commuters going home from office on their scooters. While my eyes were still haunted by angelic faces on the Chapel walls, it was difficult to step back into the world of toiling Romans on the streets.

January 10, 1979

Siri and I have just finished playing tennis. After we shower, we head to the dining hall, where we are to have dinner with the Saradhis. Lepakshi is called away to the phone. She comes back looking extremely agitated. Terrible news about the police blinding a group of Adivasis. The Bushshirt has been on the phone; the Adivasis are on their way to the clinic. We all rush there and wait, peering into the dark quadrangle, which has already been dappled by banyan leaves caught by moonlight.

Suddenly Siri gets up from the chair with a sharp cry and stands staring out in sheer panic. I am confronted with the most appalling field of terror I have ever seen.

Three scrawny figures with blood-soaked bandages across their eyes come stumbling into the schoolyard. Pain stuck in their throats, the men lay themselves down gently under the banyan. Their blood-caked hands hover over the bandages. The Bushshirt says the government-run general hospital had refused to treat them without registering the case with the police.

Lepakshi begins to clean the wounded eyes with the help of a yawning Adivasi nurse. From snatches of conversation around, I gather that these men were attacked and blinded by Golmal's constables guarding the dam site. The police had accused the Adivasis of trying to blow up the dam site. They were tied to trees and naked bayonets plunged into their eyes.

In search of wood, the Adivasis had wandered too close to the turbines in the powerhouse, damaged during a Freegunjee sneak attack the previous week. The three Adivasis were taken to a remote part of the jungle and severely beaten with rifle butts before being subjected to the ultimate savagery.

I am paralyzed by terror, because one bandaged blood-soaked face seems to follow my every move. I am spooked. A spectacle so improbable seems to require a setting far more ravaged than the moonlit schoolyard with voices of women and children from the servants' quarters murmuring softly.

Gradually, the anguished cries of the staring bandaged faces subside to low animal moans as Lepakshi administers an extra dose of morphine to them. Father Yesudas suggests we shift the three Adivasis to St Thomas's Mission Hospital in Jabalpur in the neighboring state of Madhya Pradesh, before the police squad responsible for the atrocity gets wind of it. According to Siri, the police superintendent, or Golmal, as

Lepakshi calls her, wouldn't have dared to order her men to punish the Adivasis so brutally unless prompted by her political bosses to set an example to the rest.

'I have never heard of anything like this happening, even in Vietnam,' I say. 'My brother Steve was in Nam. Pretty ghastly things were done there, by all accounts, but this gouging of eyes . . . Those men must be absolute brutes.'

Professor Saradhi looks over his shoulder and exchanges a weary smile with Siraj.

'You is talking Viet-nam,' the Bushshirt says, splitting the word in his characteristic fashion. 'But Viet-nam is war, no? This not so. Gouging eye is local custom. You not like me? You gouge out my eye. This is example of Golmal's constant war with Adivasis. Govern-ment says we give resettlement to Adivasis in other area, so govern-ment build dam. The dam sink Adivasis' village. Adivasis say no, no. We not go. I belongs here. My Mummy and my Papa lives here. I grows up here. My children, they born here. Please, this my home. I die but not leave. So government say to Golmal. Adivasis no good, destroy equipment at site of dam. Teach Adivasis lesson. Remove him by force. So police hit Adivasis hard, hard, on foot, on back everywhere. These Adivasis not responsible for damage to equipment. They innocent.'

The Bushshirt bangs his fist on the hood of the jeep. His sense of outrage has screwed up his English more than usual.

'You asking why police blinding Adivasis? So they not be able to identify police. So police go free.'

'You mean someone deliberately ordered the police to gouge out their eyes?' I ask.

'Maybe not in so many words,' Saradhi says, 'but they were obviously told to use more than their usual strong-arm methods so the Adivasis would be too scared to protest again.'

'But surely someone must have seen what happened.' I persist.

'No, not possible,' the Bushshirt explains. 'The police catch Adivasis and take in van to quarry far far. Then they puncture eye. No witness.'

According to Siraj, there may be a couple of witnesses, but locating them and persuading them to testify would be really tough. There can be terrible reprisals.

'But testify they must. We must get hold of them no matter what.' Siraj's voice suddenly rises above the roar of the engine as we prepare to leave for Jabalpur.

In that rank, confused winter dawn on the bulldozed outskirts of Jabalpur, hun-

kering under a storm of chimneystacks of factories, clutching a disposable clay mug of tea by a roadside stall outside St Thomas's Mission Hospital, I understand nothing.

The Padre, Lepakshi and Saradhi are with Father Basil of the Mission Complex. The Father phones his counterparts in Delhi and Bombay, urging them to contact other missions around the world to report the incident before the local press controlled by Golmal and her thugs can start discrediting the victims. Father Basil is an amateur photographer. He gets busy with his Zeiss Ikon, taking pictures of the victims' faces before the mission doctors dress the wounds.

January 20, 1979

Siri becomes the target of a witch hunt because he accuses Golmal of trying to sweep the blinding atrocity under the carpet. The right-wing cabal running the IUTU, Inderpur University Teachers' Union, is in cahoots with Golmal. They go after Siri for lending support to the Adivasi Bachav (Save Tribals) Movement. Disgruntled teachers, who have piled up money by tutoring students illegally and helping them get into coveted courses in the engineering and medical faculties, run the IUTU. I am still shaken by the events of last week. Never have I experienced such terror.

Although I am a stranger in this land, I feel strongly implicated in the Adivasis' fate, and not simply because I am training to be an anthropologist. That one single blind stare from that night is burned on my heart. I remember my brother Steve talking about the accusing look he had once seen in a one-eyed Vietcong they had brought into the field hospital after the guy had been tortured for information.

In Nam, Steve flew a chopper used for dusting up wounded kids from the ditches. The 'Lurps' had a peculiar name for the hilly jungle beyond the base camp. They called it Indian Country.

'If the VC didn't get you first, you could be blown to pieces by some crazy bitch of a spy on Dak To. We were busier than a bride's ass in a tourist court. Sure, there were atrocities; only a slope-head would deny that,' Steve would say. I never dared ask him what a 'gook' was, or a 'grunt'. At times my brother's language travelled too far back in time for me to make sense of it. Whenever his unit picked up the wounded, he said, 'There was at least one kid having a shit fit, vowing eternal vengeance on the VC. Then one day they rolled in a VC officer from the brush.

The guy looked as though he had been walked all over by the entire squad. He was patched up in a hurry till they could move him to the POW camp in Saigon.'

His eyes followed Steve everywhere whenever he went in to chat with the blond nurse he was screwing. Finally Steve decided to confront the Vietcong and said, 'Hey, bub, why d'ya keep staring at me like a goddam lizard?' ' But the raggedy-assed son of a bitch spat on me,' Steve recalled with a smile. 'He dirtied his own face because he couldn't prop himself up. Still, he got me so mad that I almost strangled the punk. Next day he was gone. It didn't make any sense,' Steve said. 'The guy never looked at anybody but me.'

The blinding is a watershed moment in the brief inglorious history of the dam. The national English-language papers pick up Siraj's report on the atrocity. It has shaken the nation's conscience as nothing else has ever done before. People inured to the pain of others are jolted out of their wits when the pictures taken by Father Basil in Jabalpur appear in national newspapers.

February 25, 1979

The campaign to spread the truth about the unmitigated Roopkund horrors, as the blindings came to be known, is under way. The Bushshirt escorts opposition politicians who have come out of the woodwork to the scene of the crime. Reporters from national papers have also arrived from the big cities, and the Bushshirt arranges interviews for them with the two witnesses who are under the protection of the elders of the Adivasi tribe.

The inquiry committee finds five policemen and a subinspector responsible for the actual atrocity, and they are convicted, following their suspension. Everyone knows the real culprit is Golmal; it was she who ordered them to teach the Adivasis a lesson they would never forget. Siri, in his report, exposes Golmal's pivotal role in the brutal treatment of the Adivasis. He paints a Kafkaesque landscape full of heavy silences and midnight knocks upon the door. The narrative is stark and points to Golmal as the ultimate villain.

'The real villains,' Siri writes, 'are those cynical jugglers of truth who hide behind ministerial garb, not the dim-witted police constables who merely follow their superiors' orders. The nation stands naked and shivering before the House of Justice

but someone has pulled down its blinds.'

Golmal is under Bulchand's protection, and despite Siri's write-up attracting nationwide attention, nothing is done to loosen her firm grip on power. Siri has made one hell of an enemy. The subinspector and the constables take the fall for her, and Bulchand compensates them suitably. Lepakshi is quite sure that Golmal will not rest till she destroys Siri's reputation.

Soon the Roopkund horror disappears from sight as Inderpur gets down to the business of electing its representative to the national Parliament. Golmal's men get busy gerrymandering Bulchand's candidacy.

Siraj is confident that his friend Dickey, who is the other candidate, will win the Adivasi vote because the tribal elders are still loyal to the ex-ruler's family. However, during a recent round with the mobile van, Lepakshi has come to know, through her contacts, that Golmal's men are threatening even more severe punishment than gouging of eyes if the Adivasis do not switch allegiance to Bulchand.

March 17, 1979

I have been with Lepakshi to the Adivasi areas several times in the past few weeks. It is amazing how much I enjoy being with her. Her proximity quickens my pulse, but her serious gaze allows nothing more than a peck on the cheek. I have begun to sense in her some awareness of the magical charge that passes through me when our bodies touch while going over a bump.

The Women's Action Committee, of which she is the local president, has decided to support Dicky, who is sympathetic to the Adivasis' cause. Together they might be able to lick that creep Bulchand.

Bulchand's campaign is run like a well-oiled machine. He wants to win the election in order to play a big role on the national stage. No more the narrow confines of state politics for him and the regional ministership that goes with it. He has always hankered after a place in the Central Cabinet. The only way to do that is to dislodge Dicky from his parliamentary seat.

Bulchand's alter ego, Golmal, has reinvented herself by jettisoning her uniform. She has stepped into the role of a temple-haunting sentinel of traditional values. A big round vermillion mark appears on her forehead, and she is seen driving around in an old grey Ford with her head covered modestly by the loose end of her white cotton sari.

Bulchand's jeeps, with loudspeakers attached to their hoods, rumble through the streets of Inderpur exhorting people to cast off the evil of sinful government and support the party of the pure-hearted, who are committed to stamping out all corruption and restore Ramraj, the Kingdom of Rama. Siraj and Lepakshi, who have seen it all before, are amused by my dismay.

The city is gripped by election fever, and Bulchand's lackeys have disfigured the town walls with slogans portraying him as the Savior of Inderpur and with graffiti lampooning Dicky. Siri is worried about his friend's electability. He says, 'Dicky is being dragged like a swimmer trapped in an undertow into the jagged reefs of modern-day politics, in which the prestige of his royal house is not buoyant enough to keep him afloat.'

The club is the only place in town where one can get some relief from loud Bollywood music blaring from Bulchand's jeeps touting his candidacy. Occasionally we catch sight of Dicky as a liveried chauffeur drives him across the town in his white and gold Rolls Royce with the blue insignia of his defunct princely state painted on its doors. He tours the town every day, but according to Lepakshi, the attendance at his rallies has dwindled to a handful as Bulchand continues to chip away at his image as the benevolent ex-ruler of Inderpur.

Dicky is isolated in his own old princely capital. For old time's sake, his friends agree to accompany him to the Adivasi hamlets to canvass. Saradhi, who has done extensive research on the Adivasis, is on cordial terms with the tribal elders. Lepakshi's time is divided between the clinic and the forest.

Outside in the streets, Inderpur is beginning to come to terms with its new status as a significant spot on the national map. It is transformed from a sleepy little princely backwater into the battleground for political power on a national scale.

March 29 1979

Lepakshi and I drive down to the palace to warn Dicky that Golmal is intimidating his Adivasi voters and he may lose their support. There are other candidates on the ballot, but everybody knows by now the main contest will be between Dicky and Bulchand.

When we reach the palace, we are led to a paddock at the back where Dicky stands amidst Inderpur's faded old gentry and household staff on a podium welcoming his guests. While Bulchand employs modern technology to garner support from the masses, that scion of the Royal House of Inderpur is busy playing the gracious feudal host to his old retainers at a traditional sport, a goat fight. It stirs the gambling instinct among the viewers, resulting in large-scale betting. In the good old days, Dicky's great-grandfather used to stage a combat between two mad elephants. 'Those were the days,' sighs the palace official who ushers us to the podium.

Dicky has almost reached the end of what appears to have been a rousing speech and warmly shakes hands with us, making us sit by his side. First, a well-fed goat wearing a tunic in the blue and gold princely colors of the Royal House of Inderpur is led in. It is the odds-on favorite. Two effeminate flunkeys in muslin kurta *outfits push in a reluctant, slightly mangy, older goat on whose white cloth cap is emblazoned the name BULCHAND. It is typical of Dicky and his followers to cook up such an arcane scheme of medieval vintage to fight a modern election.*

'Crack,' go the heads of the battering goats. The goat in white slumps and the crowd cheers lustily.

'Hy, Hy, Raja,' says one flunkey to the other, 'Hy Hy, our He Goat has properly goosed your She goat.'

The goat with the white colors of Bulchand begins to bleat and cringe and has to be prodded back to where the other awaits, battle-drugged, hind legs stretched, deadly black horns poised for the kill. Unable to bear the pain of those vicious jabs, the goat in white suddenly parts its hind legs and defecates.

Dicky gets up and waves to the cheering crowd; his goat has won the contest. Judging from the reaction of his followers, we assumed that the election was in the bag. Dicky is still euphoric with victory when he walks up to us after seeing off his guests.

Oblivious to the entire din around them, the cart couple goes about their daily shoeless round, eking out a meagre living.

April 16, 1979

As the date for the general election draws near, Bulchand's flunkies mount a smear campaign against Dicky, portraying him as an ineffectual yes-man who has tried to live off the good will earned by his father and grandfather during the old

212

Raj. What Inderpur wants, they declare, is a rough-and-ready fellow, your average Joe, who is not constrained by spurious old aristocratic baggage, a dynamic modern-day man who has sprung from the masses and who can hustle and grab the best deal for Inderpur in the dog-eat-dog world of Delhi politics.

While Bulchand's campaign keeps drumming his message into the minds of Inderpurians till late at night at open-air shows of popular blockbusters from the Hindi screen, Dicky spends the evenings getting his polo team ready for the forthcoming national tournament, like all the flashy royalty of yesteryear.

I find myself heading for the club every evening to get away from the incessant din unleashed by the election campaign. Dicky is too fat fo polo, and after his daily jaunt on the stump, he comes to the club and sits watching his team practice every day. His stables boast only a few good ponies, but the royal sport has to go on.

On the day before the election, all candidates are forbidden to canvass for votes. Campaigning is officially over.

April 21, 1979

Bulchand wins by a landslide. Hoisting his diminutive form onto their shoulders, the vermillion-splattered crowd marches in procession to thunderous ovation from balconies, rooftops and streets. By assuring political patronage to local smugglers and bootleggers, both Hindu and Muslim, Bulchand has managed to split the blue-collar voters, several of whom have cast their ballots under threats of death and other arm-twisting tactics, in his favor. Born in a family of petty merchants, Bulchand has now become the uncrowned king of Inderpur, making Dicky completely obsolete.

The next day, the Saradhis, the Amolinis and a few other friends of Dicky's assemble to commiserate with each other. Professor Saradhi tells us that Bulchand owns several acres of land on the outskirts of Inderpur. He has bought it for a song from poor farmers. He would now persuade the Parliament to set up a major public-sector industrial complex to boost the local economy and sell his land to the government at an astronomical price.

By beating the royal son of the soil, Bulchand has proved his worth, and even national papers carry his speech verbatim the next day. Crumpling one in disgust, Siraj tosses the paper into a nearby wastebasket.

'No need to fret,' Saradhi says, shaking his head sadly. 'Lately it's been a toss-up between tyrants and clowns in this country.'

I cannot contain myself and begin to swear.

'And where would you place that horse's ass Dicky? Is he a goddam tyrant or a freaking clown?'

'A bit of both, I expect,' Professor Saradhi replies. 'But he is from another era. His kind went out of vogue before the Second World War.'

'Did you hear about that goat fight right in the midst of the election?' I ask. 'Somebody oughta stuff the guy and hang him from a wall in his palace.'

'Hasn't the election done precisely that?' Saradhi says.

March 17, 1979

Father Yesudas has gotten involved in the conflict between the tribals and the corporations who cut down trees to make money from paper mills and cricket bats. The clinic is a thorn in the side of the state government. I think this is what they mean when they talk about brown colonialism replacing the white colonialism of British India. Saradhi is sympathetic to the Adivasis. He has made his career studying and researching them, but he also wants to be in the good graces of the government. Lepakshi, his wife, is squarely with the Adivasis. A new leadership is emerging among the Adivasis with links to the Communists.

I am about to turn into the driveway of the school when I see Father Yesudas coming up from behind me on his motorbike. He stops and asks if I have had any news from home. I feel sorry for the Padre. He seems lonely and distraught. With his public support for the dam, his parish is exposed to sporadic Freegunjee attacks. The goodwill he enjoyed earlier among the Adivasis provided a considerable protective cover. While his church has been a target of Freegunjee wrath in the past, his own person has been spared so far. Bulchand's exit from Pacheesgarh has added to his vulnerability. I ask him if something is being done to protect the new church. He merely rolls his eyes heavenwards with a sad smile.

'How many times will you let them burn down your church?' I ask.

He continues to smile and says, 'Then Peter came up and said to him, "Lord, how often shall my brother sin against me, and I forgive him? As many as seven

214

times?" Jesus said to him, "I do not say to you seven times, but seventy times seven." Matthew 18: 21–22, my text for this evening's sermon. Come and pray with us.'

I politely decline, saying I have an appointment with some friends at the club. The very next day he is set upon and beaten up mercilessly.

The Freegunjees, on whom the suspicion naturally falls, issue a statement denying their part in it. Lepakshi has a hunch that the Father's assailants are members of the extreme right-wing group who have vowed to get rid of all those who are spreading 'pollution' among their people. Golmal openly espouses the right-wing cause in the days following Bulchand's induction into the Central Cabinet, and the Padre's assailants are never caught.

With the help of the Bushshirt, the Padre manages to keep pressure on Golmal to hunt down the culprits. Lepakshi thinks Golmal will do something to divert attention from the issue. It would be difficult to tell what. Something diabolical. She certainly has the knack for suddenly creating confusion by effecting strange alignments, eliminating distinctions. Finally, the secret nexus between Golmal and the right-wing thugs is out in the open. It ticks away like a watch wrapped in cotton.

We do not have to wait long. On a muggy day, the examinations being just over, a student leader called Lakhota loses his marbles and climbs to the top of the Shiva temple in the center of town. From his heavenly perch, Lakhota entertains his gawking admirers with hair-raising acrobatics. Winding his legs around the central prong of the trishul (trident), he leans back and begins to chant through a bullhorn that all missionary activity should be banned.

It is by now obvious that the tableau on the trishul is not a spontaneous display of lunacy, a single isolated act, but a carefully orchestrated plan with objectives which belie the country-fair joviality of the occasion. The whole of Inderpur seems to have surged towards the temple.

The old couple pushes their cart in which a black mahogany cupboard stands like an upright coffin. The sea of umbrellas parts to let them through. If Golmal is the brain behind this shindig, she has taken good care to cover her tracks and is perhaps enjoying her masterwork from some unknown hideout.

'Tell the prime minister,' commands Lakhota. 'Tell him to pack off all Christian missionaries. Repatriate them immediately.'

A sudden hush falls over the mob and many a gaze is now transferred to the trishul. A few laugh uneasily. Even Lakhota's supporters realize that something is amiss.

There is a big sigh from the crowd, followed by a scream, as Lakhota stands up and striking an athletic pose, shouts wildly through the bullhorn.

'Ban the slaughter of cows. Let the prime minister declare all cows free citizens of India.' Then he loses his balance, bounces several feet down onto the terrace of the multipillared hall, and lies there in a mangled heap.

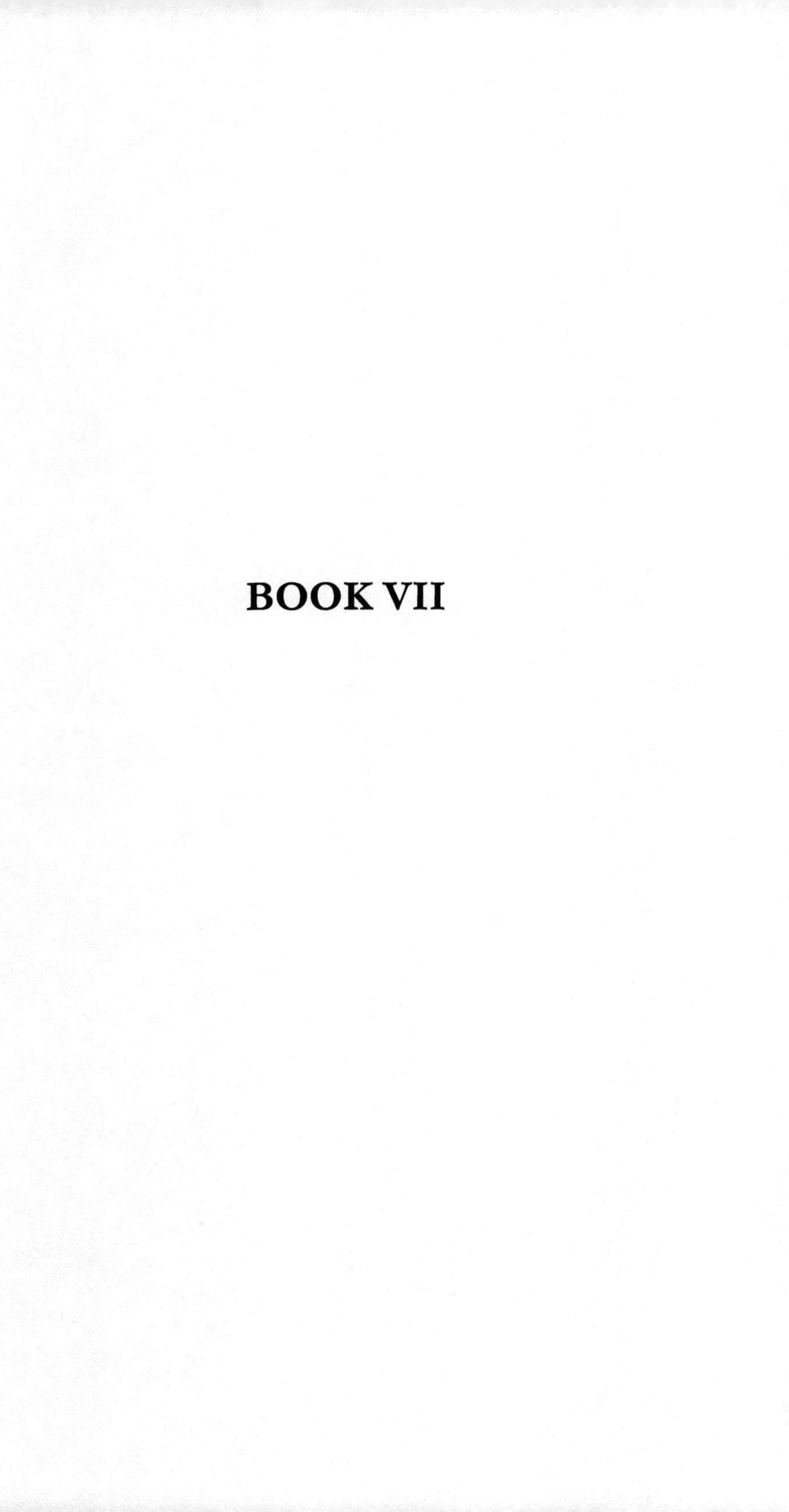

BOOK VII

One day Siri and Maury Lee had lunch at Tangra Masala, where they were served Indian and Chinese fusion food. But the diner was their favored eatery. Siri felt he was in serious danger of becoming one more colorful character, a local eccentric like the subway hermit, someone who provided a sense of continuity to those whose lives had not yet acquired the orderliness of routine. You become a local character by being hollowed out from inside. The deepest human truths that Dr Leavis used to talk about had fled; the well was emptying, its spring had dried up, with a few croaking frogs hopping about in the mud.

Looking at the IT crowd in the diner with their jeans and cool talk, Siri felt very old. They had carved out for themselves a third space, which was different from his. They were the makers of the culture in which they now lived, the titanium generation. The sense of being a wreckage when he first arrived here had returned, and he was adrift once again.

History had gone sour like curdled milk. His past was irrelevant, his knowledge gone stale, like something left undetected during the last cleaning of the fridge. His information was dated, belonged in archives of esoteric happenstance, like the routing of Bonnie Prince Charlie by the Duke of Cumberland at Culloden Moor, the debacle at Ladysmith or the Mass-Observation movement of the thirties, which was the brainchild of the poet Charles Madge; the painter Humphrey Jennings; and the anthropologist Tom Harrisson, who, according to gossip, preferred the company of cannibals to that of his fellow academics.

Siri and Maury Lee were both trying to cope with their loneliness as best they could. All that creative energy which had been channelled towards their chosen profession was looking for another opening.

Siri had always been a one-woman man. Once, Maggie Cartouche of the biology department had made a pass at him while driving him back to Queens from Manhattan, after dinner for a retired colleague. She'd invited him to go up to her place for a nightcap. Jackson Heights was still several blocks away. Siri had gently declined the invitation, but Maggie had suddenly turned to him and kissed him passionately on the mouth.

'Think of poor Cyril,' Siri had pleaded.

'Poor Cyril, indeed,' Maggie had said with a bitter laugh. 'Do you think he is alone in his hotel room at the convention? No siree Bob. Our Cyril is humping that slut Genevieve, his graduate assistant, even as we speak.'

Siri's dad had passed on in his fifties, and had such a public life that he had never had time to worry about his resurgent libido. On the other hand, his father's uncle, Badéchaha, would boldly walk into Hasina Begum's salon in Inderpur and spend the night in the arms of some nubile dancer. His great-aunt never made any fuss, even though she must have most certainly felt slighted.

Badéchacha used to return at dawn glowing with good will. His job as forest officer required him to travel the entire district, roughly the size of Rhode Island. In those days, you travelled on horseback and covered only about thirty miles, spending the night in some remote *dak* bungalow. No one ever mentioned it, but the old boy must have sown a few wild oats in the *mofussil*.

According to Maury Lee, one of the disadvantages of living in Jackson Heights was that you couldn't keep any secrets. Someone was always on the tail of teenage boys and girls who sneaked off to Manhattan for a day.

There was an elemental simplicity in the mating ritual in the England of the sixties. Siri used to spend his summer vacations in London working on his dissertation at the British Museum Library. The elderly

Iranian student in the next room to Siri's used to smuggle in plump peroxide blondes. One night when accosted by Mr Plumbley the land-lord, he'd floored the old man with a curt rejoinder.

'I don't object when you eat ham.'

As a devout Moslem, old Jamal had very strong views on the consumption of ham. Occasionally, however, he did manage to pick up a well-endowed and smartly-turned-out dolly lady. Siri didn't half fancy her.

Maury Lee knew that Bobby Franz, the music man with a higher-than-normal ego-emission rate, had tried tinkling his way into Reeny's bed with a private rendition of the *Moonlight Sonata*. He was told in no uncertain terms to back off, with a p.s. that any future attempts would result in his ass being hauled before the sexual harassment committee, of which Reeny was an active member. The poor bastard, used to having his way with dumb Dora types with cultural pretensions, had felt completely outmaneuvered.

Not too many words were exchanged between Siri and Maury Lee, but each knew what the other was going through. Both Shabnam and Judy, in their different ways, had pulled a *Lysistrata* on them.

Judy had been convinced that an academic lifestyle kept the grey cells vigilant, to a point where they went beyond their brief and kept one's hormones on a leash. As she herself moved from the financially precarious graduate teaching assistant position to tenured faculty, job security relaxed her metabolism, releasing it from anxiety about tomor-row. Grey cells were now no longer under pressure to outperform all other cells. There was truce in the world of cells, of the 'your business is yours and mine is mine' sort. Thus freed from the watchful eye of grey cells, her hormones had begun to stretch their muscles and look around for possible outlets where they could splurge and not be reined in or chided by nosey grey cells. That was the reason, according to her, why so many middle-aged academics dumped their wives and went lust-ing after younger, hero-worshipping bimbos.

When Judy decided to go west with her yoga teacher Samuel Finch,

Maury Lee had helped her pack her bags. He had suspected all along that not all those asanas she had mastered were executed solo by her. Finally, she had confessed that Finch could conflate sex with yoga, and that every time she had a session with him, she felt completely purified. Coming from a molecular biologist, it was a hoot.

As far as Maury Lee could tell, what had brought Gabriella into Siri's life was opera. Gabriella wasn't simply an ass-wiggling, large-breasted broad with a pouty mouth, as people mistakenly thought, but a lovely enormous-eyed diva, like those of days gone by. Their voices could fill Phyllis Tillinghast's living room in Inderpur with the same haunting clarity with which they aimed their arias at the fans in the far-thest balcony at La Scala. Siri said he still remembered the matron in-toning their names with deep reverence before putting the record on the gramophone—names that had a musical ring: Amelita Galli-Curci, Gina Bernelli and Celestina Boninsegna. That larger-than-life-size woman conjured up by Matron Tillinghast, surrendering her soul to music, had been reincarnated in the Junoesque Gabriella.

Lately, this vision had taken to brushing against him; her fingers handing him a cup of chocolate would linger just a trifle longer than was necessary to release her grip on the cup. Her cool touch was like sprinkles of elusive rain after a long drought. It was no surprise, there-fore, that feeling let down, first by Kingman, and left out in the cold by his family, Siri writhed in bed like parched farmland, dreaming of the carnal monsoon in Gabriella's eyes.

When her husband Jimmy had suddenly decided, at age forty, that he was gay, and walked out on her to go and live with his partner, Gab-riella had cried for days; but when Jimmy, feeling guilty about abandon-ing his wife, gave her the apartment and all their worldly possessions, she naturally looked around for a suitable bedfellow. Jimmy had shown no interest in her body for the past seven years, and in bed she had been forced to take the initiative to get any traction out of him.

For the past two years, even that had not been possible, as he had taken to spending the nights away in Connecticut under the pretext of work. He was an architect of considerable talent, but also an expert carpenter, and builders with stinking-rich clients offered him high-paying jobs. He was especially good at panelling. Come to think of it, in the past year or two, Jimmy, who was Guyanese of mixed English, French and Indian descent, had slipped into a Lord Chatterley role and more than once offered his wife, half jokingly, to Siri. In Siri's translation it had meant, 'I would do anything for a friend like you,' nothing more. But it seemed to Maury Lee that beneath the surface pleasantry was a serious admission of Jimmy's failure to satisfy his wife and a strong desire to unload her.

Maury Lee thought that, by any measure, Gabriella was a babe. She took her husband's defection to the gay community as an affront to her womanhood and was hell-bent to retaliate. Poor Siri had no choice, what with Shabnam going celibate suddenly, like Mahatma Gandhi, who had one fine day in South Africa decided that sex was only for the birds. That was the beginning of his Mahatmahood. Siri's resurgent, middle-aged libido having reached a do-or-die stage, he was at that point in his life most vulnerable to damsels in distress.

Gabriella was no Sophia Loren. 'How many women are?' Maury Lee contended. With Gabriella, Siri's mistake was that he overtured when she needed someone to lean on, and now she wanted to finish the symphony like the big B's Fifth, not just with 'Fate knocking on the door' kind of urgency but also with a thunderous finale. She wanted to have his baby.

Siri's affair with Gabriella made the biggest bang ever in Jackson Heights; it was as though a super-sized Diwali firecracker had exploded. She got pregnant.

From then on, Siri's story followed the typical pattern of the fall of the Great-Man kind that the Greeks specialized in. Siri would not give up Gabriella, sense of honor, and all that. He wanted to take care of her and her baby. Unperturbed, Shabnam went about her business, no recriminations or fits of rage. That showed class. In fact, Shabnam was so regal in her role as the betrayed wife that Maury Lee almost instinctively withdrew in awe from her presence.

To give him credit, Siri never complained that Shabnam drove him to it. But he surprised Maury Lee when he said he had grown very fond of Gabriella and couldn't just switch off his yearning for her. Guys can't do that, Maury Lee figured.

Gullu was angry with Shabnam for acting so docile against such momentous public humiliation. Immy was simply embarrassed but also secretly proud. The macho American part in him applauded his dad's prowess in bed, whereas the Indian in him was ashamed, especially because his sister was so unforgiving in her condemnation. But he couldn't quite wipe that 'who-would-have-thought-Dad-had-it-in-him' smirk off his face.

Maury Lee wanted to ask him how he got into this mess, but Siri could not be too explicit about bodily functions. He was too British, trained to keep a stiff upper lip. In the meantime, Shabnam was a picture of dignity and gravity. In order to carry on a conversation with Siri for any length of time, you had to know your Shakespeare, Dante, Dickens, Spinoza and Kant. It was weird that the guy who seemed to be practically sick with abstractions had bodily urges like any one of us. That made him human in Maury Lee's eyes.

In Jackson Heights, Siri became *persona non grata*. With the exception of Thakorji and Bookstore-Nambiar, most people avoided him.

Siri's apartment, with its Tudor exterior and the small patch in the courtyard which he cultivated assiduously, was pleasing to the eye, once you entered the side street where the entrance was, after picking your way through pedestrians milling around shop fronts. He was about to go into retirement without paying off the mortgage. Gabriella's pregnancy was expanding in direct proportion to the contraction of Siri's savings account. He moved in with Gabriella, leaving his meagre savings to Shabnam, who was now the sole mistress of their home.

224

At such a cash-strapped moment, Gabriella's cravings for food grew day by day, extending to fancy French and Japanese cuisine. Why Japanese, Maury Lee asked? Well, simply because ten years before, she had spent a week in Tokyo with her husband and acquired a taste for Sushi—not just your ordinary garden-variety Shushi but the fancy fusion kind which got written about in glossy magazines. Siri was still old-fashioned enough not to go Dutch when eating out; letting a woman pay was simply not done in Nawabi territory. As Gabriella's food intake went international, almost all the restaurants in Jackson Heights serving Argentinean, Uruguayan, Indian, Bangladeshi and Bavarian foods found among their regulars the Nawab and his paramour. Wines from as far away as Greece and Turkey were sampled, along with those of the French, Spanish and Portuguese variety. But in bed, Gabriella gave him pleasure abundantly and variously; Siri couldn't get enough of it.

He said he loved to watch her eat—she had this way of arching her body, thrusting her ass back as far as it would go in the chair and her bosom forward, so that her boobs hovered precariously over a bowl of Hungarian goulash or Kadhai fried red lobsters. She ate, making low animal sounds and flashed a satiated droopy-eyed smile at her man as she smacked her swollen lips. Siri couldn't wait to go home and roll into bed with her. This continued till the meetings at prenatal care classes stipulated that now was the time to lay off sex till the baby arrived. It was going to be a boy.

Maury Lee's loyalty to Siraj was severely tested by his growing passion for Reeny. But he was wary of making sudden moves. From his Inderpur days, he had learnt that when dealing with oriental babes, however emancipated, you must prepare the ground on solid sociological principles. Sex must be stowed away like a Halloween mask, to be taken out only on dark nights. That he was prepared to wait for the right moment must not obscure the fact that it was sheer torture for him to go back to his pad alone, while Siri and Gabriella were making whoopee.

'That about buttons it up: I rest my case,' was the way Reeny reacted to Siri's romantic escapade. She had no need to say 'I told you so.' In her opinion, Siri had reverted to type with knobs on.

This latest face-off between Siri and Reeny handed Maury Lee a diplomatic hot potato that required a finely calibrated response. With the Siri–Gabriella affair reaching its climax, so to speak, Reeny suddenly began to thaw. Maury Lee wasn't sure why. Was she putting him to an 'either Siri goes or I go' kind of test?

All of a sudden he was receiving signals that left no doubt that Reeny was intent on breaking the ice. At Kingman she acted as though she hardly knew him, but returning from a movie in Manhattan she pressed her body against his when they hugged. One day he pulled the car up under a massive billboard; as they smooched, the headlights of a truck coming round the bend blinded them. They drew apart, but not before the truck driver and his buddy began to yodel and whistle. The truck was slowing down as it passed them, and they barely managed to beat the hell out of there, otherwise who knows what might have happened.

'God, what a foozle,' Reeny said, patting her hair in place with both hands. Maury Lee was still in a state of arousal; her raised arms pushed her breasts out.

'Oh for heaven's sake, keep your eyes on the road; don't stare at me like that,' she suddenly screamed. 'That was such a dumb, childish thing to do, stopping there in the dark. What if those goons in the truck had grabbed me? You men are all alike.'

Maury Lee was stunned, and after letting her off in the parking lot, drove away instead of walking her to the door of her apartment. He made straight for a bar, ordered a double martini, downed it, and drove back home. The next day, at the meeting of the curriculum committee, Reeny tried to catch his eye, but he walked briskly away as soon as the discussion was over.

Later, on his way past her office, he heard Reeny's voice raised in anger. Bobby Franz came out looking flustered. He saw Maury Lee and said weakly, 'I was just trying to show my concern. She was crying and I wanted to help.'

'Well, don't waste your sympathy,' Maury Lee said. 'You better watch your step, Bobby.'

There were one or two complaints pending against the guy before the sexual harassment committee of which Reeny was chairperson. There was no conclusive evidence of wrongdoing, but the committee had put Bobby on notice. Maury Lee could see how Bobby's twisted mind worked. The incorrigible music man had decided that the best course to follow was to make friends with Reeny, soften her up enough to call off the inquiry.

Maury Lee knew he was finally making headway with Reeny, but she wanted him to play by her rules. She was making long-term plans, which included marriage. She made it clear to him that he was barking up the wrong tree if he thought he could move in with her without slipping a ring onto the third finger of her left hand.

The mood swings in Reeny were very unnerving. Sometimes she made him feel as though he was getting nowhere with her. Then again, on certain occasions she acted as though he was her only true friend in the world.

Late one afternoon she came to his office and said, 'I want to apologize for the other night.' A few teardrops still glistened in the corners of her eyes, making them seem unusually bright.

'No need for apologies,' Maury Lee said stiffly.

'Oh, don't be such a fuss pot; I can't stand that. I'd prefer it if you cursed me instead.'

'You know I could never do that.' Maury Lee almost choked on the words.

'Then take me home,' she said.

Wordlessly she got into his car and within minutes they were at her place. The apartment was almost completely dark. After she opened the door and turned on the lights, she led him to the sitting room, gave him a beer, and disappeared in her bedroom.

He picked up a copy of *Time* magazine and settled down on a cosy sofa. About fifteen minutes later, the door opened and Reeny came in. She was wearing a bathrobe. Maury Lee continued to flip the pages when she came and sat down next to him.

'I am assuming,' she said, her voice cracking a bit, 'that we are still friends. I had no right to snap at you the way I did. It's just that sometimes I feel you get careless.'

He could sense that she was in a confessional mood and wisely refrained from making any comment. He figured that as long as his silence deepened her resolve to make amends, it'd be foolish to spoil it by saying something stupid.

'You must forgive me if I seem cold and distant sometimes. I am very confused. When I was still at college, I was married to a man who wanted sex of the *Last Tango in Paris* variety. On our wedding night he went wild; it was very degrading. What do you expect? He was from Hyderabad in India and came from a distinguished Muslim family. I fell for his looks hook, line and sinker, and because of his family name my parents were pleased, though he was in his early thirties and I barely eighteen. I grew up in Chicago, but at home we led very traditional lives. I didn't date or have boyfriends like other girls. If he had gradually led me into it, I would have got used to his ways, but he was brutal with me and forced me to do things which I thought only beasts were capable of. That put me off sex for a long time.'

Quietly she shut the door and let the robe slide down to her feet. Although Maury Lee was shivering, he was glued to the spot. Silhouetted in the dim light of the night lamp, she looked like a statue leaning out, round breasted, supple.

Afterwards, bodies relaxed, they lay in bed. Her hand gently caressing his face, she told him how she had lived for the past ten years in a sort of limbo after her marriage had petered out. Nothing like a lasting bond was forged, though the man seemed everything that a girl could

228

wish for. Soon after their wedding, they had gone to Columbus, Ohio, where he was finishing up his doctorate.

'You are probably the best friend I have in this world,' she said rubbing her head on his shoulder.

It did cross Maury Lee's mind that although they kissed and cuddled up with increasing frequency, this new lovey-dovey Reeny was something of a surprise. Why now? he asked himself. Why did she suddenly decide to reveal her past? The story about the guy from Hyderabad was convincing enough. Earlier it was her own dad that Siraj reminded her of; now it was this Hyderabadi guy. Two strikes against Siraj. Bluntly put, why, after almost three years of playing fox-bunny, was she now willing to shake her maracas?

She had always said she would 'decide' when it was time for them to get hitched. However, the suspicion that his loyalty to Siraj was an issue with her and that she wanted to isolate her adversary completely by turning her own man into a craven traitor continued to niggle at the back of his mind. The way they had been doing things together for the past year or so, it was obvious that Reeny and he were headed toward a permanent settlement. Was she now seeking to neutralize him in what was for her a full-fledged war against Siri? Maury Lee was walking a tightrope as he struggled to remain solidly within Siri's almost depleted camp, while making every possible gesture to be her man of the hour.

His bachelor days of TV dinners and cold bed seemed to be over, but his ability to help Siri in his hour of need was severely curtailed. Everything he said or did in defending him upset Reeny, so that he was forced to carry on his campaign in secret. He looked around for possible allies who could help, without offending Reeny. Maury Lee found that Immy's wife Sally was the first to recover from the shock of her father-in-law's infidelity and was prepared to make peace with him. Sally had real talent for dealing with toddlers. She had become the mainstay at her school and was paid twice as much as any Kingman faculty.

At the same time, Gullu's strong maternal instincts had begun to assert themselves and she was next to cave in. She made plans to welcome her half brother into this world, while Sally started knitting mittens and secretly registered the baby at her fancy school.

It was a difficult birth involving a caesarean section, but the baby was deliciously cuddlesome. The infant and his mother were like one of those pictures in which baby Jesus looks up at the Madonna with a dimpled cheek and upward smiling gaze. Even Shabnam was seduced when one day word reached her that the baby was ill and wouldn't stop crying after two visits to the doctor. The door to Gabriella's apartment suddenly burst open and Shabnam picked up the child and swung it about, cooing to it in Urdu until it burped. And lo and behold it flashed a very Siri smile at her. She gathered it in her arms and pressed it to her bosom, laughing and crying at the same time.

But while his family came around, the Jackson Heights crowd who had set Siri on a pedestal in the past began to shun him. Greetings were strained, and those who used to hurry to the front of the shop for a chat pretended to be busy with customers or slunk further back into the interior. The Jackson Heights verdict was that Siri had broken the cardinal rule of an Indian public figure. He had openly committed adultery and not tried to hide it. Chitral, who had got his younger sister-in-law pregnant when his wife was in hospital, was the most vociferous in his denunciation. He had managed to get his sister-in-law married to a young distant cousin whom he had sponsored to the States. Almost everyone noticed how much the cousin's baby resembled Chitral, but no one accused him of any wrongdoing. That was the Indian way. Siri had flouted that time-honored convention by admitting paternity. His family, who should have ostracized him, rallied round him, but in general, Jackson Heights was freaked out—didn't know how to handle the situation.

❧ 2 ❧

After the Gabriella affair broke, Siri withdrew into a monastic silence. Instead of defending himself, he remained mute. When a congressman or senator gets caught with his pants down, he immediately calls a press conference, and with his wife by his side, at first denies any wrong-doing, and then resigns two days later, saying but for that one momentary transgression, which he grudgingly admits, his record of public service so far had been spotless. Then he disappears from public eye, only to make it back after a decent interval.

But Siri was made of different stuff. It was the end of the spring semester and teaching was almost over. He retreated into deep solitude.

Most saints of the traditional Indian variety scored points with a gabby crowd of worshippers by striking awe in them with their capacity to sit tight for years without uttering a word. Gandhi had used silence as a weapon to wield moral authority, similar to the sages who hid themselves away in hoary jungles and subsisted on fruit and goats' milk. The British, after a long spell of dithering, had understood Gandhi's power. In him they had found a man who had gone one better than their own famous reserve, clamped up his lips, and battened down the hatches. That silence was scary. The British understood speeches; that's why they felt closer to Nehru. They had Haileybury, the place where men of officer material were trained to dissect the discourse of possible insurgency. They had no idea how to decode silence, the nightmare of semioticians. Maury Lee had heard that in the old days, when guys like Alexander the Great attacked Indians, they'd met him with loud yells from the backs of lumbering elephants, which were shot down by

Greek archers. Gandhi's silence had proved to be lethal.

Siri's was not.

At least Maury Lee didn't think so. The older faculty tut-tutted, a bit taken aback to find Siri—always so correct and proper—in a tangy pickle. Siri had never been known to possess any hubris, but his winning the Best Teacher Award seven times over the last twenty years had stirred jealousy among those who secretly attributed his success in the classroom not to deep knowledge but to his gift as a speaker, in which his prim English accent was said to hide many a hole.

The younger faculty, led by Reeny, were out for his blood. She wrote a letter in the college paper calling for Siri to resign for misusing 'his hegemonic position' to take advantage of a disenfranchised female, a poor woman abandoned by her husband, economically vulnerable to predatory males. Reeny wrote that the marauding oriental male in Siri had finally broken through the veneer of Western sophistication; his sort couldn't see a woman except as an object of pleasure, a commodity. She knew of such people among her own relatives in Bangladesh. Underneath, they were all the same; the border may have divided the subcontinent, but the male creature on either side was still the same under the skin. Raping women was his birthright, and so on. Coming from her, an insider, the charges carried all the weight of shared subcontinental history.

To counter Reeny's move to oust Siri, his past students launched a Website called 'Support Professor Amolini.' From all over the county, old Kingmanians sent messages of protest against any move to force Siri to resign. Some said the only reason they did not transfer to other colleges after their sophomore year was because they wanted to take more courses with Siri. Some said what he did in his spare time was his business; this was America at the fag end of the twentieth century, not the McCarthy-era fifties.

Some messages from women hinted at long-suppressed transgressions by those two senior faculty who had jumped on Reeny's bandwagon to appease Hackett. One young woman threatened to expose financial fraud involving Hackett's past job in a company dealing in polymer products. Insider trading was mentioned, hastily denied by Hackett, but not with sufficient vigor, raising specters of an Enron-type disaster.

Maury Lee believed Siri had not been playing with a full deck when he screwed Gabriella. Everyone knew he couldn't do his taxes without help from H&R Block or buy his own clothes unless Shabnam was there to guide him. Maury Lee speculated that he may have been traumatized by Shabnam's accusations that he had stunted her growth. He couldn't take that. Without Shabnam, he was like a tourist stranded in Papua New Guinea after being robbed of his wallet and passport.

He had literally sleepwalked into Gabriella's bed. The guy had his eyes wide open but there was no Siri behind them, only an exposed flesh itching from a rash. To those who were eager to beat up on Siri, Maury Lee wanted to say, 'Guys, have you ever seen our Gabriella stepping out of a shower with only a towel around her head? Neither have I, but you can imagine its deadly impact, can't you? Which one among you will have the guts or inclination to slink away bashfully as your mama might want you to? For poor Siri, Shabnam was his wife and mama rolled into one, and now she was doing the pistol-packing act. The guy was disoriented. Out steps Gabriella of honeydew bosom and stands before him with open arms. He had no chance. It was carnage. He could have stopped himself only by slitting his throat, from which odd moaning sounds had begun to emanate as she wrapped herself around him. Guys, guys, have a heart, spare a thought for the vanquished. Say a prayer and admit, 'there but for the grace of God go I.'"

Maury Lee wasn't trying to condone Siri's fall from grace. Far from it. Like a good lawyer, he was merely sketching the defense, the extenuating circumstances, ferreting out the blood-stained glove that wouldn't fit the suspect's large paws, sowing doubts in the minds of the jurors as to whether it was lust-driven folly or a cold-blooded act. Cold was not the word one wanted here, as was obvious from the outcome. It was self-defense in the face of certain annihilation.

By and large, Jackson Heights, which was in the throes of its summer sale, with myriad tiny light bulbs turning night into day, remained divided on the issue. The women were too embarrassed and confused by the event to venture an opinion. The Bangladeshis treated it as a great calamity and tried to ignore it as something the Indians had to deal with. The Pakistani men, like their Indian neighbors, blamed Shabnam for letting it happen by neglecting Siri. They said such things would happen if the womenfolk get too uppity, and begin to act like American women, asking for more power at home. They said 'What is this power thing anyway?' Power was no good unless it was shared.

Durbar had the only realistic approach. He said let the storm pass. The more you goad Siri to repent, the more he will withdraw into Olympian silence. Once passion is spent, he would return to his family.

The smug crowd in Jackson Heights—yes there were a few, like Chitral—teetered among themselves, saying, after all Siraj was a Muslim, although he acted like a *gora*. Maury Lee believed dudes like Chitral were monogamous not from choice but from necessity. Most of them had wives who were a cross between Zeena the Warrior Princess and Buffy the Vampire Slayer. These guys were unused to discarding their women in favor of younger flesh. That was the way of Nawabs and Thakurs. No big deal.

For most men in Jackson Heights the Gabriella episode was like going back to the India or Pakistan of their childhood. The Nawabzada had taken a new concubine. The bazaar gossip was that the Begum had dried up and the Nawab was desperate to cast his seed; and then he accidentally stumbled upon this obliging *gori* madam. It was in the nature of things. Monogamy was overrated, a pseudo-Western concept, a postcolonial hang-up.

Mentally, the older inhabitants of Jackson Heights still lived in their village or town in Bihar, Punjab, Gujarat, or Chittagong. They had adopted only those tricks of the trade from the West as would help them rake in the moolah. Out on the street in shops, they acted like modern Western traders, put up sales signs at the drop of a hat, cooked books carefully with the help of lawyers instead of bribing their way out, Indian fashion. But at home they stayed well within the cocoon of caste and community, venturing out only when the coast was clear.

Chitral was among the most vociferous in his condemnation. Only Thakorji silenced him with one fierce reproachful stare and chided those who had so ungratefully turned away from Siri.

Once, Chitral hailed Maury Lee from his shop, invited him in, made him sit down on a stool, and told his assistant to make coffee for him. While the young man was fiddling with the coffee machine, Chitral sidled up to Maury Lee and said, 'You and I are *Ça va, Ça va* right?' He rubbed his two forefingers together as he said that. 'Why should we criticize Siraj Sahib; after all he is only human being, right?'

He meant Siraj was only human, but Maury Lee could see beneath his sympathetic pose a barely concealed leer. Right at that moment, his sister-in-law came in with his lunch box. Her second pregnancy was at its peak; it was an any-moment situation. She had deep, kohl-smeared probing eyes, and she gave Maury Lee a searching look. There were whispers, during which Chitral slipped across to her a large wad of greenbacks.

She was obviously making him pay for past favors. Maury Lee couldn't help beaming at her encouragingly a 'You go, girl' kind of smile.

Chitral almost fainted behind the counter when Maury Lee said to him, 'If you are handing out cash to everybody, I wouldn't mind some for myself.'

The young woman was not ashamed of her distended tummy, and seemed to wear it like a trophy, putting it on display like a traditional Indian woman whose sole purpose in life is to prove to her husband's family that she can breed and breed fast and good. She gave a broad smile and nudged Maury Lee with her copious tummy as she passed him. Thick beads of sweat covered Chitral's forehead, smearing his big vermilion mark.

He tried to shoo her off, speaking rapidly in Hindi. She knew that Maury Lee understood what was going on. She decided to put the screws on Chitral, taking advantage of Maury Lee's presence. Chitral looked crestfallen and silently handed over the rest of the cash from the till. Here was robbery in progress. Then she drove off. Chitral buried his head in an old-fashioned ledger; he had been gypped, and he couldn't do anything about it.

The following week, Chitral spotted Maury Lee as he emerged from the neighboring grocery and practically dragged him to his shop.

'You and me *Ça va, Ça va*, right?'

'Right,' Maury Lee said with a laugh.

Chitral's smile broadened. 'Why I like you ? Because you are spitting image of my brother who died in accident in Chicago.'

'I am sorry to hear that,' Maury Lee said politely.

'I am a graduate of Agra University. Professor Turner taught us poetry at college in Agra. What a great teacher was Turner Sahib. A real, true-blue English gentleman. Ah ha ha, I also know poetry. I've taken sudden liking to you, why um? Because,' he whined, 'because we are *Ça va, Ça va* and because you are exact copy of my brother.'

His voice shook as he touched his eyes with one end of his handkerchief. 'He died five years ago. Balaji's wish,' his eyes rose skywards. Then he put his hand on his chest, closed his eyes, and began to recite.

> Cannon to the right of them
>
> Cannon to the left of them
>
> Volleyed and thundered
>
> Into the valley of Death
>
> Rode the six hundred.

He recited jerkily, absurdly flinging his arms around to simulate exploding cannonballs. Then, traipsing to the marble-topped table, he pressed a bell and told his assistant to make coffee.

'Yes, yes, sorry. I am not happy man. You are my younger brother. You do not tell about money.'

'What money?'

'The money I gave my relative woman the other day.' Chitral said.

'Oh, you mean the cash you gave your sister-in-law?' Maury Lee said. 'No, why should that matter to me? I am sure you always give cash to poor relatives. You are such a kind and generous man.'

'So, so,' Chitral said, we two are *Ça va, Ça va*, no?'

Maury Lee didn't speak for a while. Chitral was the ultimate ass kisser.

'You know, Chitral Seth,' Maury Lee said 'those who live in glass houses should not throw stones at others. You end up breaking your own glass, understand? It costs you money to fix it.'

'Yes, yes. No throwing stone. That's good.'

'Let the sleeping dogs lie.' Maury Lee winked.

'Sleeping dogs. Yes, yes, that's good, very good.'

'Very *Ça va, Ça va*,' Maury Lee said.

Siraj began to spend most of his spare time in his office at Kingman so as to avoid meeting anyone he knew on the street. Once his misgivings about late fatherhood lost some of their thorn-in-the flesh quality, the little pink butterball in the crib, now in his sixth month, began to work his hands and feet, sticking his tongue out to run it along his wet mouth. His large brown eyes, so very much like Immy's, followed Siri around, accompanied by gurgling pleas to be taken out for a jaunt in his baby carriage, his tiny heart beating like mad.

Siri looked forward to going back to Gabriella's apartment. By the time he arrived, Gullu had come and gone, leaving behind some colorful toy for her baby brother, who registered his approval with shrieks of delight. In fact, Gullu and the baby talked to each other onomatopoeically. Siri thought women had this amazing ability to regress to the primal stage, to communicate with prelexical creatures. That's why there were so many women naturalists, like Jane Goodall or Dian Fossey, not to mention Joy Adamson with her Elsa, who spent years in dense African forests.

One Monday evening, Siri was rearranging his papers on the desk in his office. He had been working on his Inderpur manuscript and just finished a chapter on its role as a safe haven for the freedom fighters of 1857, whom the British had tried to track down without much success, when there was a knock on the door. In the dim light of the corridor there were two men, a barrel-chested fellow with hair closely cropped to the point of baldness and a smaller man, with a twitch in his bull-like neck and small darting eyes. Both flashed their badges at him, said they were from the FBI, and asked him if he would mind answering a few questions.

Even before he could step aside from the door, they walked in and distributed themselves in two different corners.

'Look here, Professor, why don't you sit down and relax,' said the small guy, his smooth eyebrowless face making him look like a pantyhose-covered crook caught on closed-circuit TV.

'This won't take long. Tell me, what kinda name is that? I mean Amolini. 'Is that Italian? Amolini?' the big fellow called Schumacher said.

'No, it's Indian. I am from India.'

'Really? Most Indian guys I know are called Patels. Ha, ha, you know, Motel-Patels,' Schumacher said laughing at his own joke.

'Quite,' Siri said, trying to sound normal. 'It's a Persian name. Originally my people were from Iran but migrated to India in the seventeenth century.'

'Really? How interesting,' said the small fellow who was called Murphy.

'You must be a Muslim then, am I right, seeing that you are from Iran and all?' Murphy's small round eyes were like shriveled jelly beans.

'I don't follow any religion,' Siri said self-consciously, feeling foolish. 'But yes, I was born to Muslim parents in India. But not all Iranians are Muslims,' he added, regaining his composure. 'There are also Zoroastrians, like the conductor Zubin Mehta of the New York Philharmonic. His people also came to India in the fifteenth century or thereabouts.' How does one give a compressed version of India's early migrants without reducing it to a few bald sophomoric statements? Siri wondered.

There was a long pause during which the agents looked at each other. Siri couldn't help noticing that Murphy's smile had stiffened and his eyes were two black holes.

'How about that,' said Schumacher, the beefy chap with a smile that revealed small, rat-like nicotine-stained teeth. 'Tell me, is it true that Muslim men are allowed four wives? You only have one, right? You looking to fill the quota?'

'That's enough,' barked Murphy. 'Apologize to the Professor here right now,' he said to Schumacher. 'There is no call to be rude, Bill.'

'Didn't mean to offend, Prof,' Schumacher said to Siri. 'Been one long tough day. Trying to be friendly like, that's all. I have great respect for men of learning, no matter where they come from.'

After nearly twenty years in the US, Siri was still surprised by the sudden descent from official formality to brash familiarity in speech and manner among a certain type of American bureaucrats. It could be unnerving and threatening to one's self-esteem. In India, too, such a sudden collapse of social barriers was getting to be routine. On trains or planes one expected to be treated to third-degree questioning within minutes of locking eyes with strangers. When trapped in a street riot, one had to be prepared to run, cutting a grotesque figure, hands flailing, mouth frothing, if one didn't want to be socked by a truncheon-wielding policeman who was trained to strike first and ask questions later. How very civilized the British Bobby was by comparison.

'Let's get to the point,' said Siri. 'What's all this about? Why are you here?' he asked Murphy.

There was a long pause during which Schumacher sucked in his cheeks, wandered towards a bookcase, and tried to read the titles.

The FBI trained its agents well; they set their own pace. Those in authority remained impervious to a citizen's attempt to establish an upper hand, especially if he or she happened to possess an air of class. Such men had to be taught who was in the driver's seat. It was an old trick, and it always worked. Government officials were the same everywhere. In India they had perfected this art of talking up to the superiors and down to those whom fate or circumstance delivered into their charge. Their type thrived on what the Bard called 'little great authority.'

Siri was tired and hungry but decided to be patient so as not to give Murphy another chance to show who called the shots.

'There are a hell of a lot of books on Shakespeare here, Ed,' Schumacher said to his colleague.

Siri didn't take the bait. The comment carried a hint that the duo would have liked to find something more incriminating than Shake-speare. He understood that the detectives were trying to lull him into a comfortable state of mind so as to catch him off guard. The two of them were enacting a slightly modified version of good cop-bad cop, with its carrot-and-stick subtext. They were rendering the FBI version of the straight-man-and-clown act, the suave Dean Martin and bumbling adolescent Jerry Lewis. The red-faced big man was a consummate performer who knew how to push all the right buttons and drive you over the edge. The hastily offered apology by Schumacher relieved Murphy of the need to pull punches. Unaccustomed to street language pared down to naked aggression, men like Siri were struck dumb.

'Tell me, Professor,' said Murphy, affecting the suave manner of a student at a graduate seminar, 'Tell me, do you seriously believe that a man should betray his country in order to save his friend?'

If Siri knew what he was getting into, he would not have answered that question. Though formulated like an academic query, it had an undertow of deferred menace. He didn't see what was coming.

'Well, I must say,' he began tentatively, 'I haven't yet been presented with that dilemma, but I do believe that if you think that your country's policies are such that they undermine certain basic principles on which our civilization is founded, than you must take strong exception to that.'

There was a long pause during which Murphy seemed to be lost in thought, his eyes closed as though he was trying to listen to a signal from outer space. Schumacher produced an apple from his overcoat pocket, and after polishing it on his lapel, began to skin it with a flick knife. As he bent down to get a better grip of the excessively polished apple, his tummy bulged out to expose a holster with a shiny object. The sight of the gun was less unnerving than the blade of the knife from which bounced off little circular spots of light. No doubt Murphy also had a gun well concealed but ready to fire when necessary.

'You must always skin the apple before eating, otherwise it sticks in your throat, don't you agree Professor?' Schumacher observed.

'Who decides which of your country's policies are wrong?' Murphy asked loudly, focusing his dull reptilian eyes on Siri.

'Well, of course a properly trained mind should be able to make the right decision without any shilly-shallying. You need to look at things in a detached, dispassionate manner and not rush to judgment,' Siri said.

'But if a democratically elected government pursues policies that violate some of these so-called moral principles, who are we to judge? You mean you are right and the rest of the world is wrong?' Murphy said.

Schumacher was engrossed in consuming the apple. He munched it, making loud chomping, sucking noises.

'It is possible for a man of sound judgment to be right while everyone else is howling for violent action that might compromise the nation in moral terms. There are several examples in history.' Siri had almost imperceptibly slipped into his professorial role.

Schumacher had polished off the apple and was wiping his mouth with a greasy handkerchief. He suddenly spoke loudly and clearly.

'Listen, Professor, do you know a student called Dan Colby?'

Siri was taken aback by this intrusion. He was beginning to warm up to the famous Forsterian caveat about choosing between country and friend, which had been fiercely debated during his undergraduate days in Cambridge. Notorious spy alumni like Blunt, Burgess, and Philby had muddied its meaning. Although it did not figure in a big way in *A Passage to India*, it set into relief the friendship between the Indian Dr Aziz and the college principal Fielding.

He told Schumacher that he did not recall this Colby fellow.

'I believe he changed his name to Pendragon when he was here. That was what he went by,' Schumacher said.

'Pendragon? Daniel Pendragon? Yes, indeed, I do remember him. He was a member of my Shakespeare class. Not a very attentive student, I am afraid. Most interested in elves and goblins, felt more at home with them, I suppose. That was a good ten years ago, in the mid-eighties; I believe my colleague Professor Irene Rumplemayer supervised his work. The medieval period was her area of specialization. She retired sometime back. I am sure Professor Miriam Shapiro, our chairperson, would have more information about him. She should be here any minute now. I am dining at her place tonight. If you don't mind my asking you, is Daniel in some sort of trouble?'

'He is and so are you, Professor,' Schumacher said sticking his hands into his pockets and looking like a polar bear.

'I must say I don't understand.'

'You will, Professor, you will. Here's the thing: How come Pendragon claims you inspired him to blow up the Queensboro Bridge?' Schumacher said.

'What? This is ridiculous. Can you explain what your colleague is talking about?' Siri said to turning to Murphy, who had been standing impassively looking at the rain falling steadily across the quadrangle.

'I am afraid you need to explain something to us first,' Murphy said, abandoning his collegial stance. His face had gone white as a sheet, and his round eyes in his yellow face flickered with frank contempt.

'If Mr Pendragon did only one course with you, as you claim, how is it that he mentions you repeatedly, not only in the margin of his sketches, but also in the suicide note addressed to his mother in which he states quite clearly that he is fulfilling a long-given pledge to his mentor, in this case, you. Here is a photocopy of his plan to demolish the Queensboro Bridge.'

Utterly bewildered, Siri sat down again and slowly read the slightly crumpled copy of the original. In the left-hand corner of the top sheet was a crude pencil sketch of the bridge with its tall scaffoldings at both ends and the long cables on which it is suspended. There were several squiggles and short illegible sentences under the diagram, which seemed to be drawn by a shaky hand. Arrows pointed to the underside struts to which explosives were to be fixed. Pendragon had also planned to kill many people while they were trapped on the bridge.

Siri realized that the FBI men expected to find something incendiary in his office to back up their charge that he had something to do with Pendragon's utterly insane plan. They were looking for some proof that would link him as an agent provocateur to the unfortunate demented fellow. It was beginning to sink in that behind Murphy's stodgy exterior lurked a ruthless Gestapo mentality.

On another sheet at the top there were certain occult looking symbols followed by a long note in Pendragon's hand.

'This is my message to the world. I am following this course to protest the policies of the National Rifle Association, advocates of capital punishment and antiabortion goons who kill innocent doctors. My country has betrayed me by not putting these subhuman monsters behind bars where they belong. Nothing is done to stop this assault on our basic freedoms, otherwise tragedies like Columbine would not happen. Who is really responsible for Columbine but those who make it possible? The government does not do the right thing. In a sense, the government is the country. As my friend and mentor Professor Siraj Amolini taught us 'if you have to choose between betraying your country and a friend, you should have the moral courage to choose the friend.' My friends are these doctors and those innocent kids who lost their lives at Columbine. I am doing what I am doing to awaken the frozen conscience of our country. Let us shake it up. Let this be a lesson to everyone.'

Actually, what good old Morgan Forster had said was more complicated and nuanced than the rather blunt paraphrase of young Pendragon's feverish imagination. Talk about impressionable kids. Pendragon had been hooked on tales of witches and fairies even before he came to Kingman. Siri recalled that the boy had been more interested in Hamlet's father's ghost or Banquo's spirit than any other student in his class. Next to ghosts, Pendragon's favorite people were Knights of the Round Table, and his senior thesis had focused on Mallory's *Morte D'Arthur*. He wore long capes and green felt hats with a feather stuck rakishly in the red band. During his junior year he'd changed his name from

Colby to Pendragon and was known to his friends as the Green Knight.

Kingman in those days attracted a few oddballs. Whereas students at other institutions stuck metal objects in their tongues and ear lobes, and painted their hair purple or red, Kingman mavericks dressed like Sir Galahad and wore historical costumes, making the lawn look like a fancy dress ball during the spring term. One Hamlet-fixated young man carried a plastic Poor Yorick skull in his coat pocket and took fencing lessons. Knee-length floral evening gowns with oriental designs were not unusual among Kingman women.

Dan Colby, alias Daniel Pendragon, was no ordinary nut. He read commentaries on medieval literature and was a favorite of Rumplemeyer's, who, while very well trained academically, was herself like something out of *Cadfaels*, the BBC series based on a medieval monk who doubles as a detective. Professor Rumplemeyer could read the poem *Pearl* in the Northwest Midland dialect of fourteenth-century England. She had retired in 1994, but when Colby/Pendragon attended Kingman, the winds of change had already swept away Chaucer as mandatory reading for English majors, and any student showing interest in her area received extra personal attention. She served food based on archaic recipes during make-up classes at her home in Brooklyn Heights, which was something like a museum of medieval art. She had her windows fitted with stained glass, where reposed saints and angels and knights sticking spears into fire-breathing dragons.

Pendragon was particularly taken with the Green Knight, who sprang up after every beheading by Sir Gawain. In his mind, Forster's statement had been translated into something like a schoolboy oath of All for One, and One for All. According to the boy's hapless mother, the virus of chivalry he'd caught at Kingman had festered over the years. When she discovered the sketches of the Queensboro Bridge in her son's room, she realized that her son had cast himself in the role of a medieval warrior ready to strike down the fierce dragon of social injustice.

'What do ya make of it? Anything ring a bell?' Schumacher asked

Siri when he handed back the diagram of the bridge.

'I can't make head or tail of it. All I can say is that I am not responsible if a former student distorts what was said in class and ten years later uses it to justify some mad scheme of his.'

'The question is, why, of all the faculty here, he only picked you and what you taught him?' Murphy said.

'I couldn't say.'

'You've still not answered my question. Do you or do you not believe that you should betray your country to help a friend?' Murphy persisted.

'Bluntly put like that it sounds dire,' Siri said. 'But that's not what E.M. Forster, who wrote that in a book of essays, intended to convey.'

Siri had this strange sensation that he had been in this situation before, but where and when he couldn't remember. Maybe it was in Inderpur, when the local rags published a vicious canard about his being a Pakistani spy simply because an old cousin of his father's, who'd migrated to Lahore after Partition, had come down to visit Ammeejan. He and his daughter had been at Ajmer to attend the Urus feast at the *dargah* of the saint Chishti, equally revered by Hindus and Muslims.

That had been reason enough for the rags to blow up the story into a vicious tale of national betrayal. Although most of his friends had stood by him, and colleagues like Saradhi had exposed the hollowness of the charge by cleverly extracting a confession from the reporter who had been bribed by Bulchand's flunkeys to publish those lies, the question of his loyalty to the country had been bandied about in the streets of Inderpur. It had destroyed his mother's will to live after her long bout with asthma.

'If you would let us look around your office, we'll be out of here in no time. We need to make a report to our boss. I would like to check your drawers first, while Billy here looks into your filing cabinet,' Murphy said.

Siri should have objected or inquired if the men had a warrant to conduct a search, but he was so taken aback by the sheer absurdity of Pendragon's plan to blow up the bridge that he could just nod his head.

The last few months had been harrowing, to say the least, but the enormity of what Pendragon had dragged him into simply paralyzed him. He was at the end of his tether, his spirit broken. He moved to the upholstered chair and tried to read the new issue of *Shakespeare Quarterly*, but his mind was racing like a car going downhill without brakes. He just sat there feeling numb.

As in Inderpur, here too a Muslim qualified as one of the usual suspects, when some fanatic went bananas and blew up a luxury hotel or an embassy. You attracted attention of every dim-witted sleuth. Political Mafiosi looking for someone to take the fall pointed their bloody fingers at you. No two ways about it. Hitler's tack for keeping his gas chambers running at full capacity was to blame the Jews for Germany's defeat in World War I. People like Schumacher got a special kick out of this 'guilt by association' sport because the rules that govern it are simple. It requires no great talent. You develop a knack for it pretty quick; it is like being able to tell by the sound of its transmission whether a car is American or Japanese.

Maybe Nasreen Babukhan was right, maybe he was a quixotic fuddy-duddy in rusty old armor with too many chinks to keep even the rain out, let alone the slings and arrows of outrageous fortune.

If your country gives you a black eye for no apparent reason, there is no guarantee that the US won't follow suit. You may take yourself out of your country but you cannot take your country out of you. That sounds clever and amusing until you find yourself at the center of the same macabre joke. Call it woman's intuition, but Shabnam was quicker to grasp this truth. Back in 1993, after the fanatical attempt to demolish the basement of the World Trade Center, she'd dreamt that someone had vandalized her parent's graves in Bombay.

If some crazy student in a misguided moment scribbled your name on a piece of paper, it brought the FBI knocking on your door. Any act of demented larceny washed away your entire past, your long career as a teacher, your Cambridge, your Shakespeare, the history of your illus-

trious family stretching back two centuries, the long chandeliered corridors of your old house with its aura of a gracious past, the chronicles
recording the exploits of your heroic forbears, the way the crowds
parted respectfully in the Kasbah to let your aristocratic mother pass,
the honors bestowed on the patriarchs of the family by the Mughal
emperor and later by the British viceroy in recognition of their contri-
bution to society, all went out the window. 'Muslim'—that one word
twisted your entire personal history into a horror comic, leaving you
only the two choices offered by Kafka's Titorelli: 'temporary acquittal
or indefinite postponement of your trial.' Nothing more.

Put that way, it sounded too pat, like one of Reeny's sound bites.
But the visit from the FBI carried that message loud and strong. You
might proclaim your secular credentials from the housetops, but when
it came to bare essentials, to Murphy and Schumacher you were a 'person of interest.'

What Siri was up against was a form of organized ignorance. Lepakshi used to make fun of his 'talk no evil' variety of political wisdom. She
always said he was a danger to himself. In her opinion, something prevented him from looking beyond people's faces into their hearts.

'You are like your hero, Nehru,' Lepakshi said, 'dreaming of the
impossible dream of nonalignment. The world will not let you remain
unaligned.'

Lepakshi was right. The world was like his old Fooaji, who even in
her nineties had continued to pull strings from deep within the *zenana*
to get every single boy or girl attached to an influential family. To her,
bachelorhood or spinsterhood was an unnatural act which would bring
down Allah's wrath. Every household in Inderpur had similar interfer-
ing aunts and uncles. His Fooaji had proposed a marital alliance between him and a politically powerful Muslim dynasty from Bhopal, to
secure his future before he went to England. If she had had her way, by
age thirty he would have turned into one of these pan-chewing, decadent aristocrats vegetating in some cobwebby *kothi*.

'You are a sitting duck for those who cannot mentally comprehend a completely neutral perch,' Lepakshi had said. 'Someone will be tempted to take a pot shot at you, even in America. So do be careful,' she had reiterated at Inderpur Railway Station.

Siri got up and pulled out his much-thumbed copy of *Two Cheers For Democracy*, in which Forster had written: 'I hate the idea of *causes*, and if I had to choose between betraying my country and betraying my friend, I hope I should have the guts to . . .'

'If you must know, this is what Forster says.'

The door opened at that moment and Miriam walked in. She stared at the two men and asked Siri who they were.

'Ma'am, we are from the FBI. We have been having a little chat with the Professor here.'

'What about?' Miriam asked Siri, ignoring the two men completely.

'They found my name scribbled in Daniel Pendragon's papers. They have been questioning me about him,' Siri said.

'Let us see your warrant,' Miriam said, sitting down in Siri's chair behind the desk and extending her hand without a glance at Murphy. 'I am the chairperson of this department and I demand that you show me your warrant, otherwise I am going to charge you for trespassing and unauthorized intrusion.'

Hand still extended she said, 'I hope you didn't answer any questions Professor Amolini.'

'Well, I did answer some of the questions put to me . . .'

'You shouldn't have without my permission.' Her voice carried just a hint of annoyance.

Looking at Siri's troubled face, the rebel in Miriam had surfaced, and when she was in that mood she was unstoppable. She looked at the visitors for the first time and in a quiet but withering tone she said, 'You have some nerve coming in here without a warrant and playing the bully. We will report this matter to Albany. We will ask our Senator Durbar Singh to find out who gave you the A-OK for unauthorized entry into official premises. This is a college, not a public park. If you don't beat it before I finish counting to three, I will get our team of lawyers to twist your tail.

Siri was so startled by Miriam's lapse into street language that he didn't even notice when the two men shuffled sheepishly out of his office. How swiftly had she taken charge of the situation, matching their menacing lingo with her simulated, underworld tough talk. She had read the scenario as soon as she entered his office and concluded from the way Schumacher chewed gum leaning against the wall that these were law enforcement bureaucrats. From the word go, she had let it be known who was the boss. That's what Americans did so well, assert their rights. That's what all this talk about the First Amendment (or was it the Fourteenth—he really couldn't tell the difference after all these years) was all about. He had reacted like a typical Indian, assuming guilt where there was none, simply because someone claiming to represent law and order had told him to do so.

Miriam was already calling Durbar's secretary in Albany. She shook her head and said, 'I hope you didn't say anything that could be blown into a federal case, Siri.'

'No. no,' Siri answered fumbling for words.

Out in the corridor a chill wind hit his face refreshingly. He knew exactly how the Finzi Continis, whose predicament he had discussed last week in his class, must have felt in detention when those overbearing Gestapo officers pushed them around.

Epilogue

❧ 1 ☙

I was done with Inderpur back in 1980 when I packed my bags and fled to the US with my family. As in 1857, the story of that royal town has moved into perpetuities which defy any attempt to resolve them. Jackson Heights and Kingman have also moved onto a new plane, new lifestyle. My sense of living on sufferance has grown acute, and my thoughts have turned homewards toward old Inderpur, my lost city. In coming to the US, I have become yet another kind of ghost, fading slowly like a robed figure on a Chinese vase.

Sometimes I see myself growing old in Inderpur, dozing in a rocking chair in the Kutcherry. Over the portico of the arcade would be flowerpots watered every morning by the maid.

I see my Ammeejan as she was when she walked down the street for the first time in her life. A year had gone by since Abbajan had departed this world. Ammeejan had surrendered the family farms to Uncle Jehangir's family and retained the *kothi*. It was difficult to maintain the old life style on the depleted income of the family, and the car was taken out of the garage only for longer excursions. It was late November, crisp and bracing—industrial smog lay in the future. As soon as the maid cleared away the tea things, Ammeejan had said,

'Let's go and get some woolens for you. It's getting chilly.'

I was speechless. My cousin Taheera, who was visiting us and was a born heretic, got up, slipped on her sandals, and dashed through the courtyard to tell Iqbal Miyan, dozing under the archway, to open the giant metal-plated gate.

'But, but Mummyjan,' I had blurted out, conflating the intimate

'Mummy' with the formal 'Ammeejan.' 'Shouldn't we ask Kwaja to bring around the car or send for a *tonga*?' I knew only two modes of transportation for my august mother.

She could tell I was agitated.

'Don't fret,' she had said with a smile. 'Let's walk; it's not far to Bijli Chowk.'

I had been too confused to argue. Out on the street, houses cast discreet purdah-length shadows around my mother. Taheera walked jauntily ahead, followed by Ammeejan, who stopped every few steps to acknowledge deferential bows from passersby. Many transferred their startled gaze to me; I merely shrugged and walked on, acutely conscious of curious eyes staring down from ornate cast-iron *zarokhas*, as word spread silently through that medieval warren of cobbled streets that the Begum Sahib, unattended by servants, was going somewhere on foot.

In another reverie, I am old and already retired from Inderpura University. In the evening, Dicky sends his car to pick me up. It's a time-weathered Daimler, and the driver, an old retainer, wears livery of red and gold, but his tunic is frayed at the sleeves. Dicky can no longer afford to dress him properly.

Save for the secluded west wing, connected to the main palace by a long jasmine-covered corridor where Dicky's quarters are located, the rest has been turned into a five-star international hotel. In its spacious Durbar Hall, *ustads*, or musical maestros, from different princely states used to hold musical *mehfils*. India's newly rich class now swills beer and plays poker with entrepreneurs from Singapore and the European Union. The new and old Inderpurs have settled down to peaceful coexistence, but we all know who runs the show.

The two *malis* that Dicky has managed to retain keep a small garden in flowers. Under the green awning, in the light of old yellowing bulbs in their exquisitely fashioned wrought-iron cases, we play bridge in the evening, eating *pakoras* and nuts with a few friends who have survived the onslaught of relentless progress.

Occasionally our game is interrupted while Dicky feeds guava slices to a pair of enormous old ostriches called Aunt Dahlia and Aunt Agatha. Each portly overfed bird snuggles close to him, snapping up pink slices of guavas to chew and slide down its raised serpentine throat. Dicky deals the cards squiffily, his blood-flecked eyes closing now and then in an effort to focus attention. Aunt Dahlia looks at us sideways with large kindly, shell-shaped eyes, steadily working her beak, her head resting dreamily on Dicky's shoulder. But Aunt Agatha tries to stare us down with a look of withering scorn. Then picking up a large slice of guava and swaying her undercarriage, she waddles away like a mother superior to a nearby trough and stands there making gurgling sounds of reproof.

To the FBI men, books and other paraphernalia of academic life in my office notwithstanding, I was a potential terrorist. How quickly their tone had changed from deferential to veiled aggression the moment they found out my antecedents.

My mind flies back to that fateful day in Inderpur when I was robbed of all dignity. In that town which my ancestors had called home and served with distinction, where my grandfather's long service to the freedom struggle was lauded in Shayari, all our history lay in tatters, stripped of meaning.

I was barely eight when India was violently partitioned, leaving in its wake borders soaked with the blood of thousands of innocent victims. The memory of that horrific harvest was rekindled in Cambridge when details of Hitler's death camps began to cut short pub chatter from Regent Street to Lensfield Road.

When Miriam invited me to team-teach her course on the Holocaust I readily agreed. She explored historical material and I handled texts by Primo Levi, Eli Wiesel, and William Styron, who in *Sophie's Choice* challenged the claim that only survivors of Hitler's murderous ethnic cleansing had a right to their memory. As Miriam put it, 'We must all help dislodge that gag from the mouth of time, otherwise in a few years' time that suffering will be just another lost dialect.'

How could I explain to Gullu, my daughter, that it was personal shame that held me captive, whenever she tried to pin me down to an opinion on what to her idealistic young mind were hot-button issues, like human rights violations in Palestine and Kashmir. I had no explanation except that shame knows no boundaries. That secret I had buried deep in my heart. The FBI visit had ripped off the scab.

My old Morris Minor had stalled the previous day and had been towed away to the garage for repairs. Returning from the campus the following afternoon, I was forced to abandon the autorickshaw that was taking me home. The atmosphere seemed tense as soon as we took the exit into the city. The traffic grew thinner until it petered out, and we found ourselves rattling down the long lonely road that led into the Kasbah. About half a mile from the city center, the road was absolutely deserted, and there in the middle of the road lay a mangled corpse.

For three months the city had been agog with wild rumors fanning red flames of suspicion.

The Women's Action Committee, headed by Lepakshi, had rescued a young widow when she was about to be forced onto her husband's funeral pyre. Prior to her timely rescue, a similar incident had ended in the acquittal of the in-laws who had been set free for lack of evidence against them. This time the Women's Action Committee had unassailable proof in its possession that would lead to an indictment. A camera equipped with a wide-angle lens had captured incriminating pictures.

One photograph showed the accused men's vermillion-spattered faces beneath the broad loose pleats of their *safa*s furled by the wind as they escorted the woman to her husband's burning pyre. In the second, a body lay strapped to a platform made of logs under a sky suffused by a soundless explosion of vermillion clouds.

Yet another shot showed a young woman in a white sari sitting motionless on a slab by the funeral pyre. She was as still as an alabaster statue.

In one crucial photograph two older men were seen dragging her to the pyre. The last was of the woman being hoisted like a puppet on the woodpile, while a police inspector and his men were seen to be rushing forward, followed by Lepakshi. The young woman owed her life to Lepakshi.

The men were arraigned. The trial dragged on for nearly three months. While it lasted the city grew tense with every passing day, and after the guilty verdict an eerie calm descended on Inderpur.

In the days that preceded the trial, the mercury marched upwards day by day, the scorching Loo winds blasted through doors and windows; at the public tap, women from families crazed with heat and thirst kicked and scratched those who did not yield the faucet. Water was cut off in the forenoon with a sinister gurgle up the spout. The city was allowed to expand without proper planning, and now the poor were paying the price. Meanwhile the vernacular press continued to publish the most egregious lies, maligning members of the Women's Action Committee.

The churning bowels of the earth sent reptiles slithering up the cracked surface; scavenging rats multiplied; a half-clawed krait, still writhing around a suffocating mongoose, was a common sight; the Loo, screaming like a banshee, coated you with grit; the Adivasis felled sparrows and crows with catapults for food. Trees stood white in the stark moonlight like surreal structures of proliferating bone and gristle; lassitude dropped the tinkle of the cart couples' galloping feet to a harsh irregular clank; dust prickled out of the body like acid granules, and night was total blindness after day's incandescence. In the interim, all the resources of Inderpur's diseased imagination were deployed in trumping up the most hideous calumnies against Lepakshi and her band of women warriors.

Under the black surface of newsprint, a festering impulse worked its powerful chemistry, and out of the ashes of long-burnt women there emerged a hideous reliquary of superstition and fanaticism. In its first phase, the suttee affair was a record of inchoate fakery rather than of personalities. Somebody declared, 'India's spiritual strength is synonymous with woman's chastity.' A so-called savant claimed, 'The suttee fills me with tenderness, which my children's children might someday feel for those who were willing to throw away their lives for their *dharma.*'

During preliminary hearings, days became a jumble of sweaty faces, whirling fans, *chuprasis* scurrying about in red and white uniforms, sounds of autorickshaws screeching outside the court room, and the drone of witnesses taking oaths and regurgitating fabricated testimony. In the stillness of the night, the constellations hung low. The Adivasi-turned-road-repair gangs, emaciated to a skeletal gauntness, drifted about, their eyes focused on the terror in the sky to avoid looking at the inflated stomachs of their hungry children. Their fly-blown women picked lice from their neighbors' matted hair and shelled them with thumbnails.

Driven out from their petrified jungles to the mirage of Inderpur, the Adivasis dug, filled out, and redug the site designated for a lake, as part of the government's effort for drought relief. About a thousand men and women first scooped out the earth from the scrubbed land. Government propaganda had it that, in remoter times at that precise location, a sparkling lake had mysteriously gone underground.

First a vast circular expanse, twice the size of a football field, was carved out, and then the official in charge of the project was transferred to an even more lucrative post. His replacement immediately set the workers filling the giant bowl to the brim with its own piled-up earth. For a month, reedy, burnished hands worked busily flattening the escarpment.

The day the bowl was filled and looked like an airfield, yet another official transfer occurred at the top, and the workers were busy gouging out the dirt in one conjoint frenzy, and in just over a fortnight the super-bowl was yawning at the blazing sky once again. The Adivasis were grateful that only fifty percent of their daily wages, instead of the mandatory seventy, had been siphoned off to line various bureaucratic pockets.

Eventually, the Adivasis developed that digging and refilling technique to such perfection that they looked like wooden dolls in jerky locomotion. The place, having acquired a life of its own, alternately disemboweled and filled itself, while up in the Office of Relief Work Agency, set up by Bulchand's local agents, a ghostly pen scratched equivocal orders.

Then the photographs appeared in English-language papers in Bombay and Delhi, and the trial was over by the end of the week. The three men were convicted of murder and sentenced to a lifetime of hard labor. The pictures sent shock waves throughout the country, now reeling under a heat wave, inflaming bazaars and back alleys alike. Telephone lines jangled in the state home minister's office, with snap orders from Delhi; the trial judge was awakened in the middle of the night and instructed to tidy up the mess.

The defense claimed that the woman was possessed by the Goddess and wanted to immolate herself willingly. A new kind of obscurantism had begun to stalk Inderpur. But the photographs told the truth.

For a month after the trial, nighttime curfew was imposed to prevent looting and burning of public property by those opposed to the verdict. The dead body that stopped the autorickshaw in the street that day was a signal to start a riot.

It was astonishing how swiftly the city grew silent when a communal conflagration was about to start. Streets emptied within seconds, people scampered for cover, and a casual passerby got trapped in some miasmic corridor, to be ambushed by crazed avengers.

I had never got my hooks into any religion. Abbajan was at best an agnostic. Almost all my friends in England believed that the God game had been played out, and here I was suddenly saddled with religion. However I might plead my secular credentials to the rampaging crowd, I was a Muslim. It was like a party game where someone passes you a book or a handkerchief, the music stops abruptly, you are left holding the tabooed object, and every one expects you to do something silly, like walk on all fours or neigh like a horse.

Only this game was not innocent.

Mongrels barked incessantly; a patter of running feet and shrieks were heard from somewhere not too far.

Once, when Maury Lee came to dine with us, a similar riot had broken out on the streets outside the *kothi* following the death of a mentally challenged student leader who had fallen fatally down from the top of the Shiva temple in the center of town. Hindu families in the Kasbah, who were defended by their Muslim neighbors in the past, were no longer safe. I was able to rescue our *bania* grocer because the men who were about to set him on fire still retained a modicum of respect for my family. I had suffered a few minor burns.

The *bania* was too far gone to recognize me, but sensing an ally, with the instincts of the dying, he had clung to my back. Telephone lines had been cut by vandals, and save for the *bania*, all Hindu families further down the road had fled to the safety of their other Hindu localities. The murderous gang was made up of Muslims uprooted from their ancestral homes in villages around Inderpur and forced into the old section of town. Three years on, I faced a crowd made up of mostly Hindu desperadoes in a different part of Inderpur.

Abandoned on that deserted road by my rickshaw driver, who feared for his life, I decided to look for a temporary shelter. It was very hot; I was in my shirtsleeves and in a hurry to get out of the locality. The rickshaw had driven away with my briefcase. I felt exposed and vulnerable. I discovered that shops on either side had all been vandalized. Shoeboxes, plastic wrappers, torn pieces of clothing covered the street. A few heads peeped out of upper-story windows but immediately withdrew, followed by sounds of windows banging shut. Then I heard a siren in the distance. I turned around and saw a police van, its windows wired and covered in a mesh, bearing down with great speed. The SRP (Special Reserve Police) were brought in from a neighboring state and didn't know local people. I stepped aside and waited on the curb, hoping to get some help. As soon as it stopped, a door was flung open, and three helmeted policemen jumped down.

I turned to them to ask for help, but before I could utter a word, one of them grabbed me roughly by the shoulder, while the other swung his truncheon and hit me on my right shin. I doubled up and went down crying in pain when the third man brought his truncheon crashing down on my back. Then the fellow who had held me, kicked me viciously in the back shouting, 'Sala take that, take that for breaking the curfew. Sala, because of you our sister-fucking bosses blame us.'

While I was still working my lips to say something, I saw the man raise his truncheon again shouting, 'Bhago, Bhago, get away you scoundrel or I'll beat the shit out of you.'

I got up, and half stumbling and cursing, ran down the road and ducked into an alley. The van turned around and disappeared in the direction of the Muslim *mohallas* further down the road. Black stinging pain where the skin had been torn radiated up from where I had taken the blow on the back. I limped on, keeping close to the looted shops, and prepared to duck behind a broken door should the police return. I must have hobbled on for not more than six to seven minutes in the alley, thinking that the police vans patrolled only the main road, when the siren sounded again.

I ran into a cul-de-sac where a shop was about to be broken into. A man with a crowbar was on the steps, and he had just wrenched the metal bar off the door as the mob cheered him on. As the siren came closer, the mob dispersed in different directions. I didn't intend to confront the police again, and dragging my right foot across the road, I heaved myself up the steps and plunged through the door, pulling it shut behind me; then slumped down behind a couple of bolsters by the wall. Coming up the steps, I had caught sight of a terrified bearded face closing an upper-story window. From the name on the shop front, painted in English, I could tell that it was a large Bohra retail establishment owned by the Tyabjee family. There were photographs of two bearded gents in round Bohra skullcaps and a calendar depicting the

Mosque at Karbala. It was a Muslim shop, and I wiped my face, breathing steadily with relief. All over the walls, on shelves rising up to the ceiling were enormous *thalis*, pots, pans, tiffin boxes, spoons, ladles, and other vessels of assorted variety.

The police van rumbled away slowly as the driver reversed it out of the cul-de-sac. I must have scared the Bohra family. While stumbling in I had knocked down some stainless steel pots leaning against the door, which had flopped down and jangled for a few seconds. I looked up from where I lay. Hundreds of eyes, peering over mouths twisted in pain stared back at me from every corner of that stainless steel mausoleum. My face looked back from scores of giant *thalis* and sides of glistening tiffin boxes, bowls, ladles and hollows of spoons. Hypnotized by those myriad eyes, I must have gone into a trance, when suddenly my face disappeared from the plates as the front door was flung open. Heavy feet charged in and the shafts of sunlight silhouetted several men. I blinked and crouched as far back as possible. Voices cursed, bodies thwacked, and vessels rattled as the mob, with renewed vigor in the absence of the police van, mounted their second attack on the Bohra merchant's property. The room was packed to capacity, and the noise of falling *thalis* and shouting was deafening. Suddenly there was a hush.

I looked up. Large bloodshot eyes stared down at me from mean looking faces distorted with frenzy and naked hatred.

'Hey, Jokhum,' a voice said, 'look who is hiding here.'

Strong rough hands gripped me by the shoulder and dragged me out to the center of the shop with cries of 'Maro, Maro, kill the Muslim swine. Let's make a *holi* of the rotten pig.'

My cries were drowned in a battery of blows that began to rain down from all sides. Even as I was about to swoon, I smelt petrol running down my eyes and nose. Shouts of 'Kill, burn, kill, finish the villain,' flew around.

'Move back, move back,' the man called Jokhum shouted.

Everyone was silent. With a tremendous effort I opened my aching eyes; Jokhum was flicking open a lighter. In a flash, I realized what was happening but try as I would, no sound came out of my mouth. Petrol trickled down my chin.

I heard someone whimper and a raw elemental scream filled the shop.

'I'm a Hindu! I'm a Hindu! I'm a Hindu! Don't kill me, I'm a Hindu.'

There was a pause while Jokhum peered at me. I caught a look of recognition on his face. I thought I was done for as he pulled and tore the front of my trousers with a knife. I had seen that face before. He was an old student whom I had helped get a job in the forest department ten years before. My teeth were chattering but through my whimpering, I could now hear my voice going on like a chant, 'I'm a Hindu, I'm a Hindu, I'm a Hindu,' over and over and over again till I felt rough fingers groping between my thighs. My whole body rocked as the cold tip of the man's knife slowly feigned to lift the missing foreskin. Our eyes met. He signaled me to be silent.

'Chatt,' the voice was filled with disgust, 'let the wretched pimp go. The mother-fucker is a Hindu.'

There were loud cheers from everybody. Somebody brought a glass of water, but my mouth hurt so badly that I couldn't drink. I was helped out of the shop and set down on the steps from where I got up and took a few wobbly steps. I was soon forgotten as the mob returned to its primary task of ransacking the shop. Blindly, I inched forward, sitting down on the stoops of people's houses to rest. The sun had disappeared behind an enormous black cloud. I couldn't go any further, and grasping the side of a handcart which was parked at the exit to the main road, I rolled into it.

The police siren sounded in the distance again. People began to run helter-skelter. I was too far gone to worry about the consequences. Giving myself up to fate, I pulled the tarpaulin cover over and lay down, not daring to breathe. Then I saw, through a little tear in the cover, the cart couple come running from the alley across the road. The old man groaned under a looted sack, while the old woman charged ahead of him. With her thin old hands she clutched her loot, a transistor radio, as she scuttled down the road on her crooked legs. The old man dumped the sack on me, and then both of them began to pull the cart. They must have sensed that there was something else besides the sack in the cart but they dared not stop to check with the siren sounding so close.

In that broken shop my life had hung by a slender thread. I must have looked ridiculous as I clung desperately to my life. That picture has stayed with me all these years. In another time, in another place, there was a professor reduced to an absurd puppet, as I was. His fate was twined with that of millions of others but in him I saw my image, a man of learning comically trying to stay alive.

How could I explain to Gullu, my daughter, that when you carry that kind of shame in your heart you are already dead? You don't distinguish between victims and tyrants with absolute certainty. The Nazis had made an old revered professor run for his life, forced to compete with younger, stronger men.

'Professor Mehring was seized by an extraordinary will to live and started running like a mad man,' George Steiner writes in *Language and Silence.*

My will to live had vanquished my pride and made me grovel like a mongrel before an old student, who perhaps out of an age-old Indian belief that one must always venerate a teacher, had decided to spare my life. Or it might have been simple gratitude for a past favor, a quid pro quo. To my ultimate shame, I would never know. I have carried that charred knowledge in my heart all these years.

No one probably knew the back alleys and shortcuts of Inderpur better than that old cart couple, and within minutes we had reached the center of the bustling Bijali Chowk, where curfew had been relaxed to allow people to shop for daily necessities.

I gave Saradhi's address to the old couple and offered to pay them ten rupees. Finding themselves in great demand by shoppers who wanted them to help transport their week's supply, the woman immediately gazumped the fare to twenty-five. My body was on fire; someone was driving red-hot spikes into my back. Delirium made the pain bearable. I was too battered to dwell on that now; the ground began to slide beneath the wheels. I opened my eyes.

Everything was in motion. The familiar tintinnabulation of the woman's anklets was soothing as we lurched forward through the crowd. There were faces, prying eyes all around. I didn't care. It was hot under the tarpaulin; it scraped my cheeks and fomented my aching limbs. The heat of that long drawn-out summer was slowly burning away my pain as we went jingle-jangle down the road. The whole world was racing backwards on either side of the cart. Livid hot flames began to lick my sore body. If one came to on a funeral pyre, that's how it must feel.

Young women, engulfed in vermillion flames, were tapering off into the clouds from where sparks came down in a profusion of shower. The pent-up monsoon had finally exploded in the sky. I tried to grab some of those brilliant sparks. Ting-a-ling, ting-a-ling, chimed the cart-woman's anklets.

Ammeejan's fingers touched my back, found the welts. She drew back, eyes popping out in horror. 'Naughty, naughty boy, Shetan Ladka,' she cried, 'playing with street boys again, dirtying his nice sailor boy suit.'

At the end of spring, Miriam urged me to go away somewhere quiet. Maury Lee's brother offered me a large room overlooking a garden in Dummerston, Vermont, not far from Naulakha, the house Rudyard Kipling had built there in 1892. The two *Jungle Books* were born in nearby Bliss Cottage while Naulakha was under construction.

So one fine day, Maury Lee drove me to Penn Station, where I boarded the 'Vermonter,' which deposited me at the Brattleboro railway station, the very place where the Kiplings had arrived one cold February day in 1892, with six-foot-high snow banks on either side of the road. Caroline Kipling's family, the Balestiers, were gentleman farmers; Kipling and his brother-in-law, Beatty, had a great public falling out, but his four years in Vermont had been the most productive in the young author's life. In addition to the two *Jungle Books,* Kipling also wrote *Captains Courageous* and sketched the story of an Irish orphan called Kim, who had grown up among the natives in the city of Lahore.

The number plate on Gretchen Carmody's pickup truck said Green Mountain State. A mass of blond hair turned platinum through outdoor work in the sun, smiling clear emerald eyes, she spoke with a slight German accent. We drove through the mellow, wood-framed storefronts and church-filled Main Street of Brattleboro to their farmhouse in Dummerston.

'Kipling had a private post office somewhere here,' Gretchen said, indicating a shopping plaza before turning left on a road winding under a dark canopy of trees.

A calm entered my heart with a gentle tap. A spider's web hanging from an old maple in evening-dew glitter was like the network of tracks jumbled in the shunting yard at Inderpur. It was along such quiet roads my old town used to unfold with its colonial style bungalows, dark purple bougainvillea entwining the front gates.

The past few months, prior to the FBI duo barging into my office, had been harrowing enough, with Shabnam filing papers for divorce and Gabriella exuberantly calling herself the new Mrs Amolini. Immy and Gullu pleaded with me to 'let Mom have her freedom.' For the first time in my life, I was alarmed by an uncontrollable urge to put an end to my life under the E Train. Instead of soothing my nerves, the Bard's words got stuck in my throat.

The FBI intervention had dampened the allure of Gabriella's flesh. The way Shabnam had rallied and fought like a tigress to secure my freedom from possible incarceration had convinced me that life without her was not an option. Suddenly, belatedly, in the third phase of my life, the mist had cleared and I saw Shabnam as she was. Nature had fashioned her as a prop to tottering, listing things, her hands automatically reaching out to catch falling objects, feckless misfits.

There must have been a whiff of something half-baked and coltish in the way I presented myself at her Aunt Bilkis's villa all those years ago, something amateurish and staged in the way I mourned for Ann, that had made her throw her lot with me. Perhaps in my voice she had detected an undertow of self-pity rather than true weft of grief. She had sensed in me something tumbledown, some flagging paralytic-in-the-making who needed ministering.

I felt that my readiness to give up Gabriella would convince my wife that I was not an abject slave to passion. The night before leaving for Vermont I had made it plain to Gabriella that I couldn't live without Shabnam, and divorcing her was out of the question. In the morning, when I woke up, after tossing and turning between resignation and hope, it was Shabnam whom I missed; it was her absence that was desolating. My life depended on winning her back. No dithering on that, I said to myself, no excuses, whatever it takes to get her back, I will do it, even pray five times a day like a good Muslim if she wants me to.

I shall have to provide for Gabriella and the baby, of course, and for the first time I began to reconsider Immy's offer to help me out with a settlement that would provide for their future.

Gretchen interrupted my thoughts, saying Landmark Trust of USA had restored Naulakha to its original shape and form. There it was, on an avalanche-prone slope, looking like a ship, its gray-green shingles a facsimile of a roadside Inderpur bungalow.

For Reeny and her kind, Kipling was just another big imperial 'Koi Hai,' whose racial arrogance had finally sullied his reputation as writer. I wasn't quite sure one could separate Kipling's India from India's Kipling. I always felt that his domain was not as black and white as those whose early years had not blossomed in its soil made it out to be. To me he would always be part of my childhood; Dicky and I singing 'On the Road to Mandalay,' with Matron Phyllis Tillinghast at the piano, and me secretly crying in bed over Mowgli's final farewell to his wolf mother. There was a part of Kipling which would forever be India.

In a local bookstore I found an illustrated *Kim*, copies of *Plain Tales from the Hills* and the two *Jungle Books*. It was like walking into one's old tuck shop to find that they still served hot cross-buns.

For me, work on the farm was light, thanks to Steve, who knew I needed time to recover from the events of the past few months. For a war-hardened veteran, Steve was unusually cordial, not just to me but also to the young students who assisted him on the farm. He often allowed them to take a break when they showed signs of fatigue and couldn't keep up with regular farmhands.

After a full New England breakfast of homemade bread and scrambled eggs, we sowed cilantro seeds in drills, and in two weeks the seedlings were out. We used liquid fertilizer to coax them to grow faster. Meanwhile, we had to use garden canes to support the chillies, which had grown more rapidly than expected. Steve was patient with me and explained to me that in order to get a hotter yield, you had to let them shrivel on the plants.

On Saturday, there was no work on the farm, and we filed into Steve's three pick-up trucks and headed for the Farmer's Market in Brattleboro. No one was the least bit curious that an obvious bumbling outsider like me was with the Carmody bunch. Landlocked Vermont was used to strangers from overseas and had offered sanctuary to writers and artists who had escaped persecution in their homeland.

The Von Trapp family, who had fled Nazi Austria, and Solzhenitsyn, until his recent return to Russia, had made their home here. Vermont welcomed its visitors without fanfare; you felt sheltered here without having to explain your past.

In India, we have this habit of creating a perspectivistic background for everyone. It is a national characteristic. That is why the moment you settle into your seat on a long-distance train, or when you are introduced to someone at a party, you are plied with embarrassing personal questions. How many children have you, and how much money do you make? We are not happy till we have painted a background that gives the other a meaning, a local habitation, a history. In India you are not left alone till at least a minibio hangs around you like a bubble in a comic strip. Your caste, creed, religion, family, and ancestry need to swirl around you like a cloud of black flies in summer.

So while my family is going bonkers—Immy lost in his American dream, Shabnam turned into a passable imitation of a well-intentioned power woman, Gullu a would-be anarchist—here in Vermont I sit quietly watching different ethnic stalls at the Farmer's Market and the people milling around them. In addition to various European cuisines on display, there is a Thai stall and an African stall. I sit smiling with forgiveness.

Forgiveness for what?

Gretchen at her makeshift bakery sells homemade breads, muffins, and scones. I have not found a decent scone since I left England, and clotted cream from Devon is missing, but what Gretchen offers is the next best thing. Tired and happy, her golden hair touched by the light filtering in through a hole in the canvas at the back of her stall, Gretchen sits like Nehalennia, the Germanic goddess of fruit, beaming at her baskets overflowing with succulent blackberries, blueberries, and raspberries.

Nights under a moonless sky are vast as an ocean, unribboned as they are by street lights, and in the morning when the sun dissolves the fleecy curtain of mist, houses on tilted tableland slide closer, like façades rolled down center stage.

On the second Sunday in August, Steve's neighbors, the Duncans, called to say they had an extra ticket to a chamber music concert in the nearby town of Marlboro and offered to take me with them. It was the final concert of the eponymous Music Festival. and the Duncans had planned a little preconcert picnic with sandwiches and coffee on the lawn outside, which was dotted with small clusters of music lovers snacking by their cars in the lush green parking lot. Inside, the cavernous venue opened like Hrothgar's Mead Hall in *Beowulf*, with arches soaring to the roof and a wide stage at the other end where technicians were testing the recording equipment. Some of that picnic informality still lingered inside, with people hailing friends as they fumbled towards their seats.

The Duncans and I were in one of the back rows, and nearsighted Mrs Duncan, who was in her eighties, slumped in her chair after straining to see the musicians as they filed in and took their appointed positions. The applause that greeted them was a fine mixture of courtesy and intimacy.

After a delectable Mendelssohn string quartet, a Mozart piano trio, and four impromptus by Schubert when the whole orchestra of roughly a hundred musicians, including a chorus of twenty led by professional vocalists crammed the stage to present Beethoven's *Choral Fantasy*; it was like boarding a magic carpet and looking down on a miracle.

I was not well acquainted with the *Choral Fantasy*, which, according to Mr. Duncan, presages the olympian *Ninth Symphony*, and was certainly not prepared for what happened to me during those brief twenty minutes of its rendition. After a short tentative, cadenza-like nosing around to find the right passage, when the London-based Japanese pianist confidently steered her keys into the heart of the orchestra, the faces in the hall disappeared beneath its oceanic swell.

Ten minutes earlier, during the brief intermission while the orchestra was still assembling on stage, all eyes had been directed apprehensively to the roof where the sky, which had been overcast with lightning bolts flashing in the distance, had crashed and then just as suddenly fallen silent.

Entire mankind seemed to be represented on that stage—the soprano with a delicate Chinese face alongside the blond Wagnerian mezzo-soprano, the African American bass baritone towering over the Mediterranean swarthiness of the tenor; the rest, a generous sprinkling of features that recalled Slavic, Gaelic, and oriental types. There was a cellist with an Indian-sounding name somewhere in their midst. Music had suddenly scrambled humanity, blending entire continents into one land mass, as seen by Astronaut Chawla from her perch in space.

The chorus sang in German, urging '*schönen Seelen*' (beautiful spirits) to accept '*froh die Gaben schöner Kunst*' (joyously the gifts of high art). There was nothing sorrowful in that sound, only a heightened sense of joy in living, and yet my frame began to rock as the sound of music faded to a thunderous ovation. I was crying silently, as if some levee had broken within me.

Mr Duncan stood up to applaud, along with the rest. Mrs Duncan passed me a handkerchief and patted me gently on the back. She acted as though there was nothing unusual in a grown-up man crying at a concert.

Tears flowed down my cheeks. I had lost control of my eyes to some nameless sorrow to which my mind could not connect. I cried, making as little noise as my self-possession would allow. At one point, I remember trying to speak, but my mouth could not formulate intelligible words. The audience was still cheering the pianist and her team, who were summoned for yet another encore. Grape-sized tears rolled down and burst onto Mrs Duncan's handkerchief. When the applause died down and people began to shuffle out, I mumbled something about a sudden attack of allergy, to forewarn the Duncans about a possible long downpour during our homeward journey.

Like well-behaved people, the Duncans made an admirable effort to shore up my fictional allergy and said all that vegetation in the parking lot must have triggered it off. My attempt to speak set off a series of hiccups that made my voice blare like a drunkard's trying to sound sober.

There are more ways of playing the fool than are dreamt of in any philosophy; from wise to sad to natural born buffoons, and heaven knows in my time I have had a shot at everyone of them, but sobbing disconsolately at a concert took the cake. At night, alone in my attic, I tried to pin down the exact moment when I had become aware of my wet cheeks in the hope of determining the cause of this wholly inappropriate, lachrymose *pagliaccio* act. Good old Ludwig Van of the noble sound was not to blame. Some inchoate, unresolved emotion had got the upper hand and sprung a leak.

I had not cried like that since the day my Ammeejan had passed away suddenly back in 1979. No one, least of all the Duncans, was fooled by the allergy excuse. The Choral Fantasy is not about 'old unhappy far off things and battles long ago.'

Then why?

Perhaps my heart had been surprised by the ecumenical power of the Fantasy that was devotional, without any particular deity being within earshot, except those green mountains.

Vermont exists in its own time zone—an invisible moat seems to encircle it—and as the train trundles in, you often have a sensation of having crossed an international boundary. Most evenings, the sky puts on quite a show in the west when the sun's effulgent sheep dogs round up the scattered clouds before going down for the night. Sometimes, distant rolls of thunder followed by exploding bolts of lightning pick up in a flash the red Carmody barn, which looks as unflappable as a ship that has weathered many a storm.

Driving past old sagging brown and ochre barns and houses that look scuffed and worn out by protracted toil, one is transported back to the late eighteenth century. The past appears silently through some crack in time as a dirt road winds through birch and maple. Only a mud-splattered pickup truck reminds you of the world outside.

Once, during an evening drive through the back roads, Gretchen stopped to let a long steady line of turkeys that had waddled out of sheltering woods cross over to a fire pond that reflected the farmhouse abutting its bank. A log drifting dreamily across its placid surface suddenly flipped and became a beaver shoring up weeds and twigs to build a dam in a dark corner. Behind the pond, land tumbled steeply into darkness. The clapboard house was impassive like a magistrate and didn't seem to notice.

Beavers build dams for many of the same reasons humans do, mainly to transform and control their environment, Gretchen said. Beavers are natural swimmers, with their webbed feet and sleek fur. But shallow water doesn't offer them much protection from natural predators such as wolves. So beavers build dams in order to raise the water level; the deeper water gives them a good place to hide. It also slows down the water's speed, which lets beavers build stable lodges to house their families.

Gretchen and Steve eat the food they grow, sit on the furniture hewn by them, and are proud that no plumber has ever been required to fix a leaky valve under the sink. They are as inventive as the clever squirrel I often see being chased away from the bird feeder she routinely plunders.

Once, Steve devised an ingenious way of hoisting and lowering the height of the bird feeder by tying it to a rope which could be rolled up a pulley clamped to a soaring branch any bird could access, but not the squirrel. After making two futile upward jumps the tiny thing just clambered up the tree, slithered smoothly to the tip of the branch, and like a trapeze artist executed an immaculate dive twenty feet down to the bird feeder. Steve just shook his head in helpless wonder. It was as if the squirrel could read human minds like a creature from the *Jungle Books*.

I have been rereading Kipling out of sheer nostalgia for Inderpur. He is the conjurer who can transport me back like no other writer I know to the sights and sounds of India. Reading *Kim* is like traveling back in time, when Inderpur was still a princely state with wide roads, palaces, and gardens.

I know now, that Inderpur is dead. It is immaterial how it died. Perhaps we all had a share in killing it.

Steve says, 'On September 13 they have open house at Naulakha if you want to find out what's in there.'

I am excited. In the old days, a golden necklace commissioned by a prince was 'nine lack' (Naulakh), about $20,000 today, but unimaginable wealth back then. Dicky's mother, the old Her Highness of Inderpur, had one. Where is it now? Probably sold by Dicky to pay for the up-keep of the palace.

Vermont is a silent state. There are no billboards here proclaiming the virtues of products. People in the state are addicted to silence. At night it is so still one can hear one's heart beat.

On September 11th, two planes change their flight path midair and plough through two of the tallest buildings in New York.

The world is silenced.

Mouth, red like Philomel's, tries to formulate a sound.

Why?

Clocks run backwards, till in ancient Egypt one day, a fisherman wakes up on the Nile to watch a pyramidless sunset. Deserts of vast eternity are still flat and barren and await the pharaoh.

Late in the morning, Immy calls to say he is coming to pick me up on Sunday. He instructs me to stay put in Vermont; he is worried about his old dad traveling alone amidst reports of revenge attacks.

The word 'pity' has lost its meaning.

'Rahem' is the nearest equivalent in Urdu to pity. I remember an old fakir who came to our door in Inderpur. '*Rahem karo,*' he would say to anyone in sight, whether Hindu or Muslim.

'*Rahem,*' says the petal that undulates through empty space before hitting the ground and bruising.

'*Rahem,*' says the smoke that chokes the lungs,

'*Rahem,*' say the incinerating flames.

Work on the farm is suspended for a day. Everyone is at the neighbor's where they have a TV set.

Friday, farmers resume their toil. Nature cannot wait; lack of water would cause a shock to the system, and plants would bolt. The chili plants have put out flowers, but they pose no danger; they will soon die a natural death.

Surprisingly, the open house at Naulakha is not cancelled. Kipling would have liked that. He said, 'If you can keep your head, when all about you/Are losing theirs and blaming it on you;'

Kipling's precocious Wee Willie Winkie talks the violent men of northwest frontier out of their evil ways and brokers a peace deal between the frontiersmen with their old tribal ways and the rule of law.

It is an impossible fantasy, delusion of the innocent.

On the thirteenth, when I go to the open house, the curator shows me a golf ball painted in imperial red.

'When Sir Arthur Conan Doyle visited Naulakha one winter, Kipling played golf with him in the snow.'

It was the time when the sun never set on the British Empire and all was well with the world.

There are sandwiches and cookies for lunch, and after that the few die-hard Kipling fans who have come to Naulakha gather outside to hear two British music men sing Kipling songs. They try to cheer us up. Serrated clouds dim the late afternoon sun prematurely as they drift past like the sad wreckage of an interrupted odyssey.

Music, like Rudyard Kipling, has lost its relevance, but the singers

press on, regardless. Their enforced cheerfulness is embarrassing, and
one by one we slink away, leaving the song gasping for breath,

> 'On the road to Mandalay,
> Where the flyin' fishes play,
> An' the dawn comes up like thunder outer China
> 'crost the Bay!

Select Glossary

(Culinary and other terms can be easily found on the internet)

attardani - perforated perfume dispenser
adab - cultivated refinement of speech and manner.
behenji - literally respected sister
bibi - wife
dhobi - washerman
goras - white folk
gulab jamun - a north Indian sweet made of condensed milk and rich light dough.
harim - more elegant term for 'harem', also a kind of hierarchical sister-hood within it.
hubsy/hubsies (pl) - from '*hapshi*' a term used in ancient India for slaves imported from Africa.
kothi - a luxurious, palatial fortified building with an inner courtyard flanked by separate wings for male and female members of an aristo-cratic Muslim family.
khus (*khas*) *tutties* - dampened vetiver grass shades
Lassi - yogurt 'smoothie' sometime enriched with mango pulp.
mofussil - rural district
nokrani -parlor maid
pugree -traditional head dress for Hindu men
pallav - loose end of a woman's sari traditionally used to cover her head.
shayar - a poet or bard who often gives a public reading/recitation of his or her work
sola-topi - short for solar-topi or pith helmet worn in the tropics
thakur - Hindu landowner of the warrior caste.
zarokhas - ornate balconies

Jackson Heights in this book is a fictional locale with common features assembled from immigrant-friendly neighborhoods around the world where hardworking honest-to-goodness traders from the Indian sub-continent, rub shoulders with ruthless entrepreneurs, reclusive antique-dealers, homeless nobodies, merchant-princes, lawyers, doctors and IT specialists. But as Siraj and Shabnam, urbane newcomers fleeing relig-ious persecution in their homeland discover there is no escape from the past. Weaving together the personal and the political *The Good Muslim of Jackson Heights* is an ambiguous elegy to a utopian ideal set free from all prejudice.

Jaysinh Birjépatil's novel *Chinnery's Hotel* was published by Bodiam Books in England and by Penguin & Ravi Dayal in India. For a number of years he taught English at Marlboro College in Vermont where he makes his home. He has also taught at M.S.University, Baroda and Brown University, and his poetry has appeared on both sides of the Atlantic.

Acknowledgments:
Without Marc Estrin's and Donna Bister's unstinted mentoring this book would not have reached American shores.
Without generous help at various stages from Mala Dayal, Tony Con-nor, John Drew, Hilly van Loon, Jennifer Mazur, Marrin Robinson, Jörge Batlles ,Virginia Schendler and Sherry Bromley, it could not have been written.

Fomite
Burlington, Vermont

Fomite is a literary press whose authors and artists explore the human condition -- political, cultural, personal and historical -- in poetry and prose.

A fomite is a medium capable of transmitting infectious organisms from one individual to another.

"The activity of art is based on the capacity of people to be infected by the feelings of others." Tolstoy, *What is Art?*

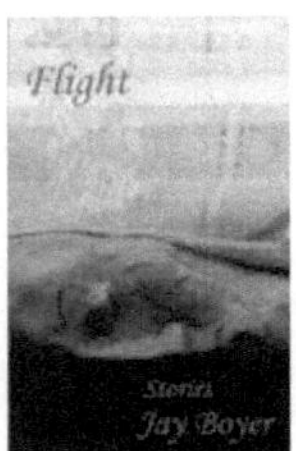

Flight and Other Stories - J. Boyer
In *Flight and Other Stories,* we're with the fattest woman on earth as she draws her last breaths and her soul ascends toward its final reward. We meet a divorcee who can fly for no more effort than flapping her arms. We follow a middle-aged butler whose love affair with a young woman leads him first to the mysteries of bondage, and then to the pleasures of malice. Story by story, we set foot into worlds so strange as to seem all but surreal, yet everything feels familiar, each moment rings true. And that's when we recognize we're in the hands of one of America's truly original talents.

AlphaBetaBestiario - Antonello Borra
Animals have always understood that mankind is not fully at home in the world. Bestiaries, hoping to teach, send out warnings. This one, of course, aims at doing the same.

Improvisational Arguments - Anna Faktorovich
Improvisational Arguments is written in free verse to capture the essence of modern problems and triumphs. The poems clearly relate short, frequently humorous and occasionally tragic, stories about travels to exotic and unusual places, fantastic realms, abnormal jobs, artistic innovations, political objections, and misadventures with love.

Roadworthy Creature, Roadworthy Craft - Kate Magill
Words fail but the voice struggles on. The culmination of a decade's worth of performance poetry, *Roadworthy Creature, Roadworthy Craft* is Kate Magill's first full-length publication. In lines that are sinewy yet delicate, Magill's poems explore the terrain where idea and action meet, where bodies and words commingle to form a strange new flesh, a breathing text, an "I" that spirals outward from itself.

Fomite
Burlington, Vermont

Loisaida - Dan Chodorokoff
Catherine, a young anarchist estranged from her parents and squatting in an abandoned building on New York's Lower East Side is fighting with her boyfriend and conflicted about her work on an underground newspaper. After learning of a developer's plans to demolish a community garden, Catherine builds an alliance with a group of Puerto Rican community activists. Together they confront the confluence of politics, money, and real estate that rule Manhattan. All the while she learns important lessons from her great-grandmother's life in the Yiddish anarchist movement that flourished on the Lower East Side at the turn of the century. In this coming of age story, family saga, and tale of urban politics, Dan Chodorkoff explores the "principle of hope", and examines how memory and imagination inform social change.

Still Time - Michael Cocchiarale
Still Time is a collection of twenty-five short and shorter stories exploring tensions that arise in a variety of contemporary relationships: a young boy must deal with the wrath of his out-of-work father; a woman runs into a man twenty years after an awkward sexual encounter; a wife, unable to conceive, imagines her own murder, as well as the reaction of her emotionally distant husband; a soon-to-be tenured English professor tries to come to terms with her husband's shocking return to the religion of his youth; an assembly line worker, married for thirty years, discovers the surprising secret life of his recently hospitalized wife. Whether a few hundred or a few thousand words, these and other stories in the collection depict characters at moments of deep crisis. Some feel powerless, overwhelmed—unable to do much to change the course of their lives. Others rise to the occasion and, for better or for worse, say or do the thing that might transform them for good. Even in stories with the most troubling of endings, there remains the possibility of redemption. For each of the characters, there is still time.

The Listener Aspires to the Condition of Music - Barry Goldensohn
"I know of no other selected poems that selects on one theme, but this one does, charting Goldensohn's career-long attraction to music's performance, consolations and its august, thrilling, scary and clownish charms. Does all art aspire to the condition of music as Pater claimed, exhaling in a swoon toward that one class act? Goldensohn is more aware than the late 19th century of the overtones of such breathing: his poems thoroughly round out those overtones in a poet's lifetime of listening."
John Peck, poet, editor, Fellow of the American Academy of Rome

Fomite
Burlington, Vermont

When You Remember Deir Yassin - R.L Green

When You Remember Deir Yassin is a collection of poems by R. L. Green, an American Jewish writer, on the subject of the occupation and destruction of Palestine. Green comments: "Outspoken Jewish critics of Israeli crimes against humanity have, strangely, been called "anti-Semitic" as well as the hilariously illogical epithet "self-hating Jews." As a Jewish critic of the Israeli government, I have come to accept these accusations as a stamp of approval and a badge of honor, signifying my own fealty to a central element of Jewish identity and ethics: one must be a lover of truth and a friend to the oppressed, and stand with the victims of tyranny, not with the tyrants, despite tribal loyalty or self-advancement. These poems were written as expressions of outrage, and of grief, and to encourage my sisters and brothers of every cultural or national grouping to speak out against injustice, to try to save Palestine, and in so doing, to reclaim for myself my own place as part of the Jewish people." The poems are offered in the original English with Arabic and Hebrew translations accompanying each poem.

The Co-Conspirator's Tale - Ron Jacobs

There's a place where love and mistrust are never at peace; where duplicity and deceit are the universal currency. *The Co-Conspirator's Tale* takes place within this nebulous firmament. There are crimes committed by the police in the name of the law. Excess in the name of revolution. The combination leaves death in its wake and the survivors struggling to find justice in a San Francisco Bay Area noir by the author of the underground classic *The Way the Wind Blew:A History of the Weather Underground* and the novel *Short Order Frame Up*.

Carts and Other Stories - Zdravka Evtimova

Roots and wings are the key words that best describe the short story collection, *Carts and Other Stories,* by Zdravka Evtimova. The book is emotionally multilayered and memorable because of its internal power, vitality and ability to touch both the heart and your mind. Within its pages, the reader discovers new perspectives true wealth, and learns to see the world with different eyes. The collection lives on the borders of different cultures. *Carts and Other Stories* will take the reader to wild and powerful Bulgarian mountains, to silver rains in Brussels, to German quiet winter streets and to wind bitten crags in Afghanistan. This book lives for those seeking to discover the beauty of the world around them, and will have them appreciating what they have— and perhaps what they have lost as well.

284

Fomite
Burlington, Vermont

Views Cost Extra - L.E. Smith

Views that inspire, that calm, or that terrify – all come at some cost to the viewer. In *Views Cost Extra* you will find a New Jersey high school preppy who wants to inhabit the "perfect" cowboy movie, a rural mailman disgusted with the residents of his town who wants to live with the penguins, an ailing screen writer who strikes a deal with Johnny Cash to reverse an old man's failures, an old man who ponders a young man's suicide attempt, a one-armed blind blues singer who wants to reunite with the car that took her arm on the assembly line -- and more. These stories suggest that we must pay something to live even ordinary lives.

Zinsky the Obscure - Ilan Mochari

"If your childhood is brutal, your adulthood becomes a daily at-tempt to recover: a quest for ecstasy and stability in recompense for their early absence." So states the 30-year-old Ariel Zinsky, whose bachelor-like lifestyle belies the torturous youth he is still coming to grips with. As a boy, he struggles with the beatings themselves; as a grownup, he struggles with the world's indifference to them. *Zinsky the Obscure* is his life story, a humorous chronicle of his search for a redemptive ecstasy through sex, an entrepreneurial sports obses-sion, and finally, the cathartic exercise of writing it all down. Fer-vently recounting both the comic delights and the frightening hor-rors of a life in which he feels – always – that he is not like all the rest, Zinsky survives the worst and relishes the best with idiosyn-cratic style, as his heartbreak turns into self-awareness and his suici-dal ideation into self-regard. A vivid evocation of the all-consuming nature of lust and ambition – and the forces that drive them – *Zinsky the Obscure* is a novel of extraordinary zeal, range, and power.

The Empty Notebook Interrogates Itself - Susan Thomas

The Empty Notebook began its life as a very literal metaphor for a few weeks of what the poet thought was writer's block, but was really the struggle of an eccentric persona to take over her working life. It won. And for the next three years everything she wrote came to her in the voice of the Empty Notebook, who, as the notebook began to fill itself, became rather opinionated, changed gender, alternately acted as bully and victim, had many bizarre adventures in exotic locales and developed a somewhat politically-incorrect attitude. It then began to steal the voices and forms of other poets and tried to immortalize itself in various poetry reviews. It is now thrilled to collect itself in one slim volume.

Fomite
Burlington, Vermont

The Derivation of Cowboys & Indians - Joseph D. Reich

The Derivation of Cowboys & Indians represents a profound journey, a breakdown of The American Dream from a social, cultural, historical, and spiritual point of view. Reich examines in concise! detail the loss of the collective unconscious, commenting on our! contemporary postmodern culture with its self-interested excesses, on where and how things all go wrong, and how social/political practice rarely meets its original proclamations and promises. Reich's surreal and self-effacing satire brings this troubling message home. *The Derivations of Cowboys & Indians* is a desperate search and struggle for America's literal, symbolic, and spiritual home.

Kasper Planet: Comix and Tragix - Peter Schumann

The British call him Punch, the Italians, Pulchinello, the Russians, Petruchka, the Native Americans, Coyote. These are the figures we may know. But every culture that worships authority will breed a Punch-like, anti-authoritan resister. Yin and yang -- it has to happen. The Germans call him Kasper.
Truth-telling and serious pranking are dangerous professions when going up against power. Bradley Manning sits naked in solitary; Julian Assange is pursued by Interpol, Obama's Department of Justice, and Amazon.com. But -- in contrast to merely human faces -- masks and theater can often slip through the bars.
Consider our American Kaspers: Charlie Chaplin, Woody Guthrie, Abby Hoffman, the Yes Men -- theater people all, utilizing various forms to seed critique. Their profiles and tactics have evolved along with those of their enemies. Who are the bad guys that call forth the Kaspers? Over the last half century, with his Bread & Puppet Theater, Peter Schumann has been tireless in naming them, excoriating them with Kasperdom....
from Marc Estrin's Foreword to Planet Kasper

My God, What Have We Done? - Susan Weiss

In a world afflicted with war, toxicity, and hunger, does what we do in our private lives really matter? Fifty years after the creation of the atomic bomb at Los Alamos, newlyweds Pauline and Clifford visit that once-secret city on their honeymoon, compelled by Pauline's fascination with Oppenheimer, the soulful scientist. The two stories emerging from this visit reverberate back and forth between the loneliness of a new mother at home in Boston and the isolation of an entire community dedicated to the development of the bomb. While Pauline struggles with unforeseen challenges of family life, Oppenheimer and his crew reckon with forces beyond all imagining.

Finally the years of frantic research on the bomb culminate in a stunning test explosion that echoes a rupture in the couple's marriage. Against the backdrop of a civilization that's out of control, Pauline begins to understand the complex, potentially explosive physics of personal relationships.

At once funny and dead serious, *My God, What Have We Done?* sifts through the ruins left by the bomb in search of a more worthy human achievement.

286